No. 1 *New York Times* and *USA Today* bestselling author and international sensation with works sold worldwide in more than twenty-five countries to date, BRYNNE WEAVER has traveled the world, taken in more stray animals than her husband would probably prefer, and nurtured her love for dark comedies, horror, and romance in both literature and film. During all her adventures, the constant thread in Brynne's life has been writing. With ten published works and counting, Brynne has made her mark in the literary world by blending irreverent dark comedy, swoon-worthy romance, and riveting suspense to create genre-breaking, addictive stories for readers to escape into.

THE *Seasons of Carnage* TRILOGY

TOURIST SEASON

BRYNNE WEAVER

PIATKUS

PIATKUS

First published in the US in 2025 by Slowburn,
An imprint of Zando
Published in Great Britain in 2025 by Piatkus

1 3 5 7 9 10 8 6 4 2

Copyright © 2025 by Brynne Weaver

The moral right of the author has been asserted.

A CIP catalogue record for this book
is available from the British Library.

ISBN 978-0-349-44654-7

Printed and bound in Great Britain by Clays Ltd, Elcograf S.p.A.

Papers used by Piatkus are from well-managed forests
and other responsible sources.

MIX
Paper | Supporting
responsible forestry
FSC
www.fsc.org   FSC® C104740

Piatkus
An imprint of
Little, Brown Book Group
Carmelite House
50 Victoria Embankment
London EC4Y 0DZ

The authorised representative
in the EEA is
Hachette Ireland
8 Castlecourt Centre,
Dublin 15, D15 XTP3, Ireland
(email: info@hbgi.ie)

An Hachette UK Company
www.hachette.co.uk

www.littlebrown.co.uk

TOURIST SEASON

Content & Trigger Warnings

As much as *Tourist Season* is a dark romantic comedy and will hopefully make you laugh through the madness, it's still dark! Please read responsibly.

- Woodchippers
- Creative use of bird feeders
- Eyeballs and also eye sockets this time. Ugh. I know. If you've been with me for a while, I think we've both resigned ourselves to this one for the foreseeable future (pun intended)
- Lawn aerators
- Scrapbooking, but make it murdery
- Gardening, but make that murdery too
- Stalking and voyeurism
- Breaking and entering, including theft
- References to physical and psychological torture
- Drowning
- Hamburgers. I'M SORRY. I didn't think it was going to happen and then it just . . . happened
- Birds that enjoy human snacks
- Vehicular collisions
- A plethora of weapons, including axes, knives, guns, needles, chainsaws, garrotes, and three-hole punches
- Explicit language and blasphemy

- Murdery use of ropes
- Sexy use of ropes
- Medical settings and details, including trauma response activities, CPR, hospitals, and long-term recovery
- Explicit sexual content, including BDSM, brat/brat tamer kink, impact play, rough sex, adult toys, pain play, and mild knife play
- This is a story of two serial killers falling in love, so expect general murder and mayhem.

While normally my content warnings are delivered with a lighthearted hand, I want to express this one seriously: elderly loved one with Mild Cognitive Impairment (MCI) and early Alzheimer's disease (AD). Caregiving responsibilities and challenges are also depicted. As a person who has lost multiple close family members to AD and who worked in the field of Alzheimer's research for over a decade, I am deeply sensitive to the emotional turmoil caused by the loss of personhood due to dementia. I know how difficult it is to be a caregiver to someone with MCI/AD. While I hope to show the beautiful complexity of this elderly character, from his fear and confusion to his humor and resilience, please know that some readers might find this exploration of memory loss triggering. More detailed information that you might find helpful:

Mild Cognitive Impairment (MCI)—subtle changes in memory and thinking that may indicate a transition to other dementia conditions, such as Alzheimer's disease. The term may be used interchangeably with "early Alzheimer's disease."

Alzheimer's disease (AD)—a progressive, degenerative neurological disease with symptoms such as memory loss, difficulty thinking, mood and behavioral changes, psychological challenges (paranoia, depression, hallucination), restlessness, and many others not listed here. It is divided into three primary phases: Mild, Moderate, and Severe. Though not explicitly stated in the story, and complicated by other medical conditions, the character in the book who has this illness exhibits symptoms of Mild to Moderate AD.

Dementia—an umbrella medical term for a number of distinct neurological conditions that represent the impairment of at least two brain functions. MCI and AD are classified as dementia conditions.

A portion of the royalties from the sale of this series will be donated to the Alzheimer's Association (US) and Alzheimer Society of Canada.

When I first announced this series, so many of you asked, "Will you ruin any foods?" and "Will there be eyeballs?"

You are truly phenomenal, and I love you.
This one's for you.

. . . Also, YES.

Playlist

Scan a QR code to listen:

APPLE MUSIC	SPOTIFY

CHAPTER ONE: Erosion
"You Don't Own Me," Lesley Gore
"Angry Too," Lola Blanc
"Man's World," MARINA

CHAPTER TWO: Anchor
"In My Room," The Beach Boys
"Something to Believe In," Young the Giant
"Wicked Love," Naomi August

CHAPTER THREE: Azimuth
"Regulars," Allie X
"Table for One," AWOLNATION (feat. Elohim)

CHAPTER FOUR: Declination
"UNFORGIVEN," LE SSERAFIM (feat. Nile Rodgers)
"Serial Killer," Slayyyter

CHAPTER FIVE: Broadsided

"DieDieDie," Erin McCarley

"CAN YOU SEE ME?" Rezz

CHAPTER SIX: Raking Fire

"eat your heart out," CRAY

"Simon Says," Allie X

"Blue," Madison Beer

CHAPTER SEVEN: Traces

"Thanks for Calling," SONOIO

"Hate You," Poylow & BAUWZ (feat. Nito-Onna)

"Granite," Sleep Token

CHAPTER EIGHT: Descent

"Minutes," SONOIO

"I Don't Even Care About You," MISSIO

"MILK OF THE SIREN," Melanie Martinez

CHAPTER NINE: Treasures

"Clone," Metric

"Love Cemetery," CRAY

CHAPTER TEN: Exhume

"River Queen," Sara Jackson-Holman

"Love and War," Fleurie

CHAPTER ELEVEN: Avast

"I'm Fine," William Black (feat. Nevve)

"Panoramic View," AWOLNATION

CHAPTER TWELVE: Deviation

"Down on Love," Cannons

"Nightmares," Ellise

"Daylight," Joji & Diplo

CHAPTER THIRTEEN: Drifting

"Too Late, All Gone," How to Destroy Angels

"I'm a Ruin," MARINA

"Hallucinate," William Black (feat. Nevve)

CHAPTER FOURTEEN: Fogbound

"15 MINUTES," Madison Beer

"Numb," Kiiara (feat. DeathbyRomy & PVRIS)

"Think Twice," SMNM

CHAPTER FIFTEEN: Harpoon

"Sloth (I Feel It Too Much)," Erin McCarley

"The Sun," The Naked and Famous

CHAPTER SIXTEEN: Running Dark

"Help I'm Alive," Metric

"Backbone," DROELOE (feat. Nevve)

"Self Destruct," Slayyyter (feat. Wuki)

CHAPTER SEVENTEEN: Fathoms

"Obsessed," Sophie Powers (feat. Ashley Sienna)

"Monster Hospital," Metric

"Chokehold," Sleep Token

CHAPTER EIGHTEEN: Towline

"Bipolar," Kiiara

"Suspirium," Thom Yorke

"I'd Be Lying," Greg Laswell

CHAPTER NINETEEN: Ballast

"Remedy," William Black (feat. Annie Schindel)

"Hard to Forget," Jane XØ

"FEEL," Beneld & BURY

CHAPTER TWENTY: Splice

"This Is What It Feels Like," BANKS

"Gloe," Kiiara

"Kiss Me," Empress Of (feat. Rina Sawayama)

CHAPTER TWENTY-ONE: Windward

"Problem Me," Modwheelmood

"Analyse," Thom Yorke

CHAPTER TWENTY-TWO: Gales

"Diet Pepsi," Addison Rae

"Bridged by a Lightwave," deadmau5 & Kiesza (Radio Edit)

"Spitting Off the Edge of the World," Yeah Yeah Yeahs
(feat. Perfume Genius)

CHAPTER TWENTY-THREE: Abyss

"dream wrld," daniel.mp3 & ZAMARO

"Drag Me Under," Sleep Token

"Bottom of the Deep Blue Sea," MISSIO

CHAPTER TWENTY-FOUR: Shrouds

"TOO GOOD," Troye Sivan

"Sugar," Sleep Token

"Odyssey," Fleurie

"Freight Train," Sara Jackson-Holman

CHAPTER TWENTY-FIVE: Foul Ground

"Sanctuary," Joji

"Renegade," Belle Sisoski

"Your Ghost," Greg Laswell

CHAPTER TWENTY-SIX: Tempest

"chaotic," Tate McRae

"Out of the Blue," Fleurie

"Black Swan," Thom Yorke

CHAPTER TWENTY-SEVEN: Squall

"Expectations," Sir Sly

"Vitamin D," SONOIO

CHAPTER TWENTY-EIGHT: Chart Datum

"Pain & Pleasure," Black Atlass

"Atlantic," Sleep Token

"Left," SONOIO

EPILOGUE

"Bear's Vision of St. Agnes," mewithoutYou

EROSION

Harper

I'M SURE NOBODY GOES ON vacation expecting to be dismembered and put through a woodchipper, but some tourists are just assholes and deserve their fate.

Like the guy in the Buoy and Beacon Pub last year who cornered Selma Dayton by the bathrooms. I was there. I heard her tell him no. When I came around the corner from the bar, he was trying to kiss her and slide a hand up her shirt. Piece of shit.

Woodchipper.

Or the guy who got drunk and high and crashed through a fence at Dale Linden's farm and then proceeded to chase his horses through the field. They panicked, of course. One of them fell and broke a leg. Dale had to put it down. Even though he called the cops, Sheriff Yates was too lazy to do anything more than write a police report. As usual.

Woodchipper.

Or the man whose dismembered hand I'm holding now. Mr. Bryce Mahoney. I saw him at Carnage Country Grocery, trying to take pictures up women's skirts with his phone. When I stole his wallet and looked him up, I found he'd already been discovered and charged with the same crime in two other states. And yet, there he was, traipsing around Carnage like he fucking owned the place, barely concealing the fact that he was up to the same shit yet again.

Definitely the woodchipper.

I hum to myself as I examine his palm, the skin pale, like a wax imitation of the real thing. It's cold. Heavier than I expected, especially with such stubby fingers. I turn the severed hand over and trace the network of veins that weaves over the bones. They were full of life only hours ago. He knew their pattern. He could probably tell me how he got the jagged little scar over one knuckle. I'm sure he had a story about how he got the stitches that marked his skin with dots of scar tissue. Maybe I should feel guilty that I took those memories from him.

"But I don't," I say as I toss his hand into the hopper of the blue woodchipper. Cookie Monster has been my faithful tool through twelve tourists now, including Mr. Mahoney. And he's always hungry for more. Just like me.

The pitch of the chipper drops a few notes as it chews through flesh and bone, spraying it onto the tarp I've set up next to the flower bed.

Maybe once upon a time, I would have felt remorse. But I left that person behind when I came to Cape Carnage four years ago. When I started a new life. When I promised to keep my past hidden and protect this sanctuary of secrets.

And I'm not about to let anyone like Bryce Fucking Mahoney ruin my town.

I cast my gaze across my garden. We're in that in-between time of year—not spring, not quite summer. Only the daffodils and tulips and snowdrops have bloomed. And yet, the tourists have already started to come. They're chartering fishing boats. They're renting equipment and booking tours of the sunken HMS *Carnage* our town was named for and the numerous other shipwrecks hidden off the rocky coast. They're exploring the museum. They peruse the artsy and quaint and quirky downtown. They trek up the one hundred and fifty-two steps to the Cape Carnage lighthouse. They head to the local distilleries and vineyards to sample whiskeys and wines.

It might be odd. A little macabre at times. But to me, it's a paradise.

Our little town only has a few thousand permanent residents, including me. When the height of tourist season peaks with the Taste of Terror food festival at the end of the summer, we'll be wildly outnumbered. And I get it, I really do. With a moniker like Cape Carnage, it makes sense that the town wants to leverage its unusual name and history to attract vacationers. These short, precious summer months will sustain us in the depths of winter when no one will come. So, I take my role in keeping the town beautiful very seriously. Just like I do keeping it *safe*.

I return my attention to the bloodied plastic bag at my feet. I've saved the best for last—Bryce Mahoney's lower leg. There's a cheap tattoo of a trout on the waxen skin beneath thick hair. Just a single hideous fish hiding a flat scar. I crinkle my nose and then push his leg into the hopper, readying myself for the deep sense of serenity that will inevitably wash over me as every last inch of flesh and bone is consumed by the machine.

Except that's *not* what happens.

The chipper screeches and whines. My hands fly up to cover my head. The smell of burning rubber floods my nostrils. It's an assault on my senses. Deafening and pungent and confusing. It takes an instant too long for it to click that I need to *move*. I hit the kill switch on the fender of the tractor to stop the PTO shaft, but not before there's a *bang* so loud that my ears ring.

I turn off the tractor engine and stare in shock at the chipper.

"Jesus, Cookie. What in the ever-loving fuck?" I hiss. Breaths riot in my lungs. I stare at Cookie Monster as though the wood-chipper has personally wronged me. But when I finally open the panels and access the blades, I find the problem wasn't the chipper at all. The problem is fucking *Bryce*, mocking me from the after-life. I yank his mangled leg from the machine. The bone is shat-tered, half of it gone. The other half is fused to a titanium plate with surgical screws. Part of the trout's tail is still intact on the torn skin. I clearly underestimated the scar hidden beneath the blacks and grays and greens of the tattoo. It never occurred to me that the asshole might have metal plates beneath that fuck-ugly trout, and I know this simple mistake is going to chew away at my thoughts until the end of fucking time.

I drop the leg on the plastic bag and heave a weary sigh. "Motherfucker."

Before I can spend too much time imagining Bryce's smirking face from beyond the grave, I trudge to the shed to grab replace-ment shear bolts and my tools. It takes me nearly half an hour to remove the broken parts and replace them. The blades are dam-aged, but they'll work well enough for now. I use my hatchet to cut Bryce's bone above the titanium plate and de-flesh it, and then I start the motor back up and toss the rest of the leg into the hop-per. This time, it goes as planned. But I'm still too rattled from the near-catastrophe of a badly broken Cookie Monster to feel much peace as I watch the last remnants of Bryce Mahoney's body splat-ter across the tarp.

When nothing further flies from the curved spout, I turn everything off. As I kneel next to the pile, a familiar *caw caw* draws my attention to the tree near the garden gate. I glance toward a black shadow hidden among the branches. "*Om nom nom.* Feed me," the raven demands.

"Give me a minute," I say. But the raven only caws and repeats his request, his voice a near-perfect replica of my own. Turns out, when you hand-raise an orphaned raven, it's incredibly easy to train it to speak with a little fresh meat. The only downside is that they're very persistent when they spot something they want. "You know it's coming. Settle down or you'll attract the gulls."

With a gloved hand, I scoop up some of the mess and take it to the bird feeder, a black platform with Gothic pillars to hold up a peaked roof. I made it just for Morpheus, who hops down to the stone wall that surrounds the garden to watch my every move, his inky feathers glistening in shades of black and indigo and deep forest green. I deposit the ground flesh and bone on the platform. I've barely taken two steps back before Morpheus lands on the feeder to dive beak-first into the muck. There's harmony in it. A shitbag person nourishing a wild creature. There's something in the closure of that loop that brings me a moment of peace.

I turn back to the pile that was once Bryce Mahoney and pick up my shovel from where it rests beside the tarp. One shovelful after the next, I unload the slop and shattered bone into the holes I've dug in the garden bed, pausing to plant flowers that aren't yet ready to bloom. Rhododendrons. Irises. Dahlias. Lilies. Before long, the body is gone, buried among the young plants. It will feed them, just like it's fed Morpheus. Just like it feeds something in me, something that grows hungrier with each season that passes. Something that never stays sated for long.

I clean up my mess. Put away my tools. Spray down the wood-chipper with Piss-Off!, which I'm just going to assume works for blood since it bleached my outdoor plastic furniture when I used it on the cat pee from Doug, the neighborhood stray. I take the remaining piece of Bryce's leg bone inside my cottage, wrap it in tinfoil, and place it in the fridge, and then I head upstairs. It's not until the shower is on and heating up that I get a good look at my reflection. There are smears of blood and dirt on my face. There are bits of Bryce in my hair, gleaming among the dark strands. I look feral. Much like I did the day I got away from that house of horrors where the vultures watched from the tree. I was all wild eyes and broken heart. I might be more settled now than I was back then, less haunted by fear and raw grief, but there's still something reckless in my reflection. Like I could take off at any moment and run into the untamed corners of the world, never looking back.

But I'm determined not to. This is my safest place. Stumbling upon Cape Carnage after trying and failing to wander away from my grief was like discovering a magical portal to a land where I could become whoever I wanted to be. Maybe not a fresh start, but as close to one as I could ever hope to find. It's my home now. And I'm needed here.

I lean closer to the mirror, closing in on myself until my breath fogs the glass. I press my bangs back from the fair skin of my fore-head. There's a thin band of lighter hair before it transitions to brown so dark it's almost black. Blond roots. Sometimes, it feels as though my body is fighting who I've decided to become.

Chewing my bottom lip, I turn my attention to my phone on the counter, logging into my sock puppet account for the Undiscovered Truths private message board, an amateur online sleuth group I keep occasional watch on. This particular group was the most active in trying to find me after I first disappeared, and every now and then my name still comes up on their site. I open the general thread where the primary conversations occur and scroll through recent posts. There's chatter about a cold case in Washington State. Some about a serial killer who was murdered in Louisiana. A few missing people. But I find nothing specific or concerning in the stream of messages over the recent posts. Certainly nothing that mentions my fucked-up past. Even stories like mine simply fade away in time. It's easier to disappear when you don't have any family left to keep your memory alive.

With a relieved sigh, I make a note in my phone to pick up more hair dye before I set it down and step into the shower.

It's just after noon when I leave the cottage on the southern edge of the estate's extensive grounds. With Bryce's mangled bone in my bag, I head toward Lancaster Manor, an imposing stone structure that casts a shadow of generational wealth across Cape Carnage. Even more intimidating than the house itself is the man who resides there. My favorite person in the town. My best friend.

I'm one of only two people who can simply walk into his home.

There's nothing to greet me when I enter the foyer. A little spike of fear hits my veins. There's usually a constant curtain of sound that seems to warm the austere stone: classical music, or old movies, or Arthur talking to himself in a low rumble. But there's rarely silence.

"Arthur . . . ?" I call out as I enter the formal living room. There's no answer. I frown and continue toward the library, where he spends most of his time reading beside the fire, even in the warmer weather. "Arthur . . . I'm here to make you some lunch . . ."

I'm just starting past the hallway that leads to the kitchen when Arthur springs from behind a statue with a knife clutched between his teeth, which is quite a feat for an octogenarian with a walker.

"Jesus fucking Christ, Arthur—"

He steadies himself before grasping the handle of the blade to brandish the weapon at me. "Who are you?"

"It's me. Harper."

He rolls a step closer with the walker and twists the knife in a threat. "If you're here to steal from me, *I'll cut you*—"

"I'm not here to steal from you. I'm *Harper*. Your gardener. I live in the cottage." A fleeting wisp of confusion passes across Arthur's weathered face at my words. "I'm here to make you lunch. Just like I do every day."

"Lunch . . . ?"

"How about your favorite sandwich today? Pastrami on rye. Are you hungry?"

Arthur blinks, his thick white brows lifting as the fog seems to fade just enough that he lowers the blade. A little piece of my heart seems to fall with it. I reach my hand out and he stares at it as though trying to uncover the secrets beneath the lines that cross my skin. "Harper," he finally says as he lays the handle of the knife on my palm. "Of course. I thought you were a thief." When I raise a brow in doubt, his eyes narrow. "Someone is coming in here and stealing from me."

I try to keep my expression neutral as I take his arm and turn him toward the kitchen. "What makes you think so?"

"My shoes went missing."

"Someone stole your shoes?"

"Yes."

"Why . . . ?"

"They're Stefano Riccis," he grumbles, as though I should know what that means.

"And someone would want to take them because . . . ?"

"Because they're *Stefano Riccis*," he says, rolling his eyes as though I'm the biggest pain in the ass to walk the earth. "They're exquisite."

"Okay," I say as we enter the kitchen and I guide him to the breakfast nook. When he's settled, I lay my bag down on the marble island before washing my hands. "So someone stole your exquisite, used, old-man shoes. But on the off chance someone *didn't* break in to take your beautiful shoes, I can have a look for them later, just in case you misplaced them. Anything else?"

"My Swarovski Signum sugar bowl."

I blink at him. "A sugar bowl. Someone stole your *sugar bowl*."

"It's an expensive piece."

"Are we talking Pauly's Pawn Shop expensive, or international black market sugar bowl expensive?"

Arthur glares at me, but I know how much he enjoys being needled. It's the reason we became friends in the first place.

When I came to Carnage four years ago, I didn't know I was supposed to be intimidated by his curmudgeonly attitude and considerable wealth, and he found that endlessly refreshing. "Pauly wouldn't know a Wassily from a Modway knockoff, you uncouth wretch."

"I have no idea what you just said."

"*Chairs*, for Christ's sake, Harper."

"Not the Wassily chairs," I say, pressing the back of my hand to my forehead. "I am *aghast*."

"I thought you promised me pastrami."

"Indeed." I give him a little bow and head to the fridge,

opening the stainless-steel door with the intention of finding the pastrami and provolone. But I find more than meat and cheese. I don't turn around when I say, "That super-special sugar bowl . . . Is it green?"

"Yes. With a Swarovski crystal on the lid."

I lift the lid of the bowl that sits eye level on a shelf in the fridge and sigh. "So . . . like . . . this one?" I turn to face Arthur with the sugar bowl in hand. The momentary burst of surprise in his eyes quickly dissolves into a glare, as though the bowl itself is at fault.

"I didn't put that in there," he declares. And though I could argue that no one is coming into his home to steal his shoes or place his sugar bowl somewhere he won't find it, I don't. It won't accomplish anything more than upsetting him, because he simply doesn't remember. Just like one day soon, he won't remember me.

He drags a newspaper close to him, fidgeting with the corner of a page as he watches me for a long moment before finally lowering his gaze. He never used to do that. Fidget with things. Stare at me as though he can't work me out. Ever since I came to Cape Carnage, he's been the one person who truly understood me. But now, it's as though walls are forming between us, ones we put up to preserve the person he still wants to be. And maybe that's the hardest part of watching his slow decline.

I clear my throat and pull my phone from my back pocket, starting a message. "I bet Lukas put your sugar bowl in the fridge by accident. I'll text him now to let him know."

> I'm throwing you under your grandfather's judgy bus.

"Yes. Thank you. He mustn't do that again," Arthur says with a disgruntled cluck of his tongue. "It must have been Lukas. Tell him he must treat my belongings with more care next time he comes."

My phone vibrates.

> Fucksakes, Harper. One of the stills just exploded. I have literally no idea what the fuck I'm doing. I don't need to be run over by the judgy bus.

> Too late. It'll make him happy. Under the judgy bus you go. Just lie there and accept your fate.

> Fuck you.

"Lukas has been a little distracted lately, I think," I say, then chew my dark grin into submission as the anticipation of winning a round of our game of sabotage buzzes through my veins.

"You're right. Lukas is a bit absent-minded these days. Tell him I need him to come clean the gutters. The fresh air will do him some good."

> Judgy Bus says you're coming to get some fresh air with the gutters.

> But I hate heights.

> You know, the septic alarm went off the other day. I was going to call

someone out to fix it, but I could offer that instead?

Tell him I'll be over on Wednesday.

I truly hate you.

"Done. Lukas will come by on Wednesday." I grin as I slide my phone back into my pocket and wash my hands a second time under the weight of Arthur's sharp, assessing gaze. His grunt of approval quickly follows. "How are things going at the distillery? Has he filled you in?"

If the revitalization of Lancaster Distillery were happening two years ago, Arthur would have given me a running list of everything going well and everything going awry. But now, he hesitates. He drums crooked fingers on the cherrywood table. "It's fine," he finally says, returning his attention to the newspaper. And I smile, because even though I know it's *not* fine, I don't want him to stress about something that will only manifest in other ways. Like sugar bowls in the fridge. Or a phantom shoe thief who stalks through the house as he sleeps.

"I'm glad to hear it."

I finish making Arthur's sandwich. He requests some light background music: Mozart's opera *Don Giovanni*. Nothing like the tale of a supernatural statue besting an arrogant nobleman to set the tone for your lunch after finding your wayward embellished sugar bowl, I guess.

But who am I to complain? It makes him happy. And despite the sharp words that often cut their way free of his tongue, he's a good man . . . I think. At the very least, a *lonely* man. So, I sit with him as he eats. We talk about the town. The tourists who are starting to appear. He reminisces about moments from long ago, ones that are still easier to remember with his Alzheimer's than the more recent experiences he struggles to recall. He tells me about the Cape Carnage he used to know, when it was an isolated place. Before food festivals, and shipwreck tours, and nighttime ghost walks with lanterns and costumes. Before repainted trim on Victorian houses and karaoke at the Buoy and Beacon Pub.

He talks about the kind of town where grief was not just a legacy, but a presence, as real as the fog that obscures the rocks that rest among the waves, waiting to crush hulls and claim lives. When Arthur was young, life was never easy in an isolated fishing village like Cape Carnage, which relies on the treacherous waters off northern Maine's remote coastline for its livelihood. Death was only a bad storm or a hidden rock or a hard winter away. It's not the town I know, though the echo of it still remains in the monuments to lost ships erected at the top of the promontory, facing the sea. But when he tells me the tales of Cape Carnage, I feel as though I'm the steward of those stories. Like he wants me to hold on to memories he knows are slipping away.

When Arthur has finished his meal, I give him his pills and wash up before settling him in the library. Even though my stomach is growling and a caffeine headache is starting to buzz through my brain, I stay with Arthur until he falls asleep in his favorite recliner for his post-lunch nap, a book splayed across his lap.

With a final, bittersweet smile at the old man, I leave the estate and walk into Cape Carnage.

My town.

ANCHOR

Nolan

THE WIND CARRIES THE GRIT of salt from the sea. I take a deep breath and let it flood my lungs. We always think the scent of the ocean refreshes us. Cleanses us. There's a rightness to that for humankind. We say it gives us peace when it's really the smell of death and decay.

A smile lifts one corner of my lips as I look across the water. It's true, I do feel reinvigorated by the scent of death.

And I can't wait to bring my vengeance to Cape Carnage.

I head to the trunk of my rental car and grab my bags, and with a final glance toward the ocean, I make my way up the steps of the Capeside Inn. My knee is stiff from the long drive. My elbow too. When I tilt my head from one side to the other, the vertebrae crunch and crack and pop. I mentally rearrange my schedule for Day One.

First, check into the hotel. Second, go for a walk to loosen things up. Maybe find a sandwich. Third, start hunting down that bitch to give her the slow and painful death she deserves for making me suffer immeasurable grief and pain and torture and indignity. Fourth, hot tub.

My grin widens as I enter the lobby.

Every year on the anniversary of the crash that killed my brother and nearly took me too, I claim another life. She's the final prize of my annual expeditions for justice. My most coveted trophy.

This is going to be a fucking amazing vacation.

There's no one at the desk when I drop my bag on the crimson carpet, but a gentle snore comes from a darkened room to the left, behind the counter. I clear my throat, but nothing happens. The snores continue. I say, "Excuse me," but there's still no response. That's when I notice the framed sign next to a little brass bell. RING THE BELL OR I'LL KEEP SNORING, the sign says in large print. And below it in smaller font: I'M NOT LYING. RING IT OR YOU WON'T GET YOUR KEYS.

I ring the bell.

There's a snort in the dark. And then, "I'm here. Hold on to your britches."

Shuffling footsteps come from the direction of the room. A short, elderly woman makes her way to the reception desk, breathing on the lenses of her glasses to polish them on an embroidered apron as she draws closer. Her cloud of white hair sways with every sliding step, her smile carving trenches into her sepia skin. When she finally stops at the desk, she slides her glasses on, then lets her cloudy eyes travel over the details of my face. Everything takes her longer than it should. Every blink. Every breath. She clears her throat. Audibly swallows. And finally: "Checking in?"

"Yes," I say, passing my license and credit card across the counter. "Reservation for Nolan Rhodes."

The woman takes my cards with crooked fingers and sets them

down as she opens a leather-bound book. "Welcome to Cape Carnage," she says, flipping through pages. "I'm Irene."

"Nice to meet you, Irene . . ." I reply, though Irene doesn't really acknowledge my words. She starts repeating my name as she trails a finger down the ledger. She leans closer to the book, and closer, and closer. Then she picks up a magnifying glass and leans closer still.

"Nolan Rhodes," she says with a note of triumph as she finds my name. "Checking out July fifteenth. Room one-seventeen."

"That's the one with the hot tub, right?"

"Yes, indeed." She turns away to a board on the back wall where keys hang from brass pegs. "You're here on holiday?"

"Yes, ma'am."

"Come to see the *Carnage*?"

I cover my snort with a cough. "Something like that, ma'am."

"Water'll still be pretty cold, but it should be clear. Wallie rents winter wetsuits if you don't have your own. You'll find Wallie's Watersports by the marina. Take Harborside Road along the cliff and then follow the signs, can't miss it," she says as she points in the general vicinity of the sea.

I know the map of the town by memory, and she's definitely not pointing in the right direction, but I just nod. Satisfied, she passes me the key. "Breakfast is served daily from six to ten in the dining room. There's a kitchenette in your suite, but there are some good spots to eat out at too." She slides a pamphlet across the counter, then rings up my credit card, declaring that she's given me the off-season rate because she "likes the cut of my jib," whatever the fuck that means. I just take my cards back with a bright word of thanks and then grab my bags, heading down the hall to my room.

Though run by someone who's truly ancient, the inn gives off a traditional but sophisticated, timeless vibe. My room is a suite with pale blue walls and mahogany furniture and French doors that face the sea. There's a small patio with a privacy fence and a hot tub that gurgles beneath a cover. I stand outside and face the cliffs for a long moment before I head back into the room, stop in front of the bed, spread my arms wide, and flop down onto the plush duvet. The handle of the knife strapped to my belt knocks against my ribs, a reminder of the amazing time I'm about to have. I wrangled a whole fucking six weeks off. Not an easy feat when you work in Search and Rescue, by the way. I've imagined this trip so many times over the last four years. And now I'm finally here, about to grasp the one thing I've been hunting for. The thing that kept me going in the darkest hours: revenge.

I pull the blade free of its sheath and turn it over, testing the sharpness with my thumb. When it nicks my skin and a bead of blood appears, I smile.

"You can't hide from me. Not anymore."

I set the blade on the nightstand, and I get up to fish a Band-Aid from my luggage before I unpack. I set out fresh clothes. My wash bag. My laptop and charger. And then, with a last glance around the room as though someone else could be watching, I pull out my prized possession.

My scrapbook.

I flip to the first page. I'm not the kind of guy you'd look at and think, *Yeah, he's into scrapbooking*. But when you spend two months in the hospital consumed by sorrow and suffering and the need for revenge, sometimes you take up new hobbies. The first pages are a little haphazard. Photos and memories glued down with ripples in their edges or bubbles beneath their surface. Laid down by an unsteady hand. But as the pages go on, the work becomes cleaner. There are photos of my first steps as I relearned how to walk in rehab, me standing with a walker next to my sister and parents. I remember what my dad said that day with tears in his tired eyes. "We're proud of you, son. There's no one on this earth more determined than Nolan Rhodes."

Perhaps it was a little hyperbolic, but he's a good dad, and that's the kind of thing good dads say when their son survives a hit-and-run. And he's got a point about determination—I definitely have a lot of that. Maybe just not the way he would expect.

Most people will probably tell you that you need to find light in the darkness to recover from the kind of suffering I endured. They expected me to embrace positive ideals that would keep me moving forward after my life-altering accident. Like acceptance of things I couldn't change. Liberation from hurt and anger. Catharsis. *Forgiveness*. But the idea of forgiving anyone was repulsive.

That is not what I did. Hope and positivity were not what drove me to wean myself from pain medications, or to relearn to feed myself, or to overcome the indignity I felt at having others bathe and clothe me. They're not what helped me survive what I lost.

I never found light in the chasm of pain.

What I did find was the deepest, most lightless void in myself. A place where the man I once knew faded away, and a new one took shape.

Why should I forgive the four people who were in the car that night for crashing into me and leaving me to die a slow and painful death alone in the dark? Why should I forgive them for the brother they took from me?

"Billy." I press a hand to my chest where it still aches every time I say his name out loud. I hardly ever do anymore. Every time my brother's name passes my lips, it's not our childhood memories that appear first. It's not the sound of his lighthearted laugh. It's not the image of his smile that I remember.

It's his unseeing eyes fixed to mine. It's the crimson rivulets that drip from his mouth to pool on the asphalt. It's the quiet hiss that escapes from his parted lips. Just a final whispering breath to warm the blood in the night.

No, I will never forgive them.

So I cling to the dark. I nurture it. I give it all my bitterness. All my hate. And in turn, it nurtures me.

It gives me purpose. Strength. A goal to work toward. A mission to fight for.

I turn to the next page of my scrapbook.

Marc Beaumont.

His face is not just stamped on the page of my scrapbook. It's imprinted in my memory, an image forever branded like a scar across my thoughts. Just like the warmth of the summer breeze, or the last light of the evening sun, or the smell of the pine needles on the steep trail that led from the beach at Calvert Cliffs in Maryland. I remember the way they crunched beneath our boots as Billy and I hiked up to the road. It was Fourth of July weekend. A quick and easy vacation to see my little brother. He'd moved to Baltimore a few months prior and I still missed him immensely. I remember thinking how good it was to hear his laugh again as I looped an arm over his shoulder. He was talking about the beers we were going to share when we started to cross the road to return to the campground. But we never made it back there. Not when that car careened around the sharp bend and struck us both.

And that moment is the brightest of all. I can still see Marc Beaumont's shock from the passenger seat of the car. I can still hear the screech of tires the instant before the blinding pain. I can still hear my brother's scream as he called out my name, the last sound he ever made.

It took me months to recover from my injuries. Several more to build back my strength. I spent every spare moment picking up new skills, learning how to hunt a different kind of prey. And on the first anniversary of the crash, Marc Beaumont was the first man I came for.

"Tell me the names of the two men in the car with you," I whisper. It's an echo of memory. I might be sitting in my room in the Capeside Inn, but it's the terror in Marc's eyes I see. I trace a numb fingertip over the photograph of his face. I can still hear his muffled pleas when I close my eyes. I remember the satisfaction I felt at ripping the duct tape from his mouth. "Tell me their names and I might let you live."

"I don't know what you're talking about. Please, *please*, let me go." The fear in his voice was an awakening. A revelation. It's what made me realize that the vengeance within my grasp was exactly what I needed. A drug that would soothe me. One I would never get enough of.

I'd already had an idea who was with him that night in the car, but I had to be sure. Marc had claimed in the police reports that he was at home alone and not with his girlfriend when she barreled into us, even though he'd been seen with her at a party not even an hour before the crash happened. He said he didn't know anything about the accident that claimed my brother's life and nearly took mine. The one that supposedly claimed the driver's life, too, when she took off but crashed a short distance away from where she left us to die, the car tumbling over a cliff and into the sea.

But I knew the truth. He *was* there. Sitting in the passenger seat, with two men in the back. I remember it, their forms and faces blurry in the distance as they got out of the car and argued about whether to stay at the scene or drive away.

It took only moments for them to decide to run away while the driver got back into the car and tore away with a squeal of tires. The only thing I remember from the brief moments before pain consumed my consciousness was my brother's lightless eyes staring back at me as I screamed his name.

My gaze shifts from Marc's photograph to the opposite page of my scrapbook.

"Trevor Fisher," Marc had finally confessed after only a few punches. "And Dylan Jacobs. He works at the Instinctive Ink tattoo parlor in Graywood."

I'd bound his arms to the chair and I remember the way he looked down at his forearm when he'd said it. When I twisted his skin, the lettering was still crisp, the edges healed but clean. The tattoo couldn't be more than a year or two old.

Memento mori.

"Let me guess," I'd said, releasing my hold on his arm. "Dylan and Trevor. They have the same tattoo, don't they?"

"Y-yes."

"That's good." I'd turned away toward the table of tools waiting to be christened with blood. "I knew I'd need a trophy."

I take a deep breath and blink away the memories, returning to my room at the inn. I look at my knife where it now rests on the nightstand, the blade as sharp as the day I'd used it to take my first trophy. My first *justice*. And then I look down at the patch of thin leather, the uneven edges bound to the page.

Memento mori.

Remember, you must die.

AZIMUTH

Harper

I ENTER A SHIPWRECKED BEAN with my bag slung over my shoulder and an eye for anything out of place in the little coffee shop. There are the usual suspects. The three Roberts—Bob, Bobby, and Bert—who spend more time in the café than at their jobs filling the potholes that appear every spring. Maddison, the studious and quiet teenage barista who works full-time behind the counter for the summer. Alex, the boy who's a year older than her, with his floppy hair and devil-may-care attitude. Maddison has the biggest crush on him, and despite several attempts at meddling with their work schedule when the Bean's owner is occupied with his other restaurant, I can't seem to get them together. I step into the line and try not to scowl at him. I'm pretty sure his oblivious stupidity is the only thing stopping these two from getting together. With a final perusal of the patrons, I step up to the counter.

"What can I get for you, Harper?" Maddison asks, giving me a sweet, shy grin as she grabs a to-go cup for me. She already knows I'm about to order an Americano, even starting to ring it into her point-of-sale system.

"The usual, please," I reply, digging into my small bag for my wallet. I wince when my fingertips don't graze it. "Shit. I forgot my wallet."

"Don't worry, I know you're good for it."

"No, it's totally fine. I know I have some cash floating around in here." I pull Bryce's tinfoil-wrapped leg chunk from my bag and dig through the remaining contents until I grab a rogue ten-dollar bill, passing it across the counter with an apology. Maddison opens the till for change as my gaze pans across the tarts and cakes and glazed donuts. I deserve a little treat for my busy morning. It's not easy work tracking down and murdering a man and chopping him up, all before lunch. Maybe a cinnamon bun—

"Anything you recommend?" a man behind me says. His voice is smooth. Decadent. Warmed with a subtle Southern accent. His tone is richer than any temptation behind the glass case. I turn. And that voice, as delicious as it is, is nothing compared to seeing him for the first time.

He's tall enough that I notice the difference between us, not easily done when you're nearly five foot ten. He runs a hand through his hair and it's almost obscene. And he *knows* it. I can tell by his lopsided grin, the way his lips tug back at one corner to reveal perfect teeth. He's full of confident charm. When his hand drops back to his side, his hair falls into place as though it's physically impossible for him to look anything less than perfect, even when he's disheveled. *Especially* when he's disheveled. Shades of honey blond streak the rich brown strands that skim his cheekbones, the kind of color that can only come from time spent in the sun. He's magnetic. And a whole hell of a lot of . . . *dangerous.*

I swallow, trying to gather my composure, and his attention drops to my throat, the greens in his eyes igniting with subdued amusement. An unusual wedge of brown at the bottom of his left iris is a stark contrast to the lighter shades. "Depends on what you're in the mood for," I say, trying to sound nonplussed. "Sweet or savory?"

His smile stretches, just a little, enough to coax out two dimples in his sun-kissed, faintly freckled cheeks. "I'm not sure, what did you go for?" At first, I don't understand what he means, not until he nods to the tinfoil gripped tightly in my hand. "What did you get?"

"Umm . . ." I swear I only blink, but that brief motion feels like it's about a thousand years long as my mind scours through every item on the menu I have memorized, landing on the only word I can seem to summon. "Meat."

"Meat . . . ?"

"Ball." The guy's head tilts. My throat strains around a desiccated swallow. "Ballmeat. I mean, *meat . . . ball*. Meatball sub. Footlong. Ish."

Our gazes both drop to the tinfoil in my hand. It's barely four inches long and maybe two inches wide at best. When our eyes connect, I can't help but cringe. Though he gives me a polite smile, something about it is pitying. "I might try something else," he says.

"Maybe the turkey," I say as Maddison passes a sandwich over the glass case to the customer in front of me. The sandwich is fucking enormous, barely contained by the wax paper wrapped around it. It's maybe three times the size of the tinfoil I shift behind the bag that rests against my hip. *Why the fuck did I lie about that?* I guess I'm not about to say, "Oh, it's some dickhead's mangled tibia," but still. I could have done better than that, right? I blame this guy. It's his eyes. Those unusual green eyes with that rare seam of brown, colors that seem to spark to life when he's amused. Just like they're doing now.

The man's grin is teasing. "Not the ballmeat. Got it."

I snort. Literally.

And then I die. *Not* literally, but I wish.

The man chuckles as though my piggish chortle was fucking adorable. I turn away just long enough to stuff the change in the tip jar and Bryce's bone back into my bag. I swear my skin is on fire. Sweat itches along my spine. But when I meet his eyes once more, the man just grins. Leans back a little. Surveys my face, warmth radiant in his eyes. "So, what drink do you recommend to go with my not-ballmeat sandwich?" he says as he moves closer to me and surveys the chalkboard above the counter.

"I should probably say something about tea bagging, to really round out my mortification."

The guy bites down on a grin, glancing down his shoulder at me. "Tea bagging is really staying on brand with the balls. Kudos."

"I'm nothing if not consistent."

Maddison reaches across the glass counter to pass me my coffee. I take it, and when I peek up at the man next to me, I find him watching the motion of my hand, his brow furrowed, his smile fading as though this moment is about to end too quickly. Maybe he feels the same tug in his chest that I'm feeling, and he doesn't want that thread to snap.

I should turn away. Get out of here. Leave this tourist guy behind. It's not like I need to flirt disastrously with some random man who's probably only here for a few days at most. That's not my way, no matter how much I sometimes long for a connection that I'm not even sure I'm ready to make. I should leave. Continue on my walk past the lighthouse where I like to stand on the cliff and look out at the sea. Toss Bryce's mangled bone into the ocean where it will sink beneath the surface, never to be seen again, just another memory claimed by black water.

But before I can convince myself to move, his hand is on my sleeve. Such a gentle touch. Only a whisper of heat and pressure. And as simple as it might be, that touch sets off a current in my skin. It steals my breath. Quickens my pulse and warms my belly and crashes through my thoughts, wiping them clean. Just a heart-beat ago, I was clinging to every argument I could think of to leave. And now they're simply . . . gone.

"I'd ask if I could buy you a coffee, but it looks like you're all set," he says as he nods down to the to-go cup in my hand. That teasing light is back in his eyes. "But if you want company while you eat some balls, I'd love to join you."

Heat infuses my cheeks. His eyes seem to brighten. I should say no. I know it. But instead I say, "Okay."

"Okay." His focus lingers on me for a moment as though he needs to be sure I'll stay, and then he lifts his hand away, turning to face Maddison. "I'll take a turkey sandwich to go, please, and an Earl Grey tea with two tea bags."

A grin sneaks onto my lips and I shake my head. When I look up at my companion, his expression is a mirror of mine.

There's something addictive about holding his attention. I forgot how fun it was to let my guard down a little. Suddenly, I find myself wanting to say something witty, or cute. Poke fun at him maybe. Like, *"Turkey and tea? You sound like trouble."* No, my God, that's fucking awful. At this rate, I probably can't trust that any-thing worthwhile will come out of my mouth.

So what if I just smile a certain way instead? Hold on to those green eyes of his that break away from mine to watch my fingers fold a lock of hair behind my ear? I thought I'd forgotten how to do this. How to flirt with a man. I thought I'd shut all that away years ago. I might be only a few months shy of twenty-nine, but I thought I'd buried those skills a long time ago. I thought they'd died the day I did.

The next patron in line steps between us to order, shattering the hum in the air that crackles like a spell. My new friend moves to the pickup counter as Maddison puts his order together, and though I leave his side to put cream and sugar in my coffee at the little stand along the wall, I can feel him watching me. But I don't return to his side when I'm done.

Instead, I pretend to observe the people around me who chat about potholes and shipwrecks and gossip from town, or museums and ghost tours and plays at the Carnage theater. But really, I'm stealing glances at him. I notice details, because that's what I've trained myself to do. Like the wear on his hiking boots, the leather scuffed, the soles caked with a thin layer of dried mud as though he spends most of his time on his feet. I catalog the lighter streaks in his hair. The tattoo that wraps around one forearm, an ouroboros. The scar that follows the curve of his elbow, disappearing beneath his rolled-up sleeve. I notice the way he tilts his head from side to side, loosening some hidden tension lodged between his bones. I especially notice the way he scans the other patrons with a cold and clinical detachment, but his focus always returns to me. And every time it does, he smiles. He seems observant, but remote. It's as though his charm is a well he can draw from when he chooses. But the rest of the time? He's stoic, like that well is hidden in a faraway landscape. A place he keeps carefully guarded.

Maybe that should scare me. But it only adds to the gravitational force that beckons me closer.

When he has his sandwich and drink in hand, he joins me to add a splash of milk to his tea. With a sweep of his gaze around the small café, he looks at me with a crease between his brows. "Busy place. There's nowhere to sit."

I shrug, though my nonchalance feels forced. "Typical for the Bean, even early in the tourist season. But we can walk, if you like?"

I'm not sure why those words just exited my mouth. I barely manage to stop short of offering to show this guy around downtown. I'm not that kind of person anymore, one who puts herself out there to strangers so easily. I used to be. And then, one beautiful, innocuous August day, it cost me more than I ever thought possible.

But there's something about this man that seems so different from the other tourists who pass through Carnage, people I only pay attention to long enough to assess as a threat to my town. Something about him is almost familiar. Maybe it's in the way he seems removed from the rest of the busy café as he gives the room one last assessing look. Maybe it's the way he appraises the coffee shop as though searching for threats that gives me reassurance. Or maybe it's in the way his expression clears when his attention returns to me and he smiles. "I'd like that," he says, and for a blink of time, a single heartbeat, the world around us disappears.

I clear my throat. Give a faint nod. Then I turn and lead the way to the door, but he reaches past me before I can touch it, pushing it open for me to pass through. And I can't stop the flutter of excitement that dances behind my ribs.

"So, how does a person wind up in a town with a name like Cape Carnage? Is it a 'come for the name, stay for the ballmeat' kind of situation?" the man asks, taking a bite of his sandwich as we amble down the street toward the quaint downtown, filled with independent shops and quirky restaurants. I chance a glance up at him and I'm met with his teasing grin, and even though I expected its pull, I still feel unprepared for the magnetic force of it.

"The ballmeat is a big draw, for sure. Premium ballmeat in Carnage." I smirk into the lid of my coffee before taking a sip.

"Not eating?"

"No, saving it for later," I say as I pat my bag where the foil-wrapped bone is hidden. I meet his eyes only briefly, hoping my smile comes off less forced than it feels in my skin. "Is that what brought you here? The premium ballmeat?"

"Honestly, no. It was the tea bagging." I huff a laugh and I can feel the warmth of his amusement next to me. "I'm here on vacation."

"I never would have guessed."

"What gave me away?"

I shrug. "I know every face in town. And I don't know yours."

"How many people live in Carnage?"

"Four thousand, two hundred and ten."

"And you know every person here."

I look up to find him scrutinizing me with narrowed eyes, the warmth in them still there, though it's veiled by a thin layer of suspicion. "Yeah. I do."

"Born and raised here?"

"No," I say, flicking a wave to Diane Montgomery, the owner of the Starlight Boutique across the street. She waves back before entering the clothing store. "Just had time and motivation, I guess." I lift a shoulder and look up at my companion, and though the suspicion still lingers in the crease between his brows, it softens. "What about you? Why are you here, of all places?"

"Bird-watching."

I pause, staring him down with a furrowed brow. "Bird-watching."

His eyes dance in a way that makes me think he enjoys my disbelief. "You heard me, Meatball."

"Don't you dare. You'll be wearing this coffee," I say on the heels of a groan. He smiles at my threat, taking a sip of his tea.

"What kind of birds?"

The man shrugs, his expression still a little teasing, but something about it has a glint of a dark edge to it, like a blade that catches the light. It's as though his bird-watching is more like a hunt, the thrill of finding something elusive in the shadows of remote and desolate forests. Some distant alarm rings in the back of my head, but his expression softens and I smother my paranoia. "All kinds, I guess. Bald eagles. Osprey. But I'm not fussy. Anything from falcons to starlings interest me."

We slow to a stop in front of the window of one of Cape Carnage's weirder shops. My heart jumps into my throat as I deliberate on my next words. I can't remember the last time I felt these feelings. Desire. Attraction. I don't want to ask my next question. But I'm desperate to know. "By yourself?"

But he doesn't hear me, not when my voice is so quiet and his own question is so much louder as he says, "Craft-A-Corpse? Is this place for real?"

I clear my throat, trying to dislodge the sensation of shrinking into myself. "Yeah," I say, my tone too bright and breezy for the way I feel inside. "It's new this year. Kind of like Build-A-Bear. Except . . . not." I point to one of the displays, a row of fake hands in different stages of decay, some of them holding silk flowers, others clutching plastic weapons, others frozen in various gestures. I catch my companion's eye in the reflection on the window, a phantom over the body parts on the other side of the glass.

"They're for the Carnival of Carnage Gravity Race. Putting together a good corpse companion for your soapbox racer is pretty critical for style points. Going the fastest down the course is one thing, but sometimes the quality of the corpse is what clinches the win, you know? And it's easier to build a corpse here than to travel in with fake body parts in your suitcase, I guess."

"Huh. That's kind of a genius business idea," my new friend says. The shop's owner, Henry, waves to us with a severed hand as patrons paint various body parts with fake blood. And though there are lifelike entrails and eyeballs and severed limbs strewn throughout the window display, my companion doesn't seem fazed by the gruesome scene. He finishes his sandwich as he surveys the body parts with an appreciative nod. "I like it," he says, though I'm not sure if he's referring to the sandwich, or the shop, or both.

"Yeah, it's cool. Definitely very 'Carnage,'" I reply with air quotes. With a final wave to Henry, we turn and resume our walk.

"It is," he says. "And I am." When I look up at him with a question written across my face, he's already waiting, a teasing warmth brightening the green hues in his eyes as they catch the sun. In this light I can see the wedge of walnut brown in his left iris more clearly, a slice of shadow among the green that feels like a familiar comfort. "I am here by myself."

My cheeks warm. I can't hide the blush with my coffee cup, but I try anyway, keeping my eyes latched to his as I take a sip of my drink. And he doesn't let me get away with an escape. He smiles as though he's caught me, and even though part of me wants to, I don't look away.

At least, not until my phone rings.

"Sorry, excuse me." I dig into my bag, trying to shove my disappointment aside that the moment between us has been interrupted. When I withdraw the phone, it's Arthur's name on the screen. I accept the call and hold it to my ear, casting an apologetic glance toward my companion. "Hello?"

"Harper."

"That's me."

"Where are you?"

"In town. Not far from the Bean."

"Where's my black bag?"

My step falters, and I can sense my companion's concern next to me. Though I dart him an untroubled smile, I don't think it's very convincing for either of us. Knowing what's in Arthur's infamous black bag, there's no way my sudden burst of anxiety can be hidden completely. "Your bag?"

"That's what I said."

"Why do you need it?"

"Maria Flores's Airbnb. The tourists staying there are awful. The man used my driveway to turn around yesterday and cut across the edge of the grass. And today, he allowed his hideous little dog to relieve itself among the rose bushes and he didn't pick it up. Why Maria made such a grand house into an Airbnb, I will never know. It attracts the most horribly entitled windbags every summer."

"Okay . . . well . . . I'm not sure those missteps fit the criteria for what you seem to have planned—"

"They do today. Where's my black bag?"

My hopes for spending a little more time with the mysterious stranger next to me are quickly slipping through my fingers. Though I hid Arthur's bag of drugs and weapons and his precious "grim-noire" in my cottage a month ago in a place I knew he'd be reluctant to look, I still wouldn't put it past him to get into his golf cart and make his way to my house so he can have a rummage around for it. And the next stop would then be the neighboring house, where Arthur would charm his way inside only to murder the occupants. That was fine when they deserved it and he had a better memory for what he did with the bodies, but these days, he's not such a great judge of what qualifies as a murderable offense.

I sigh and steal a glimpse at my watch. Hopefully, by the time I make it back to the manor, he'll have forgotten his plan to kill our temporary neighbors, and if not, I'll have to find a way to distract him until he does. "I'll be home in twenty minutes, and I'll help you look for it, okay?"

"Bring me a double-shot chai latte with soy milk and a sprinkle of cinnamon, would you?"

I roll my eyes. "Fine."

"Extra hot."

"Yes, I know."

"With cinnamon, Harper. Not nutmeg."

"I'm hanging up now."

"Extra hot, Harp—"

I disconnect the call, halting as I slide the phone into my bag. My companion stops next to me, his gaze sweeping across my disappointed smile to leave a trail of heat in my flesh. "I have to go," I say, tearing my attention away to look back in the direction we just came from. "I have to stop by the Bean again and then head to my neighbor's place. He's elderly and sometimes needs a bit of help looking for things. They get lost a little more than they used to, I guess."

"I'll walk with you," the man says without hesitation. This time, it's his turn to blush, as though he offered more quickly than he meant to. "If you like, I mean."

"Yeah. I'd like that a lot."

The electric vibration hums in the air between us, stronger than it was before Arthur's interruption. It's as though every moment with this stranger only strengthens its power. I know I shouldn't let it. This man is just a temporary presence in my permanent sanctuary. But maybe that enhances the appeal. Knowing you're going to lose something before it even starts can be a balm as much as it can be a wound.

It's a brief walk back to A Shipwrecked Bean, and though our conversation is light, there's an undercurrent to it that I find difficult to define. When I laugh at something he says, I feel the way he watches me, as though a piece of him soaks right into my skin. When he holds the door for me to enter the café, his arm grazes mine, and the pressure of his touch lingers on my flesh long after I step into the line with him. I order Arthur's latte, and we stand off to the side as we wait for Maddison to prepare the drink. With every moment that ticks by, I can feel the passage of time. And I think he can too.

"I really enjoyed our walk, as short as it was," the man says, glancing down at the cup still clutched in his hand. "Shame I couldn't have gotten the full tour on such a nice day."

"I'm honored I at least got to show you Craft-A-Corpse. I feel like that's the bare minimum accomplishment for a tour guide in Cape Carnage."

He smiles, and I can detect a hint of nerves beneath it despite the easygoing mask he tries to portray. "Maybe if you're not busy

34

sometime over the next few days, we could build a body . . . ?"
He shrugs, like it's no big deal if I say no. "I mean, if you're into
that kind of thing."

I try to withhold my grin, just to make him squirm a little. But
it still ignites, a fire that burns beneath snow and can't be contained. "I'd like that."

"Great," he says, running a hand through his hair as a whisper
of crimson rises in his cheeks. There must be some kind of sudden
epiphany that occurs behind his eyes, because they widen as the
color brightens in his cheeks. "We've been talking all this time
and I don't even know who you are. What's your name?"

"I'm—"

"Harper?" I break my attention away from the man to look at
Maddison, who holds Arthur's latte across the counter. "Here you
go," she says, and it takes me a moment to reach for my cup. I'm
still stuck in a delay, an insect trapped in amber. Because I wasn't
going to tell him "Harper." Even though it's the only name I've
used for the past four years. Even though it's my first line of
defense. Even though I've vowed to keep my real name and the
past that trails behind it hidden. But for some reason, it was right
there, ready to be exhumed.

My words feel brittle when I give Maddison my thanks. Like
the notes have been hollowed out. Scraped clean.

And when I turn back to the man, every hint of light has been
scraped from him too.

There's a pause as we stare at each other in silence, a suspended
moment that seems to stretch into eternity. He doesn't just stare at
me. He stares *into* me. Like I've turned my back on a tiger, and
suddenly it's ready to use its claws.

Maybe I'm being paranoid. This chill that ripples through my
skin might be nothing. There have been a lot of "nothing"

moments in the past few years. When you've seen the things I've seen, it's easy to think that everyone is a monster lurking beneath a mask. So it could be just a strange little moment. A weird delay. Lord knows, I've been weirder in the last few minutes than he has.

I'm the one who's the killer, after all.

A memory surfaces. One of vultures in a barren tree. They scattered when I was dragged beneath the branches that pointed skyward like bleached and crooked fingers. "They come to pick your bones," the man said as he tugged me by the hair through the dust and prairie grass. I clawed at his hands. I screamed. But he only laughed. "Pick them clean."

It won't be me, I remind myself when the moment clears as suddenly as it arose. I'm the killer now. I'm the one holding a piece of a dead man's leg and pawning it off as a sad little sandwich. So maybe this nameless guy is just having a delayed reaction that will clear in the next breath. Maybe it's just a blip.

And I could make myself believe that if it didn't take just a moment too long for his next blink to wipe the lethal patina from his expression. His smile returns. But it doesn't quite reach his eyes.

I take a step to the side, edging between the man and the glass case behind me. When I swallow, his eyes dart down to the motion. They brighten, but not with the kind of light that's reassuring. "Good to meet you," I say. But my words have a glacial edge to them. I can't ignore this sudden burst of instinct. I *won't*. I need to cut this off clean. "Enjoy your bird-watching. I hope you find what you're looking for."

I don't turn my back to him. Not until I knock into another patron and I'm forced to look away to mutter an apology. And when I glance back at the man, he's still watching me.

But his smile is gone.

DECLINATION

Nolan

I MARCH FROM THE DOOR to the dresser. The dresser to the door. The door to the windows that face the sea. Back again.

But no matter how many times I pace across the room, it doesn't change the ball of unease that burns in my guts. I don't know what it is that bothers me most. Is it that interaction we had before the barista said her name? The shade of blush in her cheeks when she messed up the name of the sandwich in her hand? Was it the way she smiled at me with light in her eyes? The shyness in her expression when she dropped her gaze and tucked a strand of hair behind her ear?

Or does it bother me that I let myself become so completely spellbound that I didn't even realize who I was facing?

Or is it something more sinister that's burning me up to the point of physical pain? Is it the need to wrap my hands around her throat and squeeze until a desperate confession tumbles past her lips? I *must* get it out of her. That admission. The final missing piece. I need to hear exactly how she saw it all unfold. She must have seen the fear in my face that second before we collided in the dark. Her speeding car. My brother's terrified yell. My unsuspecting body. A single, indelible moment that stained our lives forever.

And then she left me there. Alone. In the dark.

I don't know why, but I didn't recognize her at all. I've been planning that first meeting with Harper Starling for four years. I've imagined every moment of how it would go.

And that wasn't the way I saw it playing out *at all*.

I sit down on the edge of my bed and pull my laptop from the nightstand, settling it on my thighs. When I log in, I open the folder for Harper Starling. I click on the first picture. It's one that was pulled from social media when the local news back in Calvert County, Maryland, was reporting on her culpability in the hit-and-run collision and her presumed death. It was a story I believed too—at first. Just like everyone else. It was only logical that she'd died, her body dragged away from the car by the tides and currents of the Chesapeake Bay. But in my quest to learn more about the woman who had hit my brother and me and left us for dead, a critical piece of information floated my way.

Harper Starling's bank account was drained of its savings hours after her vehicle had landed at the bottom of the sea.

I squint at my screen. She didn't post many photos of herself online, and the few she did were either taken from a distance or heavily edited with filters, like this one. But the dark hair and light skin tone seem similar. Was it the bangs that threw me off? The gentle wave to her chocolate strands? Because other details still seem mostly the same. The face shape. The body type, at least what's visible. It's all consistent with the next photo too, though the angle and lighting make it even harder to pinpoint any distinctive qualities to her features. But in person, there's something about Harper that seems so different from a static image—something charming but mysterious that sucked me right in.

I stare at those photos for far too long. I don't understand how I could have misinterpreted the familiarity I felt when I met her in line at the café. I had hunted for every scrap of information I could find on Harper. And there hadn't been many. A mention for a gardening competition win in the *Cape Carnage Chronicle* here. A grainy photograph there. But I consumed those details as though they'd sustain me. And in the darkest hours, they did. When suffering and grief threatened to finally destroy me, hunting Harper Starling was the only thing that kept me alive.

So how the fuck could I have gotten it so wrong when I looked at her?

I slam the laptop closed and toss it on the bed before I stalk to the hotel lobby, every step I take spent trying to wrangle this unease beneath the pleasant, unthreatening mask.

When I stop at the reception desk, Irene's snore is rumbling from the side room. I sigh and ding the little bell, and a moment later, she comes shuffling toward me. "Mr. Rhodes."

"Nolan is fine, ma'am."

She nods once. "Nolan. What can I do for you?"

"I wanted to get your recommendation, actually. I was looking for a place for lunch and stopped in at A Shipwrecked Bean. I got to talking to a woman named Harper. Do you know her?"

"Yes, Harper Starling. Got magic in those green thumbs of hers."

"Gardening?" I ask, pretending that I don't already know.

"Harper does most of the landscaping around town. Her garden at Lancaster Manor has won the town's best garden award for the last two years running. You should be here long enough to see it really start blooming. Everyone always *oohs* and *aahs* over the

39

main garden of the estate, but the one in front of her cottage on the south side is also truly lovely."

Bingo. The one detail I hadn't been able to discover is where she lives.

Irene's cataract haze seems to lift just a little, her eyes dancing in a way that I do not like. *At all.* "She's a sweet girl, that Harper."

"I'm sure."

"What would you like to know?" she asks, and the lobby door opens just as I'm about to launch into some fake and meaningless answer now that she's given me exactly what I'd hoped for with so little difficulty. We both turn our attention to a man who struggles through the door with an oversized roller bag and a backpack. It's a third bag that's slung across his body that catches my eye, the Canon logo embroidered across its surface.

"Ah, Mr. Porter," Irene says as the man wheels his luggage into the inn. He's about my age, probably early thirties, his short blond hair mostly covered by a baseball hat with a circular logo in silver stitching. *Porter Productions*, it says, and it summons an alarm deep in the recesses of my darkest thoughts. "How are you making out?"

"Not bad, thank you, Irene," he says, giving me a polite nod before his attention returns to the Capeside Inn's elderly proprietor. "Would be a little better if my drone operator had been able to make it. You have no idea how long it took to get all the permits and approvals in place."

Ideas ignite. "A drone operator?" I ask.

A reserved flicker of wariness passes across the stranger's face, and he takes a breath as though he's about to launch into an explanation, but Irene beats him to it. "Mr. Porter is filming a documentary," she declares. "He's staying for the next few weeks, and his drone operator took sick so he couldn't come." Irene gives a solemn shake of her head and clicks her tongue. "Shame to miss out on such a lovely day. You know what they say, 'If you don't like the weather in Carnage, all you have to do is wait an hour or two and it'll change.'"

I wonder if this guy is thinking the same thing I am, that the reviews for Capeside Inn are pretty on the nose about Irene knowing *everything* about her patrons. "Bet you didn't know Carnage has its own retired CIA analyst," I say, testing him out with an extended hand. "I'm Nolan."

The man takes my offered greeting, shaking my hand with strength in his grip. "Sam Porter. I may or may not be on the Cape Carnage CIA watch list."

Though I give him an easygoing grin, I can tell he's not convinced by me just yet. Maybe it was my overly eager question about the drone. Or perhaps it's the excitement I battle to keep off my face. It's a struggle to keep it from bleeding into my voice when I say, "I know a thing or two about flying a drone. Maybe I could lend you a hand if you're stuck."

I can almost see the reservation dissolving from Sam's expression. "Oh, really?"

"I'm in Search and Rescue. We use them frequently on the job." I shrug, trying to seem undaunted, though I can feel the giddy anticipation climbing beneath my skin. "If you're looking to do some filming today and want a hand, I've got nothin' but time. Just let me know. I'm in Room one-seventeen."

I give him a nod and force myself to turn away, my expression a neutral mask. I keep my hands in my pockets. My steps unhurried.

I don't take more than three before Sam calls after me.

"Hey . . . you know, I'd love to take you up on the offer, if you mean it? If you're not busy, of course."

The smile I cast to the shadows of the corridor ahead is not the same as the one I give Sam by the time I've turned to face him. "I'd be happy to."

I wait for Sam in the lobby as he takes his belongings to his room, returning fifteen minutes later with a hard plastic case and a backpack. Just as we reach the door, Irene's voice pipes up from behind the counter, her tone too cheerful and teasing when she says, "What did you want to ask me, Mr. Rhodes? Something about Harper Starling . . . ?"

"Nothing, ma'am." I tip my head to her in a grateful nod, keeping my expression warm and reassuring despite the excitement that bubbles beneath my surface. "Thanks for your help."

With little more than a nod between us, we say goodbye to Irene and set off in the direction of the lighthouse. Though it's in the opposite direction of the town center and Harper's probable location, I know it's still a high point on the topography, and if I'm lucky, I might be able to fly close enough to Lancaster Manor to catch a glimpse of her.

"So, you're an SAR specialist?" Sam asks as we turn down Beacon Road. I nod. "Don't meet one of those every day. What brought you to that job?"

As if on cue, the pain in my elbow spikes, reminding me that I can never truly forget the injuries that haunt me, even when I'm able to push them to the back of my consciousness. "I was a fire-fighter. I had an accident. Just couldn't do it after I got out of the hospital." I shrug, laying my palm over the scar where the pins and plates are embedded in bone. "Search and Rescue was a good option. Went to work in the Great Smoky Mountains National

Park and never looked back. I do a lot of drone work," I say with a nod to his black case. "Not just the searches, but mapping the trail hazards, incident prevention, that kind of thing."

Sam gives me a breath of a laugh as he shifts the brim of his cap down farther against the sun. "You're probably more experienced with this thing than the guy I meant to bring. Serendipity, I guess."

"Irene said you're making a documentary?" I ask, and though he doesn't look my way, a tight-lipped smile creeps across his face. "About what?"

Crystalline blue eyes dart my way. He's nearly chewing his grin into submission to keep from spilling every one of his secrets to a stranger. "Kind of like a true crime thing." He looks at me once more, gauging my reaction. When he seems to surmise I'm the appropriate amount of both concerned and intrigued, his smile stretches. "This might come off as a quaint little town that's found a way to profit off its name, but let's just say not all the macabre vibes are for show."

"What do you mean?"

"Have you ever heard of the serial killer called La Plume?" The name vaguely rings a bell, but I shake my head, and it seems to excite Sam that he'll be the one to educate me. He pulls his phone from his pocket, bringing up a web page and searching for La Plume, holding the device toward me to display the composite sketch of a man.

His short hair is swept to one side, black-rimmed glasses framing soulless eyes. "He had a very particular method," Sam says as he pockets the phone. He nods toward a path that departs from the sidewalk we're on, a sign for WIDOW'S POINT painted on a plank of weather-beaten wood. "He'd immobilize his victims and inscribe text into their skin with a quill. The *entire* body would be covered in text. Then, once he was finished, he'd kill them. He murdered a young woman here nearly thirty years ago and then he suddenly just . . . *disappeared*. But I don't think the killing in Cape Carnage ever stopped. Since then, every so often, people who have passed through have gone missing. Sometimes, they disappear from one of the nearby towns after stopping in Carnage. Sometimes, they seem to go missing from the town itself."

I look around as though a clue might surface from the barren brown rock that lies before us. "And, what . . . they just haven't been found?"

Sam shakes his head. "Nope. They've simply vanished. No evidence. No sign of them ever again. And it's not like police want to dig too deep, you know? One murder and a serial killer who disappeared while visiting aren't really great for the tourist industry. They might like the morbid vibes that come with the name, but they don't want anyone to think it's actually real." Our attention is diverted from the path ahead as a tour bus lumbers up the road next to us, heading for the lighthouse and nearby museum. Despite the fact that it's only the start of the tourist season, the vehicle still looks packed, silhouettes taking up most of the seats behind the tinted glass. "Urban legends are good for business, as long as they're just that. Legends."

We stop at a rocky outcrop partway along the path that leads to the cliff. I can hear the rhythmic crash of the sea against the stone in the distance, the percussion of an endless battle between water and land. "But legend is what's led me here," Sam says as he sets his case down. The dark and determined look he darts in my direction reminds me of the one I sometimes see in the mirror.

"I believe someone very special went missing in Cape Carnage. I think La Plume killed her here too. And that's how I'm going to blow this place wide open."

I don't ask him what he means. I already know he won't tell me, not with the tight smile he shoots my way, like he's given me just enough crumbs to pique my interest so he can deny me a full meal. If I want to know his secrets, I'm going to have to wait. He strikes me as the kind of person who needs to be pushed by disinterest. If he thinks I'm too eager, I'll spook him and he'll shut down. So I keep my mouth shut as he sets up the drone and moves on to the technical specs and the kinds of shots he wants. I take over piloting the drone above the quaint downtown.

I can barely contain the spike of triumph that hits my veins when the camera spots Harper Starling walking down a side street not far from the coffee shop where we met. She has a duffel bag slung over one shoulder, a pair of headphones over her ears, and an oversized hoodie that nearly reaches to the hem of her black biker shorts. She seems to be headed for the gym, and just as she turns down the walkway that leads to its entrance, a man exits the building. Some douchey-looking gym bro asshole who struts straight for her. As soon as she sees him, she pulls her headphones off, a smile stretching across her face as she draws to a halt. The moment he envelops her in a hug, the triumph I just felt turns to dust in my blood.

"Let's get some shots of the south end, there's a huge manor just on the outskirts of town," Sam says, though his words barely register in my mind. My heart is climbing up my throat, trying to choke every breath as I watch Harper and the man separate from their embrace. He still has his hands on her arms. I want to fucking rip them off one bone at a time and feed them into his bright fucking smile as he grins down at her. I want to— "Nolan . . . ? South end?"

"Yeah, sorry. Got lost in thought, I guess," I say with a hint of sheepishness in my voice. Sam gives a nod and then launches into some vague references to an amateur investigative group he's part of, as though he wants to tell me more but isn't ready to. With one last look at Harper and her companion, one final burn of fury through my flesh, I pilot the drone away.

We get shots of the rest of the town. Some of the extensive gardens and the austere stone mansion of Lancaster Manor, a historic estate that looms over the town like a foreboding castle. Some of the little cottage on its southern border, much of it obscured by oaks and elms. Some of the cliffs that drop into the sea. And as the battery in the drone starts to deplete, I bring it back to our rocky outcrop to be packed away. Though I make an effort to engage in conversation with Sam, it feels like just that. Effort. By the time we're back at the hotel, I'm both exhausted and enraged, and I spend the rest of the day trying to force my anger to cool.

But it never does.

There's only one thing that will alleviate this relentless torment: *finding my prey.*

And thanks to Irene's intel about Harper's garden at Lancaster Manor, I figure that's probably the best place to start.

It's dark and there's a chill in the air when I set out on foot from the Capeside Inn with my backpack of tools and weapons, heading south, sticking to the dimly lit side streets rather than the main road through the downtown. I've memorized enough of the map to know exactly where I'm headed, and the aerial views of the property from the drone were certainly helpful. I tug my hood up when I draw close to the stone wall that follows the perimeter of

the extensive grounds, slowing as I walk past the main entrance, a wrought-iron gate closing off the driveway leading up to the manor house. I keep walking, rounding the corner at the end of the block as I head for the secondary entrance to the southwest. The driveway gate is closed off with a chain and lock, but before that is a small walkway that leads to the quaint stone cottage. The little gate is open. And the lights are on.

My fists tighten around the straps of my backpack.

I enter the property. Slowly. Methodically. With my eyes on the door of the cottage, I slip into the shadows at the left of a wide garden that leads to the house, following a decorative path toward a row of bushes and trees. There's a low stone wall and I hop over it, keeping my head down, staying close to the darkness. And then I creep closer to the house.

The wall follows the cottage, gardens and lawns sprawling on both sides. At the back of the little house are mature oak trees and more gardens, a mix of ornamental in some sections and vegetable in others, this side more a work in progress with a woodchipper and a small tractor parked close to a pile of stones. There's another small gate in the wall that leads to the backyard, most of it obscured from my view by the boughs of the trees. I imagine Harper working here in the summer, the sun beating down on her exposed back. The beads of sweat on her skin. The strength in her arms from toiling outdoors. The sound of her voice as she talks to herself. Or maybe she's talking to me.

I imagine reaching down to fold my hands around her neck, to choke that confession out of her. Those words I've been waiting for four years to hear. Words like—

"Yeah, baby. Just come a little closer."

My breath catches in my chest. I don't even blink. Fight and flight war in my limbs.

"Fuck, yes, show me those beautiful tits," a man's voice whispers from the shadows beneath a sprawling oak. "Move a little bit to the left. That's it."

Harper must be outside in the backyard with someone. Maybe that meathead from outside the gym. Maybe they're fucking beneath the stars. She could be on her knees for him. The image is branded into my brain as soon as the thought appears. It leaves a burn behind. The taste of ash. The scent of rage.

My hands curl into fists.

Part of me wants to leave. I should save my vengeance for another day. But something about the thought of Harper with this utter douchebag, whoever the fuck he is, makes me so irate that I know I can't trust myself to handle anything cleanly. She shouldn't get to make catastrophic mistakes with no consequences, enjoying pleasures as sacred as love and intimacy when she ruins lives. But as much as I want to do us all a favor and wipe her from the face of the earth, I don't want it to end in my own demise. And there's a much higher risk of that happening if both of them are outside together.

I take a step back. My leather gloves creak as my fists tense.

"Now get that toy from the bag. Such a good fucking girl."

My spine locks.

She's not outside with him at all. She's in her cottage. She might not even know he's here.

I creep forward, keeping each footfall slow and methodical. I can just make out the silhouette of a man hunched beneath the oak tree on the other side of the garden wall. Lights are on in the cabin, and though I can't see what he's seeing, I can take a guess.

I sneak a step closer. Another. Blood roars in my ears. The ever-present aches in my body fade with the burst of adrenaline

that courses through my veins. I stop and lift my backpack from my shoulder, setting it at my feet. My movement is careful. Methodical. Every tooth of the zipper is a quiet tick as I open the bag just enough to reach inside. I grasp the first weapon I touch and can't help but smile when I pull it free. *The garrote.*

I leave my bag behind in the dark.

"Yeah, baby. Just like that," the shadow whispers beneath the tree.

My grip tightens around the handles.

He doesn't notice me as I close in on him. There's a low stone wall separating us, but I can still tell what he's doing. His arm is moving rhythmically. His breath fogs in the dim light that reaches us from the cottage. He lets out a grunt as he pumps his erection. When I glance toward the house, I catch a glimpse of Harper, naked on a couch, a TV bleeding light across her spread legs and a vibrator clutched in her hand.

"Fuck *yes*," the man hisses, returning my attention to where it belongs. My heart rate spikes. A mix of fury and satisfaction floods my veins when I get close enough to realize it *is* him, that gym bro douchebag I saw on the drone's camera. I separate the two handles of the garrote, pulling the wire taut. "Put it in that pussy for me."

Fury erupts in my cells.

I rush forward. Moonlight flashes across the thin wire as I whip it over the man's head. A shocked breath empties from his lungs as the garrote slips beneath his jaw. His hands scrabble at the wire. He submits as I pull him back against the wall that separates us. It takes every last shred of restraint to stop myself from pulling it tighter and tighter until the metal slides through his flesh—until it strikes bone.

"Shut the fuck up," I hiss as he tries to beg for mercy. His boots scrape against the stone wall. It's a happy accident to have it between us, otherwise I'm sure he'd have a good shot at kicking me in the balls. But there's still no way he could fight me off completely. I know it. He knows it. And so he begs. His plea resonates against the wire, and all I want to do is pull those handles tighter. A low growl rumbles from my chest when he tries to reach back and scratch at my face. "Settle the fuck down and I'll let you go."

Though he tries to dig his fingers between the wire and his neck, he still gives me a shaky nod. I ease the pressure just enough that he can take a breath.

"W-what do you want?" he stammers.

"Your name."

His swallow is a vibration through the handles of my weapon. "J-Jake. Jake H-Hornell."

I roll my eyes. He's pissed himself. I can smell it lingering in the air, mixing with the crisp, crushed grass beneath my feet and his cheap cologne and the sweetness of an energy drink that must have spilled somewhere in the dark. "What are you doing here?" I demand.

"W-what do you think?" He thrashes, another attempt to twist free of my grasp. I pull the wire tighter and the struggling stops. "Just w-watching, okay? Watching."

My focus slides toward the cottage. I can't see Harper now from this angle, only the light from her window.

"Does she know you're here? Is this some kind of little game?"

"N-no. She d-doesn't know. I'll stay away, I p-promise."

Rage infects my veins. My molars protest the force of my clenched jaw. His panicked plea hums into my palms, my smile a caress against his ear.

"Well, then," I whisper as I jerk my body downward, taking him over the wall. I feel the tension of his skin finally give way as I drag him from his hiding place and away from the cottage. Steam rises from the torrent of blood that spills into the night. "I'd better make sure that's a promise you'll keep."

BROADSIDED

Nolan

IT MIGHT HAVE BEEN A sleepless night, but it was so fucking worth it to set up my little surprise. I feel wide awake. Much more lively than Harper, apparently. I watch through her dining room window as she trudges down the stairs, a loose bun askew on the top of her head, her bangs and wayward strands of hair framing her face. She turns off the lights she left on while she slept as she goes. Odd, that even the lamps in her bedroom stayed on all night. Her gray sleep shorts hug the contours of muscle in her ass, her defined legs bare, tapering to a pair of penguin slippers. Not that it matters to me what her ass or legs look like. Or that I can see her nipples beneath the thin cotton of her tank top when she turns a little in my direction. Maybe my cock hardens at the sight of her as she passes into the kitchen and I follow to watch from the next window, but it's *biology.* Just an automatic response to visual stimulus. Nothing more.

Watching her make coffee is a frustrating experience. Her eyes are half open and watering with a series of yawns. She manages to complete all the steps to prep a stovetop espresso maker, but only barely. It's almost tempting to burst into her kitchen and do it for her just to hurry things along when it takes her more than one try to screw the top section to the reservoir. Waiting for the water to boil theoretically takes two minutes, but it might as well be two hours. But I've learned something important in these years of waiting. The anticipation of reaching your goal is sometimes even better than the satisfaction of achieving it.

"Maybe not this time, though," I whisper as she pours the coffee into a mug with a dash of milk. She takes it to the door that leads to a patio overlooking the garden, a pastry clutched in her other hand. It's a beautiful, sunny morning in Cape Carnage, after all. Who wouldn't want to sit outside with a coffee and croissant to watch the birds?

I snicker to myself as I peer around the corner of the cottage and watch.

Harper sets her coffee on the patio table and sits, not looking up, all her attention focused on the liquid in her cup. She closes her eyes as she takes the first sip, tilting her face toward the sun to savor the simple pleasure of its warmth on her skin. Even when the croak of a raven interrupts the peace of her sun trap, her eyes don't open.

The raven croaks again.

"Shush, Morpheus," she says. She doesn't look toward the source of the sound, but I do. My heart thunders beneath my sternum. "I'll feed you in a minute."

Harper raises the cup to her lips, her eyes still pressed closed. The raven caws more loudly than before.

Everything seems to happen in slow motion. A crease appears between her brows. She takes a sip of coffee as though steeling herself for a fight with the insistent bird. Her head turns toward the feeder.

Coffee sprays from Harper's lips as she opens her eyes and finally *sees*.

The raven is standing on the roof of the bird feeder, leaning over the edge to peck Jake Hornell's eyeball, the other one already gone. The bird pulls a string of ruined flesh from the cavity and gulps it down. With a flutter of his wings, he croaks at Harper, clearly pleased with himself.

"Jake . . . ?" she whispers.

Glee races through my veins. I back out of sight behind the corner of the cottage just as Harper's eyes dart across the grounds. Maybe she'll let out a terrified shriek. A dramatic fall to her knees with her head in her hands. Maybe she'll shake her guilty fists at the sky. Surely there will be tears, at the very least. Any second now . . .

I peer around the corner. Harper is standing motionless, her head tilted to one side. Though her back is to me and I can't see her expression, everything else about her seems to have stalled.

The meltdown is coming. I'm sure of it.

Harper takes a step closer to the bird feeder. Another. A fly passes her in a slow, curling arc to land on Jake's cheek before crawling into the empty eye socket. As accustomed as I am to the grotesque indignity of death, it's still fucking disgusting. Surely she thinks so too. She's going to puke. I know it. Coffee and croissant will be *everywhere*.

Harper looks down at the phone in her hand and presses a contact before placing the call on speaker. Two rings later, I hear the quiet but gruff "hello" of an elderly man's voice.

"Did you find your shoes?" Harper asks.

There's a pause. "What?"

"Your shoes. The Christina Riccis or whatever."

"*Stefano*," the man barks. "*Stefano* Riccis, you heathen."

Though I can't see her face, she raises a hand to suppress a laugh, as though this is both an expected and amusing reply. "*Stefano* Riccis, of course. Did you find them? Did you happen to take them for a . . . wander . . . ?"

"Why would I wander in Stefano Riccis?"

"I dunno, maybe you wanted to take them on a little test drive . . . ? Last night . . . ?"

"Be specific, Harper. I'm nearly at the part where Alicia steals the wine cellar key in *Notorious*."

Harper turns just enough that I catch her eye roll before her gaze skates across the garden. I barely manage to keep my "What the fuck?" whisper to inaudible levels as confusion and disappointment swirl in my blood. "Fine. Did you take those *Stefano Riccis* over to a certain Jake Hornell's place and chop off his head to bring back as a souvenir? Is that specific enough for you?"

There's a pause. The raven caws from the roof of the bird feeder before he leans over the edge to poke at the eye socket. The buzz of the disturbed fly is muffled in the cavernous dark.

"No," the man finally says.

"Are you sure?"

"Yes."

"You know your memory sucks, right?"

"Harper, I did not kill Mr. Hornell. If this is some horrible practical joke like the time you convinced me you were finally going to let me kill that pretentious old windbag Simon McCarthy but took me to Irene Kennedy's seventy-seventh birthday party instead, I will never forgive you."

"You had a great night. You have the hots for Irene, admit it." The man grumbles a string of arguments to the contrary that sounds entirely forced and untrue as Harper chews on one of her nails. She puts her weight on one foot to rub the back of her calf with the top of the other, as though the caress of the penguin slipper is soothing. She seems to stew on his answer, but after a deep sigh, she finally says, "Okay. I'd better run."

"Wait . . . go back for a moment. Jake's *head*?"

"Gotta go. I'll see you at lunch."

"Harper—"

She hangs up and stuffs the phone into the front of her shirt to perch between her breasts on the flimsy elastic of her top's built-in shelf bra, then stares at the decapitated head, her hands on her hips as though this is merely an inconvenience. "Well," she says. "This is . . . weird."

Weird . . . ?

I nearly ask it out loud, slipping into the shadow of the cottage as Harper pivots a slow turn as though hunting through the garden for clues. She walks back inside and I retreat to the kitchen window to watch as she trades her penguin slippers for a set of Dakota work boots. The contrast of the beat-up leather against her bare legs and those ridiculous shorts has me shifting as another erection starts. I try to think my way out of that fucking biological response. *She killed your brother,* I tell myself. *She almost killed* you. *She is absolutely* not *sexy.*

She turns her back to me as she heads out the door. I catch a glimpse of her round ass in those napkin-sized shorts and drag a hand down my face as though I can swipe the image clean from my brain. "Chrissakes," I hiss, my cock not receiving the message as the door slams behind her in a stamp of sound.

I press my back to the cold stone as Harper marches past me toward a garden shed that sits adjacent to the low garden wall. It's

not far from where I killed Jake last night. If she were to lean over the wall, she might see the blood that stains the grass just past the hydrangeas. But she doesn't. Instead, she disappears into the shed and, a moment later, she strides with purpose from the building with a pair of gardening gloves in one hand and a spray bottle in the other. She returns to the bird feeder and sets the orange bottle at her feet before she pulls the gloves on, and then she's reaching into the bird feeder to yank the head free from between the roof and the platform.

What.

The.

Fuck . . . ?

When I lean farther around the corner, she's gripping his ears, trying to tug the head free. I wedged it between the roof and the platform pretty good last night, to be fair. I was a little worried about a raccoon climbing up there to run off with all my hard work while I jogged back to the inn for more supplies. It took me several hours and multiple trips to chop up the rest of Jake Hornell and run his body to the shallow burial site next to the Ballantyne River that I picked out months ago from topographic maps, the place I intended to use to dispose of Harper's body. I don't think packing dismembered limbs and a collapsible shovel into a back-pack to run them for two miles was really what my firefighter and SAR training was meant for, but at least I got a good workout in last night.

And I'm not the only one getting a workout.

"Fucking . . . just . . . comply . . . with . . . instruction . . . Jake . . . ," Harper hisses between gritted teeth as she pushes and pulls until she finally yanks the head hard enough to dislodge it. She shrieks as it faceplants into her chest, but it's really more a sound of irritation than the abject terror I was hoping for. "Even in the afterlife, Jake? Seriously? That is *fucked up*, dude."

I just . . . do not understand. And frankly, I'm a little pissed off. I spent all night chopping this asshole up and hauling him around, and I didn't even finish, for fucksakes. There's still a bag of body parts strapped to my back. It takes a long-ass time to saw a person into pieces in the pitch dark and not wake up your sleeping enemy. And I was aiming for a big reaction. Screaming. Tears. Horror. Panic. But what I'm getting just seems more like mild confusion sprinkled with a hint of annoyance, like this is nothing more than an unwelcome inconvenience to her morning routine. She's just standing there, seemingly unfazed, with the head clutched between her hands, staring down into the bloodied, vacant holes where the eyes once were.

The raven caws from the branch of a nearby apple tree. "Want to fill me in?" she asks the bird, who caws again, though I swear he looks in my direction. "For the amount of free food I give you, I think you need to start contributing more than the occasional trinket."

Harper turns a bit more in my direction, but she doesn't fully face me or notice me watching from the shadows, all her attention fixed to the head in her hands. There are two bloodied marks on her tank top from when the eye holes smacked her chest, and I'm nearly overwhelmed by the unexpected urge to find a way to resurrect that gym-bro douchebag so I can kill him again.

I shake my head, trying to clear it of the intrusive thoughts that seem to appear every time I look at Harper. It's probably just the desire to claim my prey. That guy was obviously a threat. It's nothing but more biology. I'm like any apex predator, unwilling to yield its next meal or slice of safety in an unforgiving world.

"You look like you had an eventful night," Harper says to the head as she turns it over and examines the edges of his torn skin. I never got a good look at it in the dark, but there must be marks from the ax on the vertebrae. She lets out a low and thoughtful hum, sticking one of her gloved fingers right into the flesh to pull it back and scrutinize the bone as she turns the head in the light. Her nose crinkles. She seems to deliberate. Having reached some kind of conclusion, she shrugs, and though her expression still appears unsure, she gives Jake Hornell's head a single, decisive nod.

And then, to my horror, she fucking *sniffs it*.

In an instant, she recoils. Harper's face is a mixture of disgust and confusion when she holds the head away from her as far as she can. "So gross," she whispers.

She wants to talk about gross? I'll bring the fucking gross.

"I could not fucking agree more," I say as I step from my hiding place. I hold up Jake's severed hands and give her a slow clap as Harper spins to face me. The head is still clutched in her gloved grasp. Her eyes are the color of sharpened steel, the surprise and confusion in them fleeting. Her shock quickly dissolves into a glare that's ready to flay the flesh from my bones.

"Ballmeat guy," she hisses.

I give her a dark and devious grin, and her eyes narrow. "Is that how you remember me? *'Ballmeat guy?'* Well," I say, tapping one of Jake's fingers to my cheek in the mimicry of a thoughtful countenance, "that kind of makes sense, coming from *you*."

I creep a few steps closer, but I stop the moment I see her go rigid with fear. Why I would halt so abruptly, I have no idea. It's just an ingrained response, matter over mind. And my mind is saying she's the person I've been searching for. The soul I've come to collect. If anything, it should be a struggle to keep myself from rushing forward to close my hands around her throat. It's the least that she deserves.

I force myself to take another step in her direction. "Who's Arthur?"

Harper's cheeks flush crimson. "You're . . ." she counters, eluding my question. "You're stalking me?"

"I'm not stalking. I'm hunting. *He* was stalking." I wave to the head still gripped in her hands. Her brows flicker as she tries to work through everything that's happening. When her gaze returns to me, she tilts her head.

"So you killed him for me . . . ? To keep me . . . safe . . . ?"

My mouth opens and closes, but no sound comes out.

No.

. . . Definitely not.

I feel like I've run face-first into a brick wall. Nothing about her is what I expected. Nothing about this has gone the way I wanted.

"Listen," I say, dropping the severed hands to my sides, "if we're going to be bitter enemies, I really think we need to improve our communication skills."

"Why do I want to be enemies with you?"

"Perhaps because I just killed Jake, the man you have a crush on, and left his head in your bird feeder . . . ?"

"I don't have a crush on Jake."

I sigh. "I'm starting to gather that."

"If you're stalking me—"

"I'm *hunting*—"

"You're doing a pretty shit job of it, because you clearly didn't notice that Jake Hornell is a fucking creep. Hence his nickname,

Touchy Feely Creepy Jakey. I think you just did me a favor, actually."
She shrugs, feigning a casualness that never makes it to her cutting
glare. "Maybe that makes us friends."

"We are *not* friends."

Harper sighs, as though I'm merely here wasting her time,
another inconvenience that she can just barrel through before
returning to her clearly fucked-up life. "Figured. So, enlighten
me. Why are you here?"

I take a step closer. "You really don't remember me?"

"You like tea bagging and turkey sandwiches," she says as she
edges a step backward. "I think I remember you pretty clearly,
yep."

"That's not the first time we met."

Harper's eyes travel over my face, roaming the contours of my
features so slowly that I can feel her glare linger on my skin. "I
guess I left an impression."

I laugh. It's the first genuine, uninhibited laugh I've had in a
long time, now that I think about it. Just like the smile that broke
free when I teased Harper at the coffee shop yesterday was the first
one since my accident that made my heart jump in my chest. I'd
forgotten how much I missed that feeling, the one that swoops
through you, like being at the top of a roller coaster and suddenly
free falling. "You can say that," I finally manage when my laughter subsides. Clearly, Harper doesn't think it's quite as funny as I
do, and I'm a little surprised it hasn't jogged her memory.

"Well, I think we've established that I have no idea who the
fuck you are and, contrary to whatever you think, I've never met
you before. So, thanks, I guess, for doing me an obviously unin-
tentional favor that could send you to jail for the rest of your life.
But unless you're staying to talk about hobbies over breakfast," she

says as she raises the head between us, "maybe you should just leave."

My grip around the bloodied severed wrists tightens. Harper seems to sense the threat, cataloging every minute change in the tension of my muscles, or the fury in my eyes, or the dark, merciless smile that creeps across my lips.

"I don't think I'm going anywhere just yet," I say, taking another step closer. She's only a few feet away. Just a flash of motion and she'd be within my grasp. I force myself to remember that it's not time yet—there are still a few weeks to go. But it's so fucking tempting to rush toward her now. I could squeeze those words from her delicate throat, the ones I've been waiting to hear: *It's my fault.*

"Harper?" a woman's voice calls from inside the house. Harper's eyes widen. Her mouth pops open around a silent *oh.*

"Who the fuck is that?" I hiss, but the kitchen door is already closing, someone's footsteps nearing the outside corner of the house. The raven caws and flaps away from his perch on the peak of the stained bird feeder to hide among the branches of the oak, as though he's unwilling to become an accessory to the crime that will surely spell our imminent demise. And Harper and I? We can't seem to do anything but stare at each other, both of us frozen in time.

"There you are," a woman says as she rounds the corner with a book in her hands, barely glancing up at us as she enters the back garden. She nods at me before turning her attention back to her book. "'Sup."

I give her a weak, thin "Hey," sliding the severed hands behind my back. But Harper is not so quick to move. She's still got the head clutched in her grasp, and rather than try to get rid of it, she presses the face to her chest and folds her arms around it.

"Hi, Maya," Harper squeaks out.

Maya glances up, her obsidian eyes narrowing behind gold-rimmed glasses as they dart down to the head and back up to Harper's face. "You're entering the gravity races this year?"

"Ha . . . yeah. I guess so." Harper's smile is too bright. Too forced. Her eyes move too quickly when she looks down at the head she clutches to her chest before refocusing on her unexpected guest. "Thought I'd . . . you know"—she pats the top of the head—"throw my hat in the ring."

She cringes at her own terrible joke, and Maya tilts her head as though she's trying to work Harper out. But Harper Starling is dangerous. Perhaps more dangerous than I could have imagined that night when I lay on the road, struggling to stay conscious as she drove away from the lives she'd forever ruined. She could kill this woman easily, if she wanted to. Maya is diminutive, her frame nearly frail, long black braids trailing down her back all the way to her hips, the scent of orange and hibiscus a sweet halo around her.

But another realization seems to scuttle through my brain like an unwelcome intruder. As much as I need to protect Maya from Harper, I need to protect Harper from harm too, no matter how much of a danger she might be. I can't let her be taken from me before I've gotten what I came all this way and waited so long for. And that thought is the one that forces me a step closer.

"Good thing the fake blood is water soluble," I say. Maya turns to face me and I withdraw the severed hands from behind my back, brandishing them with nonchalance. "I'm Nolan. I'd shake your hand, but this stuff makes a bit of a mess. Hopefully it'll be worth it for the style points at the race. I'm not sure my soapbox race car–building skills are really up to snuff, you know?"

Maya looks down at the hands and pushes her glasses up her

nose with the end of her pen. "Did you get the blood from Craft-A-Corpse?"

"Sure did."

She tilts her chin up and, for a moment, I wonder if I've caught myself in a lie. When I refocus on Harper, she doesn't give me any clues. She paints a ridiculous picture, with a decapitated head clutched to her chest and her full lips pressed into a tense line and her eyes wide with alarm. She's *obviously* a terrible person and completely unhinged. And I *one hundred percent* do not find her in any way adorable. *Absolutely not.*

"The Craft-A-Corpse blood can still stain," Maya says, snapping me out of my efforts to kill any intrusive thoughts of Harper Starling's attractiveness. I'm grateful for the distraction, and I make every effort to pin all my attention to the woman standing between me and my sworn enemy. I try to ignore that it feels a lot harder to do than it should. "I make a stain remover that'll get it out. You can buy it from my shop on Main Street. Maya's Magical Mixtures. And I sell better-quality fake blood too. It's even edible—you can put it on cake, in drinks. Strawberry and raspberry flavors available. Drizzle it on the whipped cream in A Shipwrecked Bean's chili hot chocolate and it'll change your life."

Maya pulls a business card from between the last pages of her book and walks forward to slide it into my shirt pocket, giving my chest a pat before she turns back to Harper. "Speaking of which, I need some strawberries. Got any?"

"Umm." Harper clears her throat and tries to force a smile, but it ends up being more of a grimace, the tension climbing into her cheeks to keep the light from reaching her eyes. "Sure, help yourself."

"Thanks." With a nod to each of us, Maya pulls a cloth bag

from her shoulder and walks away toward the gate along the garden's back wall before disappearing into the vegetable garden.

Harper stares at me. I glare back. And then, to my surprise, she marches right up to me, not stopping until she's inches from my face, the scents of death and citrus and aromatic herbs drifting from her skin.

"Leave," she snarls.

"I'm not done building a corpse."

"Go reconstruct it elsewhere. And take this with you." She shoves the head into my chest, but I don't pull it from her grasp.

"Hang on to it," I say, pushing it back toward her with Jake's severed hands. "Consider it a gift."

"A parting gift? As in, you're fucking off out of here, never to return?"

A smile creeps onto my lips, one Harper watches as it lights with a deadly vow. I feel her, like a current. A hum. A tingle in my flesh. My fingers tense around the wrists still clutched in my grip, leaving imprints on the cool skin. "I'm not going anywhere."

I expect the threat to spook her. I want to sense the terror in her. To see it in the way her pupils narrow to a pinprick, or to catch it on a scent. But it isn't there. I only hear defiance when she says, "Neither am I."

"Good. Don't waste your energy. Because you could leave Cape Carnage, but you'll never escape me."

"Harper?" Maya calls from the other side of the wall. "Do you have any of the Sweet Kiss strawberries this year?"

"Sure do. I'll come give you a hand."

I think I catch the slightest whisper of fear flicker across Harper's face. But just as quickly as it appears, she buries it, hiding it behind a vicious smirk. She knows I won't make a move with Maya here.

But what she doesn't know is that this is only the beginning. And I'm not here to rush my plans along.

I'm here to savor them.

"No matter where you go. No matter how long it takes," I whisper. I lean a little closer. There's only an inch or two of space between us. My glare fuses with hers and doesn't let go. And Harper stares me down in reply. "If you run, I will find you. You can hide in the farthest reaches of the deepest hell, and I will still drag you out. Even the devil can't save you from me."

I drop the severed hands on the ground between us.

And then I turn and walk away.

RAKING FIRE

Harper

BALLMEAT GUY THINKS VERY LITTLE of me, that much is clear.

He thinks I'm weak. That I'll run. That I'll hide. That he can bully me into submission or intimidate me into whatever trap he plans on setting.

I don't know what it is he wants from me yet, but he's obviously unhinged and dangerous as fuck. But so am I. And this is *my* town. Every square inch of it is mine to look after.

Including the Capeside Inn.

I watch from the rocky hill next to the parking lot as Nolan leaves the lobby in a sweater and a loose pair of shorts. He keeps his hood up against the misty rain that rolls in from the sea. His gaze pans across his surroundings as he stretches. Maybe he senses he's being watched, because he seems to hunt the landscape for clues. His focus passes over the bushes and boulders where I'm crouched, but he doesn't notice me camouflaged in the shadows. Instead, he bends, straightening a brace around one knee before stretching that leg. A moment later, he's putting his AirPods in, and then he's off, heading in the direction of the town at a jog, a slight hitch in the step of the braced leg that seems to soften as he establishes a warm-up pace up the gradual incline.

I turn my attention to my target. The Capeside Inn. A dark thrill swirls in my chest.

I clamber down the hill, stopping at the edge of the parking lot, just in case he turns back. Despite the shitty sleep I had hiding beneath the desk of my guest room with a gun clutched to my chest, I feel fucking wide awake now. I keep my eyes on Nolan as he reaches the end of the street and then disappears from view over the crest of the hill. And then I run for the hotel.

When I enter the lobby, there's a gentle snore from the office next to the reception desk. I slip beneath the folding counter and into Irene's domain. When I lean into the office, she's sitting in her reclining chair, her mouth gaping, a soap opera silently playing on a television that looks nearly as old as she is. Satisfied, I turn back to the reception desk, flipping to the last pages of her guest ledger, where I find exactly what I'm looking for.

Nolan Rhodes, June 6–July 15, Room 117.

I double-check the date on my watch, hoping I could magically be wrong. But I'm not. It's June 8.

"He's here for *six fucking weeks*?" I whisper-snarl. Irene snorts in the room next door and I duck on instinct, but a moment later, her snore resumes.

It's early in the season. There are only a few other bookings on Irene's ledger for this week. Most people stay for a week or two at most. Cape Carnage is cute and all, but there's only so much to do in a town our size. Unless, of course, you're here to see someone in particular. And I think it's clear with the "we need to communicate better as enemies" bullshit, the person he's here for is *me*.

Fighting the urge to slam it shut, I close the book more gently than I'd like to, then duck beneath the counter and take off at a jog to Room 117.

When I get there, I listen at the door even though I know he's out. There's no room for sloppy mistakes with a guy like this. With a glance over my shoulder, I give it a knock, but still nothing comes. Then I slip the master key I had made two years ago into the lock and enter the temporary lair of my new adversary.

There's nothing particularly revealing about the room, at first. He's made the bed. His shoes are lined up next to the door. A black roller bag is open on the luggage stand, but there's nothing in it. I flip the luggage tag over and, though there's no address, there is a phone number. I take a picture and move along. On one nightstand is a laptop. I open it just in case I strike lucky, I'm not surprised that it's password protected. I might be good at a little light burglary now and then, but computer hacker I am not. On the other nightstand is a bottle of prescription pain-killers. I head to the kitchenette, opening the cupboards and the fridge. There's not an abundance of food, but what's here is healthy and fresh. I can tell he must intend to cook for himself frequently.

I open the armoire next, moving each piece of hanging cloth-ing just enough to search for clues, but not enough to tip him off that anything has been disturbed. There's a black backpack beneath the clothes, pushed to the back of the shelf. I slide it free and open it wide.

"Oh, Mr. Rhodes," I say as I pull a garrote from the bag. The smell of chlorine rises from the polished wire. "You've come to the wrong fucking town."

I riffle through the bag just long enough to spot a pair of leather gloves and a hammer before I zip it up and toss the strap over one shoulder, closing the wardrobe before I turn toward my next objective.

The shelves across from the bathroom.

There's an iron and an ironing board. A pair of folded robes. Extra towels and pillows. And on the middle shelf, the safe.

My heart thuds heavy beats against my bones. My hands sweat in my gloves. I'm just about to push the buttons to enter the master code, the same one I managed to wrangle from Irene the time I got her drunk on an old bottle of whiskey from Arthur's long-defunct Lancaster Distillery. Irene might have puked on my only nice pair of shoes that night, but it was worth it. Especially in times like this.

And then my phone rings. I pull it from my pocket and check the screen.

"Arthur," I say, placing the call on speaker before I lay it on top of the safe. I press the first number of the code.

Zero.

"What are you doing?"

"Who says I'm doing anything?"

"You promised you'd tell me if you were up to no good. I'm an aged, dying man who is not-so-slowly sliding into the oblivion of the afterlife—"

"You're so dramatic. Shit or get off the pot, old man—"

"—and I need to live vicariously through my protégé."

I snort as I press the next button on the safe. *Nine.*

"I'm not up to no good," I say. *Two.* "I'm just having a little look around."

"A look around *where*, exactly?"

"Capeside Inn. I'm in a tourist's room."

"And where is he?"

70

"Out for a run." I look down at my watch. Something about the way he favored one leg sets me on edge. If it starts to bother him on the steep hills that snake through the town, I might not have long. I run these streets too. I know how hard it can be without persistent pain, especially in the cool mist that feels like it climbs into your bones to chill you from the inside out. "I'm nearly done," I say, more to myself than to Arthur. "I just need to get a read on how likely it is that this particular tourist will wind up in the jaws of the Cookie Monster."

I press the last button on the safe's combination lock. *Three.*

"And what is your determination?" The lock clicks as the bolts slide free. The door swings open. I pull a leather-bound book from the shadows and rest its weight on my left hand as I flip to the page that's saved by a bookmark. "Harper . . . ?"

"Pretty fucking likely," I whisper. The page is some kind of scrapbook. "Trevor Fisher," the headline says. There's a map on the left side. An *X* next to a river, drawn in red pen. Beneath the name is a list of dates and crimes. Some of them relatively minor. Theft from an electronics store, disorderly conduct. Some of them serious. An assault in a bar. A firearms charge. More than one arrest for domestic violence. On the right side of the page are photos of a man, taken at a distance. And then some taken up close. The man's face, twisted in terror. Spattered with blood. And near the bottom of the page, something that looks like leather. Preserved, dried, and crinkled—and glued to the page. But I can see the fine hairs lodged in the tissue. I can make out the warped script still written in the desiccated skin.

Memento mori.

"What is it, Harper?" Arthur asks. A thread of worry is woven through his voice. "What do you see?"

I shut the book and clutch it to my chest, sliding the phone off the safe before striding into the room. "We've got someone very bad here."

"How bad?"

I could say "someone like us." But the truth is, even if we have similar . . . extracurriculars . . . Nolan Rhodes and I could not be more different. But I know others like him. I've *survived* others like him. And so has Arthur. "He's like La Plume," I say.

There's a moment of silence on the other end of the line as I stuff the scrapbook into the empty laptop compartment of the backpack and zip it up. And I know it's not because Arthur is struggling to remember. La Plume is the last name he'll ever forget. It's the name that will haunt him until his dying breath.

Arthur's voice has dropped an octave when he says, "You need to leave there immediately. Get out."

"I'm already on it," I grit out, hanging up before Arthur has a chance to say anything more.

I stop at the nightstand and take a photo of his pill bottle, making sure to capture the details and location of the pharmacy that filled the prescription. Then I stare down at the paper and pen. I should be terrified of the trophy I saw in that book. Nolan knows where I live. He's murdered someone on my property without me even knowing. He's toying with me.

I should be running as fast and as far as I can from Cape Carnage.

But running is not enough. I've run before and been caught. I've already died once and started over. I'm not going to do it again.

I scrawl a note across the paper, my smile stretching with every word.

I fold it and put it where I know he'll find it.

And then I leave the Capeside Inn with a backpack slung across my shoulder, my thoughts taken up by war.

Irene is still asleep when I stride through the lobby and pause at the door, taking my time to survey the parking lot. It's raining, misty. There are only a few cars parked here, and aside from Irene's old Hyundai, which I'm ninety-nine percent positive she can't legally drive, the others seem to be mostly rentals. A nondescript SUV. A silver sedan. There's an Escalade with a personalized license plate, so I discount that one. With a menacing smile, I run into the rain, headed straight for the black SUV.

When I get to the vehicle, I huddle next to the passenger side front tire, drop the backpack from my shoulder, then retrieve a sheathed knife from its depths. A heartbeat later, the blade is lodged to the hilt in the tire, and I give it enough of a twist that it will slowly leak air. Then I rise, putting the backpack on and tightening the straps. With a quiet laugh, I turn and run, leaving my gift of his weapon behind.

I'm soaking wet when I make it into my cottage, my bra and panties slick against my skin, water sloshing in my boots with every step as I march to the kitchen table and drop the bag on its surface. Fear and excitement and anticipation sear my veins and tremble in my fingers. I grip the zipper and open the main compartment to pull out the weapons hidden inside. Knives. Screwdrivers. A Glock and two magazines of ammunition. There are cutters. A folding saw. Even a cheese slicer, which makes my skin crawl when I think about Nolan's book. His bag contains everything a psychopathic killer could ever dream of for a holiday pack.

Even his trophies.

I stuff everything except the gun and ammunition back into the main compartment, and then I unzip the laptop section, withdrawing the book to set it on the table as I lower myself onto a chair. I take a deep breath and flip to the page I saw in his room.

"Trevor Fisher," I whisper. I trace the name written at the top of the left side, letting my fingers drift across the paper to what is surely preserved human skin. "Who were you?"

I don't recognize anything about him. Not his crimes, or the place marked on a map, or the *memento mori* tattoo affixed to the scrapbook. I flip to the previous page, where there's a similar layout of petty crimes and a map and a desiccated piece of human skin, another *memento mori* tattoo imprinted in the leathery slice. Dylan Jacobs is the name at the top of the parchment above photos of the unfamiliar man. He was a tattoo artist, judging by the candid shots of him working in a tattoo parlor. And he must have died a similar torturous death to Trevor Fisher's. His face was twisted in pain in the second set of photos, his terror frozen in time. The photo that interests me most is one of Nolan standing next to Dylan in the shop, the ouroboros tattoo fresh on his forearm. Dylan smiles with pride at his work. Nolan smiles too, but there's an edge hidden in its sharp borders. He's not just happy with the ink on his skin. He's basking in the humor of a joke that's only funny to him. He's a hunter toying with his prey.

I might not know who Nolan Rhodes is. But I know his kind, and not just because we're similar creatures on different branches of the same evolutionary tree. He's not the first serial killer I've crossed paths with, after all. But he's the first who has come to hunt me down specifically. I'm not just a random opportunity to seize. I'm the prize he's been waiting for.

And I have no idea why.

There's a *tick, tick, tick* at the window.

I jolt in my seat and reach for the gun, swiveling to point it in the direction of the sound. But it's only Morpheus, perched on the flower box, a shining string of silver chain dangling from his beak. I expel a long and shaky breath and head to the window with the gun still clutched in my hand.

"You scared the fuck out of me," I say when I open the window and take a piece of homemade jerky from the container on the counter to offer it on my palm. With a knocking greeting and ruffled feathers, he sets his gift in my hand before taking the meat and moving a few steps away. I know what it is before it even hits my palm. "Oh, Morpheus." My thumb traces the engraved silver panel on the bracelet. A^2BC. Cracks in my heart that never seal seem to split a little wider, and it takes a long moment for me to swallow down a sudden well of tears. Morpheus must have followed me when I went to the Lancaster family plot last week, and has brought it back in case it was lost. "This is lovely, but I meant to leave it where you found it. You shouldn't take things from the cemetery, you could make people very upset."

Morpheus caws and knocks, then imitates my voice as he says "good boy," his attention fixed on the jar of jerky. With a sigh and a tense, fleeting smile, I leave the bracelet on the counter and give him another piece of beef, casting a wary look around the garden. The rain has stopped but the mist still lingers, obscuring the manor house from view. Chances are strong that Nolan has returned to his room at the Capeside Inn. Maybe he won't notice I've been there just yet. But I can't be sure. I might not have much time.

I set a few more treats out for Morpheus to keep him occupied, and I leave the window open, knowing he'll raise an alarm if an intruder comes from the direction of the garden. And then with a final glance out the window, I return to the table with the gun at my fingertips as I sit before Nolan's book of sins and secrets.

I flip to the next page closer to the front of the book, working my way back farther in time. There's a third man. Marc Beaumont. Another name I don't recognize. Another strip of skin, another set of photographs. No crimes listed this time, but a map with an X at the bend of an unnamed river. He's probably buried there, what's left of him, anyway. I chew my lip, trying to pull these pieces together, but still nothing comes.

I turn the page.

This time, there is no slice of skin, no name at the top of the page. Instead, the name is in a photograph, carved into a granite gravestone: WILLIAM EMERSON RHODES. There are photos of a young man—some of him on his own, some with Nolan and a young woman, a family resemblance woven through the shapes of their lips and angles of their noses and the dimples in their cheeks. Two brothers and a sister. I stare into William's eyes, trying to force a connection that feels hidden from my view, as though if I just scraped away another layer of sediment, a picture would emerge.

A picture.

My focus trails back to the gravestone. I almost know what I'm going to see there before I read it.

July 5, four years ago.

"Billy," I whisper, but it's not my voice I hear. It's a man's desperate voice in the night. It's grief, trapped in a gurgling cry. *Billy.*

My hand is shaking as I turn the next page.

Nolan Rhodes, standing with a cane, his parents and sister flanking him, a sign for Wycombe Memorial Hospital over their heads in white block letters. Nolan Rhodes, in a rehabilitation facility, working with a physical therapist, the scar on his elbow still red and freshly healed. Nolan Rhodes, learning to walk. Learning to write. To feed himself. I turn the page. Nolan Rhodes in a hospital bed. On a ventilator. In a halo of metal. Surrounded by tubes. His face swollen and unrecognizable. Nolan Rhodes, clinging to life.

There is no photograph for the moment I see in my memory. A man on the deserted highway, his broken arm reaching for a man whose open eyes are unseeing. Every breath he takes is an agonized rumble. Every exhalation is a whisper. A plea. *Billy. Wake up, Billy. Please wake up.*

I turn the final page to the first one in the book. There's only one thing on the page. A handwritten list.

Marc Beaumont, front passenger side.
Dylan Jacobs, rear passenger side.
Trevor Fisher, rear driver's side.

And last of all, the woman who drove the car that hit him. The woman who took his brother's life. The one who left them to die and drove away. My blood turns to crystals of ice that dance in my veins as the final words of the list are branded onto my soul.

Harper Starling, driver.

Harper Starling. The first person I ever killed.

TRACES

Nolan

THERE'S SOMETHING KIND OF ENDEARING about this town, even in the fog and the misty rain. The Victorian houses of mismatched bright colors. The endless dark water and the waves that crash against the cliffs. The way the people who live here stop to talk to their neighbors over freshly painted fences. They wave to one another as they drive down streets lined by antique gas lamps and banners that flap in the never-ending breeze. But to the tourists, the locals are friendly yet reserved, protecting the true Carnage from visitors like me. They ask where I'm from. How long I'm here. What I do for a living. What I've come to see. But they won't remember my answers. Most of my responses aren't truthful anyway.

The run takes its toll on my body, the hills steep and unforgiving, the chill of the mist seeping through my sweat-slicked skin. After two loops through town, I decide I shouldn't push my knee much farther, and I turn back for the inn, cooling off at a walk when I reach Main Street. I near A Shipwrecked Bean and think of Harper standing in the line, her dark hair cascading over her

shoulders, the aroma of coffee and pastries masking her gentle scent, which I didn't catch until we stepped outside. Sweet, soft herbs, musky and wild. Orange blossoms and bergamot. I can still remember it, as though it lingers in the fog that rolls through the town.

It takes me a second to realize I've stopped in front of the café. I'm looking at the line behind the ordering counter, but I'm seeing Harper. I'm reliving that moment I asked her for a recommendation and she turned around. Those full lips. Glowing skin. Bangs that skimmed her brows, the dark strands offsetting her gray eyes, irises the shade of the overcast sky. Features that seem so delicate, but she is not fragile. She is *fierce*. I knew it the moment she turned and looked at me, so fucking beautiful she nearly brought me to my knees.

My heart stutters beneath my ribs and I press my hand to my chest, closing my eyes. I still don't understand it. How could I not have known who she was? How could I have been caught so easily in her spell? She's the same woman who crashed into me. Who stole my baby brother right out of my grasp. Who ripped my life apart, and then simply . . . *drove away.*

When I open my eyes, it's my future I see. My hands wrapped so tight around Harper's throat that she can't even beg for the mercy I won't give.

She can fake her death. Run away into some idyllic secret life in a seaside town. She can stash her secrets and dodge time. But she cannot escape me.

I turn away from the coffee shop and stride through the mist, refocusing on my hunt, letting my vengeance reemerge to cut through the murk that seems to bleed into my mind whenever I think about the woman I've come here to kill.

By the time I make it back to the inn, I feel realigned with my mission. I know who she is and what she's done, but she clearly still has no fucking idea who I am. It's somewhat infuriating, honestly. But at least I have the upper hand.

I've got Jake's body buried away in a secret spot along the river, ready to be exhumed whenever I feel like tormenting her. Nothing says psychological pressure quite like a random foot showing up in your mailbox or a femur in the cupboard when you go to grab a mug for your agonizingly long coffee-brewing process. I cling to these little fantasies. They give me the clarity I need amidst the confusion of the last two days. My steps might be painful, but they're lighter. I'm even smiling as I enter the inn and make my way down the hall. I've got the upper hand, after all.

Until I don't.

When I enter my room, I take only one step before going rigid. I stand unmoving as the door closes behind me with a quiet *snick*. The hairs on my arms rise. The details around me sharpen. There's nothing different about the room from when I left it, but whether it's a scent or an energy or an echo of intention, I know it.

She was here.

I stalk to the armoire first and throw the doors open, sliding the hangers across the metal rod to reveal the back of the wardrobe.

My backpack is gone.

I take a useless spin, desperate to believe that I just misplaced it. That it hasn't disappeared. But it has.

My heart climbs into my throat to choke every breath with furious beats.

"Fuck. *Fuck*."

I race to the shelves across from the bathroom sink, where the safe sits in a cubbyhole. My fingers tremble as I press each number. *Zero. Seven. Zero. Five.* I pull the handle.

It doesn't budge.

Sweat rolls between my shoulder blades. My skin is burning. My vision narrows at the edges. I try again, counting out loud as though it might change the outcome.

"Zero. Seven. Zero. Five."

I rattle the handle this time. But it still doesn't budge.

Rage and panic flood every cell in my body. I twist away from the shelf to smash a fist down on the counter. The pain doesn't soothe the feral fury that threatens to emerge in a scream. I stare at my reflection. Eyes wide. Brows drawn, creases notched between them. Hair damp with sweat and rain. I lean closer, until my unsteady exhalations fog the mirror, my hands shaking as I grip the edge of the sink. Who the fuck knows what Harper has done with my belongings. She could be at the police station right now, laying my weapons out one by one on a table, relishing her macabre game of show-and-tell. She could be showing them my book . . .

My fist crashes onto the counter a second time, pain radiating through my bones.

"I'm going to fucking *kill her.*"

The promise lingers in my breath on the glass.

I march down the hall, glaring at every corner I pass that doesn't have a camera. Which is *all of them.* It's one of the reasons I picked this fucking hotel in the first place. The total lack of security is kind of a big plus when your sole purpose for being in town is to commit fucking *murder.*

At least it is until someone steals your precious trophy book from the *fucking safe* when you've been gone for not even an hour.

A growl escapes my control as I round the corner and the reception desk comes into view.

As usual, the cadence of Irene's snore flows from the darkness of her office. I roll my eyes and huff out a sigh as I hit the bell with more force than necessary.

There's a startled snort in the dark. "I'm coming, I'm coming, keep your panties on."

I ring the bell again.

"I said I'm coming, Jesus H. Christ in a chicken basket." Irene shuffles into view, straightening her glasses with crooked fingers. "Mr. Rhodes—"

"Irene," I say, swallowing my irritation, though only barely, "I seem to have locked myself out of my safe and I need to access it for important documents."

"Oh, oh. Just a minute." She waggles a finger in the air and starts pulling open drawers on the other side of the counter, shuffling through their contents. I figure she must be searching for a key, which gives me at least a tiny shred of hope that maybe my book is still safely stored inside if a nondescript master key is buried among her belongings. But that little wisp of hope evaporates completely when she withdraws a Post-it note and slides it across the counter. "There you go."

Zero, nine, two, three, the note reads.

And above that:

Master code for room safes.

I close my eyes. Take a deep breath in. Let it out slowly as I pinch the bridge of my nose.

"Irene," I say as I open my eyes and level her with a flat glare, "do you really think you should be giving me this?" I slide the paper back to her, but she merely waves my concern away and places the note back into the drawer.

"I've been running this inn for forty years. Seen all types come and go." She pins me with an unwavering stare over the acetate rims of her glasses. "*All* types. Good and bad and indifferent. I can tell, Mr. Rhodes. You're a good man."

All the admonishments I'd like to make, or the snarky retorts, or even the frustrated sigh that was building in the back of my throat seem to vanish. She smiles at me as though she really believes the words she just said. As though, somehow, she knows I don't agree.

I should tell her I'm not a good man. And I don't know if I've ever been one. Maybe the monster in me was always lurking in the shadows, waiting for the right moment to come into the light. And when Billy died, there was no reason to keep it caged anymore. With the first bite of revenge, all it wanted was more.

Sometimes, I do wish I could tell someone about the kind of man I really am. I might not feel guilt about the things I've done, but my sins still grow around me like the impenetrable wall of a remote forest. I can't really be seen when I lurk in those shadows. I don't show anyone my true self. Not unless I have a blade in my hand and I'm carving my darkness right into them.

I clear my throat, ridding it of protests and confessions, giving Irene a weak smile. "Thanks for the code," I say, nodding toward the paper before I turn away and head back to my room.

By the time I'm inside, the reality has truly sunk in. There's no way my book is going to be sitting in that safe, particularly not when all my weapons are gone. I head to where it sits on the shelf, mocking me, and punch in the master code. *Zero, nine, two, three.*

The mechanism unlocks and the door swings open.

Just as I suspected, my book is nowhere to be seen. But, to my surprise, there's something left in its place. I pull out a folded note, turning away from the shelves as I unfurl the torn paper to read the curling, precise script of an unfamiliar hand.

Hello, Ballmeat. I have your little art project. Maybe you should just fuck off out of town while you still can.
   Sincerely,
   Your bitter enemy

PS How's this for communication, asshole?

I catch my reflection when I turn my attention away from the paper in my hands. It's not just fury I see. It's the thrill of a chase. The challenge of someone who isn't just prey, but another predator, perhaps one who is not all that different from me. I saved Harper Starling for last because I knew she would be the best prize. I just didn't realize how right I would be. How worthy she would be of destruction.

"I cannot wait to kill Harper Starling," I say to the man in the mirror, every word a deliberate, decisive vow.

I fold the paper along the creases she left and place it on my nightstand, then grab my car keys and leave.

Or, I *try* to.

There's only my vehicle and an Escalade in the parking lot when I get there, and I don't even make it halfway to the road before I realize there's a critical problem with my SUV. I throw it into park across two empty spaces and slam the door shut behind me before walking around to the passenger side.

My knife is lodged to the hilt in the flat tire.

"Jesus fucking Christ," I snarl as I pull the blade free, the last of the air hissing through the slit left behind. My knee protests in the brace as I scan the space around me. There's no other option. I can't really call an Uber to take me to the home of someone I might possibly murder with my bare fucking hands.

With a heavy sigh, I hide the blade beneath the cuff of my sleeve, and then I start a painful jog toward Lancaster Manor. I stay off the main roads. Stick to the quiet side streets with their mix of Victorian houses and wartime bungalows and the occasional new build that's always too modern for its surroundings yet somehow seems to work as a contrast to its more colorful neighbors.

The fog is so thick that I can only see a few feet in any direction. There's no one on the roads, but I hear things in the gloom. A door slamming shut. Children's hushed whispers, one of them starting a countdown as they take up a game of hide-and-seek. My haunted surroundings do little to dilute my obsession, Harper taking up all the space in my thoughts, so much so that I make a wrong turn and end up on a dead-end road. My knee throbs. My neck aches. My back hums with the threat of pain, a drum that echoes every footfall it took to get here. But I don't stop. I just grip the knife tighter, imagining the moment I can hold it to Harper's throat, when I can feel her heartbeat through the polished steel. I push myself to keep going, not letting myself slow to a walk until I get to the secluded side street where Lancaster Manor looms on the hill, staring down at the town shrouded in fog.

But when I finally arrive at my destination, I find that I'm not alone.

Sam Porter stands across the street from the main entrance of Lancaster Manor, his camera mounted on a tripod, panning across the estate as he makes notes into a voice recorder. It's not until I get a little closer that I catch the occasional word. *Serial killer . . . Murder at the cottage . . . Never the same . . .*

"Maybe La Plume was here all along. And maybe he never left," he says, giving me a dark smile as I draw to a halt a few steps away. He turns off the camera and pockets the voice recorder, pushing the hood of his raincoat off his Porter Productions ball cap. "Hey, man. Great day for some atmospheric shots, don't you think?"

"Yeah, sure is. Not such a great day for a jog, though. Think I'll head back to the inn soon," I say, the lie rolling off my tongue with ease as I cast my gaze up the hill to the foreboding home, a sentry lurking in the oppressive mist. "How's your film coming together?"

"Good, thanks." When I nod and make no move to ask prying questions, he says, "I'll start interviewing some of the townsfolk this week, actually."

"Oh, yeah?" I jerk my head in the direction of the manor house. "Lookin' to start with whoever lives there?"

Sam's cheeks puff out as he blows a long breath through pursed lips. "I wish. Somehow, I don't think the old man is going to give me an interview, all things considered." I tilt my head, my brows furrowed, and Sam smirks. He knows he's piqued my interest, and I've given him just enough of a reaction to warrant the crumb of a reward. "You really don't know the story about that place?"

I shake my head. This time, my reply is honest. I swallow the swell of anger I feel at myself for being so focused on hunting Harper that I didn't research the town's ancient history, and now I have to defer to this frat boy–looking prick with his polo shirt and his stupid bleached teeth and country club–bland yet conventionally "good" looks. I grind my teeth in irritation before I paste on a lazy smile and say, "I heard it won a gardening competition or two, but beyond that, no."

"Lancaster Manor is as old as Cape Carnage. The Lancaster family owns half of the businesses in and around town. A silver mine, back in the early days. A distillery. The general store. The list goes on. Problem is, when you're looming over a town like this one for generations, it might give you wealth and success, but it makes you a target, too." Sam stares up at the house for a long moment before turning his attention to his equipment, pulling the camera off the tripod, then removing the plastic cover protecting it from the rain.

"You mean for that Plume guy?" I ask, purposely flubbing the name even though I remember it with clarity from the last time we spoke.

"La Plume, yeah. Have you ever heard of Sleuthseekers?" When I shake my head, a thread of disappointment weaves itself through Sam's expression. He straightens his cap and places the camera into its padded bag before starting to dismantle the tripod. "I'm one of the founding members. It's an online amateur investigative group. We've solved two murder cases already. You really not into true crime stuff, huh?"

"I mean, it sounds pretty cool," is all I can manage with a shrug. I guess he's not that different from me, in a way, considering I hunt down criminals in my spare time, too. But I don't relish the thought that Sam Porter and I might share similar pastimes. I don't know why that bothers me. Maybe it's an aura about him, something I can't see or hear, but something I feel. Or maybe it's just the fucking hat. "So what, you're after La Plume now?"

"You could say that. We've been trying to track down his real history for the last five years." Sam huffs a laugh. Shakes his head, then jerks it in the direction of the estate. "As far as anyone knows, this place is the location of the last kill by La Plume. Poppy Lancaster was the woman's name. He killed her right there on the property, in the little stone cottage where she lived with her son. As the story goes, her father was the one who found her body. He ended up raising his grandson on his own."

My first thought is Harper, alone in that same stone cottage with a man outside her window, watching her intimate moments from the shadows of her garden. My fingers tighten around the handle of the knife, the quiver of Jake Hornell's final breaths a memory imprinted into my skin. I would kill him again, if I could.

You want to kill her too, I remind myself. *You just want her to yourself, that's all.*

"But the way I see it," Sam continues, breaking me free from the storm that's rolling through my thoughts, "if Poppy Lancaster came across a secret her father was hiding, who says he didn't kill her to keep himself hidden? What better way to throw suspicion off himself than to murder her with the same method and then cover his tracks with a weak alibi and the burden of a grandchild? And then if he changed his modus operandi entirely after murdering Poppy, he could have kept killing in Cape Carnage without ever being caught."

"I thought serial killers don't really change their methods. You really think he completely gave up his pattern and managed to stick to it all this time?"

Sam's brows knit and he tugs the zipper of the camera case closed with more force than necessary. "It's not totally unheard of," he says, his eyes meeting mine only briefly, as though he's struggling to hide his irritation at my dismissive comment. "He's a smart guy. If he really did kill his own daughter to remain undetected, changing his pattern isn't much of a stretch. He wouldn't be the first to do so."

"Interesting. You know more about this stuff than me, that's for sure," I say, and he preens at the acknowledgment. "Guess that makes sense if the disappearances around here haven't stopped, like you were saying."

"Exactly. And the police aren't going to get off their asses and do anything to solve it. They only care about keeping tourism alive and the dollars flowing. It's not like they'd want to bring attention to it, you know? Cape Carnage used to be just another sleepy little seaside town on the slow path to abandonment until several years ago, when they elected Mayor Patel and she ushered in the plans that overhauled its tourism industry. They're making money hand over fist now with all the weird and creepy Carnage shit. And this town belongs to Arthur Lancaster, just like it's belonged to the generations before him."

Arthur.

I fight to keep a devious grin from slipping across my features and unmasking my hidden desires. Harper Starling might have taken my most prized possession, but I have something just as powerful. I have a wolf on a chain. One who has scented his precious beast. One who clearly will not be deterred from flushing out his prey. *Arthur Lancaster.*

"I mean, I guess that all makes sense," I say, trying to temper my excitement with notes of skepticism. "All you need is proof, I guess."

Sam slips the tripod into a carrying case and slings the camera bag over his shoulder. "I have something better. I have the story of a lifetime. And all I have to do is wait for the sun and moon and sea to align to get it. At the next spring tide, Arthur Lancaster's biggest secret will surface, and even he doesn't realize just how big it is."

"Spring tide?" I ask. But Sam doesn't answer. He just smiles in a way that's meant to bait and control, to keep me hooked on a line he's not ready to reel in.

He claps me on the shoulder, a gesture that should feel friendly, but seems hollow. "Need a ride back to the inn?"

"Nah," I reply. "Thanks, though. I'll keep going for a bit."

"See you around." With a tip of the brim of his hat, Sam heads to his car. I watch him drive off in the rain. I wait until the road descends into silence. In nothing more than a handful of heartbeats, it's just me and the manor on the hill. It's the branches that reach toward me in the mist, offering their secrets. It's the ghosts that Harper Starling can't outrun.

A raven caws in the fog. A throaty diesel engine starts up from the direction of the little stone cottage.

I smile.

DESCENT

Harper

"Good boy," Morpheus says above the rumble of the tractor engine as he picks at the mulched flesh on my gloved palm. "Pretty murder bird."

I shake the glove off my other hand, and with a slow and fluid motion, I raise it to pet his back. "That's right. You are a pretty murder bird." His feathers shimmer beneath my fingertips, iridescent blues and greens and purples vibrant despite the dim light of the overcast sky. I turn and set him down on the garden wall with a hunk of Jake Hornell's mangled right hand to eat. "I'll bring you some more treats in a minute."

I check my watch and press my arm against the gun that's holstered at my side to ensure it's still there, as though it could simply disappear and leave me unarmed. It's nearly noon, almost an hour since I made it home from the the Capeside Inn. Nolan has probably finished his jog by now, and who knows how long it will be until he realizes I was there. It could be days, depending on how often he needs to use his bag of tricks. He could be checking his safe even less frequently if he's here for several weeks. Maybe he doesn't indulge in frequent scrapbooking. And it's not like I can wait around all day until he figures it out and either leaves town like he should or comes to Lancaster Manor to get himself killed.

I probably should have planned this better. Bought some cameras and hidden them in his room, perhaps. Taken his point about communication and written a more comprehensive letter. Spelled out my almost-innocence. I could have made it clear that he's right—I am no saint. I did leave him behind on that road, after all. I left him to die so I could start a new life. But I'm not the person he thinks I am. And I will not break my word to Arthur. I'm not about to give up the life I've worked so hard to create just because he's mistaken one monster for another.

I don't owe Nolan Rhodes, or anyone else, an explanation. Not anymore. I have a town to protect from shitty tourists and an elderly serial killer with memory loss to look after, for fucksakes. I can't put my whole life on hold for some ridiculously hot psychopath who wants to kill me.

"This is not the best use of my time. So fuck that guy and his murder dimples," I say to Jake's severed hand, trying to rid myself of the memory of Nolan's smile in the coffee shop and the way it ignited a dormant, long-neglected flame in me. I fold Jake's fingers down, leaving only the middle finger upright in a *fuck you* gesture, then I toss it into Cookie Monster's hopper. He's one person to wind up in my woodchipper that I actually do feel a bit bad for, and I'm not even the one who killed him. I mean, he was Creepy Jakey, maybe creepier than I even realized, but he's from town, and Arthur's instructions have been explicitly clear. *I will keep your secrets, Harper, but you must promise me. Promise me that you'll always protect this town, no matter what it takes.*

I heave a deep, regretful sigh as I watch the machine chew

through the last of his flesh and bone, spitting it across the tarp. I'm bending to pick up Jake's head by the hair when it suddenly turns off in an abrupt cessation of sound.

My heart lurches to a halt as I unholster my gun. I drop the head and pick up the bottle of Piss-Off! spray instead as I straighten, both nozzles pointed at the cab of my tractor.

Nolan Rhodes saunters into view, a dark smile coaxing out his deep-set dimples.

"Hello, Harper," he says, pushing the hood of his sweater down from his damp hair. "I believe you have something of mine that I would like back."

Morpheus caws a much-delayed warning as I stare down the barrel of the gun, keeping Nolan's face trained within the sights while I release the safety on the side of the weapon. "I see you got my note. I thought my communication was pretty clear, but if you're here, I guess it was missing something. So how about this?" I clear my throat, giving him a dramatic pause. "*Fuck. Off.* Get the fuck out of Cape Carnage and never come back, and I'll ensure that your book stays safely hidden. Is that clear enough for you this time?"

Nolan's smile brightens. Something flashes in the dim light at his side. It's the blade I left behind in his tire, his fist tight around the handle, its deadly edge ready to kill. "I'm not going anywhere just yet. Not until you give me my book."

"You think I'm just going to hand over my leverage? I'm not giving you shit," I declare, firming my grip on the gun. "You need to leave, before you get everything even more ass-backwards than you already have. You're making a mistake. I'm not who you think I am."

"You're right. I thought you were a coward, just running from your past. Turns out you're actually a soulless monster." Nolan scoffs, his eyes slowly dropping to my feet and back up again, a look of disgust surfacing in his expression. For some reason, that hits harder than any of the vitriolic comments he's made to me in the brief time I've known him.

Stalemate.

The word comes out of nowhere and crashes into me with enough force that I nearly lose sight of the present. The voice that delivers it is still so clear in my mind despite the years that have passed, a memory that has no right infiltrating such a fraught moment.

I shake my head only slightly, barely a perceptible motion as I try to rid myself of the echo. I don't expect Nolan to notice, but I think he does, a crease settling between his brows. It's not concern, even though it might seem that way on the surface. It's just confusion—I know that. But even if it was some kind of fleeting wisp of empathy, I don't want it. Not from him.

I suck in a breath to resume the argument about his trophy scrapbook when another voice interrupts my thoughts.

"Pretty murder bird," Morpheus says from the garden wall. Our gazes cut toward him as he pecks the last of the morsels off the stone. "Nom, nom. *C* is for *cookie*."

Morpheus gives three knocking clucks and then mimics the sound of the diesel tractor engine.

Nolan's eyes slide to the woodchipper and then back to mine, disbelief now mixing with the revulsion that still simmers in his face. "Did you name your woodchipper after the beloved Sesame Street character Cookie Monster and then teach a raven to beg for human snacks made from the people you murdered?"

A thick swallow slides down my throat. "It's not as bad as it sounds."

"No," Nolan says as all the light leaves his eyes. "It's worse."

"*That's good enough for me,*" Morpheus recites in a painfully accurate replica of my own impersonation of Cookie Monster.

I'm desperate to drag a hand down my face, but I'm unwilling to let go of the gun or the bottle of Piss-Off! Neither feels like enough of a weapon when Nolan stares at me with such unforgiving malice. There's enough heat in his glare to ignite a violent eruption in a dormant volcano.

"You're a terrible human being," he says, as though he's affirming it to himself as much as he is to me.

"You don't know anything about me," I whisper.

"Oh, really? I think I know plenty." He takes a step closer, and though everything in my body screams at me to run, I stay right where I am with the gun aimed at his face. "I know you kill people and drive away. I know you dispose of dead bodies with a woodchipper."

"You kill people and make them into a scrapbook, so that's a bit of the pot calling the kettle black, don't you think?"

"At least I dispose of them properly. You do realize bone chips don't just magically disintegrate in the soil, right? I guess I know how you get all those gardening awards now. Maybe the police would like to know too." Nolan frowns down at the tarp and then over to the beds of freshly planted flowers before he settles his ire back on me. He takes another step closer, his grip tightening on the handle of the knife. "Tell me, do you hunt with the old man? Or is it just his messes that you clean up? Is that why he lets you live in this cottage? Maybe you're the daughter he always wished he had."

Bile churns beneath my sternum. I don't know if he understands what he's saying, or if it's just a cruel coincidence. Either way, his words crawl beneath my skin, heating my palm in the glove as I firm my grip on the gun. "Get the fuck off my property and maybe I'll let you live," I snarl as he takes another small step closer. I should back away. Or I should shoot him, just accept the risk that the bang will draw the attention of neighbors and tourists staying nearby. I can tear my name out of his book and hand it over as evidence. Work quickly to try to clean up the mess of what's left of Jake Hornell and hope to fuck Cape Carnage's inept Sheriff Yates won't look too closely at anything other than Nolan, the man who was trespassing on Arthur Lancaster's estate and threatening my life.

I'm still weighing the risks and benefits of shooting Nolan Rhodes in the face when he says something that slices through every thought spiraling through the confines of my skull.

"Since the police can't seem to solve shit around here, maybe I should just let that amateur investigator Sleuthseekers group know, seeing as how the old man's already got their attention."

All the fire that was just coursing through my veins suddenly turns to ice. "What did you say?"

"The Sleuthseekers. They're here, and it's only a matter of time before—"

"Who is here?" I demand, taking a step back. "*Who?*"

A flicker of intrigue ignites in Nolan's eyes, nearly hidden by the malice and hatred he seems to wear like armor. It's as though he's contradicting his better judgment when he unleashes a name I dread to hear. A man who was on my trail when I first disappeared. One who is tenacious. Determined. And worse, one who hunts fame like a bloodhound scenting a fox. One I haven't kept close tabs on since I thought my story had faded away when their group started favoring other prey. But I know I've made a colossal fucking mistake when Nolan says, "Sam Porter."

I falter under the weight of those two words. And Nolan sees it. That one heartbeat where my finger separates from the trigger. When I lower the gun just enough to leave an opening.

And he takes it.

The weapon flies from my grasp and lands on the grass. I have just enough time to hit the flat side of his blade with the bottle of Piss-Off! spray to knock it to the ground. But even as it's falling, Nolan's other hand is already gripped tight around my throat. He leaves me just enough air to breathe. His palm tightens beneath my jaw, his fingers firm and unforgiving in my flesh. My pulse hammers into his warm skin as he draws me closer, staring down into my eyes as though he'll consume my fucking soul. "Where. Is. My. Book?"

Mint and rage flood my face with every breath he takes. Fury radiates from him, charging the air between us. That wedge of brown in his left eye seems to darken, as though the demon in him is rising to the surface. And I stare right back at it, daring the devil to come out. My words might be choked, but they still hold venom when I say, "Go fuck yourself."

His grip hardens and I struggle not to cough. "I could torture you until you tell me."

"I've been tortured before. Go ahead," I hiss, the pressure building in my head with every heartbeat, my vision throbbing. Nolan's brows knit tighter, just for a flicker of time, his scowl dropping to my lips before rising once more. "Except you should probably know . . ." My gloved hand grips his wrist and I haul myself closer, until there's only an inch or two of space between us. "Your precious book will go straight to the FBI along with every scrap of information I've collected on you so far. The license plate of your rental vehicle. The medication you take. The pharmacy that fills your prescription. Your fucking phone number. Hurt me or kill me. Go right ahead and watch your life unravel. I'm sure your parents and sister will be so proud to find out who Nolan Rhodes *truly* is, especially after everything they've already lost."

At the mention of his family, I see the first true moment of unease burrow beneath Nolan's ruthless scowl. A muscle feathers along his jaw as though he's trying to clamp down on his fear. His grip loosens just enough on my throat that I can take a full breath in.

"There's only one way you're getting that book," I say. A shadow of rage passes across Nolan's face, his lips set in a tense line. "Help me protect Arthur. Get Sam out of here."

"If you want me to kill him, I'm not going to do that."

"*Fuck* no." I glare at him, resisting the urge to roll my eyes. "If you do that, the fucking Sleuthseekers will descend on this place. We'll be overrun by those fucking tin hat conspiracy weirdos. Just make him leave."

Nolan lets out a bark of a laugh. There's no joy or warmth in the smile he gives me. "So you want me to help you protect your serial killer benefactor from the guy who seems to be legitimately on his trail? That's rich."

"That's the offer. Take it or get fucked."

"Why don't you just lead Sam off course by yourself? Judging by your little setup here," he says with a jerk of his head in the direction of the woodchipper, "I'm sure you can manufacture a reason for him to take his focus off your friend and put it elsewhere. Maybe try being magnanimous for once in your life and take the heat for Arthur yourself."

I swallow down the vows I've made. The promises I'll do

anything to keep. "If I could take the heat for him, I would," I say. Though I'm sure Nolan won't believe me, that's the truth. I know enough about Porter to know that he's not just here to solve a mystery. He's here for fame. And no one could give him a better story than me. If I let Sam Porter get too close to me, he'll thrust me back into the spotlight, and who knows what that bright light could uncover. Every promise I've ever made—to Arthur, to myself, to the ghosts I left in my past—will crumble like dust in my hands.

If only it were that simple.

I can't do this on my own. Nolan Rhodes might have come here to kill me, but he's suddenly the only person who can save me. "Help me or your book is going to the authorities."

He scoffs, his eyes scouring my face as though he could flay the flesh from my bones with nothing more than a look. "Let's say I do help you. Then what? You're just going to give me my book back and let me go on my merry way?"

"Yes."

"How do you know I won't turn around and kill you the second it's in my hands?"

"I guess you could." I shrug. "But I suppose the rest of the evidence could still be a problem for you."

Silence descends between us. His hand tightens once more around my throat and I capture a breath to hold it. *Stalemate*, I hear again as the edges of my vision start to darken. My eyes press closed only long enough to will the memory away, and as soon as they do, Nolan's grip relaxes just enough that the hum in my head subsides.

"I will help you with Arthur. And then you'll give me the book and anything else you have stored away," he finally says.

"I'll give you the book and your weapons. You'll leave town. Anything else stays with me, since I'm sure you'll be gathering evidence against me during our super fun time together that I'm so looking forward to. Take it or leave it."

I can see how desperately he wants that book. It's a war behind his eyes. But just because I have leverage and need his help, doesn't mean I can trust him. No matter what I keep after our deal runs its course, he'll kill me the moment that book is in his hands. I know it.

The only way I'll survive is to kill him first.

"Pretty murder bird," Morpheus says in the mist, his voice a flawless imitation of my own.

I swallow, unfolding my hand from Nolan's wrist to hold it up between us for him to shake. "Do we have a deal?"

Nolan looks down at my offered truce. He gives so little away in his expression, his eyes fixed on my bloodstained glove. It takes a long moment before his focus finally meets mine once more and he uncurls his grip from my throat, one finger at a time. Morpheus caws in the shadows. Maybe it's a harbinger of doom. Or fate, sealed in an ominous song. His cry falls into the background as Nolan tugs the gardening glove from my hand and tosses it to the grass, then slips his palm against mine, his stare unblinking. "Make no mistake," he says. "If I go down, I'm taking you with me."

"I'm sure." I can't help the wicked smile that creeps onto my lips as I pump his hand twice. "Starting tomorrow."

With my other hand, I raise the bottle of Piss-Off! and spray him in the face.

Nolan drops my hand and backs away, raising his arm in defense. "What the fuck? What are you doing?"

"Getting you to *Piss-Off*! I've had enough of your shit for one day."

"It *burns*."

"Good," I snarl. Three more sprays land on his hand. "Get the fuck off my property. Take your fucking head with you. I'm not interested in cleaning up your mess."

I toss Jake's head at Nolan and it hits his chest with a dull thud. He's wiping the spray from his eyes with the sleeve of his hoodie when I open the valve on the garden hose lying next to the tarp and toss it in his direction.

"Come back tomorrow afternoon and we'll figure this shit out," I say, picking up the knife and the gun as he fumbles for the hose, a string of curses tumbling from his lips. He points the end toward his face and blinks into the trickle of cold water. "And if I see you before then, I'll be putting you through my woodchipper before our deal even begins."

With a final glance, I turn my back on the man who has come here to kill me and walk away.

TREASURES

Harper

"YOU'RE SURE ABOUT THIS? THE Pocket Rocket is basically a death-trap," Lukas says as I whip back the canvas cover from the old soapbox racer.

"Aren't they all?" A cloud of dust envelops us, catching the morning sun through the filmy window of the shed. I wave a hand in front of my face as I step closer to the makeshift car, its body constructed from two whiskey barrels that have been cut up and welded together with extra panels of steel. Arthur's ingenuity might as well be stamped right next to the Lancaster Distillery logo that's branded into the aged oak. "I can't believe Arthur let you name it the Pocket Rocket."

Lukas chuckles, sliding a palm over the faded name painted above a decorative wing. "He wasn't really up on his penis slang, you know? When Bert nearly pissed himself announcing my turn and started cracking some pretty obvious innuendos while commentating on my run, he caught on pretty quick. I was grounded for a solid two weeks after that." Lukas's smile turns bittersweet and his gaze grows distant, as though he's looking back in time. "Even still, it was worth it. That was the best day."

My heart sinks as I watch Lukas run a hand through his short black hair and rest it on the back of his head, something he always does when the weight of his life seems too heavy a burden to bear. Though he meets my eyes for only a fleeting moment, it's long enough to see the raw edges of a wound that's never healed. A wound named Maxine, the girl he loved all his life. The one who picked up and left Carnage in the dead of night on their graduation day with no explanation, as though she couldn't wait another moment to get away.

It broke him irreparably. And despite being tall and fit, independently wealthy before thirty, and painfully good-looking in a broken soul kind of way, I'm ninety-nine percent sure Lukas is a virgin. Not that it's any of my fucking business.

"Are you sure you're okay with me using the Rocket?" I ask, pulling my thoughts away from the "Is Lukas a virgin?" debate I've had with myself many times, even though it skeeves me out a bit as he feels like he could be my brother. Lukas is already shaking his head and dismissing my concern. "I can find something else—"

"No way. It's totally fine, Harp. I'd love to see it reclaim its former glory." Lukas whacks the barrel with a loving pat and something clunks in the undercarriage and falls to the floor, rolling off into the shadows. "Yeah . . . I suppose a decade of sitting idle hasn't done the recycled parts any favors. You're gonna have to take her apart and really make sure she's at least more roadworthy now than when we first made her."

I only have two weeks before the race, so realistically a full overhaul is not in the cards. But I just smile and nod. "Yeah, I'll make sure she's ready to fly. Might give her a new name, though. I don't need to throw myself under your grandfather's judgy bus."

"I'm still pissed at you for sacrificing me to the bus. Those gutters are such a bitch. It's going to take me all afternoon, and I'm not going to have time for a shower before theater rehearsal. Ross is still jealous that I scored the Beast role in the production. He's definitely gonna call me out on my stank in front of the cast."

"Then you should *definitely* be thanking me for not suggesting the septic system." I smile as Lukas rolls his eyes and tosses a dusty rag in my direction. "Don't worry, I called the guy to come in and fix it. That job is off your shoulders. For now."

Lukas's expression softens as he swipes a hand over the surface of a stool and lowers himself onto the cracked vinyl. "Thank you for always looking after my grandfather. This place would be falling apart without you."

"It's no trouble."

"It's Arthur Lancaster. It's always trouble."

Lukas is right about that. Arthur is *always* trouble, but in a way I admire. And his most troublesome behavior reflects a hidden life that even Lukas isn't privy to. I'm one of only two people who know what he's truly capable of. Me, his greatest ally. La Plume, his formidable enemy. And I guess now a third person.

Nolan Rhodes.

My focus cuts toward the bag I shoved beneath the soapbox racer yesterday before Nolan showed up at my cottage. "Actually," I say, picking up the backpack, "I do need to call in a favor."

Lukas's brows hike in a silent question and I give him a grave smile in reply as I hand him Nolan's backpack. "I need you to hide this. Put it somewhere I won't find it. And don't tell anyone where it is. Not unless something happens to me."

His brows knit. He stares at the backpack as though it might blow up if he touches it. With a swallow, he finally takes it, settling it on his lap. "What do you mean, 'unless something happens to you'?"

"Like I go missing. Or if I wind up badly hurt, like the kind of hurt where I'll never wake up to tell you what happened. Or if I turn up dead."

"What the fuck? Are you in trouble?"

"Everything is fine."

"It doesn't sound fucking fine. What's going on?"

I shake my head, placing a hand on his when he starts to open the zipper. Lukas is not a man of darkness, despite how it has enveloped his life, often without his awareness. I'm not about to let Arthur's lifetime of work collapse because of me. "This is a *need to know* situation. And the less you know, the better it is for everyone." With a single nod, I squeeze his hand. "Please. Just put it somewhere safe and don't look inside. If something happens, send it straight to the FBI."

"The FBI? Are you fucking kidding me?"

"Sheriff Yates is about as useful as tits on a rock. It needs to go to someone with two brain cells to rub together."

Silence descends in the shed. Lukas searches my face, dust motes twisting in the wedge of light between us, an ethereal boundary between two creatures who might as well belong to different realms. Lukas Lancaster is the angel of Cape Carnage. And I'm the devil who claims the souls that come to pollute his heaven.

When he tugs the strap of the backpack over his shoulder and gives me a nod, I can't help but feel like I'm failing to keep his sanctuary safe.

"Are you sure you're okay? I'm really worried about you," Lukas says, his rich brown eyes searching mine, concern woven into his furrowed brows. For a guy who looks the way he does, with his dark hair and stubbled, chiseled jaw, his athletic frame and broad shoulders, you wouldn't think he is the way he really is, all his worries laid out on the patchwork of plaid sleeves that are rolled to his elbows and smell like malt mash. "I'm sorry you've taken on so much of the work of looking after Arthur. I can spend more time here—"

"No, Lukas." I toss the canvas back over the Pocket Rocket, a plume of dust erupting around us like a pyroclastic ghost. "I love spending time with Arthur. And it makes him so happy that you're restoring the distillery. I know it takes a lot of time. I'm good."

"Are you sure?"

"Trust me," I say, patting his arm on my way toward the door. Lukas rises to follow. "If I need your help, I'll definitely let you know. It won't be long now before you're back to a more normal schedule, don't worry. And it'll be worth it. The whole town is going to be so excited to see the distillery up and running again properly."

Lukas shrugs, turning to thread the chain between the shed's door handles and close the padlock after us. He stops at my side, and we take in the view. You can see the whole town from our perch on the hill of Lancaster Manor. Puffs of white cloud shift high above us in the relentless coastal wind. Spears of sunlight pierce through their soft edges in search of the water, boats traversing its shining surface far in the distance. The Victorian homes in the heart of the downtown face off against the sea, bright colors that fight the gloom of depths that hold death and dark memories for those who have been here long enough. Every piece of this town exists in the shadow of Lancaster Manor. Even the people who live on its grounds.

"I don't know if they will be," Lukas says, as though he's plucked my thoughts right out of my head. "Some people, sure. But not all."

I look up at him, squinting as I take in his pensive expression. "What makes you think that?"

"I dunno. I just feel like they'll never be ready to let some things go. Like what happened to my mom." He lifts one shoulder, not pulling his focus away from the town as his grip tightens on the strap of the backpack. "When I went into Maya's this morning to get some stuff for cleaning the gutters, she said some guy had come in to ask her questions about the estate for some documentary he's filming. A *documentary*, Harper. It's like someone is always looking to exhume my family's past. You know?" He shakes his head, not looking down at me, which I'm grateful for. Because if he did, he might see the tension in my jaw as I clench my teeth, or the color that infuses my cheeks. "Apparently, he was talking to Daryl Winkle the other day about our piece of land out by the Ballantyne River."

My eyes narrow, and he looks down at me as though sensing the alarm that suddenly pulses through the chambers of my heart. "Why would he want to know about that?"

"Probably because I sold it last month, though I'm not sure why that would matter to him."

I nearly choke on a breath of air. "You *what*?"

"Sold it," Lukas repeats, a crease notching between his brows. "We didn't need it anymore, and the council fast-tracked a development application—"

"To whom?" I realize too late that my tone is harsher than it should be, and a note of suspicion now sharpens the angles of his face as Lukas stares back at me. "I'm sorry. Arthur told me he signed over the power of attorney to you and it's none of my business or anything. I guess I'm just surprised, that's all."

"Does this have anything to do with what you're asking me to hide?"

"No." I shake my head as though trying to dislodge that lie from my throat. "No, I'm really just curious, that's all."

Though he is still scrutinizing my expression, Lukas's concern gradually eases, and the tension in his clenched jaw unlocks. "Some property development company called Viceroy. They approached me a while back about building a new boutique hotel along the river. They're pretty eager to get started. I heard from Bert that they've already gotten their permits and rented the diggers. Guess I've been so caught up with everything at the distillery that I just forgot to mention it—I'm sorry. That place has kinda sucked up all my time."

"No, don't apologize." I muster a smile that I hope will be convincing enough. "That's great," I say, another complete fucking lie. A pang of guilt snaps at my heart. My existence is already full of enough deception that I try to limit the number of direct lies I tell to the people I care about. Aside from Arthur, Lukas is the only person I really let myself get close to, and I already feel guilty enough on a regular basis that he doesn't know the kind of woman I truly am. I don't like making that worse. "When does the sale close?"

"Three weeks from today."

"Three weeks from today," I parrot after him, swallowing the urge to bark a bitter laugh. "Cool . . . cool. Well, I'd better get going." I try to temper the suspicion rising in Lukas's eyes once more by giving him an easy, untroubled smile. With a brief yet awkward salute, I turn for the path that leads down to my cottage at the edge of the property. "Have fun with the gutters."

"Next time, you're the one going under the judgy bus," he calls after me, but I just toss a middle finger back at him and fight the consuming urge to run the rest of the distance to my house.

When I get inside, my breath is uneven, my heart hammering every beat against my bones. *Three fucking weeks.*

I march toward the staircase, taking the stairs by two, turning toward the guest room when I arrive on the landing. The air seems to never move in the room that belonged to Lukas when he was only a baby. Aside from the kitchen, it's the room I know Arthur would be most reluctant to enter if he came searching for his bag, the memories of it seared so deeply in his brain that I don't think even his illness would force them out. I only stay long enough to grab the bag from where I've stashed it beneath the bed and take it back downstairs.

"From one murder bag to the next," I say aloud as I sit on one of the overstuffed couches and drop it at my feet. "What the hell have I done with my life?"

It's definitely not what I ever expected. I had a good home. A happy childhood. I thought I'd have a normal life. But the universe loves to prove you wrong. One day, it upends everything. One day, you might even wind up captured by a serial killer and thrown in his cellar as the universe really says, "Fuck your expectations."

And now, here I am, pulling Arthur's "grim-noire" from his bag of tricks.

"Chrissakes. This is so . . . *Arthur*." I run my fingers across the title stamped into the soft leather, each letter embossed with gold that Arthur must have pressed into the calligraphy himself. This is the first time I've ever dared to take a very close look at his prized record of names and dates and manners of death. I flip open the worn cover. Inside, there are recipes for poisons. Notes for noxious gasses. Ratings for weapons, methods of decomposition. Over many years, he's detailed the disposal of each body, with locations marked with numbers on maps of his properties.

I flip to the one for the parcel of land at the Ballantyne River.

I'm pretty sure blood stops coursing through my body.

I close my eyes and expel a long, resigned breath. "I'm so fucked."

My gaze tracks up to the chessboard on the little table by the unlit hearth.

Stalemate.

His voice surfaces again.

I close my eyes and press them into the heels of my palms.

"Neither of us won," his voice echoes in time.

"Let me lose this time, Adam," I remember saying. It was that day we waited for a tow truck to come and collect our broken-down vehicle from a deserted dirt road. I can still smell the smoke of palo santo burning in the half-moon incense holder that Adam loved, the one that lived on top of the tiny wood-burning stove in the van we called home. It was the day our lives shattered and splintered and collapsed around us.

Sometimes, it feels like the five years that have elapsed since then never existed. Not when I hear his voice so clearly in my mind.

"I'll always lose for you." Adam's words were warmed by his ever-present grin as he tipped his king over on the chessboard, forfeiting to me like he always did when there were no moves left in the game.

It was just a moment later when a knock rapped three times on our sliding door.

I force my eyes open, willing myself away from a time I keep pushing away, one that will drown me, if I let it. I stare at the pieces, set up and ready for a new game. Just stare and stare, one deep breath after the next, until the memory of Adam's smile finally fades.

I need to keep my promises. The one I made to Adam, to never give up hope. The one I made to Arthur, to protect this town.

The ones I've made to myself.

I force my attention back to the book splayed out on my lap. I'm still staring down at the map when I pull my phone from my pocket, barely glancing away long enough to hover my thumb over the new contact. *Ballmeat Guy.*

I press it and put the call on speaker.

In two rings, I receive a heartwarming greeting from Nolan Rhodes. "Who is this?"

"Who do you think?" I resume staring down at my near future, drawn in ink and brown splotches that look suspiciously like old blood. I raise the book close to my face and squint at the droplets, then give it a tentative sniff. The scents of ink and leather lift from the page, a mustiness lingering like a phantom in the fibers of the deckle-edged cotton paper. I crinkle my nose. "What is it about these men and their books of blood and skin?"

"What did you say?"

I roll my eyes, closing the grim-noire and setting it next to me on the couch. "Still want your precious scrapbook back?"

"You know, I do have other shit to do. You can't just say 'scrapbook,' and I'll come rushing to your door."

"We both know that's a lie. You came here for me. To make me into one of your little tannery trophies. And now that I have your trophy case, the way I see it, you have time at your disposal."

"So you expect the whole world to revolve around you. Color me shocked."

I bite down on a sharp retort. That urge to tell him he doesn't know who he's talking to slips between my enamel until I swallow it down. My gaze slides back to the chessboard. No matter how far I try to get away from the person I used to be, she's still there, ready to claim a past I've tried to wash away. But I haven't kept her hidden for this long just for someone like Nolan Rhodes to bring her to the surface.

"It's a simple question, Nolan. I could have it sent to the FBI if you prefer."

There's a measure of self-satisfaction in his voice, and I imagine he must be smirking as he says, "If it were that easy, you would have done it by now. But it's not that easy, is it? You need my help."

For the love of God. I truly despise this man. And not just because he's right.

"Do you want your fucking book or not?"

There's a long pause. For a moment, I think the line has disconnected, but the seconds tick away on the screen. The book by my side seems to whisper to me in the silence. There are too many names on the map of the Ballantyne River property. Too many bodies for me to unearth on my own in such a short time. Enemy or not, Nolan Rhodes is the only person I can rely on to help me protect Arthur's secret, to keep Lukas and the rest of Cape Carnage safe. And I don't know what I'll do if he says no.

It's just a single word, but in his rich tone I can hear both wariness and determination when he finally answers. "Yes."

"Then we have some work to do."

EXHUME

Nolan

"Three weeks before the deal closes. *Three fucking weeks.*"

Harper gives a single nod. "Three fucking weeks."

"And how many bodies?" I ask, even though I heard Harper perfectly well the first time she told me. My hard stare drills into the side of her face, but she doesn't look away from the silty floodplain stretched before us, dark water flowing just beyond the reach of her headlamp.

She swallows. Clears her throat. "Sixteen."

"*Sixteen* fucking bodies. That's almost a body per night, and it assumes we'll have perfect conditions and zero mistakes."

"Yes," she says, her eyes glinting in the dim light as they roll. "Thank you for mansplaining math. Don't know what I would have done without that groundbreaking contribution."

I huff an irritated sigh. "I'm not trying to mansplain math to you."

"How about you mansplain to me your surely elaborate plan of how you're going to get Sam to leave instead? That would actually be useful."

Right. That too. I'd already started keeping tabs on his whereabouts this morning so I could work out any behavioral patterns that I might be able to upend or exploit. So far, I haven't come up with many grand solutions except for maybe sabotaging his equipment and his vehicle. "I'm working on that," I grumble.

Harper huffs. "I'm sure. Well, you'd better work faster, Ball-meat," she says, thrusting the handle of a shovel into my chest with precision, even though she doesn't turn or even look my way. "We have a Sleuthseeker to drive out of town and exactly zero-point-seven-six bodies per day to exhume in the glorious three weeks we'll be spending together, so we'd better get cracking."

She marches away toward the shallow slope that drops onto the swath of silt by the river where vegetation is sparse and landmarks are few.

I could kill her. Bash her over the head with the shovel in my hands and take my chances that she wasn't bluffing about my book. Disappear into the wilderness. Resign myself to never seeing my family again, further breaking the already shattered remains of their hearts. At least they would know I served justice to those who deserved it.

My grip on the handle loosens just a little as I watch Harper lay her duffel bag on the ground, setting her shovel next to it. She has her back to me, a pool of light tracking over the dirt as she surveys the space around her, as though she's projecting her thoughts onto the ground. She's scared, but not of me, and not for herself. She's worried about the old man. So worried she's willing to risk her life to wrangle me into her control. And I want to know why.

Though I hate the idea very much, I can understand why she might send her car off a cliff and fake her own death after a deadly hit-and-run. I get why she'd hide in a strange little town for four years. Self-preservation. But I *don't* understand why she'd risk everything for an elderly man who might have killed his own daughter. How could someone with no qualms about leaving me and my brother for dead be so loyal to him that she puts herself in harm's way?

There's something about Harper that pulls questions from the dark recesses of my thoughts, and they're not the same ones I came to Cape Carnage to ask her.

Harper bends down and unzips the bag to rummage through the contents. The fantasy that I've been living for these last four years is only a few feet away. I've dreamt so many times about choking the confession free from her lips. I take a few steps closer. In only a handful of heartbeats, I could have her under my control. But instead, I lower the shovel, take a deep breath, and walk calmly toward her, making enough sound so as not to startle her.

I will get the answers I came for, I promise myself. *I am here to deliver the consequences of the choices she made, ones that neither of us can escape. But I want to know all her secrets before I do.*

"So," I say as I draw to a halt next to her. "Where do we start?"

I squint against the light of her headlamp as she eyes me, her attention flicking to the shovel in my hand before returning to my face. I'm making her feel unsafe. I should probably be relishing the discomfort my presence is giving her. But I don't.

I push the shovel into the dirt next to me and make a point to take a step away from it and fold my arms, and as though she's giving me something in return, she turns off her headlamp, switching on a camping lantern instead.

"I figure we can start at the edge over there and work our way from left to right," she says as she nods past me toward a cluster of granite boulders in the distance. She pulls a tape measure from the bag and tosses it at my feet before rising with a spray bottle in one hand, the lantern illuminating her from below in a way that would make most people look like shit. But not Harper. She's hauntingly beautiful, ethereal in the bluish glow of the lantern and the moonlight. Even more so when she starts spraying a mist above the crown of her head, the droplets shimmering as they fall over her hair.

"What is that?"

"Bugfucker."

I snort a laugh. Her lips don't even twitch as she mists a cloud of spray around her head. A mosquito lands on my neck long enough to pierce my skin and I slap it. "Seriously?"

She shrugs. "Maya likes to get creative with her names. But she has a PhD in chemistry from MIT, for fucksakes. Everything she makes is fucking incredible. This is the good shit." Harper mists her arms, her eyes never leaving mine, as though she's ready to turn the nozzle on me if I so much as twitch in a way she doesn't like. I'm pretty sure she would flay the skin right off my face with her fingernails if she could, judging by the merciless glare she pins on me. It's murderously adorable.

No, it's fucking not. What the actual fuck?

I shake my head, maybe hoping to clear my wayward thoughts, maybe hoping some of the cloud of citronella-scented droplets might drift closer to cover my skin in the light breeze.

"I'd like some," I say.

Harper's eyes narrow to thin slits of malice. "Where's yours?"

"At the inn."

"You're telling me you do Search and Rescue *for a living*, and you come to a nighttime body removal party at a body of water without bug spray?"

I swat at another mosquito, but two more land on my body in the time it takes to kill just one. "First of all, you're playing fast and loose with the word 'party.' Second, when you said, 'Pick me up at ten o'clock and help me with something for Arthur,' you left out the part about digging up dead bodies by a fucking river. So. *Can I have some?*"

A snide little smirk flickers across her lips. "Not so good with manners, are you? Maybe if you'd said 'please' in the first place, I would have given your book back when you asked for it."

"No, you wouldn't have."

"You're right. And I'm not feeling so inclined to give this to you either," she says as she sprays down the front of her body, her eyes still locked to mine. Blood roars in my ears. I don't know if it's rage, or the enticing boldness of her challenge, or the way the mist coats the exposed skin of her chest to shimmer on her collarbones. Maybe it's all three that set me aflame.

My jaw presses tight as I take a step closer. "I could take it."

She's mere inches away, staring up at me with total defiance, her full lips set in a determined line. "And I could spray you in the face. That worked so well for you the last time."

I inch closer. She still doesn't shrink from me. Instead, she slides the spray behind her back in a way that almost dares me to take it. To reach around and fold her in an embrace and pull it from her hands. No matter how hard I try not to, I imagine the feel of her against me. Her warmth. The rise and fall of her chest against mine. The cadence of her heartbeat.

Her hard stare bores right into me, digging through every layer until it feels like she's embedded herself into my heart, piercing me from the inside out. "Please, Harper," I finally say, not missing the way her gaze finally drops to my lips and lingers there when I let her name slowly roll from my tongue, "can I have the bug spray?"

Her words come out a little breathless when she says, "Will you complain less if I give it to you?"

"I'm sure I'll find something else to complain about, don't worry."

One hand slowly comes from behind her back to lift the bottle into my peripheral view. "I can't wait to find out what joys you'll bring next."

Our fingers graze as I take the bottle from her. An electric hum sizzles in my skin even after that momentary touch has passed. And I wonder if she felt it too. If she did, she gives nothing away. As soon as she releases the bottle, she's bending to grab the lantern and tape measure with one hand, the shovel with the other. "Follow me," is all she says.

I pick up the duffel and my shovel, covering myself in the Bug-fucker mist as Harper leads the way toward the boulders that sit on the rise at the end of the plain. When we arrive there, she sets her shovel and lantern down, then passes me the end of the tape, keeping the wheel in her hand.

"Do you have a map?" I ask.

She slices me with a glare. "I *am* the map. Six meters from the middle of the biggest rock. There should be a little line," she says, running her finger over the surface of the boulder. "It's here."

I lean close to where her fingers rest, and sure enough, there's a small notch in the stone made by a human hand. When I straighten, we both turn to evaluate the floodplain. "But how do you know you're going straight? It could be there," I say, pointing to a spot on the ground close to the shore, "or there." I shift in an arc and point again. "Or it could be somewhere in between.

Unless you have a second point to anchor from, it could be any-where around there."

Harper's focus tracks across the wide, slow-moving river, lock-ing onto another set of boulders on the opposite shore. Her shoul-ders fall a fraction, enough for me to notice. "There is another anchor point. The rock closest to the water."

"Okay . . . well . . . that's helpful, I guess. Except for the fact that it's on the other side of the river."

"Yeah." There's a long, silent pause. I would have expected her to march right up to the riverbank and dive in with the tape mea-sure and probably a knife between her teeth. But she offers noth-ing. She just gnaws at her lip before lifting a shoulder as though she can hide her concerns beneath a nonplussed gesture. "I think it will be fine if we just measure from this rock," she says as she motions for me to hold the end of the tape against the notch in the boulder. "As long as I go straight-ish—"

I let out an audible sigh and stop her with a touch to her arm that makes her jolt. "You said yourself, we don't have much time. We'd better save ourselves the trouble of digging all over the place. Do you have another tape measure in here?" I squat down to start rummaging through the contents of the bag, glancing up to catch Harper shaking her head. She might not have more than one measuring tape, but she does have a brand-new, sixty-meter-long nylon cord rolled up in the bag, and I'm hoping that might do the trick. "What's the distance on your map from the boulder across the river to the first body?"

"Forty-four meters."

"Okay. Here's what we're gonna do." We measure out the length of cord to forty-four meters, tying a knot at that marker. Then we measure out six meters on the tape, locking the position on the wheel. When everything is ready to go, we head to the shore with the lantern and rope. There's only one more thing to do.

I take a deep breath and reach behind my head to pull off my shirt.

"What the fuck are you doing?" Harper whisper-hisses, her eyes darting around us as though someone might be lurking.

I chuckle, unfastening my belt buckle next. "Going for a swim."

I'm sure she's blushing. I can almost hear the blood rushing to her cheeks. Though she tries to look away, it's as though she can't help herself. Her eyes keep returning, settling on my abs, or my pecs, or my shoulders, or on my hands as I take my time with the button at the top of my jeans. Basically anywhere there's exposed skin or the possibility of more.

What the fuck. I am *not* flirting with the woman I might kill.

Will kill. I *will* kill her.

Later.

"So I guess I get it now," I say.

"Get what?"

"Why you've been hiding out for so long in Cape Carnage specifically." I toe off my shoes and unzip my jeans. Harper's eyes fuse to mine and her head tilts, and I swear I can feel the absence of her gaze on my skin, a chill that has more to do with her than the cooling night air.

"And why is that, oh wise one?"

"At first I thought you only liked it because it's . . . *quirky.*" I tug my jeans over my hips, and though I expected she'd look down, she doesn't. A twinge of disappointment stings in my throat when I swallow. "But if you're spending all your spare time looking out for La Plume and doing his murderous dirty work in exchange for room and board, that makes more sense."

If I had been flirting with her, which I *wasn't*, my words would have killed my chances stone dead. The look she gives me is more than lethal. It's incendiary. "I can't believe *you* are the person trying to take me out. A man who couldn't be more ass-backwards if he tried. Congratulations on getting literally *none* of your assumptions about me or anyone else right." Her eyes are knives of malice, but I think I see a flicker of hurt in their depths before she tosses the end of the rope to my feet. "Don't drown. It would be such a tragedy to lose your brilliant mind from this fucked-up world."

With a sneer, she turns her headlamp on in my face long enough to blind me and then pivots away, heading back toward the boulder. Though I can't see her clearly with the halo of the bright light burning in my eyes, I doubt she even gives me a backward glance. If she feels the weight of my gaze on her shoulders, she doesn't let on.

The halo slowly dissipates from my eyes, leaving only the pale blue of the lantern and the darkness of the forest on the opposite shore.

I tie the rope to my ankle and wade into the water that bites at my skin with bitter jaws.

The soft sand gives way beneath my toes as I move away from the shore and I'm enveloped by the current, slow enough to be easy to fight, fast enough to push me a little off my target. The fragrance of fresh water mixes with the citronella oil still clinging to my body. I push my way into the darkness, keeping that silver rock in sight. I should be thinking about how the hell I'm going to get my book back or how to strategize my way out of this exhumation plan. But I'm not. I'm thinking about Harper. I'm remembering that flash of hurt I just saw in her eyes. It didn't feel the way I thought it would knowing it came from me.

I close my eyes and dip my head beneath the surface, trying to force that image from my mind. But it's stuck there. Unwilling to let go.

A shiver racks my body as I climb onto the narrow bank. I tilt my neck from side to side, the negative pressure popping between vertebrae. I stretch and flex my arm against the pain in my elbow. My knee throbs from running too far to get to Harper the other day. Scar tissue and broken pieces that never perfectly healed. When I look back across the water, she's watching, her headlamp off, just the gentle lantern light pooling at her feet. I wonder what she thinks about the marks she saw in my skin when I undressed. If she imagines the suffering it took to endure them or the grief that lies deep beneath their warped edges.

It's too dark and distant for us to see each other clearly. But neither of us moves, not for a moment that seems to stretch as long as the river that snakes between us.

It's Harper who breaks away first. Harper who bends to pick up the other end of the rope that's still tethered to my ankle. "Are you ready?" she calls to me. And I still haven't moved.

I finally lower to one knee to untie the cord and then bring it to the rock where a notch is carved into its surface. Harper pulls it taut and lines it up with the other tape. When she's found the point where the two measurements coincide, she spears the shovel into the silt. No words pass across the water. She starts digging. And I start swimming.

By the time I make it back to shore, she's already made good progress in the soft soil. I watch her fluid, metronomic movement as I get dressed, still soaking wet. She stabs her shovel into the earth and shifts it next to the pit she's creating. She's strong. Graceful. She doesn't break her cadence, not even when I pick up a shovel and join her. We don't talk. I don't think she really looks at me, at least not the way I do, sneaking the occasional glance like a thief. It's not until she strikes a foreign texture with the point of her shovel that her eyes meet mine.

"Guess your plan worked," she whispers.

I nod. "One down."

"Fifteen to go."

With a single, grim look shared between us, we dig up the body, nothing left of it but bones in a decaying polypropylene sack with a faded black stamp that says RYE in large black letters. When the hole is filled back in and our tools are packed up, we stand for a moment and survey the floodplain and all the work we still have left to do. And she's probably thinking the same thing as I am when we turn and start heading back toward the road. I know I should not be looking forward to it, but some traitorous little voice in my brain claims otherwise. It's the anticipation of the hunt—that's all it is. I'm gathering evidence and learning the habits of my prey. Tonight was just setting the stage for what I can learn about Harper that will take her down. It was nothing more than an indulgence in my curiosity.

"Thanks," Harper says, breaking the silence that I didn't even notice in the riot of my own thoughts.

"Sure."

"What's wrong?"

I blink at her. "What do you mean, 'What's wrong?'"

Though she lifts a shoulder, I don't miss the way her brow furrows as she assesses my face, as though she's hunting for clues. "You've looked miserable all evening, but now you're . . . *extra* miserable. I didn't think that would be possible, and yet, here we are."

"Maybe I'm just thinking about how fucked up this situation is."

"Didn't really take you as the type to be put off by a little body relocation, given your scrapbooking hobby. But yeah," she says, pausing to run her fingers along her jaw as she surveys the road ahead. I want to remind her that she's been handling a body sack and that human decay juices have definitely passed through those fibers. But I don't. "I guess it's a little messed up."

"A bit. And now I'm helping a woman I want to kill to cover up murders committed by another serial killer. This is the most incestuous murder party I've ever heard of."

"You have no idea," Harper mutters as she tosses the sack of bones over her shoulder and walks away.

"Wait . . . what? What do you mean by that?" I jog a couple of steps after her before she tosses me a quizzical look in return. Inexplicably, my blood feels a hundred degrees too hot in my veins. "Do you and Arthur have some kind of . . . situationship . . . thing?"

"*The fuck?* No. Oh my God. Do you get anything right *ever?* Arthur has the hots for Irene." She scoffs, and though she turns away before I can see it, I swear I *hear* her eyes roll. "Forget about it, Ballmeat guy."

Harper walks out onto the shallow gravel pull-off where I'm parked. I follow her, but when she reaches my rental vehicle, she just keeps going, heading for a path that slices into the woods on the other side of the road.

"Where are you going? I'm your ride," I say, walking to the middle of the unlit road.

"I'm good. See you tomorrow."

Without another word, she disappears. And just like the first time we met, she leaves me alone.

In the dark.

AVAST

Harper

THERE IS NOT ENOUGH COFFEE in the world for me to survive today, let alone another seventeen days of this shit. I can barely even think straight long enough to *make* coffee, for godsakes. Yesterday, I even forgot to turn the fucking stove on. *For a full ten minutes.*

It's day four. But I swear it feels like day four hundred and eighty-five. These late nights are killing me. It's not just staying up until two or three in the morning, or the additional physical work of digging up bodies after an already demanding day of preparing Arthur's extensive gardens for another season of decimating Sarah Winkle's hopes and dreams. It's not just trying to fix the rusted old Pocket Rocket or worrying about Sam Porter suddenly showing up at my doorstep with triumphant jazz hands.

No. It's the stress of being in a secluded place with a man who wants to kill me, and the only thing stopping him is a bit of evidence currently in the possession of the endearingly naive and perpetually distracted Lukas Lancaster.

And the other part that makes this whole corpse relocation program so completely unbearable?

Nolan Rhodes is *hot as fuck*.

Those dimples. They'd be my undoing if he smiled at me with anything more than contempt. His skin. A man's skin has never rendered me close to speechless until Nolan. The moonlight settles on him every night as though it's determined to illuminate the planes of muscle in his ridiculous body as he undresses to swim across the river. Sometimes, the shimmer slithers across the scars that cross his elbow. His shoulder. His back. His lower abdomen. Christ, that one is the worst. It follows the diagonal ridge of muscle that leads to the waistband of his briefs. They always hang low on his hips, like a purposeful taunt, daring me to look down when he strips his clothes off so he can walk to that dark water and slip beneath its treacherous embrace. I've never been jealous of fucking *water* before. But here we are.

But it's not just the way he looks. It's his presence. Even though I know he'd probably rather clock me in the face with his shovel, there's something oddly comforting about his menacing silence at my side every night. The most dangerous monster is the one right next to me. When he's there, I'm not afraid of the dark.

This is like some super-fucked-up Stockholm-syndrome-adjacent thing I've got going on. Rationally, I know that in his mind, I belong to him. Nothing and no one will stand between Nolan Rhodes and the life he's come to claim. But to my not-so-rational mind, that is *so fucking hot*. It's wildly intoxicating to be such an object of someone's obsession that they would decimate anyone who threatens you. I realize that sounds pretty messed up. And I know with every fiber of my being that I need to kill this man before I wind up as a souvenir in his skinbook. Though I should be running in the other direction and testing out his theory that he'd find me no matter the distance, the idea of him traveling to the ends of the earth to chase me down somehow makes him even hotter.

My self-imposed, years-long dry spell isn't doing me any favors right now. It's tempting to picture an alternative ending to our acrimonious story, maybe even a happy one, but the reality is he would kill me, that's what he would do. One hundred percent chance of death.

I sigh and roll my eyes, my hands braced on either side of the stove. "Get your shit together," I whisper as I finally realize I haven't turned the burner on to boil the water in my stovetop coffee maker. *Again.* "He's just a guy. A completely psycho serial killer guy with a decent skin suit and muscles for days and some cute dimples." I squeeze my eyes shut and turn to lean against the counter. "You should just feed him to Cookie Monster and be done with it."

Even though I say those words out loud, I know it won't transform the way I really feel into an opposite reality.

My enemy is right where I can see him. I don't just need his help. I *want* it. Maybe part of me even wants *him*.

"No, you absolutely do *not* want him," I say to myself as the water starts to boil in my coffee maker. "You just need caffeine."

I turn off the gas, still chastising myself for the treacherous, intrusive thoughts that refuse to leave me alone. I'm finally pouring my coffee and trying to make a mental list of parts for the Pocket Rocket when a sudden crash comes from the grounds beyond the cottage garden. The shock of sound makes my hand jerk, and half the pot of boiling hot coffee spills onto my other hand and across the counter. "Goddamnit," I hiss as pain erupts across the back of my hand. There's no time to run it under cold water to soothe the burn. I grab a tea towel and dab it dry as I rush toward the door. "Nolan Rhodes, if this is your fault I am going to *fuck you up*."

I head outside and through the back gate in the stone wall to find Arthur climbing out of his golf cart, the front of the vehicle wedged against a tree stump.

"Jesus Christ, Arthur," I say, taking his arm to steady him. "Are you all right?"

"I'm perfectly fine."

"What the hell are you doing?"

"Crashing this piece of junk," he says, whacking the crumpled hood with his cane. "What does it look like?"

"On purpose?"

"Of course not." He stabs his cane into the turf and starts hobbling in the direction of my cottage as though nothing happened. "The accelerator was stuck."

"Under your foot? Because you were pressing it instead of the brake?"

Arthur grumbles an inaudible reply.

"Where's your walker?" I ask, surveying the dented fender of his golf cart before trailing after him. A quiet rustle of feathers pulls my attention away to the wall where Morpheus has just landed, shaking out his wings as he watches us with interest. I manage to subdue a groan, but only barely. "Did you leave it in the house?"

"Yes."

"Why?"

"I don't need it. It will slow me down." This is never a good sign. When determination to kill makes its way into his bones and roots itself there, Arthur tends to forgo the more cumbersome walker in favor of one of his handmade canes. Especially the one he has now, made of rich red oak with a bronze wolf's head on the handle. I can see that dark energy coursing through him as he grips the cane and makes his way toward the garden gate with purpose. I know exactly what he's going to say before the question even leaves his mouth. "Where is my black bag?"

I swallow and train my face into an innocent mask as he shoots me a glare over his shoulder. "I don't know, Arthur. Where did you put it?"

"I know you took it. I saw you on the security camera when I looked back through the footage to identify the thief of my Pasotti umbrella."

"Someone stole your umbrella?"

He doesn't answer.

"Did you find it?"

"That's beside the point, Harper," he says as I chew my lip under his sharp scrutiny. "I want my bag."

"Why?"

"None of your business."

"Murder," Morpheus pipes up from the wall. A look of distaste creases Arthur's features as his foreboding stare slices to the source of the sound. "Pretty murder."

"Pretty murder *bird*," I correct.

Morpheus flies to the peak of the bird feeder, tracking Arthur with his onyx eyes. "Nom nom cookie."

"Harper. Why do you insist on feeding that vermin?"

"He's not vermin. He's a highly intelligent corvid."

"A highly intelligent corvid who would gladly poke out your eyes if given the chance." Arthur waves a hand in the bird's direction, but Morpheus only caws a defiant refusal to be subdued, followed closely by a string of "nom-nom-cookie" requests as we pass the feeder. "I need my bag. I know it's here."

Arthur slows as we step onto the flagstones of the patio, halting when he reaches the table. He stares at the cottage. His grip loosens and firms around the handle of his cane, his fingers flexing as though he could squeeze the images from his thoughts. He shuffles his feet but doesn't move closer to the door, his determination slowly ebbing away.

Pain surfaces in his features. Grief is a phantom that never gives up. It never grows tired of haunting our hearts. It clings on, somehow surviving even when other memories drift away. It's so imprinted on his soul that I think everything else about him could change as his disease pulls his identity apart, and yet it will persist. Maybe it will be the same for me one day. The grief that still clings to me like a cloak might linger on when everything else fades into darkness. The fear too. Terrors that seem carved into my bones.

I hate everything about this moment. I hate the loss Arthur was forced to endure all those years ago. I hate having to hide and not give back the tools with which he copes. I hate losing the friend and mentor I love to such a cruel decline.

I slip my hand into Arthur's. He startles, but he doesn't take his eyes from the cottage. His lips press into a firm line as he squeezes back.

"I'm sure you must want that bag for an important reason. But why don't you sit down and I'll make you a tea. We can talk about it." I pull a patio chair back from the table for him, gesturing to the padded seat. "Please?"

There's a pause, and I think for a moment he might argue, but instead he nods and I let a breath pass through my pursed lips. I help lower him onto the chair and then leave him with the raven while I head inside to make tea and another pot of coffee, slapping a large gauze pad over the back of my blistered hand with a wince as I wait for the water to boil. When I take the drinks out on a tray with a couple of pastries and a treat for Morpheus, Arthur is staring at his folded hands, fidgeting with the tension in his fingers. In one way, I'm relieved he's still sitting there. In another, I wish he'd taken off, because then at least I'd know he's still determined to do what he wants.

"Are you sure you're okay?" I ask as I set the tea in front of him before delivering a piece of fish to the bird feeder for Morpheus. When I take the seat next to Arthur, he's still looking at his hands. "Did you hurt yourself?"

"No," he says, unlacing his fingers just long enough to wave me off.

"What do you want that bag for, Arthur?"

I expect he'll tell me he wants to kill that man who's staying in Maria Flores's Airbnb, the one with the ugly dog who shit in the rose garden. Or maybe he's found another candidate, someone who's actually worthy of being murdered by a prolific elderly serial killer who has deemed himself protector of Cape Carnage for the last sixty years, long before he lost the daughter who died in the cottage standing before us. It's the kind of place that's always needed protection in one way or another, and who better to offer it than a brilliant and principled man with deep roots in the community who just so happens to also enjoy a bit of calculated killing when the need arises? So I'm sure he'll tell me about someone's misdeeds. Maybe a more egregious sin than shit in the garden or tire marks on the grass.

Arthur doesn't meet my eyes when he finally says, "So that I remember who I am."

I feel as though I've been punched in the chest. The wind is sucked clean from my lungs, leaving my lips in a whoosh. A sudden sting climbs up my throat and pricks at my eyes. "You're Arthur Lancaster," I whisper.

"I know my name," he replies with a frown. The creases in his brow soften far too quickly, their sharp lines dulled by distress. "But I feel like I am disappearing. I am losing who I truly am."

My hand covers Arthur's as I swallow a ball of blades. "You don't need that bag to remind you. I can do that." Arthur meets my eyes, a glassy sheen coating their cloudy surface. "You like Hitchcock movies. You love classical music. You have great taste in shoes. The Christina Riccis are truly impeccable."

He gives me a lethal scowl. "*Stefano Riccis*, you obdurate philistine."

"Of course. *Stefano*. My bad," I say through a grin that feels too fragile beneath the weight of these heavier emotions. It fades as I squeeze his hand, and he grips my fingers in reply. His eyes search my face, and I level him with a serious stare as though I might be able to imprint his identity back onto him. "You're the most formidable man I know. You're sharp, but you're caring. You're tough, but you're kind. You're my best friend."

An ember of surprise ignites in Arthur's eyes. He swallows. His lips press closed in a tight line. He gives me a single nod before he squeezes my fingers a final time and then slides his hand free to grip his teacup. "Well. You're . . ." He clears his throat and nods again, taking a sip of his tea. "You're . . ."

"An obdurate philistine?"

"Yes." He chuckles, a rare and precious sound. "But you're a good girl when you're not being purposefully obdurate. And I am . . . I am grateful that you're here."

I can't help the smile I beam at him, even if he's unwilling to keep his eyes on me for longer than a moment. Morpheus caws from the bird feeder—three sharp, loud squawks.

"I still think you should give me my bag back, however. And you should get rid of that vermin."

Morpheus barks three more caws. The smile that was just on my face disappears. "I don't think so," I say as a hum buzzes from the direction of the road on the other side of my house.

"He's irritating."

"He's also warning us."

A chill races down my spine as I stand and look toward the cottage. It's the same sound I heard the other day, when I was going to the gym and stopped to talk to Jake Hornell.

Nolan's words come back to me from the morning he stood in my garden as I gripped his bloody gift in my hands. They slid into my brain and branded themselves in my memory, but in the turmoil of the moment, they didn't make sense to me. They just lodged there, a thorn beneath my skin.

Perhaps because I just killed Jake, the man you have a crush on . . .

"Warning us?" Arthur says, his voice dampened beneath the veil of furious heartbeats that roar in my ears. "Why . . . ?"

A drone rises above the roof to hover over us. The same one I saw at the gym the other day and didn't think much of at the time. The one that must have been piloted by a certain enemy who stood in my garden with Jake's severed hands just a few days ago. The one who's clearly back to spy on me again. "Because someone has come to spy on Lancaster Manor."

The want I've been feeling for Nolan? That inexplicable desire? It seems to shred apart in the spinning white blades of the device that hovers above my home. It's a venomous sting that hurts more than it should. But pain can be a cleansing fire. One that leaves only one truth behind.

Nolan Rhodes needs to die.

DEVIATION

Nolan

I'M IN THE GENERAL STORE on Davis Avenue, putting things into my shopping cart that I *should not* be buying for my mortal enemy.

Just like I've done for the last three days in a row.

After the first night when I swam through the frigid current of the Ballantyne River, I bought a laser measurer so we could just point it at the rock across the water and have the correct distance in a matter of seconds. I convinced myself it was for me, so that I wouldn't have to brave another night swim. But when I picked her up that night to drive us there, I kept thinking about the way she watched me as I undressed. The way her gaze slid over me like the caress of fingertips in the dark. I could feel it, even when I looked away. I thought about the way she chewed the corner of her lip. Maybe I shouldn't have wanted her thoughts on me for a second night. Or a third, or a fourth. But I did, and I still do.

The laser measurer has stayed in my new backpack, the box unopened.

The next day, I bought Harper a better-quality shovel. I told myself it would make the whole experience of digging up bodies much faster. We only have a little over two weeks left before the land sale is complete, and we'll still need to cover our tracks when we're done. Actually, I got the new shovel because it has a sharp and pointed end. Since she insists on walking home every night with a sack of bones slung over her shoulder, I figured she should at least have something she can use as a weapon in case another Jake Hornell comes along. Fucking creep.

Maybe I should have more seriously considered that she could use said shovel on me. But every time I think about her watching me undress to swim, I don't believe she would. She might be uneasy around me, but I don't think it's purely because of the threats I've made or the kind of man she knows I am.

Yesterday, I got her bear spray. What if a shovel isn't the best weapon? I don't want her within striking distance of a fucking bear. The thought of its claws raking through her skin makes a twinge of nausea swirl in my stomach. I didn't tell her that when I gave it to her, of course. I blamed it on the book in her possession, which she was pretty clear would go to the authorities if anything happens to her, and she's brash and smart enough to back up that promise. I'm not about to call her bluff. "I don't want to go to jail if you're mauled by a wild animal," I'd said as I thrust the can of bear spray in her direction as though it was an inconvenience and not a gift. "Don't let anything get close."

She'd scrutinized the can as though there might be explosives hidden inside before she finally said a quiet "thank you" and slid it into her jacket pocket. And then, with the bag of bones slung over her shoulder like a sack of vegetables from the farmer's market, she said her curt goodbye and slunk off into the night. I watched her go, berating myself for not walking with her, and cursing myself even more for worrying about the woman who ruined my life.

The problem is, every time I remind myself of how she ripped

Billy from me, or how she broke my bones and shattered my existence, or how she drove away and left me to die alone on the road, insidious questions rise through the murk of latent rage:

What if she didn't ruin it? What if she gave me a purpose when I had none?

"That's stupid," I say aloud as I place a mosquito repellent device back on the shelf. A woman pushing a toddler in a stroller crinkles her nose at me with a look of distaste. I give her a sheepish smile and a nod, placing the device back into my cart. Her eyes only narrow as she passes me and continues down the aisle. I pick up a box of extra repellent cartridges and look for the next items on my mental list. A tarp. An expedition-sized backpack. A brighter lantern than her current one. Is that too much?

I pick up a little Coleman stove at the end of the aisle. Fuck it. I don't have to give it to her. I can keep it for myself. Maybe I'll make hot chocolate and drink it all myself in some petty-ass move to antagonize her. She's pretty fucking adorable when her feathers are ruffled.

No, she is not.

My fingers tighten around the box before I shove the stove into my cart.

I find the rest of the items I'm looking for and pay before heading to my rental vehicle to place them in the trunk. It's early afternoon and still sunny, but it's supposed to turn into a miserable evening with a cold rain by the time we're out looking for the next burial site. We've been making good progress so far, a body every night. Harper works hard. She never complains, never balks at the late hours or the tedious labor or the persistent insects, not even when a huge June bug pinged off her headlamp and fell into her top. She screeched and flapped and turned away to fish it out of her bra, then merely switched her light off and kept working in the moonlight. "Cheeky fucker," she'd muttered as I pressed my lips together to kill my smile in case she looked my way. "Could have bought me a drink first."

I swallowed a laugh, but only barely.

Even now, as I slide into the driver's seat, I catch a glimpse of my smile in the rearview mirror.

"Shut the fuck up," I growl at my reflection before I key the engine and pull away from the curb.

I turn the corner onto Main Street. Harper is still at the forefront of my thoughts when I catch sight of her dark hair and her now-familiar gait as she enters Maya's Magical Mixtures, and I slip into an empty spot along the road before I even fully realize what I'm doing.

I could drive away. Go about the rest of my day like what she does is none of my business right now, at least not until our deal is done. Some separation would probably do me some good, so my obsession with her doesn't fully rule every waking hour like it already does my dreams.

I'm jogging across the street before I give my protests another thought.

I try not to linger at the missing person flyer stapled to the telephone pole outside the shop, Jake Hornell's name in block letters and his smiling face grinning back at me. A coil of rage tightens beneath my ribs before I refocus on my destination, and I slow my steps to watch through the bay windows as Harper moves through the space, the handle of a basket tucked against her elbow as she heads to an aisle that says FIRST AID. She picks up a jar to examine the label. There's a bandage covering the back of her left hand.

In my next heartbeat, I'm yanking open the door and striding toward her.

"What the fuck is *this*?" I hiss as I catch her wrist and loom over her. Surprise ignites in her eyes, brightening to a flame of white-hot irritation.

"Hello to you, too, psycho stalker." She tries to tear her arm from my grip, but I don't let go. "What the hell is wrong with you—"

"What is this? Did something happen last night?"

"I—"

"Was it on the walk home? I fucking told you I'd drive you—"

"It wasn't—"

"Did someone do this to you? Was it a wild animal? Why didn't you use your bear spray?"

"On a fucking coffee pot?"

I blink at her, then pull the jar from her grasp, turning it to read the label. "Crispy Skin Burns and Blisters . . . ?"

Harper rolls her eyes, her cheeks crimson. "It's burn ointment, you fucking weirdo," she grits out. "And you're making a scene. What the hell is wrong with you?"

She tosses a brittle smile toward the counter behind me and I follow her gaze. Maya pushes her glasses up her nose, her eyes as sharp as obsidian blades behind their lenses. She assesses the tension in my shoulders, the grip of my hand around Harper's delicate wrist that I can't seem to let go of. I give Maya a fleeting smile and an untroubled wave with the ointment in my hand before I turn my back on her and place all my attention where it feels like it belongs. On Harper.

"I don't understand what the fuck has gotten into you," she whispers, twisting her arm until I finally let go. My palm feels cold in the absence of her warmth. Before I can delve too deeply into why this unpleasant chill is traveling into my flesh, she rips the jar out of my hand and thrusts it into her basket.

"You burned yourself?"

She pierces me with a glare, her silver eyes shards of pure malice. "Yes, and what the hell do you care? I'm not going to have your precious book sent to the FBI because of a fucking coffee incident," she whispers before walking away down the aisle.

I should get her a Keurig, a traitorous little voice in my head declares.

No. I *will not* buy her a fucking Keurig, goddamnit.

"Are you . . . ? Did you . . . ?" I clear my throat, unsure what I'm even trying to ask. I want to know if she's okay, but it shouldn't matter. I want to sluice the guilt from my veins for letting it happen, but I don't know why I feel like it's my fault. I don't think she appreciates my concern anyway, judging by the lethal stare she cuts me with. We're enemies. She killed my brother. She destroyed my fucking life. Some things cannot be forgiven. Harper is clearly sticking to the brief. So why can't I?

"Like I said. Coffee accident. But I'm surprised you didn't know that already, seeing as how you spent the morning stalking me."

"What?"

Harper shrugs, though there's nothing nonchalant about it. "I figured if you went to the trouble of flying a drone over my house, you've probably been looking through my windows the whole time too."

My brows draw together with confusion, but Harper barely looks at me as she makes her way down the aisle, feigning interest in different ointments and concoctions on the shelves. "I didn't fly a drone over your house," I say.

"Oh, really? Because you've spied on me with one before, *haven't you,*" she whisper-snarls, not a question but an accusation. She flicks her bandaged hand in my direction and I suppress a sudden urge to snatch it out of the air so I can get a proper look at the wound beneath the white gauze. "You were flying that thing as I was going to the gym the other morning. That's how you got the dumbass idea about me having a crush on"—her eyes dart around us before she leans closer—"*you know who.*"

Fucking Jake Hornell. I would kill him again if I could. And I would take my time about it. I would make him *suffer.*

I shake my head to rid it of those murderous fantasies and all the questions that threaten to arise about why it would be so fucking satisfying to do it all over again. "I swear to you, I wasn't piloting any drone today."

"Sure. I almost believe you."

"I'm telling you the truth."

"Then who was?"

"I don't know." I scratch my stubble, worry gnawing at my guts as Harper watches me, notes of fear hidden deep beneath her tough exterior. I did spend some time following Sam around the first couple of days. It wasn't very enlightening. He had busied himself interviewing locals in the privacy of their homes or businesses. But when I'd been close enough to eavesdrop, the conversation centered around uncovering anything that would prove Arthur Lancaster is the infamous La Plume. He was obsessed. And judging by his furrowed brow and deep frown as he scribbled notes in a leatherbound journal, he wasn't getting the big hit he was looking for. *Yet.*

So far, he's been staying away from Lancaster Manor.

How do I know?

Because I have not been staying away from Harper Starling.

Whenever I've felt reasonably sure that Sam has been occupied with his interviews, I've let myself succumb to following Harper, as though I'm indulging in a drug I can't say no to. I've hopped the stone wall surrounding her cottage and watched from the bushes like a proper fucking creep as she's worked in the garden of Lancaster Manor, edging the beds, planting new flowers, trimming hedges and trees.

Other times, she's tended to the public gardens around town. The flowers that frame the WELCOME TO CAPE CARNAGE sign. The park on Randall Road. The hanging baskets that line Main Street. She had help putting those up from a trio of guys that I recognized from the coffee shop the other day. They're all older men wearing wedding bands, but it scratched at my nerves all the same. I could have been the one to help her. Maybe if I had, she'd let her guard down and give me enough information to figure out what she's done with my scrapbook. Then I could get back to my real reason for being here. At least, that's what I keep trying to tell myself.

"Sam's drone operator," I finally answer. Irritation crawls beneath my skin like scuttling insects. I thought I'd built enough of a rapport with Sam that he would ask me if he needed help with the drone again, but clearly I was wrong. "He must have arrived this morning, I guess."

"You guess? I thought that was part of our deal, that you were supposed to be keeping tabs on Porter and leading him away."

"I have been."

Harper snorts. "Clearly."

"Maybe I've been too busy with *other projects*." I pick up a small bottle, Corpse Reviver Hangover Juice written above the image of a dancing skeleton on the black label. I toss it into Harper's basket and she hits me with a vicious glare.

"You're not the one who also has to work all day. *And* I have to rebuild a fucking soapbox racer too so I can cover your ass for your little bird feeder present. You're welcome, by the way." She picks up several bottles of fake blood and drops them into her basket. A little spark seems to dance in her eyes just long enough to arouse my instincts for self-preservation, and then she turns her back on me to continue down the aisle. "I hope you're enjoying your stupid fucking holiday in my town. What are you even doing with yourself all day? Aside from *not* keeping up your end of our deal."

Watching you, my very unhelpful internal monologue volunteers with cheerful enthusiasm.

"Right," she says before I have a chance to cobble an answer together. "You've been doing sweet fuck all, which is *super surprising*. I'm truly shocked. And *now*, since you haven't been deflecting him like you promised, Sam is flying drones over Arthur's fucking property, spying on us as we're trying to have a cup of coffee. And what recourse do I have to stop him? It's not like I really want to call Sheriff Yates, you know?"

"Why not? Does La Plume have bodies buried on the home estate too?"

Harper reaches the end of the aisle and turns on me, and though I expect the vicious look in her eyes from my needling remarks, that's not all I see. There's a glassy sheen over their gunmetal depths. She swallows, staring up at me in a challenge. "Believe whatever you want about me. I know what you think I've done, and I don't fucking care about trying to change your mind. But you are *wrong*, Nolan. Arthur Lancaster is not La Plume."

I could argue back. Say something about our nightly excursions that seem to prove otherwise. But the conviction in her eyes gives me pause. And Harper takes that beat of time to push past me, brushing the fingers of her bandaged hand beneath her lashes as she goes.

"Harper—"

"Leave me alone."

I watch her walk to the counter and unload her basket, Maya's obvious concern shifting between Harper and me. She whispers something to Harper, who only nods before paying for her goods in cash she pulls from the chest pocket of her faded plaid shirt, hastily packing her purchases into a backpack, then slinging it over her shoulder. When Harper stalks toward the door, she darts a brief glance in my direction. It's only long enough to imprint the image of her pain and anger into my memory, and then she's gone.

I move closer to the bay window, watching as she heads down the street. Her bandaged hand swings in the sun as she strides away from me as fast as she can without running. I contemplate exiting the store so I can track her from the sidewalk, but I linger there, watching through the window as though she might return.

With a deep sigh, I shift my attention across the street, my focus passing over the increasingly familiar shops. A Shipwrecked Bean. Craft-A-Corpse. Bhandari Law Offices. Disco Barber. A new office that just opened, Viceroy Properties.

And standing across the street at the entrance of Viceroy is Sam Porter. He's got papers clutched in his hand. A camera bag slung over his shoulder. He's facing the same direction where Harper just left. His eyes are fixed on something in the distance.

Or someone.

A breath later, I'm leaving Maya's shop and striding toward him.

He catches sight of my brisk walk and gives me a brief flash of a smile and a wave with the papers in his hand before he opens the flap of his bag and slides them inside. I catch the pale greens and blues of a map before they slip into the shadows. My heart knocks against my ribs.

"Hey, Sam," I say, trying to keep my voice light, though it's more of a struggle than I thought it would be.

"Rhodes. Hey, man." He extends a hand and I shake it, and he's barely touched my palm before he's nodding in the direction Harper just walked. "You know her?"

I follow his gesture and look down the street, spotting Harper's dark hair blowing in the breeze. I keep scanning the sidewalk, not wanting to let my attention linger on her in case he notices. "Who?"

"The woman there," he says, pointing to her. "The one with the plaid shirt. She was just in the same shop as you."

I shake my head and shrug, not taking my eyes from Harper until she disappears around the bend of the road. "Nope. Sorry. Don't know her."

Sam gives only a thoughtful hum that's colored with a note of disappointment. I offer him an untroubled smile, but the one he gives me in reply is only faint. I can tell his thoughts are else-where, and when his gaze darts to where Harper has faded from view, it's not hard to track their whereabouts. "How's the docu-mentary going?" I ask, trying to swallow the sudden need to throw him off her scent. "Making progress?"

"Getting there." He pats his camera bag with a little more enthusiasm than he had moments ago. "Finished a few interviews, waiting on a few more."

"Need any help with the drone again? I've got free time. Happy to lend a hand if you need."

"Thanks, man. My guy showed up, so I should be all set, but I'll let you know." Sam smiles, though his eyes slide back down the road, narrowing just long enough to betray his thoughts of pursuit. If he's seen Harper sitting with Arthur outside the cottage that once belonged to Poppy Lancaster, I'm sure Harper is a new target. Another layer in an already complicated history.

But the spark in his eyes makes me feel like there's something more. His expression now is the antithesis of the one I saw painted on his face after the interviews, when it was obvious that there was something missing from the picture he was trying to pull together.

The man before me now is a hunter. He's got the expression of a predator who has caught the scent of its prey on the wind. I know it, because I've seen that same look in my own eyes when I've stared in the mirror and imagined the blood I was about to spill. I've seen it when I told the mirror I was going to kill Harper Starling.

"Well," Sam says, patting his bag where the papers are hidden, "I'd better run, got lots of work to do. I'll see you around?"

"Sure will," I reply.

Sam leaves me on the sidewalk, but the growing dread remains long after I watch him drive away.

DRIFTING

Harper

It's ABSOLUTELY PISSING IT DOWN. And it's fucking cold. I'm used to being outside in miserable weather, but in the daytime. Being alone in the dark and the pelting rain is another matter entirely. It's pushing me a little too close to thoughts of a past I try my best to forget. It reminds me of that first gasp of freedom after terror so consuming it had eaten everything good left in me, leaving only a raw alloy behind. Something that could be fashioned into a blade but was still too weak to be deadly. I had only seen the forge. I'd not yet been embraced by its flame.

I grip my shovel tighter where it rests across my shoulder as I walk on the unlit path that leads to the Ballantyne River and the floodplain. Though the footing is uneven, marred by rocks and roots, I'm not paying much attention to the trail or the hazards in the dark. I'm still caught on the past, even though I hate thinking back on that time. Not just the derelict house I'd been dragged to, or the oppressive cold of the cellar, or the smell of piss and shit, fear and death.

It's not just the memory of the heavy footsteps above us, or the way desperation and despair chewed through my soul when Adam was torn from me. It's not just the sound of the chainsaw or Adam's screams or the maniacal laughter of the man as he murdered my boyfriend a floor above me. It's not the memory of pressing the heels of my hands so hard to my ears that I hoped I would crush that sound out of my skull. I hated those first days after I'd escaped from that hell house too, when I was sucked into the whirlwind of police and lawyers and reporters. When I was forced to face my vulnerabilities.

The truth is, I didn't feel like a survivor. I felt like a failure.

I wanted to be like the woman who'd been thrown into that cellar with me the day Adam died. While I was stammering a helpless chant about Adam's death, she was cool and calm, even though her face was streaked with blood and her shoulder was badly dislocated. "Yes. He killed Adam," she'd said. "And I promise you, Adam will be the last person Harvey Mead ever kills."

Then she gave me her fucking shirt.

Sloane Sutherland. She wasn't just a survivor, she was a *warrior*. Courageous. Determined. Indomitable.

You'd think I'd look back on my first moments of freedom after escaping that cellar with a sense of relief, or maybe even pride. But I don't. Because as I hid in the rain to watch Sloane and her now-husband exact their revenge on that fucking monster Harvey Mead, I understood how weak I really was. Sloane wasn't just tough, she was a killer too, one even more dangerous than Mead, something I didn't fully grasp until I tracked her down and uncovered her deepest secrets. The infamous Orb Weaver, a killer of killers, a woman who hunted serial murderers and made them into art. But even in those earliest moments, just watching her and Rowan bring down the man who had abducted and nearly murdered me, I realized I had so far to go to become a woman as unconquerable as she was.

Maybe I never will.

I'm sure I'll never be exactly like her. She probably never sleeps with a light on. I bet she's not afraid of being alone in the rain and the dark. I bet she would have killed Nolan ten times over already. She would have said, "*Fuck you* and your skinbook and your murder dimples and your stupidly beautiful eyes. I won't be swayed by a hot psychopath." Then she would have plucked out his eyeballs, slit his throat, and exhumed all the bodies by herself. She'd know what to do with Sam and how to protect Arthur without getting caught. She wouldn't need anyone's help.

A heavy sigh passes through my pursed lips, the air cold enough for my breath to leave a plume of fog among the raindrops. I'll definitely never be exactly like her. Because I almost regret telling Nolan to leave me alone back at Maya's shop. I'd rather have him around during these exhumations, even if he's just another asshole who wants to kill me. That's so fucked up.

And what's even worse is that I'm not just angry with him about the drone or his lapse in fending off Sam, or his cutting words about Arthur, or even all his erroneous beliefs about the things I've done. What truly burns is the hurt beneath all that. I think I'd started to convince myself he gave a shit about me when he gifted me that bear spray, or when he met my eyes as he took off his clothes to swim across the river, watching me in a way that was meant to leave heat behind. I swore I felt a thread pull tight between us, energy crackling across the fragile filament. But the reality is, that's only a ruse. He's just helping me so he can get his book back. And I guess he doesn't care too much about that either, seeing as how he didn't text or call or pick me up for our nightly excursion.

I just wish I could remember that every kindness he offers, no matter how small, has only one purpose: to get him closer to his objective. Kill Harper Starling.

I gnaw at my lip and hike the strap of my backpack higher up my shoulder, then turn off my headlamp as I near the quiet road, the rain reflecting off its surface in the ambient light. Nolan's car isn't here. He usually parks on a narrow section of gravel that dips into the property so it's not as obvious and out of place, though there's hardly ever traffic on this road anyway. A conflicted swirl of emotions tugs at my guts. I'm relieved. I'm dismayed. And, thankfully, I'm enormously pissed off. Anger is the only useful emotion of the bunch, so as I march across the road, I focus my attention where it belongs. On fucking up Nolan Rhodes.

How dare he squirm his way out of our deal? How dare he assume the worst of me, even though I'm also a serial killer and clearly protecting another serial killer? How fucking dare he give me bear spray and then leave me to walk alone in the night when there could be bears to use it on?

How dare he . . . make hot chocolate . . . ?

I draw to an abrupt halt at the edge of the floodplain. Nolan is at the left by the boulders where we always ditch our tools, sitting on a folding stool beneath a tarp suspended on the branches that stretch above him. He's bent over a small camp stove, stirring steaming liquid in a pot. Two mugs and a can of whipped cream are resting in the glow of the lantern next to his feet.

"I was starting to think you weren't going to show," he says as I come closer to stare down at the scene before me. He doesn't let his attention linger long enough for me to read anything from his expression. I let the silence stretch between us, determined to hold on to the rage that still simmers beneath my skin. I just stand there, the rain pelting the hood of my coat, my hands shoved into my pockets. Nolan darts a wary look my way and I raise my brows in an unspoken question. "Figured I'd make some hot chocolate to keep us warm. If we're going to work in the rain, might as well make it worth our while."

I could find other ways to do that, I think as the image of Nolan stripping to his swimsuit in the rain appears in my mind. I shake my head to clear the unwanted thoughts, the motion deepening the crease between his brows.

"No hot chocolate?" he asks, and though he tries to look non-plussed, I think I still catch a wisp of disappointment in his face.

I want hot chocolate. But I also don't want to take a single thing he has to offer, that fucker. I know his game: He's just trying to get back in my good graces so I don't mail that scrapbook off somewhere. So I shake my head. "I'm fine, thanks," I reply as I set my bag down, unzipping it to grab the lantern from its depths. As I do, my fingertips graze a bottle in the bottom of my bag. I pull it out to check the label. Berry Blissful Bloodbath. Maya's strawberry-flavored fake blood.

It'll change your life, she'd said to Nolan in my backyard the other day as he stood there with severed hands clutched in his grip.

I've tried her edible blood before. And it will, indeed, change your fucking life.

"You know what," I say as I set the lantern down and pop the cap of the bottle, giving it a sniff. The sweet scent of strawberries floods my nostrils. I can't detect the earthy, musky smell of the other ingredients. But I know they're there, and I keep them and the red warning label on the front of the bottle hidden beneath my fingers. "Maybe I will have some. We can put some of Maya's Bloodbath on the whipped cream. I haven't had it in ages. She was right when she said it'll change your life."

Nolan's eyes sweep over me, leaving a tingling current behind. I don't react. I try not to look too interested in the prospect of hot chocolate, as though I really don't care either way if I have some. But suddenly I do. *Very much.*

"Okay," he says. I detect a measure of relief in his voice as he turns the stove off and grabs the mugs, pouring the steaming liquid into them. "This is the packaged chili hot chocolate from the Bean. I hope that's okay."

I try not to let my smile stretch too far. "Perfect."

Nolan shakes the can of whipped cream and dispenses a healthy dollop of white foam onto the top of each mug before passing one to me. I deposit a couple of drops of the strawberry blood onto my whipped cream before reaching over and drenching his with a generous drizzle of the viscous red liquid. "I'm not a huge fan of the strawberry flavor," I say with a saccharine smile as I continue squeezing the bottle until he finally pulls his mug away. "I prefer raspberry, but most people enjoy the strawberry more."

"Thanks," Nolan says as he looks down at the crisscrossed red streaks on his whipped cream. When he looks my way, I take a sip of my drink.

"Thank *you*, for this." I raise my mug as though giving him a toast. "It's thoughtful of you."

Nolan nods. When he takes a sip of his drink and downs a mouthful of the whipped cream, I struggle to smother a wicked smirk. "The rain is supposed to let up in about half an hour or so," he says, casting a thoughtful frown across the floodplain. "Maybe we should hang back a bit. No point in making it worse than it has to be."

"Sure." I bring my cup to my lips, positioning my finger to sweep it beneath the cloud of whipped cream. When Nolan isn't looking, I flick it into the shadows behind me. He must still notice the motion in his peripheral vision, because his gaze shifts to me with a hint of suspicion in the crease between his brows. "The bugs of Cape Carnage," I say, flapping a hand in front of my face as though waving a mosquito away. "They're not deterred by a little rain."

He nods, pulling a second folding stool out for me before shifting his over to make room. Even still, there's not much space beneath the tarp when I join him. I can feel his heat at my side. His presence seeps into my skin despite the layers of fabric between us. We don't speak for a long while. It shouldn't be a comfortable silence, but it is. I've grown accustomed to his quiet countenance in the night. I'm not sure if he actively tries not to talk to me, like I try not to talk to him. Or maybe this is just his nature. Stoic. Sparing with his words when he doesn't have any desire or need to be charming. But as much as we try to keep our conversations impersonal and centered only on our work, there's often still a pull to say more. At least, there is for me.

"Bet when you were a kid you never thought you'd be here," he says, not taking his eyes from the pan of silt that stretches into the dark. I follow his focus. Our recent excavations are hard to discern in the darkness, the disturbances in the soft and sparsely vegetated soil washed away by the heavy rain.

I take a sip of my drink. "Can't say it was on my dream boards, no."

"Did you really have those?" I dart a questioning glance in Nolan's direction and find he's watching me with more interest than I expected. "Dream boards?"

"Yeah," I reply, a wistful smile tugging at my lips. "I did. For a long time, actually."

"What was on them?"

When I look over at Nolan this time, I let my attention linger on him as I push the hood back off my damp hair. Why is he asking? Does he genuinely want to know? How much do I say? How much do I keep to myself when that thread between us tugs at me like a plea to give a little something to see what I might get in return?

"Disney princess shit at first," I say. "I wanted to work in a zoo or train animals. So it was a lot of outfits for my dog when my parents finally let me have one."

"I didn't peg you as a dog-wardrobe type."

I shrug, shifting my attention away. "Different life. Different time."

"Did your parents indulge your dog-wardrobe fixation?"

A bittersweet smile flickers across my lips. "While they could."

I don't elaborate. I don't even look in his direction. I just keep my eyes trained on the graveyard that stretches before us. Looking back, I feel as though every time I begged for death to leave me alone, it only dug its talons in deeper. And when I finally decided to embrace it, I found death was the key to living. I'm immersed in it now. Wielding it. Protecting it. Fighting for it. But that first sting of loss? That first kiss of grief? I'd still trade anything to not feel it.

"You don't have them anymore," Nolan says.

"The dog outfits? No. I got rid of those when Pips attacked Mr. Taylor's pant legs and then shit on the stage during my sixth-grade talent show. I was forced to face the stark realization that I was a pretty crap animal trainer."

Nolan chuckles. It might be small, but it's a genuine laugh, and I haven't heard one from him since the first day we met in the coffee shop. It hits like a dart, scrambling my senses. "I would have paid good money to see that."

"Yeah," I say with an eye roll, "I'm sure you would have reveled in my humiliation."

I take a sip of my hot chocolate, and I feel the weight of Nolan's gaze on the bandage that covers the back of my hand. His presence looms in my periphery, and at first I think he won't push me for more. But then he says, "I didn't mean the dog outfits. I meant your parents. You don't have them anymore?"

I swallow. Shake my head. "No." I look down at my hands as though there's something I'll find there that I haven't seen before. "It was a car crash. Drunk driver. I was at a sleepover so they could go to dinner for their anniversary. We were having pancakes when the police showed up at Caroline's house."

I'm just staring down into my mug, blinking, fighting away the memories. I'm sure Nolan thinks a thousand horrible things about me. Maybe some of them are true. I might not have been the one to hit Nolan, but I did see him on that road. I did leave him there to his fate. And my moral compass was skewed long before we met. Because since the day my parents died, all I could think about, all I could *wish* for, was the destruction of those who had done evil deeds. Even if I had to become like them.

"Is that why you left when you hit me on Division Road?"

I turn to face him, my motion slow and purposeful. He stares right into me. Just like every night, the light is too dim to make out the wedge of brown in his eye. But I saw it today. The way its darkness seemed to deepen when he thought he'd struck a mark with his comment about La Plume. And I wonder if that's what's happening now too.

He will never think anything differently of me. So why fight to convince him that I'm a better person than the one he thinks I am?

I only give him one word in response. And I deliver it with precision, and clarity, and finality when I say, "*No*."

I'm the first to break our connection, shifting my attention back to the shoreline as I force us into silence. I finish my hot chocolate but hold on to my mug, and Nolan does the same. We don't talk as the rain gradually diminishes to a drizzle and the drum of droplets eases to a gentle patter on the tarp above us. I'm thinking about voicing a suggestion to start working when I hear a sound in the distance, something from the direction of the road.

I sit straighter, twisting on my stool.

"Did you hear that?" I whisper.

"No . . ."

I strain to listen, hoping that it was just my imagination, but then I hear it again. The sound of a car door or trunk closing. That unmistakable clunk so deeply ingrained into daily life that it's still recognizable despite the distance.

"What's going on?" Nolan asks.

"I heard something. It sounded like a car door." I duck from under the tarp to look in the direction of the road. There are too many trees and thick bushes to see anything from here. I take a step in that direction, straining to listen for any other sounds. "It could be nothing . . ." I say. But I never discount my instincts. And my instincts are telling me that I most definitely heard something.

I take another step toward the path that leads to the road.

"Did you see that?" Nolan asks, and he sounds so genuinely freaked out that I spin around to find him crouched down, staring at the lantern with his mouth agape in shock.

Oh *shit*. "Umm . . . see something . . . ?"

Nolan edges closer to the lantern, his head weaving side to side as though he's searching for something within the light. "It *moved*."

"I'm sure it's just the wind."

"No." He frames the lantern with his hands, disbelief painted across his face. "There was some kind of . . . creature . . . inside the light. Did you see it?"

"Shh." I wave a hand in his direction and strain to listen for anything coming from the direction of the road. "It's your eyes playing tricks on you. Lack of sleep, probably."

"No, Harper. I'm not making this up. *Look* at it." The distant sound of a quiet voice reaches through the trees. We're not alone. "It's *moving*—"

I yank the lantern from him, tossing it over the bank and into the water to the sound of Nolan's horrified gasp.

"It'll drown, you *monster*—"

I drop to my knees and slap my hand over his mouth, catching his distressed protests in my palm. "Listen to me right now, Nolan Rhodes," I hiss. His eyes are wide with alarm, and I stare into them in an attempt to reach whatever deteriorating clarity might be lurking in their depths. "There is nothing in the fucking light, okay? No creature or fairy or sprite or whatever. It's all in your mind. I might have . . . given you something."

His muffled question vibrates through my hand.

"When Maya said her fake blood will change your life, she wasn't fucking around." I keep my hand clamped to Nolan's face and my eyes trained on him as I reach for the hot chocolate pot in my peripheral vision and toss it into the water. The stove quickly follows. "It contains psilocybin. Magic mushrooms."

Nolan tugs my hand free of his mouth. "You *drugged* me?"

I shrug. "Maybe a little bit," I admit, chucking both our cups over the embankment. "And by a little bit, I mean probably a lot. Who knows."

"What do you mean?"

"I kind of free-poured, you know? It's not like I measured your BMI beforehand, is it?"

"You're a terrible person," he whisper-snarls.

"You already knew that, remember?" I yank the stool from where he's about to plop himself down so he can probably question all his life choices and hurtle it into the water as his ass hits the damp earth with a thud. "But you can take it up with me later, because someone is here, and we need to hide. *Now.*"

"I can't believe you fucking drugged me," he says, his eyes wandering over our surroundings as though he's seeing a whole different world than the dark and dreary one that envelops us.

"And I can't believe you're moving at a fucking glacial pace when I said I heard someone approaching our little gravedigger situation. Get a move on." I toss my backpack over one shoulder and his over the other, and then I grab hold of Nolan's wrist and tug him to his feet. I thrust my shovel into his hand. "You were a dick in the shop today. What did you expect?"

"I was?" Nolan's brow furrows, his eyes tracking to my hand as I scramble to pull the tarp off the branches. A fresh bandage covers my blistered skin. "I was just worried about you."

My motion slows as his words take root in my mind, warmth blossoming in my chest. And I'm sure that's exactly what he's hoping for, even though he looks as though he's telling me a truth that's emerged in a drug-induced haze. But it's a ploy. He wants the book. He'll say anything to get it.

I shake my head and refocus on my task in the hope the heat still slithering around my heart will wither and die. "I'm not going to have you sent to jail for a little burn, Nolan. You were weird about the hand, sure, but you were a dick about Arthur."

I tuck the tarp under my arm and survey the terrain around us, but I'm not sure there's a good place to hide. The trees are too sparse. The rocks are too exposed. If we make a break for it across the plain, we might be seen, and even if we're not, we'll leave a fresh set of tracks behind in the mud.

Nolan takes my hand. "Come on," he whispers as the voice draws closer. He pulls me along after him, heading toward the bank and the river that snakes through the woods.

"No—"

"It's the only place left to go."

He's right—it's the only viable hiding spot. And I'll be even more vulnerable there than I will be sitting out in the open. Because I can't swim.

Adrenaline bursts through my veins as I clutch his hand tighter and follow him down the slope to the narrow shore. Nolan doesn't stop at the water's edge, he just keeps going into the inky water, pulling me along as though he can't feel the hesitation of my steps or the tremor in my hand. A cold current fills my boots and sweeps around my ankles. It rises up my calves to swirl around my knees. I manage to transfer my phone into the chest pocket of my jacket before the water reaches my hip. By the time the river grazes the bottom of my breasts, I'm shaking, whether from the cold or the fear I don't know.

"Stop," I whisper.

Nolan turns, his eyes slowly dragging over me. It's not his usual sharp, scrutinous stare, but he still seems to understand through his psychedelic haze that I can't go any farther. He opens his mouth to say something, but a voice comes from the dark to stop him.

". . . drone footage to follow the river," a man says from the bank above us, "with a voice-over about the purchase of the property following the disappearance of the previous owner . . ."

"It's Sam," I whisper.

Nolan nods and tugs on my hand to pull me closer, shielding me from both the current and the view of the bank. "I saw him today, coming out of the Viceroy office on Main Street."

"That's the company that bought this land."

". . . dusk shots, fog or heavy cloud. Bring a metal detector . . ."

We remain still and silent in the river, Sam's voice growing more distant as he continues scouting the grounds that he doesn't have permission to be on. My lips tremble. I keep my focus trained on the direction of Sam's words, even though it becomes harder and harder to hear him above the hiss of rain on the water and my heartbeat humming in my ears. Though I feel Nolan's eyes on me, I don't meet them. Not until he whispers something so unexpected that the threat of Sam suddenly seems like a distant memory.

"You're so beautiful."

I meet Nolan's eyes, trying to decipher his expression despite the shadows. "You're just saying that because I'm made of light worms or some shit."

"No." I don't know if he realizes he's still holding my hand beneath the water. Or that his thumb is tracing a repeating pattern over my bandage. Or that he could hurt me if he wanted to. Just a little pressure against a wound, a reminder, a clear communication that we're still enemies. But he doesn't. Instead, he raises his other hand, moving slowly as though not to scare me, and traces the curve of my cheek to leave the scent of the river behind. "I mean, now that you mention it, there are light worms in your face."

"Great."

"But I thought you were beautiful the first time we met too."

His caress follows my jaw, lowering to my neck to glide down the pulse that hammers through my flesh. He watches the progress of his touch, one that feels as reverential as it does forbidden. I fight to keep my eyes from drifting closed. My heart erupts beneath my bones. "And then you realized who I was."

"It didn't change anything."

"No. It changed *everything*."

He meets my eyes, his palm resting on my neck. He could so easily wrap his hands around my throat and squeeze. It would only take a heartbeat to subdue my body beneath the river. Only moments to force the air from my lungs and fill them with water.

Maybe he thinks about that too, because Nolan holds my gaze as he lifts his fingers one by one, then lets his hand fall away. It feels like a shadow descends between us. Something dark and cold and otherworldly. We're still staring at each other when Sam's voice returns as he seems to backtrack toward the road. Our connection doesn't break as he passes by. Not even as the car door closes a few moments later. It's only once we hear the car travel over the nearby bridge that the thread between us snaps, and we walk back to shore.

But it's not until we're standing on the rocks at the top of the bank, staring down at the graveyard before us, that he finally lets go of my hand.

FOGBOUND

Nolan

"I HAVEN'T DRIVEN IN A long time," Harper says, her eyes fixed on the rearview mirror as she adjusts it. She chews on her lip, ribbons of light erupting from each bite. I need to stop staring at her mouth. It's just fucking hard to do when she's so beautiful that my heart implodes every time I'm forced to look away. She's like an angel, her skin illuminated with shifting colors, glowing from within.

She's not an angel, for fucksakes. She drugged *me. She's a fucking* demon. *But don't think too much about that because then I'll probably see fucking demons everywhere and freak the fuck out.*

I peel my gaze away and press my eyes closed, leaning my head back against the passenger seat as the world seems to pulse around me. "I can't imagine why."

"Not for the reason you think."

I turn my head just enough to see her face. "It wasn't reason enough?"

Hurt erupts in Harper's eyes before she shutters it away and keys the engine. It never feels the way it should when I manage to slip an arrow past her defenses. I keep expecting satisfaction for hitting my mark, but the closer I get to a bull's-eye and the deeper I strike, the more it feels like I've missed the target entirely.

She doesn't say anything in reply, just puts the car in drive and coasts away from the abandoned lane where I hid the rental, just in case Sam happened to pass by the Ballantyne River property as we were working. Fucking Sam Porter. He's getting too close to her. I could rip his fucking face off. It would be so satisfying too, feeling the flesh pull away from his bones, stripping his skin off with my bare hands. That would probably be a bad idea though, and I need to keep my last wits about me. So I take a deep breath, closing my eyes again as I press myself back into the seat until it feels like it's absorbing me.

"Well," Harper says, her tone grim, "I guess I'm not taking you back to Capeside in that case."

"Why not?"

"Because you just said you wanted to rip Sam's face off with your bare hands."

"I said that out loud?"

Harper's eyes dart to me. I think I see a blush in the pink light that rises in her cheeks. She doesn't answer me as she slows the vehicle and navigates the turn that leads to Lancaster Manor.

It might take us six years to reach our destination, or maybe only moments. Time makes no sense to me anymore. The one thing I'm sure of? Harper Starling is my lifeline to the planet. If I'm not with her, I might end up stuck in this other dimension. I need to touch her. I couldn't help myself at the river. I can't help myself now either. So I reach out, laying my hand on her arm, moving with her as she startles.

"We're here," she says, turning off the car. She pulls away from my grasp. Why do I feel the loss of her heat in my hand? Why am I trying to touch her in the first place? She's clearly sticking to the plan. Enemies until death or destruction. Why can't I do the same?

I trail after her as she leads the way from the street to the gate of her cottage, holding it open for me. When she gets to the front door, she unlocks it and doesn't look back to see if I follow. I've seen her house through the windows, of course, but this is the first time I've been inside. It's exactly how I'd expect Harper's place to be, aside from the way I'm pretty sure the shifting geometric pattern on the stone floor has enveloped my feet, anyway. It's simple. Practical. The decorations are sparse, but I'm sure that each one is meaningful. A chessboard whose pieces I'm sure are moving on their own. A carved wooden orca. A brightly colored macramé of a southwest desert landscape. A photo of a man and a woman with a blond girl, maybe four or five years old. I pick it up and stare at their faces. It must be Harper and her parents. There's an ease in her smile, a lightness to it that just doesn't exist in the version of her that stands in the kitchen. The woman I know is forged by destruction. Maybe that's the only way to survive this world. To become the destroyer.

I look over at Harper, tracers of light following every motion as she strips off her coat. She glances my way over her shoulder as though she can feel me watching. "I'll get you a robe and we can wash your clothes," she says, unbuttoning her plaid shirt. I'd give anything in this moment for her to turn and face me. To see if the bioluminescent glow covers her whole body. To see the curve of her breasts as they rise and fall with unsteady breaths. To see the light on her skin. The flare of her hips. The softness of her flesh. To see if her pussy glistens with arousal for me.

Jesus fucking Christ.

"Okay," I say as I drag both hands down my face, my cock aching with sudden need.

Harper gives me a perplexed look, one that seems to linger. The light within her deepens to shades of red and orange. For a moment, I think she might turn toward me. But she doesn't, heading up the stairs instead. I'm still standing there with my hands on my face, trying to will my erection away when she comes back down in a robe, another one draped over her arm, her wet clothes clutched in her bandaged hand.

"Here," she says as she comes close enough to offer the garment to me. I take it with a tentative hand. "Follow me." She leads me to a short hallway off the kitchen, pointing to a bathroom as she throws her wet clothes into a washing machine in the closet on the opposite side. "You can put your clothes in when you're done getting changed. Just close the lid and it'll start."

I nod, doing as she says, though the simple task takes a lot longer than it should to execute when I end up staring at my reflection, trying to make sense of the person staring back. I've come all this way and waited all this time to avenge my brother. And now I'm standing in his killer's house with a hard-on for the woman who took his life?

It's just the mushrooms, I tell myself. *They're just clouding your thinking.*

The problem is, every time I tell myself that, it feels more and more like a lie. What if they're not clouding anything? What if they're peeling back the fog?

By the time I come out of the bathroom and start the washing machine, Harper is cracking open a beer, an empty one already resting next to where she leans against the kitchen counter. She's got a bottle of tequila out too, and chases a sip of lager with a shot. "You're going to have to stay the night here, because I'm not driving you anywhere," she declares as I approach. "So I guess I'll be looking after you. Joy of joys."

I chuckle. At least one of us can stay focused on our situation. I need to do the same. "Seems fitting," I say as I pull the tequila from the counter and take a sip straight from the bottle. The smoky burn slides down my throat and I hold on to that feeling. I need to scorch her right out of my veins. "You kill Billy. I come to kill you. You steal my book and drug me. Then you look after me. Seems full circle, doesn't it," I say as I raise my arm to show her the ouroboros tattooed there. I know she's looked through my scrapbook. She's already worked out who gave me this tattoo and what I did to him when it was finished.

I take another sip from the bottle and she watches every motion with haunted eyes, the luminescence in her skin cooling to a blue light. Her voice is firm, but I detect a melancholy edge beneath it, the tremor of something deeper and hidden when she says, "I don't want to argue with you right now, if that's what this is."

"What argument could you possibly make? You did what you did."

"Oh, I could make *plenty* of arguments." She rolls her eyes before taking a long pull of her beer. "Problem is, you're the kind of person who would argue with me if I told you the sky was blue. If you want to believe it's green, you're going to be fully committed to your bit. It wouldn't matter if you're *dead fucking wrong*. You're going to believe what you want to believe, and no one is going to change your mind."

"Since when have I given you the impression that I'm *that* unreasonable?"

"I don't know," she snarls, the volume of her voice rising with every word, "how about the time you left a severed head in my fucking bird feeder? Does that seem like something a reasonable person would do?"

"And you're some bastion of morality? You called the old man killer up on the hill to ask if it was his doing, then promptly yanked that head out of the feeder to sniff test it and give it a little cuddle. Quite possibly, that's something that a hit-and-run murderer might do, don't you think?"

She rips the bottle from my grasp and takes a long drink before slamming it down on the counter. "*I wouldn't know.*"

"Right." I step closer to Harper, hemming her in against the counter. She doesn't balk, doesn't back down. Not even as I lean in until I can smell the tequila on her every exhalation. Her eyes drop to my lips, and when they rise to meet mine once more, I swear I see more than just fury in their mercury depths. "You run away from everything, don't you? You run away from me."

"Do I? Because you've threatened me, you've intimidated me, you've spied on me, and yet I'm standing *right fucking here*."

She's right, but she's also wrong. And I don't just mean the accident. I mean *now*, in Cape Carnage. In Maya's shop. Every night that we dig and she insists on walking home. In the car, when she pulled away from my touch. Just moments ago. I know she saw the way I was looking at her. She let her gaze rest on me until I felt the undeniable tug, an invisible cord that seems to pull taut every time she's near. Even now, she's staring up at me with her fucking intoxicating defiance, but on the inside, I know she's retreating, folding in on herself. Running away.

And if she thinks I can't find her there, she's wrong. Because I'm in her thoughts, just like she's always in mine. I can see it in the shifting flecks of silver in her eyes. It's in the rosy hue that illuminates her cheeks. It's in the pulse that strobes currents of light in her throat, and the unsteady breaths that tremor in her chest. It's in the desire that haunts her features when her focus drops to my lips and lingers.

There's a single beat of time where I just stare at Harper Starling. It's a moment that might stretch to infinity, balanced on the cutting edge of a blade. It's an ouroboros, consuming itself, violence and desire intertwined.

And in the next moment, we're crashing into a brutal kiss.

There's nothing tender about it. There's no kindness. No mercy. It's teeth biting into lips. Nails digging into skin. Blood threading across tongues. It's pure fight and sheer want. When I frame her face with my hands, she clamps down on my bottom lip. When I grip her hair and wrench her head back to expose her neck to my bites and kisses, she rakes her nails down my chest hard enough to draw blood. And when I push her back against the counter, she moans and tears the robe from my shoulders, shoving her thigh between my legs to feel my erection against her skin.

"If you hate me so much," she says as I cup her breast and pinch her nipple to draw a gasp from her parted lips, "you'd better fuck me like you mean it."

In a flash of motion, I whip her around, caging her in with her ass facing me, the terry cloth robe still covering her body. "Do not say that to me unless you mean it."

"What makes you think I don't?" She presses her ass against me like an invitation, one I should be trying to resist. But I can't. I tug the robe down her back to expose her to me fully, keeping the tie balled in my hand as I let the rest drop to the floor. She shivers as I run my other hand from her neck to her ass, not stopping until

I reach between her thighs and cup her pussy. Arousal, silky and warm, coats my palm. My cock grows impossibly harder. I don't know if it's the drugs scrambling my brain or if it's just her, but no woman has ever felt as good as Harper. Her heat, her scent, the way she seems so soft and pliable in my hands despite all the lethal barbs that fly from her mouth. I've never needed anyone as badly, the one person I should never want.

I close my eyes and take a long, deep breath, forcing my hand away from her heat. I'm sure I feel the softest whimper vibrate through her spine.

"You're going to have to ask me nicely," I say as I loom over her to speak in low tones against her ear. "Because I might be here to kill you, but I'm not the kind of man who would fuck a woman who doesn't want it. You need me to fuck you? You tell me. You want me to stop? You tell me."

She trembles as I bite her neck and soothe it with a kiss, but the gentle press of my lips lasts only long enough to bite her even harder for keeping me waiting. "Fuck me like you hate me," she breathes.

I chuckle, running my hand down the length of her body to smack her ass. She yelps, but it dissolves into a moan as she pushes harder against me. "That wasn't very nice."

"Fuck me like you hate me, *please*."

"That's a little better. But you still sound like a brat."

"Fuck you."

I smack her ass harder and she braces her hands against the edge of the counter, her knuckles bleaching. "I can do this all night. And I mean that, seeing as how I probably have another six or seven hours' worth of mushrooms in my system. I wonder whose fault that would be?"

My palm connects with her flesh once more, waves of light erupting from the impact to spider across her hip. Every sensation is magnified. The sound of pained pleasure that escapes her lips becomes a wave of color in my vision. She's softer than cashmere when I glide my palm across the globe of her ass to soothe the sting. Even the network of tiny moles across her shoulders becomes fractal patterns, a constellation of desire mapped across her skin.

"What do you want?" I grit out.

"I already told you. But as usual, you aren't fucking listening." I smack her again. "*Jesus fucking Christ*, just fuck me, for the love of God, you stubborn asshole."

My voice is saccharine when I press my lips to her ear and whisper, "But I don't have protection."

"I'm on birth control. And I'm clear."

"How do you know that I'm clear too?"

"I . . ."

She stalls, her words lost to a silence that pulls tight around us like a film that clings to this moment. My hand folds around her throat, and though some distant thought urges me to squeeze until she begs for air, I keep my touch gentle, little more than a warning. "Tell me."

"I . . ." Her throat shifts beneath my palm as she swallows. "I trust you."

The breath stalls in my lungs. Maybe Harper doesn't mean what she says. I shouldn't believe her. But though it might be a lie, even the slim possibility that it could be the truth still ignites every cell in my body.

I was right when I said I'd need to scorch her out of my veins. I just didn't expect it would be impossible. That she would claim every piece of me first.

I grasp the base of my erection, kick her feet wider, then thrust into her pussy with a single, brutal stroke.

Nothing has ever felt as good as Harper's warmth enveloping my cock.

Breaths saw from my chest. Her heartbeat rages through her back as hard as mine resonates through my chest, and we haven't even started. We're stalled, unmoving, trying to come to terms with what we're doing, this detour from fate that we've both accepted, even if it only lasts for a fleeting moment of time.

I'm supposed to fucking *hate* her. I hate how she tore my brother away. He was everything to me, the person who made me want to be a decent man. I hate how she's eroded every plan I've had since arriving in this town. It was supposed to be easy. Come to Cape Carnage. Kill Harper Starling. Feed the vengeance that consumes my thoughts until it's finally sated. Then get back to the business of living. Find a nice woman, someone friendly and easy-going who fills a few of the holes left by Billy's absence. Go on to live a normal, healthy, productive life. I was never supposed to be here, buried to my balls in the woman who nearly killed me. And most of all, I hate myself for my weakness. Because there's nowhere else I'd rather be.

But I can still punish us both for that.

I pull out to the tip of my erection and thrust all the way in again. God, she really is a fucking angel, the way her cunt grips tight around my cock. Her moan is so otherworldly that I *see* it, ripples of colors that surround me. Another merciless thrust and her freshly bandaged hand lands on mine. She tugs at the tie bunched in my fist, the one I forgot was even there in my mindless need to bury myself in her pussy.

When I loosen my grip on the fabric, she pulls it from me to lay it across her throat, draping each end across her shoulders. I'm unmoving, my cock still lodged to the hilt in her channel, trying to process what's happening when she turns enough to give me a sidelong glare. I see everything in that brief connection. All her bitterness, her acerbic rage. But I see pain and loss and grief too. Even a hint of the guilt that I've been searching for, there in the glassy sheen that gathers at her lash line.

"Like you mean it," she says, dropping a weighted look at the tie lying over her shoulder before she turns to face forward. "Punish me. Fuck me like you'll never forgive me."

I'm sure I leave my body.

I wrap both ends of the tie around my hand and twist until it's flush against her neck, and then I pull out of her, banding an arm around her waist, and lift her away from the counter. I carry her to the living room and drop her on her knees on the couch, leaving just enough slack in the tie to not choke her. She lets out a whimper when I lay my free hand between her shoulders to press her chest down, keeping her ass up, her pussy glistening in the dim light. I settle behind her and twist that tie again, just tight enough that she shudders, but the breath still flows unobstructed through her lungs.

"You heard me earlier," I say as I notch the crown of my cock to her entrance. And I don't think it's just a reminder, but a veiled plea when I say, "Tell me to stop. Tap out."

A dark, mirthless laugh escapes her. "And you heard me. You loathe me. So go ahead. Try to fucking *destroy* me. I deserve that much after everything, don't you think?"

With a growl, I smack her ass hard and then push into her tight heat as deep as her body will take me, her moan rippling through the tie clutched in my hand.

I glide out to the tip and slam back in, picking up a punishing rhythm of deep, merciless strokes. Her pussy cinches tight around my girth as though she can't bear to let me go. Arousal smears down her thighs. My palm hits her ass, connecting over and over until it reddens. Her sounds of pleasure rise around me, lingering in the air on the musky scent of sex. Every time I grip those loops of fabric tighter, she somehow still matches my thinning restraint and dares me to take everything I can. With each brutal thrust and every impact of my hand against her ass, I'm the one who is shredded apart, destroyed by my desperate desire for her.

"More," Harper grits out as I reach around to swirl my fingers over her clit. Sweat shimmers over her back, illuminated by the glow in her skin. I swear I feel every one of her heartbeats pulse around me as she climbs closer to an orgasm. "Give me more."

The tie tightens in my grip and she moans out a breath. "I"—I thrust so hard she pitches forward with a yelp—"fucking"—I do it again, and her moan fills the room—"hate"—another vicious thrust and her arousal coats my hand—"you."

"I fucking hate you too," she rasps as I fuck her mercilessly. "And if you don't make me come, I'm going kill you with my bare fucking hands."

I thrust faster. Harder. I work her clit with slick fingers and she lets out an agonized cry of need. A hiss escapes my lips as an electric current crackles at the base of my spine. "*Goddamn.* I could fuck you right into the afterlife."

Her channel tightens around me. She loves those threatening words that could be a promise as much as a fantasy. So I tell her more, leaning closer to her ear to whisper desires shaped by darkness and sin. *Maybe I should grip your throat between my palms and squeeze until you can't breathe. Is that what you want? To beg me for air as I fill your pussy until it fucking overflows? Maybe I should spin you around and tighten this noose as you choke on my cock. You'd look so pretty with your face all red and your eyes bloodshot as you swallow me down. You want my cum to be the last thing you ever taste?*

It's not just my dick stretching her pussy or my touch on her clit that throws her over the edge. It's those fantasies I whisper. She screams my name as she comes apart, and I fall over the cliff with her, my length pulsing, my cock lodged deep as I fill her. I don't loosen my hold on the tie until the last ropes of cum have been spent and my heartbeat riots in my ears, muffling all the sounds in the room. Only then do I let the belt around her neck go, but still I remain buried in her warmth, not ready to leave. I'm not sure I ever will be. And that thought terrifies me, because as exhilarating as it is to be embraced by her warmth, it still feels forbidden. Like I'm taking something I never should have. Like I'm betraying everything I've set out to do since the day I woke up in that hospital bed four years ago. But I still want it, as much as I want justice. I want *her*.

And I have no fucking idea what she's thinking.

Her back still to me, her forehead pressed to her arm as she recovers her breath. I'm trying to find a way to ask when a chime sounds from the direction of the hallway. The washing machine. It's a dart of the mundane that bursts this cocoon of sweat and skin and unsteady exhalations.

I pull out of her slowly, riveted by the sight of my glistening cock sliding out of her swollen pink flesh, tracers of light and color following the motion. "Stay there," I say when I'm free, watching as the first drops of cum gather at her entrance to slide down her thighs. "I'll be right back."

She doesn't answer. I leave her to transfer the clothes into the dryer, then head to the bathroom to gather a warm washcloth and a towel so I can clean her up. I'm distracted a second time by my reflection. I don't recognize this version of me. One who is motivated by something other than revenge, if only for a moment. One whose purpose seems fogbound. This moment seems so far away from the cataclysm that propelled me here. Maybe I want to see where I end up when the fog clears, if it's somewhere different than I thought I would be.

I give myself a final once-over, then return to the living room. But Harper is already gone. Her robe is no longer on the floor. Mine is laid neatly across the back of the couch alongside a blanket and towel and two pillows. There's a glass of water and a bottle of ibuprofen on the side table. I hear a creak upstairs, and I know by the position it must be coming from her bedroom.

I stand naked in the center of the room for a long while, the washcloth cooling in my hand. I don't know what I wanted in the aftermath, but it wasn't this.

Eventually, I put the robe on and sit in the armchair, staring at the geometric patterns that shift across the floor. Maybe the mushrooms are starting to wear off a bit, because that's the only thing that seems strange around me. There are no more vibrant lights, no sounds that become colors across my vision.

I don't move at all for a long while, not until the dryer beeps to snap me out of my daydream as I try to relive every moment of this night with Harper, from the way her eyes drifted closed when I touched her face and told her she was beautiful in the river, to the one where I pulled free of her pussy, staining her thighs. With a deep sigh, I head to the closet and fold the laundry, setting mine on an armchair before I hesitate at the bottom of the stairs with her clothes balanced on my palm. And before I can talk myself out of it, I'm carefully taking every step in silence until I'm on the landing of the second story.

Her bedroom door is ajar, light pouring through the crack. At first, I think she might be awake, but she's not. Her deep, even breaths spill out into the hall. Just like the night when I killed Jake, she's sleeping with not one lamp on, but two. It seems strange, like it did then, to sleep with not just a night-light to guide her way if she wakes, but two lamps to keep out the shadows. Her life seems surrounded by darkness, and as I slip into her room, I can't understand why she would find discomfort in it when she sleeps.

I stand at the threshold of Harper's room and watch the rise and fall of her chest beneath a patchwork quilt. The things I would have done in this moment if it happened mere weeks ago.

And now, I feel as though I shouldn't enter her private space uninvited. Every step I take closer to her, I know I should stop. I shouldn't set her folded clothes on the dresser, or stop beside her bed to loom over her sleeping form like a specter. I shouldn't be lowering to my knees, my face so close to hers that I can smell the mint of toothpaste on her breath, or lifting my hand to shift a lock of damp hair away from her neck. I definitely should not place a kiss to her cheek. But I'm as powerless as the sea is against the moon. I'm caught in the gravitational force of her despite the dark chasm that spans between us.

I lay my lips to her skin so gently that she doesn't stir, doesn't wake. But when I pull away, Harper glows.

HARPOON

Nolan

THE LIGHT STREAMING THROUGH THE gap between the curtains lands on my face like a slap.

"Fucking hell, I feel like shit."

I stretch, my body already protesting a crappy sleep on a couch that's too short for my six-foot-three height. My elbow aches. My knee throbs. My neck protests when I try to turn to the left to look at my watch. It's nearly ten-thirty in the morning. I'm the kind of person who's usually awake by six. But then I guess that's what happens when someone drugs you with mushrooms and you don't come down from your high until four in the morning.

With a groan, I sit up and take in my surroundings. "Harper?"

There's no answer.

I look toward the kitchen. The window is open, but no sound comes from outside to signal that she might be around. I don't smell any coffee either, but from here I can see a to-go cup sitting next to a red kettle, a box of Earl Grey tea, and my car keys resting beside it.

"Harper . . ." I call again, louder this time in case it reaches outside to where she might be able to hear me. At first, I'm met with silence. And then the rustle of feathers.

The raven lands on the windowsill, something shiny dangling from his beak. He sets it down next to his foot, the sound of his caw drowning the metallic clink when it tumbles off the narrow ledge to fall into the sink.

"Murder bird," he says in an imitation of Harper's voice as he sidesteps toward a glass container on a shelf within his reach. He eyes me and then pecks the lid of the jar. "Nom nom."

"I haven't even had caffeine," I protest.

"*Murder.*"

"Fine." I roll off the couch, fixing the robe around my body, memories of last night fleeting through my mind as I knot the terry cloth belt around my waist. My dick aches at the thought of plunging into Harper's pussy again. Christ. I cannot believe we did that. That was a wildly horrible, impulsive, ridiculous idea. I should be using my time in her cottage to tear it apart and search for my scrapbook and weapons, not fantasize about all the many, *many* ways I'd love to fuck her again. "Maybe you should murder me," I say to the bird as I approach the window. He flaps away to land on the patio table in the garden, watching me with interest. "Because I did something monumentally stupid last night, and, at this rate, I fucking deserve it."

I grab a handful of what I hope is beef jerky from the jar and toss it onto the patio stones to the sound of the raven's delighted caws. Setting the kettle to boil, I pick up the gift he dropped, a silver bracelet with thick links and an engraved panel in its center. A^2BC, it says in a simple script. I'm not sure where he could have found it, or who it might belong to, so I keep it in my hand as I wait for the water to boil then pour my tea, leaving it to brew on the counter before grabbing my clothes and heading to the bath-room to change.

I've just finished getting dressed when I hear the staccato trill of an impact driver in the distance, coming from the direction of the hill where the manor house sits. When I stand in the claw-foot tub and open the frosted window, I can just make out Harper's form bent over what must be the soapbox racer through a tangle of rhododendron branches. She sets the tool down and then pushes the car back and forth a few times. Seemingly satisfied, she tosses a cover over the vehicle, then stares down at it, unmoving.

I can't make out her expression at this distance. There's no way to see if she's gnawing her bottom lip like she does when she's anx-ious, or if her brow is crinkled in anger, or if her stormy eyes sud-denly brighten like when she's trying to suppress a smile. But I can still see a conflict warring within her. She turns, marching a few steps in the direction of the cottage. Then she stops abruptly. She pivots and strides a few steps in the direction of the manor house. Stops again. Spins to face the cottage and stomps once, and I nearly smile at her frustration. She shakes her head and, with a final turn toward the mansion, she strides away, disappearing from view.

My guts twist with the ache of disappointment.

If I'm being honest with myself—which I truly hate having to do these last few days—I was hoping that she would return to the cottage. Every time she faced my direction, longing and anticipa-tion soared in my chest. Every time she turned away, my hope plummeted as though its waxen wings had melted in the sun.

I drag my hands down my face as the distant sound of a door closing rolls down the hill, a stamp of finality on the idea that Harper might actually want to see me. As though the to-go mug wasn't enough of a "get the fuck out of my house" message.

"You should be looking for the fucking book, dumbass," I say as I start to turn the handle to close the window. "You should be getting back on track with your fucking plans, not worrying about why she doesn't want to see you."

The window is almost sealed shut when I hear a buzzing sound. One that blankets my vision with thoughts of red mist.

I know that fucking sound.

I race from the bathroom, grabbing my keys but leaving my tea untouched as I dart through the back door. A drone soars over the garden in a smooth arc toward the manor. She's in the main house, thank God. But it could have been watching when she was still outside without her knowledge. And it shouldn't be anywhere fucking near her.

"Fucking Sam," I hiss, taking off at a sprint through the back gate, keeping my eye on the drone in the distance as it continues toward the mansion. I head to the left and stay out of its view, running across the lawn to where I can pass through a gap in the thick shrubbery and jump over the stone wall. When I land on the sidewalk, I brush myself down, take a calming breath, and then backtrack toward the cottage gates.

A man I don't recognize is standing on the opposite side of the quiet street next to what looks like a rental vehicle, his attention consumed by the screen and remote control in his hands. My SUV sits between us, parked close to the entrance of Harper's house.

I'm watching him, weighing my options as a *caw caw* sounds from the direction of the cottage. When I look up, the raven is in the branches of the tree that leans over the stone wall, watching me. *Great.* All I need is for that fucking bird to start screaming "pretty murder bird" at this drone operator who is clearly here for Sam's search for anything that will tie Arthur Lancaster to La

Plume. And it's a search that's endangering Harper the longer it goes on.

I swallow a swell of darkness that chokes up my throat as I cross the road, stuffing my hands in my pockets to keep them from tearing the device free of his grasp and ramming it down his fucking throat.

"Hey, man," I say, laying my easygoing Southern drawl on a little thicker. He gives me a brief flicker of a smile. With only a single nod in reply, I know he means to dismiss me. "Cool house, huh?"

He chuckles. "Yeah, I guess."

"Is it going up for sale or something? You taking shots for a real estate agent?"

"Nope." His lips press tight in a silent *fuck off*.

Irritation churns through my blood as the drone buzzes in the distance. The mere sound of it stokes the fury coursing through the chambers of my heart. "Okay . . . cool . . . Well, if you're looking for buildings with history, you should try the old Victorian B&B on Ortolan Drive. An old guy at the coffee shop downtown told me some famous serial killer stayed there back thirty-ish years ago. La Flume? La Gloom? La Something . . ."

"La Plume?" the guy says, his eyes sharp with interest as they finally settle on me for more than two consecutive seconds.

"Yeah, that's it. La Plume. Buddy said the La Plume guy stayed there before he killed a girl and disappeared. Said he was an odd dude, I dunno. Had some weird story about pancakes or some shit." I shrug and clutch the bracelet tighter in my pocket, inviting the pain of the metal links as they dig into my palm. "Anyway, good luck with . . . whatever this is."

With a single nod, I keep walking. I don't know shit about the

B&B on Ortolan Drive, I just know it's old and on the other side of town. Far away from Harper.

It takes every shred of restraint to keep my head down and not turn back to split the guy's throat open with my bare hands. When I get to the end of the block, I allow myself a glance over my shoulder. A dark smile kicks up one corner of my lips as I see the drone returning from over Harper's house. I know he's taken the bait.

As soon as I'm out of view, I dart behind the wide trunk of an elm tree, hiding there until I hear his engine start and his car drive past. When I'm sure I won't be seen, I return to my vehicle and start it up, my hands gripping the steering wheel so tightly my fingers ache. The more Sam closes in around Arthur, the more Harper could be threatened by the fallout. If she's been covering for his crimes, which seems to be the case given the exhumations she's wrangled me into, it's only a matter of time until she's caught in the web too.

Whether I want to kill her one moment or kiss her the next, I cannot let that happen.

With a furious growl, I hit the steering wheel with my fist. It's not nearly as satisfying as crushing Sam's cheekbones would be, but it will have to do. I inhale a steadying breath that fills to the bottom of my lungs, then pull away from the curb, heading for the outskirts of town.

Ten minutes later, I'm parking at the one place I never thought I'd voluntarily show my face. Particularly not on Harper Starling's behalf.

I give myself a final check in the mirror. Eyes a little bloodshot, haunted by dark circles. Hair a bit disheveled. I need caffeine and a shower, but this will have to suffice. This is a batshit, reckless idea. Not the kind of thing I would normally do. But I need to put some heat on Sam. Something official. Something that will eat up his time and make him think twice about infringing on Harper's privacy.

I practice my best guiltless, "I'm a good citizen and absolutely not a murderer" smile, and then leave my car to stride toward the entrance of the Cape Carnage Sheriff's Office.

A man in his early forties looks up from the reception desk as I enter, pushing a pair of black-rimmed glasses up his nose. "Can I help you?"

"Maybe," I say, giving him a smile that I hope has the right mix of concern and helpfulness. "I saw something that's maybe a little suspicious, and I thought I should probably let you know."

"Okay." The guy taps his mouse and brings up something on his computer, flicking a bland, disinterested look my way. "What's your name—"

"I'm not busy, Tom," a man interjects. He saunters out of an office behind the desk, a set of beige plastic blinds obscuring the interior behind him. He's tall, even more imposing in his full uniform, likely in his late fifties, though it's hard to pin down a specific age. His hair and close-cut stubble are silver, only a few dark hairs clinging to their youthful shade, but he's putting in effort to stay in shape, the muscles in his arms and legs obvious despite the formal attire. He smiles at me, his eyes a colorless kind of blue that takes on the traits of its surroundings. "Come on back, son. I've got time."

I return his smile and pass the reception desk, entering the office of Sheriff Yates.

Sheriff Yates stands at the door, his hand stretched toward the vinyl-covered chairs in a gesture for me to take a seat. I give him my thanks and do so without delay, doing my best to stay in my concerned-citizen-non-murderer character as I lace my fingers and wait with rigid posture. He shuts the door and sits on the other side of the desk with a long, contented sigh. The office is decorated with photos of what must be his wife and two daughters, fishing and hunting photos interspersed among the happy family pictures. Yates with a fish. Yates with a dead deer. Yates with a perfect small-town life.

Light streams through the blinds behind him and it sets off the start of a pulsing headache that I do my best to ignore.

"I'm glad you came in," Yates says, his smile crinkling the corners of his eyes. Despite the wrinkles that say he's spent his life giving easygoing, welcoming smiles, unease still creeps across my spine. "It's a welcome delay to reviewing the Carnival of Carnage plans. I think I've gone over them with the town council no less than sixty times already."

"Glad I could be of service," I reply with a deferential nod. "I'm sure it'll be worth it. I hear it's quite the event."

"It is. A little chaotic, but so is Cape Carnage during tourist season." Yates folds his hands on his desk and leans back, his smile dimming to something more serious as he scrutinizes me. "So, what can I do for you, Mister . . . ?"

"Rhodes," I say.

"Mr. Rhodes. Did I hear you tell Tom that you saw something suspicious? Why don't you tell me about it."

I clear my throat, expecting Yates to take up a pen and paper or fire up his computer, but he doesn't. He just raises his eyebrows, giving me a faint but encouraging nod.

"Well, it might be nothing, but there's this man who's staying in the same hotel as me, the Capeside Inn. He's here filming a documentary, something about some kind of amateur investigation group he's part of. The Sleuthseekers."

"Ah, yes," Yates says, a bemused smirk lifting one corner of his lips. "I know the type. They show up here from time to time."

"Yeah, well, he seems a bit . . . obsessive. And I'm not sure he's playing by the rules." I jerk my head in the general direction of the town, arranging my features into a look of earnest concern, a departure from the simmering rage that still boils in the depths of my chest when the image of the drone operator resurfaces in my thoughts. "Last night, I saw him snooping around some place by the Ballantyne River that has No Trespassing signs."

"The Ballantyne River?"

"That's right, sir."

"You've got a fishing permit?"

"Umm . . ." My brain seems to flip over, trying to process his question with insufficient caffeination. "I wasn't fishing, sir . . . ?"

Yates's head tilts like a curious dog. "That's the usual reason people find themselves out at the river. You're not hunting off-season, are you?"

"No, sir." *Unless we count human game*, an unhelpful voice in my head declares. "Absolutely not."

"You're sure? I'll let you off with a warning, but you need to be honest with me. Deputy Collins is a vegan and he takes poaching very seriously. If he gets wind of it—"

"I swear, sir. I wasn't hunting at the river," I say, trying to think my way free of the whirlpool I seem to have dropped into. Yates visibly relaxes at my assertion, his shoulders dropping, the softness returning between his eyes. "But this Sam guy, I don't know why he'd be out there, walking all over private property. And just a little

while ago, I saw his drone flying all over the big estate on the hill, the old Victorian place. There was a woman outside a stone cottage on the property who looked pretty upset about it."

Yates's expression turns grim. Lightless. He leans a little closer to his desk, his eyes pinned to me, unwavering and shadowed beneath his drawn brows. "He was flying over Lancaster Manor?"

I give a single nod. "Yes, sir."

"And you weren't the pilot?"

Blood drains from my limbs, leaving crystals of ice behind. My heart rages, carving alarmed beats into my ribs.

"Sir . . . ?"

"You were piloting the drone recently for Mr. Porter—six days ago, correct? The day that Jake Hornell was last seen."

The bitter taste of fear lingers on my tongue as the moisture evaporates from my mouth. I never gave him Sam's last name.

This isn't how I operate, recklessly putting myself in the searchlight. I stay in the shadows. I know I'm good at charming people when I want to, at manipulating them into moving their pieces on the board, placing them right where I want them to be. But I also know I'm not indestructible. I don't swan into a police station figuring that I hold all the power.

But that's exactly what I've just done. And not only is it a consuming, obsessive need to protect Harper that's driven me to this moment, but now I might have put not only myself in danger, but her too. Because she's on that drone footage that I shot. She might be one of the last people who saw Jake Hornell alive. Pieces of him are in her *fucking garden*. And the rest of him is buried along the Ballantyne River, on Arthur's land, not far from where we exhume his victims every night. In the grave I dug. The one I intended for her.

These thoughts cascade through my mind in mere seconds, some other part of my brain slipping into self-protection mode as I say, "I piloted the drone for him a few days ago, yes. But only that one time. He was a little . . . weird . . . about things he wanted me to focus on. Insistent. He wanted me to film certain people. It just didn't seem right. It felt . . . invasive." I shake my head and shrug, masking the partial lie with nonchalance. "Anyway, I guess his drone guy must have shown up."

"So you *weren't* the person flying the drone over Lancaster Manor?"

"No."

"Then why were you there?"

"I was just walking by."

"You were just walking by," he repeats. He taps a long index finger on the desk, the ghost of a smile lingering on his lips. It doesn't reach his eyes. "Look," he finally says, leaning back in his chair with a deep sigh. "Cape Carnage is a small town with an unusual history. Guys like Porter show up every few years, searching for something they think they're going to find. Some truth behind the urban legends, maybe. But they don't uncover anything, because there's no old, hidden secret to find here. Every small town has something dark in its past if you look back far enough, just like Cape Carnage. That doesn't mean there's a murderer lurking around every corner. And, more often than not, their meddling messes up things for the likes of Deputy Collins and me when we have *actual* work to do. Like figuring out what the hell happened to Jake. It's possible he just skipped town, all things considered." He taps on a manila folder on his desk, which I assume has something to do with Jake. But his eyes don't leave mine as they narrow. "However, I guess I could be wrong. You wouldn't know anything about Mr. Hornell's whereabouts, would you?"

I shake my head, conscious of every micro expression I make as I hold his gaze. "No, sir."

"Hmm." I'm not sure if that's a good *hmm* or a bad *hmm*, but I just wait, my expression bland and guiltless despite the bead of sweat that rolls down my spine. "Well," Yates finally says, rolling his chair backward and rising to his feet, "I appreciate you raising a concern. I'll keep an eye on things."

He extends a hand across the desk and I take it, wondering what he thinks of the temperature of my palm as I say, "Anytime, sir. Happy to help."

With a nod and a brighter smile, Sheriff Yates lets go and walks around the desk to open the door to his office, stepping aside for me to walk through. Just as I pass the threshold, he lays a hand on my shoulder. "Oh, and son . . ."

"Yes . . . ?"

"If you run into Mr. Porter, tell him to pop by the station. I've been trying to get that drone footage from him in case Mr. Hornell was on it, but for some reason, he seems to be avoiding me. Best to cross every T, and I'd rather not have to issue a warrant. Not a good look during tourist season, especially not when the Sleuthseekers will descend on this place if they think I'm antagonizing their queen bee."

"Sure thing, sir."

With a fatherly pat to my shoulder, Sheriff Yates lets me go, and I keep my steps measured as I get the fuck out of the station. It takes everything in me not to speed from the parking lot in a squeal of tires.

It isn't until I'm sitting on the edge of my bed at the inn that I feel like I can finally take a breath.

Since the first day I arrived in Cape Carnage, nothing has gone the way I thought it would. The imagined future I came here with has been split through a prism, fracturing into shards that are unrecognizable from the simple, colorless beam of light I started with. It began the very moment I met Harper in a coffee shop. And now, I feel like I'm crashing through every one of those meticulous plans I made, desperate to get closer to her no matter how hard I try to fight my way back on course.

What would happen if I stopped trying to hate her?

More and more, it's an effort to hold on to my anger toward Harper. I see how fiercely loyal she is to Arthur. She puts herself in danger to keep him safe. I see how much she cares about Cape Carnage, from her refusal to leave despite the threat of my presence to her efforts in making the town more beautiful, even though she must be exhausted. I think I even see how much she cares about me. It's in the long glances in the lantern light. It's in the guilt that glazes her eyes. It was there last night, even when she tried to hide it. And she's right to be wary of me. Just like she's said, I've threatened her. Intimidated her. Spied on her. I've never given her a safe space. I've never even allowed that concept to thrive in me, constantly battling to crush it into submission.

So what would happen if I just . . . stopped fighting it? What would she do if I let myself care? *Really* care?

I look toward the wardrobe where I once stored my backpack of weapons. The one Harper stole after I stuffed a head in her bird feeder and left her with a threat. When I promised that no matter where she hid or how far she ran, I would still find her. Somehow, even that vow has changed color in the prism of time.

With a sharp inhale, I rise from the bed and stride to the shower. Within fifteen minutes, I'm leaving my room, headed for the general store to replace everything that she tossed into the Ballantyne River. Maybe I even pick up a few more things. When I get back to my room, I text her.

I stare at the screen for a long time. But her response never comes, even after the last shades of indigo have bled from the sky. Despite the lack of reply, I still drive past her cottage on my way to the river, slowing as I near the gate in the stone wall. There are no lights on in her house.

I park on the lane near the river where my vehicle will be hidden from view. With my new stove and lantern and tarp shoved into my damp backpack and an unused shovel over my shoulder, I head to the boulders that overlook Arthur's burial ground. I set out two mugs. I make hot chocolate. But Harper doesn't show.

It's nearly eleven-thirty by the time I finally take the leftovers in the pot down to the river to wash the cooled chocolate away. When I'm done, I turn toward the silt floodplain, my focus panning over the expanse of secrets. Without Harper, I don't know the measurements. I wouldn't know where to start to look for the next of Arthur's victims.

But that's not why I'm here.

I head back to the boulder and pack my belongings, then walk along the shore, wading into the water until the bank narrows and disappears and granite creeps into the water. Within a few moments, I arrive at a smaller silt plain. One that's familiar. I don't need a map. I know where to dig.

I plunge my shovel into the soil.

In the dim light cast by a crescent moon, I open the grave I dug for Harper Starling.

RUNNING DARK

Harper

> I'll swing by at 9 to pick you up?

NINE O'CLOCK WAS OVER THREE hours ago. I never replied, though one could argue that I had several good reasons.

Reason one: I hate him. Seriously. And I refuse to be dickmatized by that asshole.

Reason two: No matter how hard I keep trying to find evidence to the contrary, Nolan Rhodes hates me too. He told me so. Multiple times. *He hates me he hates me he hates me.*

Reason three: I do not need him right now. Absolutely not.

And most importantly, reason four: Arthur. I was lucky I found him on the kitchen floor when I did. Though I try not to think about how he could have died after a fall like that, the thought still haunts me, refusing to let go.

I look over to where he's sleeping soundly despite the beep of his heart rate monitor and the harsh scent of disinfectant and the voices of nurses and patients on the other side of the curtains that separate us from the rest of the emergency ward. A white gauze bandage is taped to his forehead. Dried blood dots the collar of his hospital gown.

I frown, the inside of my bottom lip raw between my teeth. Sometimes I don't go to the main house after dinner to check on Arthur a final time before bed. I might have so easily rationalized that he didn't need me. Or assumed he was already in his room and left without checking the kitchen. He could have spent all night on the cold and unforgiving stone. He could have been there alone. He could have—

I shake my head, forcing myself to banish my worst fears.

I don't need Nolan. I'm not lonely. I'm not afraid. I can do this on my own.

I don't miss him.

I groan and press my head against the wall behind me in the hope it might absorb me into another, less complicated dimension. Having a mortal enemy is a lot harder than I anticipated. Because I shouldn't want him here. I shouldn't miss him. *At all.* Except I think that I do.

I shift on the vinyl seat, the ache between my legs a persistent reminder of my night with Nolan. I should not be thinking about that right now. But every time I close my eyes, I hear his whisper in my ear. I feel his calloused palms on my skin. I catch his scent in the air, bergamot and spice. And it's not just the sex. It's the connection that came with it. It felt like I had been cracked open just enough that I could let a little of myself out into the light. After hiding for so long, I felt seen. For a moment.

But he hates me. I think.

A text buzzes in my hand, and in one heartbeat, Nolan's name flashes through my mind. But it's not him. It's Lukas, and I try to push away the shard of disappointment that lodges in my chest.

How's grumps?

Grumps? I bet Arthur loves being called that.

AUTOCORRECT! Gramps. But grumps is also pretty accurate.

Grumps is sleeping. I'm just waiting for the doctor to come by. Hopefully we'll be out of here soon.

Okay. I changed to the earliest flight tomorrow, so I should be home by noon. I'm sorry for the shitty timing for being away.

Not your fault. Don't worry about it, I don't mind.

Still, I appreciate your help so much. Thank you.

Don't thank me yet. I'm going to throw you under the judgy bus with "grumps" the first chance I get.

Fuck you, Harps.

I chuckle and pocket the device just as the curtain is swept to the side and the doctor enters with a nurse whose hospital scrubs stretch over her pregnant belly. With a smile that deftly straddles the line of comforting yet professional, the doctor gives me a nod in greeting as the nurse gets to work changing Arthur's IV fluids.

"I'm Dr. Reid," she says with a warm Jamaican accent. I recognize both her and the nurse from town, though we've never officially met. "You're Harper? Arthur's granddaughter?"

"Oh . . . no, I mean yes, I'm Harper, but we're not related. Just friends. I understand if you need to wait and give his medical information to his grandson. He's away for a meeting but I can call him if you'd rather speak with him directly."

She taps on her tablet. "No, it's fine. Arthur authorized you on his medical records." I glance at Arthur's bed. He's still asleep, unaware that my heart has grown two sizes in my chest. "There doesn't seem to be any sign of a stroke or internal hemorrhage after the fall. He's got some bumps and bruises, of course, but nothing is broken. However, his bloodwork came back with a B_{12} deficiency. Has he been particularly irritable lately?"

"It's Arthur Lancaster. He's always irritable."

Dr. Reid does her best to suppress a smile, its faint traces fading as quickly as they appear. "What about any mention of pins and needles in his hands or feet?" I shake my head. "Problems with coordination and balance?"

"He crashed his golf cart yesterday."

The doctor lets out a thoughtful *hmm* as she taps her stylus on the tablet to note the detail. "Have his Alzheimer's symptoms noticeably worsened recently?"

Blood threads across my tongue as I worry my bottom lip. I feel fucking terrible that I could have missed a constellation of symptoms that pointed to another health problem that could have been fixed. "It's hard to say. He's been losing things more often. He's a bit paranoid that someone is breaking into his house to steal his belongings. But this kind of thing has been happening for a while."

The doctor nods, giving me a polite smile. "I understand. We're going to keep him in for a few days so we can get his B_{12} levels up and monitor for other symptoms. He'll be transferred to the geriatric ward, where he'll be much more comfortable. Once we get him stabilized—"

The doctor's next words are lost to a sudden cacophony outside our curtained room—a crash of metal across the floor, slurred yelling, and raised voices. I share a worried look with the doctor and nurse, and then they're rushing into the corridor as I follow on their heels.

A huge mammoth of a man is facing off against a doctor in a room across the hall, a stainless-steel cart lying on its side at the edge of the curtain, metal instruments scattered across the floor. Vomit glistens on his wiry ginger beard and stains the top of his white shirt. There's an open gash through his brow, a suture needle dangling from a thread sewn into his flesh. The doctor who was treating him raises his hands in a placating gesture, and I can tell he's nervous about being hemmed in between the gigantic man and a tangle of medical equipment and wires. "Mr. McMillan—"

"What is your fucking problem?" the man bellows, every word slurred and stretched. Two orderlies and the doctor and nurse who were attending to Arthur come closer, a halo of "calm down, sir" rising around him.

"Please sit down so Dr. Aspen can finish your stitches," Dr. Reid says with calm authority. She's only met with a tirade of drunken vitriol despite her polite request. "Sir, police will intervene if you do not calm down."

"Stop telling me to fucking *calm down*." The man rushes forward and tumbles over the cart, knocking over the pregnant nurse as he falls to the floor. She lands hard on her ass and lets out an agonized yelp. Both of the doctors immediately rush to her side while the orderlies keep the drunken man pinned to the floor. A police officer jogs in a moment later, and the doctors help the nurse up, her eyes shining with unshed tears, a protective hand cradled around her belly.

Fury rages through the caverns of my heart. My hands are folded into fists, fingernails pressing crescent imprints into my palms. When I look over my shoulder at Arthur, he's awake, watching me with grim determination.

I turn back to the man subdued beneath the knee of the officer. The details of the room seem to sharpen as this unfamiliar man is handcuffed and dragged to his feet. I'm not sure if he really sees me when he meets my eyes across the corridor. But I see him.

When Dr. Reid returns, she only stays long enough to see if I have any questions. And after she departs, I turn all my attention to Arthur. I fill his paper cup with water and hold it to his lips. I unplug his phone from where I left it to charge and lay it beside his hand. He says he doesn't need help as he shifts on his bed, but I still push his pillows around until they're right where he wants them. He insists that I leave for my own benefit. I know he wants to rest, so I don't linger, even though I feel like I should be doing more to make him comfortable. With a kiss to his cheek that he pretends to be disgruntled about even though he pats my hand, I leave him with the promise that I'll return as soon as I can.

It's nearly two in the morning when I get home, even later when I finally fall asleep. But I'm wide awake at six, ready for a full day of activity. I make coffee. Feed Morpheus. Check my garden for body part presents from my frenemy Nolan. There are none. I frown at my bird feeder, though I don't know why I should feel a needling sense of disappointment at the absence of a decapitated head. Then I head to the main house and clean up the blood on the marble tile in the kitchen from Arthur's fall.

As soon as I speed through these mundane chores, I'm enacting the plans that kept me tossing in my bed until two in the morning.

I pry the loose floorboard up in the guest room of the cottage, where I hid some of the reminders of my old life when I first arrived in Cape Carnage.

This is a huge risk.

Sam was interested in my true identity and my disappearance four years ago when I first went missing, maybe just as much as he's interested in the story of La Plume now. I was already trying to disappear before I made it to Maryland and fate intervened to give me the gift of Harper Starling. But I was careful to do everything I could not to leave a trail here. Though he's given no indication that he's figured out I wound up in Cape Carnage, he's already spying on the property where I live. It's not a stretch that he could recognize me despite the darker hair and stolen name.

But this might also be a once-in-a-lifetime opportunity to kill the rumor that Arthur is La Plume and get Sam off the old man's back for good. And after feeling so fucking helpless at the hospital, it'll be good to take charge and do something productive to keep my promises. With a deep breath, I steel myself and commit to my plan.

I pick a few keepsakes from my hiding place that might be interesting to Sam but not conclusive proof that I was here. An incense holder shaped like a crescent moon. It lived on the wood-burning stove of the van I shared with Adam. A Higonokami pocketknife. I used that in a few videos we took when we explained to our followers how we set up camp at the various stops on our cross-country road trip. The unusual angle of the blade's tip is easily recognizable to anyone as detail oriented as Sam Porter. A Texas Tech sweater that was Adam's. I borrowed it so frequently that he finally declared it mine. I press my nose to the fibers and inhale. It doesn't smell like us anymore. I sigh as I run my fingertips over the embroidered letters. I haven't looked at these mementos in at least a couple of years, and there's something reassuring about their presence in the house. But even in these last few days, I feel less attached to them. Maybe I'm not ready to give up some of the more personal relics that I keep hidden in this hole, but as I put the floorboard back, I think maybe I'm ready to let a few of them go.

I put the knife, sweater, and incense holder into a bag along with a few additional supplies, and then head to the garage next to Arthur's house, borrowing his ancient Jaguar sedan to drive to the abandoned farmhouse off Clarke Road, twenty minutes outside town. I don't even know whose land it is. I just know it's not Arthur's, and that's the only thing that matters.

It takes me a moment of staring up at the decaying roof and graffitied siding to convince myself to follow the overgrown path that leads through the weedy lawn. Every step I take, the memory of vultures in a tree threatens to push me all the way back to the car. My palms sweat. My heart riots in my ears. *This is my chance to protect Arthur*, I tell myself over and over as I hurry over the threshold where the faded white door hangs from rusted hinges. *It's not the same house.* I climb the rotting staircase to the second level. *It doesn't smell the same. Doesn't look the same. There's not even a cellar.*

I find a loose floorboard in a bedroom on the second story and ram it with my heel until it shatters. My pulse is still humming as I take a steadying breath, and with a silent goodbye, I shove my belongings beneath the shattered remains of the splintered wood. When I've snapped a quick photo with my phone, I head outside and take a last look at the house, then I drive back to town.

Once I'm parked a few blocks away from the Capeside Inn to keep Arthur's distinctive vehicle out of sight, I head to my perch on the hill to hide among the rocks where I first watched Nolan as he left the inn for a run. His car isn't in the parking lot now, and I try not to think about where he might have gone. "It doesn't fucking matter what that asshole is up to," I whisper to myself as I log in to my sock puppet account on the Sleuthseekers Discord server.

My eyes drift up to Sam's rental car, and then to the empty spot next to it, the one that Nolan seems to prefer. Heat twists behind my navel, that ache from earlier throbbing between my legs. I wonder what would happen if I broke into Nolan's room and waited in my lingerie for him to return. Would he turn and walk away? Or would he pin me to the bed and fuck me so hard I see stars? What if I brought my Lelo Enigma dual vibrator? What if—

"Oh my fucking God. Get it together, bitch. Stop thinking with your neglected vagina and think with your brain."

With a shake of my head, I refocus on the device in my hands, tapping out a short private message to Sam. I include the location details of the farmhouse on Clarke Road, claiming I found the items when I was snooping around the abandoned house. Once the photos are sent, I wait.

It takes only a few moments before I receive a reply, and though he seems a little hesitant at first, the excitement is still palpable despite his short messages. In less than ten minutes, Sam and his drone operator are packing up his rental vehicle and leaving the Capeside Inn.

A dark smile creeps across my lips as I jog to Arthur's car and set off for my next destination.

You'd think the next stage of the plan would be the hardest part. But really, it's not as much of a challenge as it seems. Sheriff Yates never likes to keep anyone longer than he must, so it's likely the charming Mr. McMillan has already been released. And a guy like that is neither the Capeside Inn nor the bed-and-breakfast type, so chances are he's staying in the shady Lionshead Motel just off the highway that leads into town. He'll either be sleeping off his hangover, or he'll be in Gus's Tavern within walking distance of the Lionshead, drinking himself into his next oblivion.

I swing by the dumpster behind Milo's Pizza first to grab a discarded box, then I start with the Lionshead, betting that it's early enough in the day that he might not yet be ready for the pub. When I'm parked just out of sight of the motel, I take out my phone and select the contact for the reception desk.

"Lionshead, how can I help?" a man says after picking up on the second ring. I know by the timbre of his voice that it's the young guy who started working there last season, and the wicked grin that's been lodged on my face since I departed from the Capeside Inn grows a little wider. He's the quiet type, a little shy. He's just there to make enough to pay his rent. And he doesn't give a shit about things like rules, or privacy.

"Hey, I'm the delivery driver for Milo's Pizza," I say, keeping my voice disaffected. "Some guy with the last name McMillan ordered delivery to the Lionshead, but Milo's handwriting is shit and I can't make out the room number. He's not picking up the phone either. Can you tell me which room I'm supposed to go to so Milo doesn't ride my ass for a late delivery?"

"Yeah, sure. Give me a second." My smile could be seen from space. I reach toward the back seat and grab the empty pizza box along with a couple of choice goodies from my bag as the sound of keyboard tapping fills the line. "Room three-twenty."

"Thanks so much. You're a lifesaver."

"You got it."

I disconnect the line and leave the car with the pizza box in hand, my blood fizzing with adrenaline. *I'm a pizza delivery driver*, I tell myself as I walk around the hedges that frame the Lionshead parking lot. There are a few cars scattered in front of the motel rooms, but all the curtains are closed. There's no one around.

My attention homes in on the door for Room 320.

I'm meant to be here. I'm just doing my job. And it's funny how easily you can slip through society when you don't just tell a lie, but you *embrace* it. If you make the effort to believe it, often everyone else does too.

I take a deep breath, dim the wicked edge in my smile to something less sinister, and knock three times on the door.

"Pizza delivery," I call, my voice chipper. A disgruntled groan rumbles on the other side of the door. "Pepperoni with extra cheese? For . . . McMillan?"

A string of weary expletives and slippers dragging over tile grow louder as he approaches the door. My expression brightens as the dead bolt turns. The door swings open and McMillan glares at me, his stained T-shirt and boxers barely covered by a fraying gray robe. "I didn't order no fuckin' pizza—"

I lift the pizza box enough that he can see the gun I hold beneath it, the silencer aimed at his navel. Surprise ignites in his bloodshot eyes.

"Come with me, Mr. McMillan," I say, releasing the safety with a threatening click, "and I might just let you live."

FATHOMS

Nolan

IT'S NEARLY NOON. AND I'M standing on the street outside Harper's cottage like a fucking obsessed loser.

I push the sleeves of my charcoal-gray Henley up to my elbows. She likes my forearms. I think. She stares at them a lot. Unless I'm fucking delusional, which . . . probably tracks. She seems to like these tactical work pants I wear sometimes, too. "Is that part of your uniform?" she'd asked a few nights ago, gesturing to my trousers and work boots.

"I don't really have a uniform other than a vest and jacket, but . . . I guess so."

I still feel the heat beneath my skin from the way her gaze dropped down the length of me a fraction slower than what would be deemed appropriate for a nemesis, unless she was searching for the most painful place to knife me. "Hmm," was all she'd said before returning to her work. But I still caught the little glance she tossed my way.

I brush away the nonexistent dust from my clothes. Maybe she'll like what she sees? It shouldn't matter, but increasingly, it feels like it does.

This is stupid. Leave her alone.

With a frustrated sigh, I turn away as though I'll actually manage to convince myself to walk back to the Capeside Inn. And then I turn again, facing her house once more.

When she didn't reply last night to my text about picking her up, and then never showed to excavate Arthur's victims, I tried to convince myself that she just needed some space to process our mind-blowingly hot sex from the night before. Well, *I* thought it was mind-blowing. The best sex I've ever had, and I know it's not just the mushrooms talking. It just felt *right* with her. Natural. Like our energy fit together, two magnets snapping into place. But maybe she doesn't feel the same way, and it chews me up. She still didn't reply this morning. And when I texted her an hour ago, she didn't reply to that either.

As the minutes have trudged onward, I've become increasingly worried about her. She's usually so responsive. This isn't like her. It's bad enough that she might be avoiding me, though I could understand that, given the circumstances. But what if it's something worse? What if she's sick? Hurt and alone? She operates in shadowed circles. What if some of those ghosts have caught up with her? What if Arthur has turned on her? What if she's—

I cut my thoughts off before they can spiral into my darkest fears and march through the gate, not stopping until I'm pounding on her door.

"Harper . . ." No sound comes from within her cottage. I knock again and press my ear to the door. Still nothing. "*Harper.*"

I catch a muffled groan that sounds as though it's coming from the back of the house.

In a heartbeat, I'm striding down the flagstone path that skirts the side of the cottage. I'm nearly at the corner when the front door opens and I halt abruptly at the sound of my name.

"Nolan . . . ?" Harper's head pokes out the door, her eyes flicking toward the street before landing on me once more. "What are you doing here?"

Relief is a flood that washes through my veins. It's followed quickly by a wave of embarrassment.

And then, suspicion.

There's something wild in her eyes. A sharpness in their silver shards. She retreats just a little, backing into her lair like a feral creature. She looks like she's ready to run. What I wouldn't give to see a wicked smile flash across her face before she bolts away from me with a challenge to catch her. Maybe she's wearing those tiny sleep shorts that highlight every curve in her ass and that low-cut tank top that hugs her breasts. The sudden fantasy of chasing her down and fucking her brutally as she screams my name goes straight to my cock.

I clear my throat in the hopes that it might somehow clear my mind too as I walk closer to the door, my steps careful and cautious.

"I was . . ." What do I say? *I was obsessively worrying about you until I finally decided to trespass on your property, which I've already done several times, though you don't know that . . . ?* Fuck, that sounds awful. "I was at the river last night. Alone, despite the fact I don't know where to dig. Figured I should stop by to make sure you were coming this evening, seeing as how we've got a strict schedule to adhere to."

"I'll be there."

Her assurance is delivered with no biting edge, no roll of her eyes. And *that's* what worries me the most. She retreats farther as I near the door, shielding her body behind the slab of wood so that only her face is visible in the narrow crack of light.

What if she's naked?

What if she's naked and *not alone*?

Jealousy explodes through every cell in my body, incinerating my earlier fantasies into bitter ash.

I do my best to convince myself that whatever she's hiding is none of my business. That the only reason I care about her well-being is because it has the potential to affect me too. As soon as I'm sure she's all right, I promise myself to go back to the inn and leave her the fuck alone. "Everything okay?" I manage, my words slow and measured.

"Yep." She nods emphatically. "Great."

"Can I come in?"

"Why?"

"Why not?"

"Because you hate me and you want to kill me?"

Touché. "Not . . . right now."

"That doesn't fill me with confidence."

I lay my palm on the door and her eyes dart to it before landing back on me with enough fury to set my skin on fire. When I put just a little pressure on the wood, she pushes back. "Why are you being so weird?"

She snorts a sardonic laugh. "You're the one who's pushing on my door like the fucking psychopathic serial killer that you are. I have your precious book, don't forget. If you think you're going to stop by to kill me, think again."

"I'm not here to hurt you," I say, my heart scraping my ribs on its way to my guts as her glare intensifies beneath the dark bangs that frame her eyes. I've been unraveling my grip on the idea of vengeance, one talon at a time. But it's obvious Harper would never believe that. And it's going to be fucking difficult to convince her. Maybe even impossible. She might need my help so

badly that she's willing to go out into the night and dig up bodies with me. But despite what she said when I fucked her, she doesn't truly trust me.

And in this moment, as I'm standing as an uninvited guest at the doorstep of her home, caught in the corrosive power of her mercury stare, a realization hits me so hard it steals the air from my chest. That as much as I've wanted justice for Billy's murder and the injuries that will haunt me forever, the need for retribution has kept me trapped in the past. If I'd come here wanting to meet Harper and, unfathomably, forgive her, a whole different life might have risen around me. But I've been so focused on our history that I might have destroyed the seeds of our future before they even had a chance to grow.

My hand slips from the door, landing back at my side. A thick swallow grinds down my dry throat. "I'm sorry, Harper," I say, and her brow furrows with wary surprise. "I shouldn't have—"

Another pained groan comes from the back of the house. And it sounds like a muffled plea for help.

Alarm detonates across Harper's features. Her eyes are impossibly wide, her full lips parted in a sharp inhale. I'm sure my expression is a mirror of hers. And for a suspended heartbeat, we're trapped in time, unmoving.

In the next breath, she slams the door in my face as I pivot and take off running down the path that hugs the cottage.

I make it to the back corner of the house just as the kitchen door slams and Harper bursts out onto the patio.

"Harper . . ." My shocked stare travels from her toes to the top of my head and back down again, trying to make sense of what I'm seeing. "What the *fuck*?"

She's wearing her gardening gloves and overalls, a black pair this time, and her favorite leather work boots, but they're covered with makeshift plastic booties fixed to her ankles with duct tape. Her hair is tied in a messy ponytail with a red bow, as though she's ready to do a musical song-and-dance routine with the ax that's clutched in her left hand. Her bangs and wisps of stray locks frame her flushed face. But it's her cropped T-shirt that really grabs my attention.

Craft-A-Corpse! the retro font says over the white fabric that's stained with splashes of blood. And I am *one hundred percent* positive that it's not more of Maya's Berry Blissful Bloodbath. Especially when another desperate plea for help comes from the other side of the garden wall.

Her eyes dart to the sound. I creep a step toward the gate. Harper catches the motion in her peripheral vision, and in the next blink, she takes off running with me close on her heels. By the time she makes it to the gate, I'm right behind her, and just as she's passing through it, I wrap an arm around her waist and scoop her up off the ground.

"Well, well, well," I say against her ear as she thrashes. Her sweet scent of fresh herbs and citrus floods my nostrils. "I am going to hazard a guess that you've been up to no good."

"Let me the fuck down," she snarls. She scrapes at my arm with one hand, but she's still wearing her gardening gloves and can't dig her nails in. With awkward steps, I walk in the direction of the pleas that now come in earnest, keeping her pressed to my body with her feet lifted from the ground. A man's desperate sobs come from around the corner, the spot near the freshly planted flowers where Harper likes to use her woodchipper.

"I think it's best we first check out this rather odd sound coming from your back garden, don't you agree?"

"Not really. No."

The *caw-caw-caw* of the raven sounds from the branches of the oak tree. I chuckle against her neck, relishing the way she shudders as I keep her trapped against my ribs. "Are you sure? Because it sounds like your bird has come for cookies. He wouldn't be ready to say something about 'murder,' would he?"

"Let me *down.*" Harper whacks my shin with the blunt edge of the ax. She's not delicate about it either, but I guess I should take a little comfort knowing that she chose not to use the sharp side. *Small victories,* the unhelpfully optimistic voice chimes in my head as I curse. I manage to limp us past the corner of the stone wall before I set her down, her macabre stage coming into view.

A huge man with a thin smattering of ginger hair over a sweaty scalp is lying on his stomach, his ankles and wrists tied to metal stakes that are driven into the earth at sharp angles like tent poles. He's facing our direction, a dirty cloth stuffed into his mouth and tied at the back of his head. His thick slab of a back is covered in small bleeding wounds that trail rivulets of crimson over his shuddering ribs, leaking into the grass. The scent of piss and boozy sweat lingers on the breeze. A garden tool with a long, silver handle leading to a roller of blood-covered steel spikes lies a short distance away. An even more menacing gas-powered machine that looks like a push mower is also nearby, though I can see from here that the hollow tines at the front are still clean.

With a slow blink, I turn to face Harper, who impatiently waits for me to catch up, one fist planted firmly on her cocked hip, the ax dangling from her other hand like a threat.

"What . . . is that?" I ask, not taking my eyes from Harper as I nod toward the scene beside us.

"A spike lawn aerator."

"No. *That*."

"A hollow tine lawn aerator."

I sigh and drag a hand down my face as a devious little glint fires up in her silver eyes.

"*That guy*," I say, pointing to the man who thrashes and whines on the grass. "That whole . . . situation over there."

Harper gestures to her shirt. "I'm crafting-a-corpse, what does it look like? I'm killing this asshole."

I look at the guy, then back to Harper, then back to the guy again. The raven drops down to the grass, walking at a safe distance around the man as though he's sizing up his future buffet options. When I turn my attention back to Harper, she's chewing on her bottom lip, her brows raised as though she's waiting for all my next questions so that she can hurry this along. "Why . . . ?" I finally ask.

She shrugs, swinging the ax like a ticking clock. "Pushing over a pregnant nurse was a good start. Threatening hospital staff. Acting like a complete asshole. I'm sure there's a laundry list of other stupid shit he's done in his miserable life." She leans to the side so she can get a better look at him. "Isn't that right, dickhead?"

The guy shakes his head against the lawn and begs around his gag.

"Sure. That's super believable." Harper straightens, rolling her eyes before leveling me with a no-nonsense glare. "Look. I don't have time to trawl through his entire backstory. But, if it helps—and I must say, I'm genuinely shocked that you of all people would care—I can guarantee he's a total piece of shit and a waste of the planet's finite resources. He'll be put to much better use *here*," she declares as she thuds the top of the ax onto the ground.

The guy's sniveling pleas grow desperate. He garbles a string of denials, his eyes pinned on me as he begs for help. But he's looking for hope where it can't be found. I have numerous mounting concerns about this moment, but every one of them centers on Harper. On her well-being.

As his panic escalates, I look over at her. She doesn't return my gaze. All her attention is homed in on that man. There's more than just hatred, or anger, or determination in her face. There's a very particular brand of fury. One I've seen in my own eyes. The kind that only blooms when the world peels back and you see the abyss of grief and loss and anguish that lurks beneath it. You might claw your way out, riddled with scars. You might hide your deepest, unhealing wounds just to make it through each day. You might survive it. But that's the worst part. Because you can't unsee it. You always know hell is there. It's a creature lurking in the night, ready to rip another piece from you.

You can live in fear of the next bite, or you can bite back.

And Harper Starling is ready for a meal.

I can feel the rage surging from Harper, charging the air around us until she can't contain it. Jaw clenched, she drops the ax to the grass, marching past me to the spike aerator. She picks it up and stops at the man's side.

"Did you know that the nurse you pushed over has been receiving IVF treatment for longer than I've been in Cape Carnage?" she snarls to the man as she raises the device to bring it down on his back with a sickening thwack. The spikes lodge into his flesh, his scream leaking around his gag. But Harper is merciless. She closes her grip around the metal handle and guides the roller from the base of his spine to his shoulder, laying down a fresh row of punctures that weep rivers of crimson. "Seven years. *Seven fucking years* of injections and tests and God knows whatever else she and her husband had to endure to make that baby. And you nearly took it away, you fucking piece of shit." Her voice is nothing like I've ever heard from her. She struggles to keep it steady beneath her fury and the threat of tears, and somehow, that hint of vulnerability makes her even more terrifying. "You're just another shitty tourist who thinks he can waltz into my town and hurt whoever he wants. As long as you're 'having a good time,' nothing else matters, right? So tell me, Mr. McMillan, are you *having a good time* yet?"

Harper lifts the tool off the man and stares down at him for a long moment, her back and shoulders heaving with deep breaths as she seems to force herself into a calmer state. I'm considering approaching her when she runs her forearm across her eyes, tilts her head side to side, then turns and tosses the aerator on the ground. Blowing a puff of air into her sweaty bangs, she flashes me a brittle smile and walks calmly back in my direction, leaving the injured man to sob and shake alone.

"So," she says, bending to retrieve her ax. When she straightens, she fixes her hair with a bloody glove, a slight tremor shaking her fingers. She squares her shoulders, tipping her chin up. "As you can see, I'm having a very busy day, but I can assure you I'll be at the river tonight. You can run along now to do . . . whatever it is you do here in Cape Carnage."

I open my mouth to say something, but not a single word lands on my tongue. I'm not exactly sure what to make of this situation. I assess the scene. First there's Harper, who looks fucking adorable with her cropped shirt that just barely covers the bottoms of her breasts and those baggy overalls, feral but focused determination bright in her eyes. Then there's the guy, set up like he's cosplaying a medieval torture scene at a Renaissance fair that's taken its commitment to authenticity a little too far. My eyes land next on the raven, who boldly hops close enough to snag a flap of loose skin off the man's mangled back as he lets out an agonized cry.

Dear God.

I knew Harper was game for some fucked-up shit given the situation with Arthur, but I have clearly underestimated her. And while the fact that she's into a little torture and murder should give me more reason to return to the idea of seeking vengeance against her, it's having the opposite effect. It takes every last shred of my resolve not to grab her and press her to me. To reassure her that the darkness she nurtures is safe with me. But I can tell she's not ready. It's in the way her brows knit as she watches every minuscule movement and facial expression I make.

"You know Sam has been flying drones over your property. He could see you," I warn as my heart kicks into a new gear at the thought of him being anywhere nearby.

Harper is resolute when she says, "He and his drone operator are busy elsewhere. I made sure of that. It's fine."

The man on the ground falls into silence and though I hold on to a momentary hope that he might have died of a heart attack, he's still breathing, his face now turned away from us. In the privacy afforded by his absent gaze, I take a step toward Harper. She doesn't budge, and I take another step, pushing my luck at getting a little closer. "What's going on? Why are you doing this?"

"Did you miss the part where I told you he's a waste of skin?" She scours my face with brutal scrutiny, her steely eyes narrowing. "Have you been dipping into Maya's supply of mushroom-laced blood again?"

"You're taking a big risk here," I say, dismissing her joke. "You don't take big risks."

She snorts and waves a hand in my direction, nearly grazing my chest. "You want to kill me and you help me dig up dead bodies at night. So, I beg to differ."

"You take *calculated* risks. This seems different."

"It's not, actually. Because Arthur has an infallible alibi, one that even Sam can't spin. That asshole on the ground over there is my best chance to finally convince him that Arthur isn't La Plume." When my brows furrow with an unvoiced question, a thread of pain weaves through her eyes. "Arthur is in the hospital. I went to make him some dinner and found him on the floor of the kitchen with a nasty gash on his forehead. He's . . . not doing so well. That's why I didn't come last night."

Fuck. *Fuck.* I should have thought to go find her. I should have been there. I know how much he means to her. It's obvious with how much she's willing to put herself in danger on his behalf. This is the first time I've felt guilt in . . . I don't even know how long. "Why didn't you call me?" I ask.

"Why would I do that?"

"Because I would have come."

"Why?"

She watches me like this is a legitimate question. As though she really doesn't know. Do I even know? Maybe I have for a while now, but I've just been refusing to acknowledge it. And now it strikes me with the power of a lightning bolt, spidering through my consciousness to burn my delusions away.

I'm falling for Harper Starling.

No. I can't be.

But I am.

I force a thick swallow down my throat. If Harper sees the startling revelation in my eyes, she doesn't let it show.

"I would have helped," is all I can manage.

"It's fine." She dismisses my assurance with a shake of her head, though a heaviness rests in her features, a weariness germinated from more than just one night of worry and stress. It inhabits the creases that line the space between her brows and the dark circles beneath her eyes. Her lip is swollen from biting it raw. With a metronomic cadence, she tenses and releases a fist around the handle of the ax.

"Something else is bothering you," I say. "Is it the fact that you're killing some random guy with garden implements?"

Her face scrunches as though the mere idea of that suggestion is detestable. "*Fuck* no."

"Then what's going on?" Harper looks away. She can't hold my eyes. Something is weighing on her with pounds of pressure that she can't shake off. When she chews at her bottom lip, I can't resist. I press my thumb to the pulp of flesh and pull it free of her teeth, letting my fingers trace the slope of her cheek. "*Talk to me.*"

When her eyes meet mine, they shine. Something cracks inside my heart, a fissure beneath the strata of time and anger. A sliver of space that she climbs inside, like roots between fractures in pavement. And her presence in that crevice only grows when she blinks her tears away. They mount a protest at her lash line, refusing to be subdued.

"We don't talk," Harper whispers, a dying protest. She backs away from my touch, and it stings more than I thought it would.

I let my hand fall to my side. "We're talking now."

"We are not."

"Then what are we doing?"

"We're . . . I don't know . . ." Harper looks away again. She's fighting herself with every moment that passes. A tear finally breaches her lash line. Her voice is hushed when she says, "I'm losing my best friend." Her lips tremble as she swipes at her cheek with the edge of her bloody glove. "I'm a shitty caregiver. I missed the symptoms, and now he's in the hospital when it's something I should have caught. I'm out of my depth."

She sniffs and looks down at the ground. Maybe that weight she carries is a little lighter with her confession. If I could, I'd reach out and reel her into me. Let her cry against my chest. "I don't think most people who have the responsibility of looking after another person get a guidebook. You're doing the best you can," I say instead, and her tear-filled eyes snap to mine.

"Why are you voluntarily being nice to me?" she asks. Wariness rolls from her in waves.

"Because . . . I don't want to see you upset."

Her eyes narrow. "But you've come here to inflict the maximum amount of suffering on me as possible."

"Maybe I did," I admit. "But that's not why I'm here now."

"Is this part of your game to get your book back?"

"No, I—"

A roar of sound rushes toward me, my next words cut off as I'm thrown face-first to the ground, the air shoved from my lungs. Sudden pain burns in my shoulder as a heavy block pins me to the lawn. A heartbeat later, the weight is gone, though it leaves behind something lodged deep in my deltoid. But the searing pain barely registers as fear takes over, all of it concentrated only on Harper.

When I look up, the man from the grass is stumbling toward her, ropes trailing after him with steel pegs bouncing in his wake. He has the spike aerator clutched in his hands, swinging it like a mace as Harper backs away from him. Her ax is raised, but he's got the more powerful weapon. And he's the one with everything to lose.

I grab one of the ropes, twist it around my fist, and *pull*.

The man stumbles. But he doesn't go down. He turns on me and swings the aerator in my direction. I raise my arm to take the hit. He only catches me with a wheel, but the strength of his blow radiates through my elbow in a shock of pain. I swear I can feel it vibrate through the titanium screws. I let out an agonized rasp, but a louder sound drowns me out. One of determination. *Harper.*

"Get the fuck away from him," she snarls.

Harper's ax slices through the air and lands in his neck with a sickening *thwack*. Blood lashes across my face.

Everything goes quiet. Everything goes still.

The man's wide blue eyes are fixed to mine as his fingers unfurl from the handle of the aerator. It drops to the ground next to him as he falls to his knees, his other hand rising to graze the ax lodged at the juncture of his shoulder. With a garbled, liquid swallow, he falls flat on his face and dies.

For a moment, neither of us moves. Harper's eyes coast over me to alight on the source of the pain that now throbs in my shoulder. She reaches out a tentative hand toward me, but stops herself. "Are you okay?"

A thousand images of what could have happened to her fly through my head as I rise.

"*No.* I am fucking *not okay*," I say, barely managing to keep my voice from a yell as I reach behind my shoulder to pull the peg from my flesh. I toss the bloody spike at her feet. "Jesus fucking Christ, Harper." I drag a trembling hand through my hair. Breaths saw from my chest. I want to grab her by the arms and stare into her eyes and shake her to her senses. Then I want to crush her to me and never let her go. "Don't you know what could have happened?"

A look of hurt flashes across her face. And then it dissolves into something lightless. Something *deadly*. Before I have a chance to take a breath and clarify, all her pent-up fury comes pouring from her mouth. "Oh, I fucking get it. Just like I thought. It all comes down to your fucking *scrapbook*. That's what *everything* is about, isn't it? Including the other night. You're fucking toying with me. If you can't put me in your book, you're going to find every possible way to make me suffer until you finally get it back. And then, all bets are off."

"That is one-hundred-fucking-percent *not* what this is about."

"You told me yourself that you fucking hate me. Two nights ago. As you were fucking me, remember?"

"And you asked me to fuck you like I hated you—"

"That's the difference between us. You actually do hate me."

I blink, momentarily thrown off by her words. Judging by the shaken expression that fleets across her face before she subdues it, she is too. "I do not."

"I don't believe you, Nolan."

"Then I guess we're not that different after all, are we?" I snarl as I crowd her space and stare down at her. "Because you're determined to believe what you want to, no matter what contrary evidence is staring you in the fucking face."

She eats the remaining distance, leaving only a thread of space between us. "That's *exactly* the kind of shit an enemy would do. Use their opponent's own words against them. And they certainly wouldn't say 'thank you for saving my life.'"

For the briefest moment, her gaze drops to my lips. She's so close that her chest touches mine with every heaving breath. I want to crash into her, to claim those plump lips. To claim all of her. But she shoves past me with a derisive snort, stopping beside the dead man to press a boot to the back of his head as she works the ax free of his neck. When it finally releases, she notches it over her shoulder, and with a final, cutting glare, she marches away.

"You're fucking welcome," she yells as she reaches the garden gate. Middle finger tossed over her shoulder, she disappears. The image of the ribbon bouncing in her ponytail as blood drips from the ax to spatter her shirt with drips of crimson burns through my mind long after the back door of the cottage slams shut.

I look to the body on the ground as the raven swoops down from the garden wall to survey his next meal. "Pretty murder bird," he says.

But it's only Harper's voice I hear.

TOWLINE

Harper

I RUN MY HANDS DOWN my skirt, one that has an almost Victorian-era feel despite the hem landing just below my knees, its black-and-white stripes unusual and quirky, perfect for the evening's festivities. With a short-sleeved black top and black tights and a pair of retro deep red velvet oxford heels, I'm cute as hell. Then I loop a red ribbon around my ponytail. *Even cuter.* I just wish Nolan could see me in something other than muddy or bloody clothes.

No, I don't. That's fucking stupid.

Is it, though?

It feels like the most asinine thing I could ever do would be to put my trust—my *real* trust, not my tenuous "I have your skin-book and you will do what I want" trust—in a man who has explicitly said that he would hunt the deepest reaches of hell to find me. One who has come here to kill me. Of all the women in the world, I cannot be the one to roll over and say, "Take me now, Murder Daddy."

Fuck no. Not after what I've survived.

A deep sigh fills and empties from my lungs and I press my eyes closed, rolling my neck where tension has been endlessly building until it feels ready to snap. My head says I can't do it. But my heart sees the hurt in his eyes when I told him I didn't believe that he could care about anything other than the belongings Lukas hid on my behalf. It looked real.

But appearances can be so deceiving that they're deadly.

I leave the floor-length mirror to open the top drawer in my dresser. Beneath my lingerie is a small, nondescript jewelry box. One I don't open often. I couldn't bear to put it beneath the floor-boards or on the makeshift gravestone in the Lancaster family plot of the cemetery. But I can hardly look at it either.

I take the watch out and lay it on my palm.

There's no strap. Just the shattered crystal and scratched dial of a TAG Heuer Autavia. A faint smile passes over my lips as I remember Adam's twenty-first birthday. We went to dinner with his parents. They gave him this watch. Adam was so surprised. He was always joyful, generous with his laughter and kind words. But that night, he was so vibrant he lit up the whole room. That was the day before we left on our adventure to live the van life for the next two years.

My smile fades.

"I can tow you. I've got a garage. I'll fix that van right up for ya," Harvey Mead's voice echoes from memory, corrupting my mind like ink on pristine paper.

Adam had given him the same glowing grin he gave to every-one. "That would be so great, thank you."

I remember Mead smiling at Adam in return, but it never reached the lightless abyss of his eyes. He walked back to his tow truck as I whispered to Adam, "Are you sure about this?"

"Yeah," he'd said, running a hand over my hair before placing a kiss on my forehead. "He seems all right."

I open my eyes as the image of scattering vultures flutters through my mind.

I blink down at the watch. It looks just the same as it did when I pulled it from the ashes of Harvey Mead's house. Just the same as when I tried to give it to Adam's parents. When Mrs. Cunningham's hand folded around mine and she told me to keep it. She never once tried to make me feel guilty for being the one to survive that hell where her son was torn apart. But I still felt it anyway.

There were many times I wished it had been me who died there. Grief debrided me like teeth on a grater, shaving away every piece of me until only ribbons of my life were left behind. And every time I tried to pick them up and mold them into something that looked vaguely familiar, they fell apart. I had to let go of the woman I used to be and glue my shredded pieces together with shadow and sin to feel anything close to whole again.

I can't just give that up. I can't force that broken woman back into the light. I can't unravel this life I've created here in Cape Carnage. I cannot, *I will not*, let Nolan Rhodes take it from me.

I set the watch inside the box, staring down at it for a long moment before I place it back in the dresser and walk into town, forgoing the opportunity to ride with Lukas so he can have some one-on-one time with his grandfather. It feels good to just walk for the sake of it. Lately, it's just been a constant swirl of gardening, refurbishing the soapbox racer, crafting a fake corpse, and, for the last three nights, ever since I dispatched Mr. McMillan on my lawn, working in near-silence with Nolan to exhume Arthur's long-buried victims.

I finally mustered up the courage last night to apologize for nearly getting him killed and then yelling at him, though he didn't give me much of a reaction, unless a bottomless, indecipherable stare of molten darkness qualifies as tacit acceptance. At least I tried, I guess. It won't be a bad thing to get a break from Nolan for a night. I should probably be getting ready to head to the river right now, but I just can't bear to miss one of Arthur's favorite annual events on his first day out of the hospital.

So on this warm, clear evening, I soak in the details of my town on a leisurely stroll instead. From the ornate wooden scrollwork on the peaked roofs of houses to the hanging baskets I take care of every summer, Cape Carnage is a place I finally feel at home. It looks after me. And I look after it, just the way Arthur has taught me.

Tonight kicks off the time of year when I need to be most vigilant. The official start of tourist season. The opening event of the Carnival of Carnage Festival.

There's already a lineup outside the theater when I arrive on Maple Street. It's a mix of visitors and townsfolk. Some of them are dressed in costumes aligning with tonight's show. Others are like me, festive but not going so far as dressing like candelabras or teapots or burly nineteenth-century hunters. Some, mostly tourists, are casual. I eavesdrop on conversations and soak in the atmosphere until my ticket is finally taken and I make my way inside, grabbing popcorn and a soda. I find a seat in the center of the seventh row, using my handbag to save the one next to me for Arthur. I settle in, reading the playbill as I wait for the auditorium to slowly fill up.

"Well, well," a familiar voice says to my left after only a few moments of blessed serenity. I close my eyes for a beat and blow out a long, slow breath that does nothing to alleviate the irritation that seems to drown me from the inside. Okay, maybe a little excitement too, but I do my best to trample that. "What a surprise seeing you here."

A waft of sandalwood and cedar drifts around me as Nolan

Rhodes takes a seat at my side. I keep my eyes closed, unwilling to be assaulted by his infuriating hotness. "I'm sure."

"Cape Carnage Theater presents *Beauty and the Beast*. That's fitting, don't you think?" he asks.

I crack open a single eye and glare at him. The instant I catch his gaze, one corner of his lips pulls back into a lopsided smile. I barely repress a groan.

"Since I'm so beautiful and all." He runs a hand through his hair with dramatic flair.

"And I'm such a monster, right?"

"You're the one who said it, not me." His smirk dissolves into an unflinching stare, a mirror of my own. It feels like it takes far too long for him to drop his attention to the paper in his hands. "What is this?" Nolan asks as he reviews the playbill, a crease notched between his brows.

"Do you have reading comprehension problems? You literally just read the title to me."

Nolan rolls his eyes and reaches over for a fistful of my popcorn.

I slap his hand. "Get your own."

"I got the title part. But what I don't understand is why there's a content warning for *Beauty and the Beast*. It's Disney."

"This is Cape Carnage. Nothing is Disney. This is the antithesis of Disney." I scowl at Nolan, and he returns my irritation with a steely glare of his own. "If you don't like it, leave."

A sardonic smile sneaks across his lips. "I'm comfortable right here, thanks."

Something darkens in his expression, and it summons heat beneath my bones, deep in the cavern where my soul should be. There's no light in his eyes. No air between us. The voices and laughter, people moving to their seats, the instruments warming up in the little orchestra pit—it all fades away. There's only Nolan and the way he watches me, as though he would tear my heart out with his bare hands if I didn't have his precious book hidden away. Like he would hunt me to the darkest hidden corners of the earth if I ever tried to disappear. I almost want to run, just to be chased by him. To be caught and bound, forced to face whatever fate is lurking in his predatory machinations. But I'm too ensnared by him to go anywhere.

And I'm too slow to react when he steals a fistful of popcorn from the bucket on my lap.

I blink as though clearing my mind from a haze and move the bucket, holding it on the empty seat next to me and out of his reach. When I face him once more, he seems quite pleased with himself, as though he's fully aware of the effect he has on me, whether I like it or not. "Go. Away."

"Too late. I paid the ticket price."

"I'll personally reimburse you."

"There's no amount of money that would mean more to me than your suffering, no matter how minute. Isn't that what you think?" he says, that darkened, mocking smile of his still fixed on his face. I roll my eyes and lean forward to look beyond him before I twist in my seat, searching the patrons entering the theater. "What is it?"

"Stop pretending like you care, Nolan. It doesn't suit you," I mutter, leaning from one side to the other as I try to catch a glimpse past a small group of tourists entering the theater. "He should be here already. He hates being late."

"Who?"

I glance in his direction, and I'm surprised when I catch the faintest glimmer of concern in his furrowed brow. But I know him. The only thing he cares about is that fucking book, and the only reason he'd ask is either to assess the risk to his prized possession or to explore the opportunity of getting it back. "It's not with him, so don't even fucking go there," I warn, continuing my thoughts out loud. Nolan's head tilts and he frowns as though he's genuinely confused.

I slice him with a final glare and then shift my attention to the back of the room where I finally spot Arthur in an impeccable three-piece suit, one hand wrapped around the indigo handle of his black oak cane, the other gripped to Lukas's bicep. I let out a long breath through pursed lips. "Thank fuck."

I can feel Nolan's gaze on the side of my face, burning beneath my skin. But I don't look his way. I turn my back on him instead, watching as Arthur and Lukas progress down the shallow steps that lead to the row where I'm sitting. When they get to my aisle, I rise, surprised when I sense Nolan do the same beside me.

"I was getting worried," I say as Arthur takes my hand and we exchange a *bise* greeting.

Arthur grunts, casting a vicious glare at his grandson. "I despise being late."

"We know," Lukas replies as he leans around the old man to give me a brief hug. "You mentioned it no less than forty thousand times on the drive here."

"Who are you?" When we separate, Arthur is sizing up Nolan, a look of suspicion folding his skin into wrinkles that seem even more menacing than their resting state, particularly with the stitched gash that's still healing on his forehead.

"Nolan Rhodes, sir." Nolan extends a hand past me, and though it takes Arthur a beat to move, he accepts the handshake. "Pleased to meet you."

I suppress the urge to groan, but only barely. *Of course* Nolan would lay his accent on a little thicker and put on his most charming facade for Arthur. All I need is for these two to suddenly become friends. "Nolan, this is Arthur, and that's Lukas."

"Good to meet you," Lukas says, and though Nolan replies with the same, it feels cold, summoning a chill across my skin. When I peek up at Nolan, he's closer than I thought he'd be, his presence looming only an inch from my back. His attention shifts from Lukas to me, dropping to linger on my lips. Blood dances in my veins. I give him a quirked brow, an unvoiced question. When his eyes latch to mine once more, he backs up a step, then sits. The distance between us is a cold whisper in my flesh.

I clear my throat and give a little shake of my head. When I turn my attention back to Lukas, he looks puzzled. "All okay?"

"Of course," I say, squaring my shoulders. "Just wondering what took you so long."

A slow, sardonic grin slides across Lukas's lips, summoning a ball of dread into my flip-flopping guts. "You must have put the house keys in the dishwasher, Harper. It took me forever to find them."

Shit. "I absolutely *did not*—"

Arthur hits me with one of his lightless, menacing stares. "Why would you put them there? If you wish to clean them, Harper, use the silverware polish if you must. It was an infuriating search."

Judgy bus, Lukas mouths over the top of Arthur's head as he settles his grandfather into the seat next to mine.

"But—"

Lukas's eyes light with sparks of vengeance. "Judgy bus, Harper," he whispers. "Just let it happen."

"Harper," Arthur barks, and I cringe. "The hedges need to be trimmed."

I dart a glare at Lukas, whose smile only widens. I try not to look too petulant when I turn my attention to the old man, who glares at me over the rims of his reading glasses. "I can start them this week—"

"Into *shapes*."

"W-what?" I ask, though Arthur has shifted his focus to his playbill, pinching the arm of his probably ridiculously expensive reading glasses as he skims the details. A thick swallow slides down my throat. Dread slinks down my spine. Lukas can barely contain his glee. I cast a glance to Nolan on my other side, though I don't know why. He might look a little perplexed, but I'm sure he's busy trying to devise ways to increase my future suffering. I return my attention to Arthur, my voice thin and tight when I say, "What kind of shapes?"

Arthur waves a hand toward me, not looking up from the paper. "Animals. A swan for the boxwood in the center of the circular drive—"

"But—"

"And a series of native species for the yews in the front garden. Perhaps a bear. Maybe a moose, but it must be majestic. Befitting of Lancaster Manor."

Lukas hides his laugh in his fist, barely keeping it under control when I reach past Arthur to smack him in the arm. "I've gotta go get ready," he says, backing away toward the aisle. "Don't want to be late for opening night. Have fun."

"Break both legs. Maybe also your hands while you're at it."

"Doesn't sound like such a bad idea. You'll get to do the gutters next time if I do." With a wink and then a nod to Nolan, Lukas turns and strides away.

"Arthur, I don't know anything about topiary," I say, clutching my popcorn to my chest as I lower to sit between the two men. "How am I supposed to make a moose?"

"Practice, Harper. Use your own garden." Arthur takes a fistful of popcorn without even looking in my direction. "We nearly lost the best garden award to Sarah Winkle last season. We need to come out with something spectacular."

He's right, we do need to come out with something spectacular. Arthur is too curmudgeonly and I'm too taciturn to join something as sociable as the gardening club, and those fuckers have been banding together to take us down. I'm afraid there aren't enough deserving dead tourists to win against their creativity on the quality of the blooms alone. "I'm just not sure a topiary moose is going to seal the deal for best garden of Cape Carnage, Arthur."

Nolan takes his own successful swipe at my popcorn. "Especially not if it winds up looking like a hunk of ballmeat."

When I slice a glare in his direction, his eyes brighten with amusement. And while I'm distracted, Arthur takes his chance to steal another handful of popcorn. With an exasperated sigh, I shove the whole bucket in his direction and stand, rogue kernels falling from my skirt. "Trade places with me please, Arthur."

"I'm comfortable."

"If you move, you can more comfortably share your popcorn with this"—I wave a hand in the general direction of Nolan behind me—"*thing* over here, instead of both of you reaching over me. Plus, you'll be smack in the center of the row. Best seat in the house."

"Where are you going," he demands, rather than asks.

I start moving past him, the patrons a few seats away shifting to make room for me to exit the aisle. "To get my own popcorn. Maybe I'll go backstage and see if Lukas needs help with his costume."

"Hmpf."

"Trade places with me and I'll bring you back Milk Duds. You know they're contraband."

I barely get out my last word and Arthur is rising just enough to slide into my vacated spot. When I shift my glare to Nolan, he's leaning forward in his seat, watching me with an intensity that hums through the confines of my skull. I feel tilted from my axis. Off-center. Like someone has shoved me to the edge of reality.

I blink and turn away. I just got up too fast, that's all it is.

With a shake of my head, I shimmy my way down the aisle until I reach the stairs. And though I don't look back, I still feel his eyes on the back of my neck. When I touch it, there's a current beneath my skin. It doesn't leave until I'm at the top of the stairs. But even when I'm consumed by shadow, the electric murmur is there.

I head into the bright lobby, where people are still mingling and standing in line for refreshments. I join the line, deciding I'm going to get myself a cocktail along with my popcorn. I need something much stronger than soda to deal with Nolan. I'm watching the bartender make a pair of cocktails with gummy eyeball candies stabbed with cocktail sticks when I feel a presence behind me. Someone watching me with intense, obsessive interest. But unlike the weight of Nolan's gaze, which ignites a resonant pulse in my veins, this observer leaves only frost behind. I know who it is before he steps to my side and says, "You look so familiar."

My heart lurches into my throat as I turn and give Sam Porter the most bland, unaffected look I can manufacture. "Really?" I squint and cock my head to one side. "I'm afraid you don't look familiar to me at all, sorry."

Like me, Sam also arranges his face into a mask. But it's not infallible. Though his smile is benign, he can't manage to subdue the kaleidoscopic gleam in his eyes. There's excitement there, and the anticipation of a hard-earned victory. But there's urgency too. Maybe a bit of concern. He extends a hand to me, and I hesitate a beat before I slip my palm against his. "I'm Sam Porter. Pleased to meet you."

I pump his hand once, and two of his fingers slip against my wrist as though he's hoping to feel the beat of my hammering pulse, his eyes fused to mine. I slide my hand free. "Harper," I say.

"Harper . . . ?"

A beat of time seems to pull apart around us. All the sounds of the reception hall fade as my options are snipped away. "Starling."

Sam nods, as though this is the response he expected. "That's a unique name."

"Is it?" I face forward, keeping my eyes on the reprieve of the ordering counter, which seems like a continent away with several people still in line before me. Sam stands at my side. I don't know why it bothers me so much that people around us could think we're some cute little couple on a quirky first date, me with my striped skirt and retro heels and red bow, Sam with his blond hair combed into place and button-up navy shirt and features that I qualify as "sensibly handsome." Fuck, I hate the idea that people might think we're together, though I don't know why. It feels like a skin I need to shed.

I turn the opposite way from Sam to look over my shoulder, but I can't see the familiar face I'm searching for. The person who would feel right at my side.

First, I can't get rid of Nolan. And suddenly, it's his presence I crave.

"You don't look like a Harper," Sam says, pulling my attention back to him. He leans a little closer to me as we move a step forward toward the counter. His voice is low and earnest when he says, "The only Harper Starling your age was presumed dead when her car crashed into the sea after a hit-and-run accident in Maryland four years ago."

"What a weird thing to say to a complete stranger." Adrenaline siphons into my veins. My stomach churns. A swallow drags down my throat before I do my best to pin Sam with an unwavering stare. "I guess your data is wrong. Because I didn't hit anyone and I'm certainly not dead."

"Or maybe you're just a different kind of ghost," he says, his voice barely more than a whisper. He stares back at me as though trying to reach the most hidden crevices of my soul. "Maybe one who goes by an entirely different name?"

My lungs seize around air. "What do you want?" I ask, reining in the sting in my throat.

"The truth."

"My name is Harper, and Arthur Lancaster is not La Plume. There you go. Truth has been served. You can leave now."

"From what I understand, you live in his cottage."

"I'm his gardener. But I'm sure you know that too."

"So you don't have a vested interest in protecting him?"

"Arthur is an elderly man who is *dying*. He was just released from the hospital. Of course I want to protect him from anyone like you who's clearly got him all wrong," I hiss, managing to restrain my knowledge of whispers of McMillan's disappearance. Those rumors already hit the Sleuthseekers Discord server thanks to one of my sock puppet accounts. "Leave him alone. He and I have both been through *enough*."

I feel the eyes of nearby patrons turn to me with the tension that hangs in the air, even if my words were too quiet to hear. Furious tears blur my vision no matter how hard I try to suppress them. Sam's expression softens when he sees them, and for some reason, that angers me even more. I step forward to the counter and try to focus all my attention on calmly ordering Arthur's candy, hoping Sam will leave. But he doesn't. When I turn with the Milk Duds in hand to stalk back to the theater, he's right behind me, blocking me in among the crowd.

"Look, I'm sorry. That was unfair. I don't mean to upset you, truly. I'm just looking for answers. I know something strange is going on in Cape Carnage. You've been here long enough, you must know it too. And you could be in danger here." Sam slides a hand into his pocket and withdraws a business card, holding it up between us. "Please. I just want to talk. Even if it's off the record. You could be the key to understanding what's really happening in this town." I stare at him, the card lodged like a white thorn in my peripheral vision. Someone in line behind us clears their throat in a wordless prompt to encourage us out of the way. But Sam and I remain unmoving. "Please," he finally whispers.

I take the card and leave.

"I found some things that I think you might find familiar," he says before I can move out of earshot. I turn and scrutinize Sam with a cautionary glare. But the look he gives me is a warning in reply. "They were hidden in an old house on Clarke Road. I'll keep them safe until you're ready to talk about how they got there and why they suddenly showed up three days ago."

"I'm afraid I don't know what you mean," I say. With a final nod, I give him my coldest stare, and then I walk away.

Breaths shudder in my lungs as I weave through the patrons and make my way back to the auditorium entrance. My hands are shaking. Sweat itches at the nape of my neck. I suck in air like I'm drowning, trying to calm my raging pulse. With a longing look toward the entrance of the ladies' restroom, where I'm tempted to let tears fall in the privacy of a bathroom stall, I keep going, reluctant to leave Arthur alone with Nolan for longer than necessary.

And when I sidestep my way back to my seat, that concern is proven to be valid.

"Why are you there?" I ask, pointing to where Arthur sits. There's an empty space between him and Nolan. "You're supposed to be in *that* seat. Next to *him*."

"It's the tourists. They kept trying to take that seat," Arthur hisses at me in a whisper of disgust. He waves a hand in Nolan's direction without looking his way. "This man suggested I move over one place and he would help me keep the one in between us free for you, so I obliged."

"But I promised you Milk Duds," I say, rattling the box.

"He offered me Maltesers."

Arthur gives me a smug look as he digs into the half-eaten pack of Maltesers for another ball of chocolate-coated malted milk. My mouth drops open. *Fucking traitor.* This is the last thing I need after the encounter with Sam Porter in the lobby. My thoughts are already spiraling through my grasp, pinging through my brain as though my skull can't contain them. I can't even manage a cohesive retort. I just close my mouth and shimmy past Arthur to drop into the empty seat between him and Nolan.

"I thought you were getting popcorn," Nolan says, though I barely register his words, my thoughts consumed by the encounter in the lobby as I scan the audience in my hunt for Sam.

"Yeah . . . popcorn. I was . . ."

I don't know where Sam went. Though I turn enough to dart a glance behind me, I face forward after only a moment, unwilling to let him see how much he's rattled me if he's still watching.

I try to anchor my focus to the stage where the drawn curtains rustle, the stagehands on the other side finalizing their preparations for the show.

How do I keep my past out of this place? How do I stay hidden on the other side of the curtain when someone is gripping the rope, ready to pull back the darkness and force me into the light? What more will everyone be able to see if he thrusts me onto that stage?

"Harper." It's the concern in Nolan's voice that shoves me out of the alternate realm I've dropped into and back into the real world. It's as though he doesn't even try to hide it. Like it's real. Not part of a game, not a trick. Not a lie.

"What?" I ask, though it comes out weaker than I wanted it to.

Nolan searches my face. There's darkness in his eyes. It has an edge that will cut to the bone, if I let it. "What happened?"

"Nothing." I try to break my attention away, but it returns to him as though I can't fight the pull of his tide. He's washing me out to sea. "I'm fine."

"What happened?" he repeats. He lays a hand on my arm. I swear it sends a current all the way to the base of my spine.

I give him the slightest shake of my head. Maybe most people wouldn't even notice. But I know he does. When I bite my lip, his gaze drops to the motion. "It's nothing you can fix."

"Who are you?" Arthur demands on the other side of me. We both turn toward the elderly man sitting to my right. Suspicion is a thin veil for the confusion in the cataract haze of his cloudy gray eyes. "Are you bothering my daughter?"

A sting bites at the back of my throat. I can see Arthur trying to match up connections that don't fit. Flickers of emotion pass across his face. He knows I'm not Poppy. But he also knows he loves me like the daughter who was stolen from him. Just like I love him like the father I lost. Like the friend I needed most when I was alone in the world. It's fucking heartbreaking to know that someday soon, he won't remember me at all. But the hardest moments of Arthur's dementia are the ones like this, where his most painful memories are dragged out to sea and muddled in the churning waters of time, only to crash in on him once more. It's the cycle of forgetting life's most devastating moments and jumbling them up with the present. And then, most cruelly of all, remembering them all over again.

When I return my attention to Nolan, his brow is furrowed, his eyes searching. They traverse every detail of my face, hunting through flesh and bone. I'm not sure what he sees. Maybe a wisp of panic, though I do my best to hide it. I hate the thought of him finding the chinks in Arthur's formidable armor. I hate the thought of him finding a weakness in *me*. I know he sees something beneath the unyielding mask I'm trying and failing to maintain. There's some kind of awareness blooming in his features. It's in the lines that deepen between his brows. It's in the curves and creases of his eyes. It's in the flesh of his lips as they part to let a breath slide free. And then, with a blink, his expression clears. His hand lifts from my arm. He leans forward and extends it over my lap to Arthur with a faint but welcoming smile. "I'm sorry, I forgot to introduce myself. I'm Nolan Rhodes, sir. Pleased to meet you."

Arthur looks to me as though searching for reassurance before shaking Nolan's hand.

The lights dim. The two men settle back into their seats at my sides. A spotlight flicks on. The band starts up, wind instruments in a melody that weaves through hushed whispers and quiet coughs and shuffling fabric.

Nolan's hand finds mine in the dark. He doesn't look over to see a tear slide down my cheek. But he squeezes my hand like he knows it's there. I close my eyes. And I can almost see it, the way a little light glimmers in my heart. His touch is a beacon in the night.

The curtains slide back from the stage.

And then the real show begins.

BALLAST

Harper

NOLAN HOLDS MY HAND THROUGH the entire first half of *Beauty and the Beast*. When the show really gets going Cape Carnage–style and the fake blood starts spraying and my eyes stop leaking, his thumb begins to draw gentle circles, tracing the skin that's almost healed from the burn. An absent-minded pattern, as though this touch is so easy and natural that it's second nature.

I can even picture it, us as a couple sitting comfortably in the dark. What if it were a real date? Would we go for dinner afterward? Would we talk and laugh like normal people do? It's been so long since I've allowed myself the indulgent daydream about being with someone that I didn't truly realize how much I've missed it. The empty space in my chest aches in a different way than it does when I think about Adam and the way he was taken from me. I know I miss him. I know I'm lonely. But it's in *this* moment, with Nolan's warm hand wrapped around mine, that I realize the truth of what I've really been doing these last four years. I think I'm starting to understand the true impact of the trauma I've been trying to hide from. I've been so focused on surviving my grief that I've forgotten about living.

It's a nice change to ache for want, rather than for loss.

When the lights come up for intermission, Nolan squeezes my hand before finally letting go. I face him, trying to blink away the feeling that I'm waking up from a long sleep. "I'll get that popcorn," he declares, as though he won't take any argument. "Anything else?"

My mouth suddenly goes dry. I somehow manage to scrape a word together, though it sounds like a rasp. "Ballmeat."

Nolan laughs. I forgot what it sounded like. It's so infrequent that I hear it. At least, not a real, genuine laugh like this. It's resonant and warm. His face lights up, and those murder dimples come out, and *oh my God*, he's so fucking beautiful it hurts my eyes. "Not sure they have ballmeat on the menu."

"Eyeballs will have to do." I give him a weak smile when he quirks a brow in an unvoiced question. "They have a cocktail that has eyeball candies. I'll take one of those too, please."

With a nod, he checks in with Arthur, who's now finished his chocolate and is nearly done with my former popcorn, then heads off to the concession. I can't help but watch him go. His cool authority, his predatory grace. He moves as though lethality is coded into his DNA. Why does he always have to look so fucking perfect? Whether it's the work clothes he wears to our nightly adventures, or this charcoal dress shirt rolled to his elbows and black pants that expertly show off his ass, there's never a time he's unattractive to me. And it's not just the way he looks. It's something about the man beneath the shell. The way he notices the most minute details. His calm and calculating authority that swims just below the surface of a charismatic mask, one he only wears when he wants to. I'm the only person in the world who knows exactly who he really is. And that's intoxicating.

I know I should be careful when it comes to Nolan Rhodes. But I can't shake the way Nolan looked at me that day I killed McMillan. It was as though desperation and distress had chewed their way to his surface, and he couldn't hold them back.

Because you're determined to believe what you want to, he'd said. *No matter what contrary evidence is staring you in the fucking face.*

"You were holding hands with that man," Arthur says, scaring the shit out of me even though he's been next to me the whole time. I'd been too immersed in the details of Nolan's hot ass and enigmatic serial killer appeal to think about my surroundings.

God. I really need that fucking drink.

"More accurately, he was holding hands with me," I reply, as though I'm some teenager trying to downplay her first crush to her dad. It's hard not to feel that way when Arthur gives me an unblinking stare.

"Do you want me to cut his hands off?"

I snort, trying to calm the blush that burns in my cheeks. "Jesus, Arthur. No."

"I didn't think so," he says in his most curmudgeonly grumble. I shake my head and survey the seats behind me again for Sam. Satisfied there's no sign of him lurking nearby, I close my arms around my middle and I settle deeper into my chair. "So. Who is he, this man whose hand you were holding as equally as he was holding yours?"

That blush just refuses to go away. "His name is Nolan," I reply, in case he's forgotten again. "He's a tourist."

Arthur rumbles a low, disgruntled note. He's not a fan of tourists, though like all Cape Carnage residents, he understands how necessary they are for the town's flourishing economy. But with tourists comes trouble, and for a man who has spent his entire adult life looking after our odd little home, there's a built-in level of suspicion toward visitors that he'll never get over.

"Is he good to you?" he finally asks.

That simple question seems to dismantle my thoughts. It should be so easy to answer. *No*, I want to say. He came here to murder me, slowly and painfully. To slice pieces from my body and glue them into his fucked-up trophy case. But also *yes*. I know that he's helping me to help himself, but it feels like more than that. The shovel, the bear spray, the hot chocolate—though he tries to make them seem like practical things that benefit himself, he watches me as though he hopes I'll be happy when he gives them to me. The way he looks at me feels real, despite how hard I try to convince myself it's all part of his game. The hurt in his eyes the other day. I don't think that could be manufactured. Even holding my hand tonight. If he truly wanted me to suffer, if he really hated me so much, would he offer such a simple but meaningful comfort?

"I don't know," I say, though I'm not sure if it's an answer to Arthur's question or a continuation of my thoughts. "I'd like to hope so."

"That's not an encouraging answer."

"It's the best one I've got."

"Sensible," Arthur mutters before his attention wanders away. "It's difficult to judge character these days."

I don't know if he's referring to his own deteriorating health, or the general state of the world, or both. "A guidebook would be helpful. Some criteria."

"Perhaps you could ask him if he would allow his hideous little dog to relieve itself among my award-winning roses and not clean it up," he says, his eyes fixed to a bald man in his sixties who's sidestepping down the aisle three rows ahead. A woman with fluffy blonde hair follows close behind him, chunky gold chains layered around her neck. The couple looks like snowbirds, with their golf club clothes and their over-bleached smiles and their sunglasses tans. Arthur despises tourists like this. Garish. Entitled. When I first arrived in Cape Carnage, crimes such as indiscriminate dog shitting wouldn't qualify as a murderable offense—these people would have to do something legitimately heinous for Arthur to consider that. But lately . . . ? I'm not sure his barometer for what qualifies as a "murderable offense" is very accurate.

"I don't think he would allow that, no," I say.

Arthur doesn't pay me any attention. His focus is entirely homed in on this couple as they take their seats to talk and laugh just a decibel too loudly for Arthur's taste. He's still watching them intently when he suddenly says, "You can't tell him."

"Tell him what?"

Arthur turns his attention my way, his eyes clearer than they've been all night. "Who you are."

"I had no plans to. I promised you I wouldn't tell anyone, and I'm not going to break my word," I say, laying a hand on his arm and squeezing gently. "I'll look after the town, don't worry—"

"It's not for the town, Harper. It's for *you*."

My brows knit. "What do you mean?"

"The wrong man discovered my true nature, my identity, and it made me a prized target. And look at what that cost me," Arthur says. His eyes shine as he raises a hand to my face. "Keep your past safe. Or the whole world will descend upon you, and you don't know what kind of creatures will be coaxed out of hiding. I cannot bear to lose another daughter."

I can't trust my voice to form words, not when my heart is crumpling in my chest like crushed flowers. I don't tell him that

Sam is closing in. Or that keeping my identity buried might be a lost cause. I don't whisper about all the worries that are piling up around me in a suffocating embrace. I just place my hand on his. Lean into the warmth of his palm. With a nod, I reaffirm what I promised to do four years ago.

Arthur gives me a weak smile and then refocuses his attention on the couple ahead. "You're a good girl, Harper. Even though you put my keys in the dishwasher."

A breath of a laugh escapes my lips as I sneak a finger beneath my damp lashes. "Are you sure you didn't—"

"I am absolutely confident I would never put keys in a dishwasher, if that's what you were about to insinuate." Arthur's brows lower when the woman three rows ahead laughs too loudly at something the man says. "I'm looking forward to your topiaries. Perhaps you should start with a beaver."

"I don't know shit about topiaries."

"You'll learn. I have faith in you."

"Please don't."

Arthur ignores my protests as the couple continues to talk and laugh, his aggravation deepening with every moment of their existence. Though I try to pull his attention away, he seems happily steeped in his irritation, and maybe a little worn out by the emotion of our conversation. So I let us slip into companionable silence. Before long, Nolan returns with a box of popcorn in one hand and two cocktails balanced in the other.

"One Orbit-uary," he says, passing me the drink with a flummoxed expression. "This place is fucking bizarre."

"That's what's so great about Carnage. It's unapologetically weird," I say. Nolan seems to ruminate on that as I take the popcorn from him under the guise of making it easier for him to get settled next to me, but when he reaches for it, I hold it beyond his reach. "Where's yours?" I ask with faux innocence. "You didn't forget it at the counter . . . did you?"

The flat glare he gives me tastes better than the sweet cocktail I take a sip of. His eyes drop to my lips and darken. I can feel the hunger in him that has nothing to do with sugar and salt. A lick of heat coils deep in my belly. I'm flirting with him. And it's working.

Hold on a second . . .

I'm flirting with *him*.

And it's—

"Have you had dinner?" he asks. It looks as though it takes effort for him to peel his focus away from my mouth. I shake my head. He reaches over and wraps his warm palm around my forearm and reels it in until the box is resting on my lap. "We'll get dinner after."

My brows hike. My heart is flip-flopping in my chest like a fish drowning on air. "Don't we have work to do?"

Nolan just shrugs. He keeps his attention on the stage as the lights lower and a hush descends across the crowd, but I still feel the pull of his thoughts, as though he wants to meet my eyes but denies himself the indulgence. "We need to eat," he finally says.

Right. It's just eating. Normal human biological stuff. It's not as though it's a date or anything. We haven't even really gotten past the whole McMillan thing from the other day, despite my apology last night. A bit of empathetic hand-holding and some popcorn doesn't fix a murder-induced argument. Probably.

I'm not sure my heart gets the message. It reminds me of its existence with every thunderous beat. It only gets worse as the show nears the end and Lukas's Beast is shot by Gaston in a spray of blood, falling onto a crash pad just behind the set. Belle gets her revenge by bodychecking Gaston into a fire, and in a halo of pyrotechnics, the dramatic climax moves swiftly to a happy ending. I'm barely invested in the song-and-dance finale, despite the juggling act of severed limbs, not with Nolan taking up so much of my thoughts. With the final bow from the cast, I help Arthur out of his seat for the standing ovation, looping his arm through mine so I can keep him steady. When I look up at Nolan, he's watching me as though he doesn't quite know who he's looking at.

People start filing out of their seats. I move to pull Arthur with me as I start following Nolan down the row, but Arthur twists free of my arm and sits back down. "What are you doing?" I ask.

"Waiting here for Lukas," he replies, settling his cane against the empty seat on his other side. He keeps his eyes on the stage. "Go to dinner with the tourist man."

When I hesitate, he waves me off. I've been dismissed, but not without the barest hint of a smile tugging at the corner of his lips. Nolan waits at the end of the row when he realizes I'm not right behind him, and that perplexed expression is there again, as though I've defied some kind of expectation and he doesn't know what to make of me.

There's still no sign of Sam among the crowd as we pass through the foyer, nor on the street as we head outside, where a warm evening breeze envelops us with a faint scent of the sea. Many of the attendees make their way toward the Buoy and Beacon Pub for the *Beauty and the Beast*–inspired karaoke and half-price drinks. Others head toward Main Street or the shoreline where the fancier bistros and restaurants will be open late. But Nolan and I move as though caught in our own slipstream, drawn to somewhere darker and quieter in the opposite direction of the crowd, ambling slowly away from the voices and laughter and the glow of the ornate Victorian lamps that line the street. Nolan stays close to my side, and though he doesn't touch me, the heat of his presence warms my skin like a phantom caress.

"Are you going to tell me what got you rattled on your failed trip for popcorn?" Nolan asks, looking down his shoulder at me.

I let out a long, slow breath as I tamp down the urge to scan our surroundings with obvious panic. "It was Sam."

"You saw him?"

"I more than saw him. I talked to him."

A flicker of unease passes over Nolan's face, a muscle fluttering in his clenched jaw. "About Arthur?"

I shrug, pressing my nails into my palm to keep myself from biting my bottom lip. "About me."

"About *you*," he repeats, his voice incredulous. Fury cascades from him in thick waves. "Why? What did he want?"

"My story." It's not a lie. But Nolan watches me as though he knows it's not the truth either. "He wants to interview me for his documentary. I think he's still convinced that Arthur is La Plume. And he definitely knows there's more to Cape Carnage than meets the eye."

"Do you think when it comes out more widely that this McMillan guy is missing that it will throw him off course?"

"That's what I'm hoping, but I don't know," I reply. "I thought that if it happened while Arthur was clearly in the hospital, it would be a perfect alibi that could finally put that whole 'Arthur is La Plume' theory to bed. I'm sure another disappearance will keep Sam interested in Carnage, but at least Arthur will be safe, and I figured that if he doesn't have a body or the suspect he wanted to pin everything on, he'd be forced to leave eventually. But what if

Sam's too distracted to focus on anything other than the story he's determined to tell? Maybe this has all been a waste of effort."

"It's not." Nolan takes my hand. There's such a relief in the warm touch. I don't know what's changing between us, or why. I can't understand the tortured expression he gives me. I just know I don't want this feeling to end. "I'll find a way to steer him on the right path."

"The 'right' path leads straight to me. Maybe I . . ." I swallow, looking away to the growing shadows that surround us. "Maybe I made a mistake. Let my emotions take too much control until I talked myself into making the wrong choice."

"The 'right path' leads out of this fucking town. And that's exactly where he's going to go. That's a fucking promise, Harper," he says, his voice low and laced with a vicious edge. His hand tightens around mine. When I look up at Nolan, there's no doubt written in his face, no trepidation. He's not a hero. This is not a promise bound by morality. Nolan Rhodes is a villain. He'll lie, he'll manipulate, he'll even kill for this promise. He would burn this town to ash to keep his word. "You did what you had to do, and he'll leave when he doesn't get the story he wants. We just have to stay the course."

I give him a weak smile, a nod. But I know it will be hard to refocus Sam on one injured quarry when he's already closing in on the bloody trail of another.

Nolan might not know the full details of my encounter with Sam, but I wonder if he's thinking the same thing when he keeps hold of my hand as we follow a winding path of packed gravel that leads to an empty playground. Or maybe he's thinking about all the ways he intends to throw Sam off course. Though I steal glances at him from the corner of my eye, I can only see stern determination in his expression as he keeps his sights on the path ahead. And maybe I shouldn't trust too much in his promises. But as we slow to a stop and look down over the trail we took to get here, I find that I do believe him. I might not have faith in heroes. But I trust the man at my side to make a vow and keep it.

For a while, we just stand in silence to observe the town and the growing dark. From our little hill, we can see the attendees making their way in different directions. The sea shimmers in the distance, picking up the last light of the fading day. "We should let them all figure out where they're headed," he says. "So we don't have to fight for a table somewhere."

I sit on one of the swings, rocking back and forth. "Though I'd like to see a fight to the death over the Buoy's nachos, I agree. I've eaten my body weight in popcorn anyway."

Nolan gives me a faint smile before taking the swing next to mine. For a long while, we don't talk, letting the swings squeak in harmony instead. I spot Lukas emerging from the theater with Arthur. He helps him to the curb, and though we can't hear the words, I can make out the body language clearly enough to see that Lukas is about to chuck himself under the judgy bus. When Arthur pops his grandson on the head with the handle of his cane, I snort a laugh.

"How did you meet him?" Nolan asks as we watch Lukas jog down the street toward the nearby public parking lot.

I have a lie ready for exactly this question, one Arthur himself made up for me four years ago. I could feed Nolan the same story about being distant relatives. But instead, I say, "I was boondocking near the Lancaster Distillery. I walked into town to get supplies one day and I was passing by this same park when I saw an old Chevy Nova drive by. My dad used to tinker with vintage cars, so I noticed it right away. But then a few minutes later, it passed me again, heading in the same direction. And then again, a few minutes later."

"Someone was following you?" he asks, and though he tries to keep his voice even, there's still a thread of malice woven into its notes.

"That's what I thought at first. So I stopped and pretended to tie my boot and watched for the car to come again. I thought maybe I was just paranoid. But sure enough, the old Nova drove past a fourth time. Just one man in the car. Going slow. But he wasn't looking at me. He was watching three little girls playing tag at the park with no grown-up around. I just . . . had a feeling . . ." I swing back and forth, looking toward the street as I recall the instinct that fired to life in my veins. And the *rage*. Nolan's fist tightens around the chain in my peripheral vision, and I can feel that same fury churning within him. We might have started as enemies. Two monsters who are missing their souls. But our shadows share a likeness. "I came up here and sat on the swings, just close enough to keep watch on the girls. And that night, I hunted him down. Except Arthur had found him first, and I waltzed in just after the kill."

"And Arthur didn't try to attack you?" Nolan asks.

"He was pretty surprised, but no. Not at all. We kind of hit it off, actually. Shared interests and all that." A wistful smile rises on my lips as I watch Lukas park in front of the theater just long enough to help his grandfather into the passenger seat of the old Jaguar, and then they're off, headed for the estate. "By the end of the night, he offered me a permanent home if I promised to learn how to look after Carnage the same way he always has. The rest is history."

I feel Nolan watching me, but I don't return his gaze. "That's a lot of responsibility."

"Yeah, but it's a strange town. It attracts a lot of great people, sure. But a place like this summons the shitty ones too. It would quickly turn to chaos if someone weren't here to protect it. Yates and his deputies certainly aren't up to the task, and it's not like Arthur can do it forever. Someone's gotta take his place and look after Cape Carnage."

"Don't you find it exhausting?"

"Sure," I say with a shrug. "Sometimes."

"You look after Cape Carnage. You look after Arthur." The weight of all his attention burrows into the side of my face. "Who looks after *you*?"

My swinging slows to a stop. My lungs stall around a breath. The scent of sandalwood and cedar still lingers in my senses. My thoughts leap in several directions all at once. When I turn to face him, Nolan is watching me intently. "I do," I say.

We stare at each other for a long moment, neither of us moving. I don't know what he makes of my answer. But I do know that no one has ever asked me that question before. Aside from Arthur, Nolan is the only other person who knows my true nature. But he also seems to understand everything else. The weight of this responsibility. The pain of the loss I'm powerless to stop. Nolan sees it all. He sees *me*. And he looks at me now as though he wants every piece of my broken soul.

Nolan rises from his seat on the swing next to me. His eyes never leave mine as he stops in front of me, blocking my view of the street and the sea and the moon that hovers in the sky behind him. The whole universe around us seems to fall away.

"Maybe you should let someone take care of you for a change," he says.

My heart riots. *I should leave*, the rational voice says in my head like a repeating plea. But that voice grows quieter every second that he watches me, until it fades into silence. "Maybe. Any suggestions on who? Your version of 'taking care of me' might be tossing me into the ocean with concrete shoes."

Nolan drops to his knees in front of me, gripping my ankles to keep me in place. His eyes shimmer in the dark. I could kick him off. Push him down. A dark thrill courses through my veins when I wonder if he'd pursue me. But I already know he would. He wouldn't stop until he caught me. He would revel in every second of the chase. And he'd probably love punishing me for it.

So would I.

"I'm not going to hurt you," he says.

It might not be delivered as a promise, but I want to believe that. I want to trust him in this too. And if I could just tell him the truth, that I'm not who he thinks I am, maybe everything would be easier. I know I'm no saint, not after the things I've done. Not after I left him for dead. Even still, I wonder if he could forgive me for that if I were honest. But I will not break my promise to Arthur. "I'm not the person you think I am" is the closest I let myself come, and even that is only a whisper, as though anything louder will shatter my vow.

"You're right, you're not," he says as he slowly pulls one of my feet away from the other, dragging it through the rubber mulch. "You're so much more than what I thought you would be."

He could mean anything by that, good things or bad. But the heat in his touch sets off an electrical storm in my veins. I can feel the dampness of my panties. My nipples tighten. A shiver trembles through my flesh, one that has nothing to do with the deepening dusk.

"I'm desperate for a taste of you, Harper." He pulls my other ankle through the mulch, spreading me wide. "I'm fucking starving for it." My breath comes in shallow pants as his hands travel the length of my lower legs, gliding over my knees. He grasps the hem of my skirt and slowly pushes it up my thighs. "It's all I can think about."

It's all I can think about too. I don't say the words, but he can see them in me, as though I'm projecting them into the space between us. His eyes are still fused to mine as he drags my skirt higher and higher until it reaches my hips. "Will you let me have just one taste?"

"No," I say, and he goes as still as marble. There's relief in knowing he will immediately stop without any hesitation. The earnest questions and concerns burn so brightly in his eyes that I nearly laugh. I might love his words and all the fantasies they evoke. But I love antagonizing him even more, perhaps because I know that he'll never stop meeting whatever gauntlet I throw down. The wisp of fear that he's crossed a line still lingers in his eyes until I lean a little closer with a devilish grin. "Not just one taste. I'm not some fucking snack."

I spread my legs wider. A ravenous shadow descends across Nolan's face.

"If you start, you're going to finish your fucking meal."

SPLICE

Harper

THERE'S A FLASH OF METAL in the dim light. He holds a knife in his hand, the blade curved like a tiger's claw. "You're a bit of a brat, aren't you?" Nolan says as he shifts closer, the heat of his body settling between my thighs. He drags a finger along the seam of my tights, the fabric damp, and then pinches my clit. I gasp. It treads the line of pleasure and pain as he lets the bundle of nerves slip free, the fabric of my tights and panties still pinched between his fingers. "You know what happens to brats, don't you?"

"They're punished?"

"Yes. But I believe that punishment should come second . . ." The tip of the blade pierces through the fabric in his grip. Every muscle tenses as I lock my body in place, anticipation coursing through me. The blunt edge of the curved blade touches my folds in a cold kiss of metal. It presses just hard enough to be a threat, a warning not to move. And I don't. I barely breathe as it drags up to my clit, the cutting edge shredding the fabric in a long, slow slice. "A brat needs to be tamed first."

I let out a long breath as the blade pulls away from my center, but detours toward my right thigh. Nolan watches me with an intensity that burns through the shadows descending around us. He turns the blade so the tip is now flush with the tender skin at the crease of my thigh. Then he drags it slowly down my inner thigh in a straight line toward my knee, tearing through the fabric as he goes. I stay perfectly still, aside from my racing pulse and the ragged breaths that shudder in my lungs. The tip of the blade coasts over my leg just hard enough to leave a line of discomfort in my skin, but not hard enough to bleed. When the tights are cut all the way to my ankle, he shifts to my other leg, doing the same but from the bottom up. His touch is such a gentle contrast to the hint of pain, his free hand sweeping up the path of the blade in a soothing caress.

I swallow a moan when the blade arrives at the crease of my left leg. He catches the edge of my panties and glides it over my lower abdomen, pulling them and my tights taut against the cutting edge until they both fall away from my skin.

Nolan lifts the blade away, closing it before sliding the knife into his pocket. I'm bared wide to him. A tremor vibrates in my bones. I can smell the subtle musk of my arousal rising on the cool breeze that caresses the moisture gathered at my entrance. Nolan licks his lips, a slow smile stalking across his glistening flesh. "What a good girl you were for me. You stayed so perfectly still, and I didn't even have to ask. It was almost as though you were . . . *tame*."

Well . . . *fuck*.

His smile widens at the scowl I give him. "Don't get used to it," I say.

I can just make out his dimples in the dark when he laughs. He runs his hand through his hair and it falls back into place to skim his cheekbones in that perpetually disheveled way that makes my heart ache.

His smile fades. He leans closer to my center. A line of cool air flows from his pursed lips, teasing across my pussy. When I shiver, he leans back. "Maybe it's time to be punished."

I surge forward to grip the back of his neck with my hand, my face so close to his that his breath of a laugh floods my senses. "Nolan fucking Rhodes—"

"I sure hope you're about to say 'please' when you tell me to eat your pussy."

My lips clamp shut. I was definitely about to say something along the lines of "eat my pussy or I'll cut you into ribbons of flesh," no hint of a "please" in sight. And as he leans a little farther away, his hands braced on my thighs, I know he'll toy with me if I don't give him the one little word he wants.

"I thought you said you were going to take care of me," I finally venture.

Nolan's eyes track upward as though he's digging through his memory, his expression pensive. "Actually, I suggested you should let someone take care of you. I never said that was going to be me."

My chest feels like a burning pit of rage, and Nolan's loving every minute of my descent into madness. "I truly hate you—"

"But . . ." he interjects, trailing a single finger up my inner thigh, crossing over to my pussy. With a long, slow stroke, he drags his touch through my arousal and then swirls his finger over my clit in a caress that's far too gentle to be anything but a tease. "If you ask me *nicely* . . ."

"I . . ." Any protest I hoped to make dies on my tongue, my brain short-circuiting as he presses a little harder on my sensitive bud of nerves. His wolfish smile. The dark and dangerous shine in his eyes. He's watching me like he knows he's about to win. "Nolan Rhodes . . ."

He bats his long lashes at me in faux innocence. "Yes . . . ?"

"Would you, pretty please with a cherry on top"—I lean closer, holding his eyes—"take your hand off my pussy?"

He swallows, and judging by the sudden pain that surfaces in his expression, it could have been blades that just passed down his throat. But he does so immediately, lifting his touch away from both my clit and my knee without delay.

It takes every last fraying thread of my self-control not to smile. If he was still touching me, surely he would feel the rush of my pulse as adrenaline surges in my veins.

I lean back. Spread my legs wider. "And put your face there instead so you can devour me," I say.

I see the exact moment my words click together in his mind. With one blink, rejection turns to desperate hunger that burns even hotter than it did moments ago. He surges forward, his hands bracketing around my ass as he buries his face between my thighs.

And Nolan does exactly as I asked. He fucking devours me. He feasts as though he's addicted to me. Like I'm the only thing that will keep him alive. He sucks on my clit hard until I buck in the swing and then he lavishes it with swirls of his tongue. He catches me between his teeth in a gentle bite and I yelp, fear and pleasure and just the slightest hint of pain an intoxicating mix that threatens to undo me.

"You know what I love?" he whispers as he pushes a finger into my pussy, curling it to stroke my inner walls. I let out a quivering moan. Another finger slides into my entrance, pumping in slow thrusts. "I love how much you get off on your fear of me. I give you a little whisper of it, maybe a little hint of pain, and you fucking soak my hand. When I slapped your ass and told you I would fuck you into oblivion, your pussy cinched so tight around my cock that I nearly came on the fucking spot."

Nolan covers my clit with his mouth and works his fingers as his free hand withdraws the knife from his pocket. With a flick of his wrist, the blade clicks free of the handle. He keeps his eyes on me as he touches the point to my outer thigh, dragging it gently over my skin, just hard enough to leave a mark. I whimper, my core clenching tight. And he laughs. Laughs right into my flesh as my arousal floods his hand.

"See?" he says, his face glistening in the moonlight as he withdraws his fingers to show them to me. They shine in the dim light. With a grin, he lays them on his waiting tongue and sucks the juices off. When he drags them free of his lips, he slides them back into my pussy to the sound of my shameless, shuddering moan. "Fucking delicious."

This time when he buries his face between the apex of my thighs and groans with desire, I know he won't stop until I'm falling apart. And he's right. I am spellbound by the fear and the pain. With Nolan, I feel like I can reclaim them, like I can dictate the terms of what I'm willing to feel. He transforms terror and torture into alchemical pleasure.

It's not the way he worships my clit, or slides his fingers in my pussy, or even drags the knife over my thigh that breaks me apart. It's the realization that Nolan understands me in a way no one else can. And he's taking care of me in a way that no one else ever will. He chases every second of my orgasm like he can see my epiphany unfurling like a night-blooming flower.

I'm shaking. Panting. My eyes are squeezed shut. My biceps

burn from holding on to the chains of the swing. The blood rushing through my head is so loud that it muffles the sounds around me. Even the shuffle of fabric as Nolan shifts between my thighs.

In a sudden flash of movement, he pulls me from the swing and flips me over, trapping both my wrists behind my back in one of his calloused hands. The thin rubber is braced across my waist and my bare knees rest on the cool mulch.

He hastily pushes my skirt up and plunges his cock into my pussy with a single stroke.

"Jesus fucking Christ," he hisses as I let out an agonized cry of pleasure. He pulls back and thrusts, burying his cock even deeper in my channel. I can already feel a fresh wave of pleasure rolling through me. "You might have been sent from hell to torment me, but you feel just like heaven."

I'm completely at his mercy. And he fucks me with none.

I love every second of it.

He grips my wrists tight and digs the fingers of his other hand into my hip until it aches. He picks up a rhythm of long strokes and uses the momentum of the swing to drive into me. I rock away from him as he glides out to the crown of his cock. He pulls me back and slams to the hilt. The pace quickens and I hear the pained restraint in the curses and praise and promises he whispers in the night.

"I'm going to fucking ruin this perfect pussy," he says as the swell of another orgasm threatens to crash over me. "Next time I fuck you, you're going to look into my face and I'm going to watch you fall apart. And then I'm going to fucking *claim* you, Harper Starling."

I close my eyes, imagining everything he could mean with those words. Maybe he'll make good on his fantasy to fuck me into the afterlife. Maybe he'll slice my throat and fill me with cum as I shudder my dying breath. Or maybe he'll choose a worse demise and take my heart instead. I've been trying to keep it safe in a cocoon of fear and promises. But he keeps pulling it apart. Shredding my defenses. One day, he might strip it right out of my chest, and I'm not sure that he'll keep it safe if he does. That fate terrifies me more than any other.

"What if I claim you first?" I finally ask. My question breaks his cadence. He stalls, but only for a moment.

"You already have."

His fingers dig into my hip and he picks up his rhythm and fucks me so hard I see flashes of light in the darkness of my closed eyes. I don't just break apart. I shatter. I'm fragments and shards, mindless with pleasure. My core seems to coil tight with it, and Nolan suddenly roars behind me, slamming into me as he fills my pussy with his spend. I can feel him trembling as much as I am. I can hear his ragged exhalations, every breath as uneven as mine.

It takes a long moment for us both to recover. When he pulls away, he does it slowly, carefully. He wraps an arm beneath my chest and raises me off the swing with care, not letting me go until he's sure I have my balance. And then he cleans me up as much as he's able to with a section of my torn tights. He could be quick about it. Or he could leave me to do it myself. But he doesn't. He takes his time, his touch gentle as he makes slow passes over my skin.

"I can take you home to get cleaned up properly," he finally says as he balls the shredded tights and panties into a fist to place them in a nearby trash can.

"No," I reply, and if it were a little brighter out, he'd be able to see the crimson heat that rises in my cheeks. "I'd still like to get that dinner. If you want." And though I don't say it, maybe I like the thought of his cum smeared on my thighs. Of being marked. And the way his smile surfaces, maybe he's thinking the same thing.

Nolan gives me a single nod. He reaches out a hand.

I slip my palm into his, and we walk toward the lights.

WINDWARD

Nolan

I TRIED TO CONVINCE MYSELF it wasn't a date as we walked here, but I gave up before we even made it through the door.

Harper is luminous. She glows in the candlelight as we have dinner at Nightfog, a restaurant perched on the edge of the rocky shore. I turned on some of the Southern charm to score us a table on the busy covered patio that rests on stilts covered with barnacles. She seemed to like that, judging by the smile she tried to bite free of her lips. We share a starter of mussels in white wine and garlic sauce. She devours a plate of scallops and linguine. It should be harder than it is to talk to her, but in reality, it's not hard at all. She asks genuine questions, not just superficial ones. When I tell her about the time Billy burnt his eyebrows off when he tried to make Bananas Foster, she asks me everything about his dream to be a world-class pastry chef. When I mention that my sister, Amelia, is finishing her PhD in nanorobotics, she wants to know the minute details about her field of research.

But no matter how hard I try, I can't seem to pry much from her. Sometimes, I notice a glimpse of a pause, a catch of her breath, as though she knows she shouldn't show much of herself to the man who is supposed to be her enemy. She only talks about her earliest years or the most recent ones, leaving a black chasm in between. She tries to focus on things I'm already familiar with, like the soapbox racer or the corpse she's been crafting for tomorrow's gravity race. But Harper gives up nothing of the person she was just before she came to Cape Carnage. I came here thinking I needed every detail about the night she crashed into my life so I could find some kind of peace, but I'm starting to think that's not what I want anymore. The woman I really want to know is the one sitting a candle away.

When we've finished dinner, I drive Harper home, waiting in my rental car for her to change her clothes before we head to the Ballantyne River. We have more bodies to exhume and not many days left to do it. We can't take more nights off. It gnaws at me, knowing we're running out of time and she's the only one who knows the places to dig. If she'd tell me, I'd do it on my own and work later into the night so she could rest. But the truth is, I know I can't ask. Her trust in me is fragile. She's always looking for a reason to break it. The best thing I can do for her is to keep my suggestions to myself and follow her lead, even if we're up against the clock.

We manage only one exhumation tonight, agreeing we'll dig up two bodies tomorrow. It's going to be bright weather and a busy day in town with the Carnival of Carnage Gravity Races, and festivities afterward are due to continue into the night. We can risk starting a little early, since it's unlikely Sam would miss the opportunity to film one of the town's most important annual events. When we leave the river and get to the road, I think for a moment that Harper might let me drive her home. Maybe she'll even ask me to stay. But she doesn't. She slings the bag of bones over her shoulder and gives me a tentative smile, then starts toward the path, disappearing into the dark.

I watch her walk away, and I linger there on the road long after she's gone.

It's a restless sleep. All I can think about is Harper. How Sam is getting too close to her.

And *why*.

There's something she's not telling me. A secret she's harboring. I'm more sure of it with every day that passes. And the way he must have approached her on his own?

It just doesn't seem right.

When I finally fall asleep, I dream about that night four years ago. Everything happens just as it did. Crossing the dark road. The crash. Opening my eyes, my face flat against the cool asphalt. Even the taste of blood. But I don't hear Billy's voice. I'm not reaching for him with my broken arm. It's not his sightless eyes that watch me back. It's Harper's.

I awaken just after five with a sudden start, drenched in a cold sweat. My body is aching. A dull throb pulses in my elbow where a bruise colors the flesh in streaks of deep purple. My neck radiates pain into the base of my skull. I press my fingertips against the tender wound on my shoulder, prodding the puncture beneath the bandage. With a groan, I pop a couple of painkillers and run through my stretches, and by six, I'm sitting by the unlit fireplace of the lobby with a cup of tea as I watch the morning unfold in the Capeside Inn. Despite my insistence that I can lend her a hand, Irene refuses my assistance, shuffling from the kitchen with my plate of French toast and bacon held at a precarious angle. It's a fucking miracle it doesn't slide onto the floor.

261

"Any big plans today, Mr. Rhodes?" she says as she places a glass jug of maple syrup on the table with an unsteady rattle.

"I think I'll take in some of the soapbox races. That's about it."

"Nothing else . . . ?"

Aside from more pining after a woman I shouldn't want, buying industrial quantities of hot chocolate, and digging up dead bodies? "No, ma'am. Nothing in particular," I reply as I stir a splash of milk into my tea and raise it to my lips.

"So you haven't already planned a second date with Harper Starling? Such a shame."

I cough my sip of tea back into my cup and onto my lap.

"You need to hop on it. None of that 'wait three days to call her' bullshit," Irene says as she pulls a tea towel off her shoulder to dab at the wet spot on my lap. "Otherwise, you'll be left with one of those dating apps where it's either swipe left or you finally pick someone and find yourself catfished."

"You're on dating apps?"

Irene flips the tea towel back onto her hunched shoulder before she pushes her bifocals up her nose. "I'm one foot in the grave already. If I wait any longer for Arthur Lancaster to make a move, I'll be ashes in the wind."

"I . . ." I'm legitimately not sure what to say.

"Get Harper to give Arthur a kick in the pants and ask me to dinner. Unless you screwed up your first date so badly that she doesn't want to talk to you again."

"Who said I was on a date with Harper?"

Irene looks to the ceiling as though searching through a lengthy list, holding up a hand so she can tick names off with her fingers. "Jimmy Baker. Maria Flores. Bert Wilson. Sarah Winkle, that crusty bitch—"

"So, the whole town."

"Pretty much." Irene pushes the teapot in my direction so I can replenish my spilled drink. "Not much gets past the residents here. Especially not when it comes to romance."

Irene shuffles away, but she leaves me with a spreading sense of unease. If a simple dinner has caused ripples through Cape Carnage, what does that mean for our other activities? What if we haven't gone so unnoticed in the night?

I'm mulling over this question when Sam's drone operator and assistant who I saw the other day by Harper's house, a guy named Vinny, enters the small dining area, the first of the other guests to appear. He gives me a curt nod before he finds a table on the other side of the room, pulling a tablet from his bag as soon as he's seated. There was no warmth in his greeting, only the most basic amount of civility to cover a cutting edge in his eyes. Either he's pissed about the goose chase I sent him on, or Sam has been talking. Maybe both.

Sam enters a few minutes later with his camera bags in tow. When he sees me, his smile and words of greeting appear much more genuine. But Sam is slick. He knows he needs to manufacture something believable so he can avoid making waves as he's slithering through the murk. He might consider himself on the other side of the law from a creature like me, but we're just different branches of the same evolutionary tree. And I can recognize my own kind. This is the way the darkest creatures operate. We keep the surface still until we're ready to take a bite.

I take my time eating. Pretend I'm minding my own business. The pair of men make it hard for me to mind theirs. They speak in low tones, leaning over their meals, passing the tablet and papers and Sam's notebook between them. When they drain their coffee cups, Vinny heads to the parking lot with his gear as Sam packs up his belongings.

"How's that documentary going?" I ask over the lip of my cup as soon as Sam's surly companion is out of earshot.

Sam turns, flashing me a polite smile. "Good, thanks. How's your vacation?"

I do my best to keep my smile consistent, despite the cutting edge that threatens to creep across my face. "Great. Very relaxing." Sam's eyes track down to the bruise on my arm and narrow. It's too late to hide it, so I turn my arm so he can get a better look. "Even got some mountain biking in. Albeit not always successfully."

Sam's head tilts. I don't like this level of scrutiny that he doesn't even seem eager to hide. "You brought a mountain bike here from Tennessee?"

Shit.

"I rented one," I reply.

His head tilts the other way. "Oh really? Where from? I used to compete in single track. Wouldn't mind hitting some trails on the coastline in my spare time."

Double shit.

I lean back in my chair and take another sip of my tea, letting an untroubled smile drift into my features. "Wallie from Wallie's Watersports hooked me up. I'm sure he could help you out."

Sam's head rights itself, complete with a smile that looks a little too predatory for my liking. Maybe I'll get lucky, and he won't call me on my lie. But, somehow, I think he's too thorough for that.

"Good to know. Well," he says, placing his Porter Productions ball cap on his head, "I'd better run. See you around." With a little salute, Sam pivots and starts walking toward the door. But he only takes a few steps before he turns to face me once more. My stomach drops through my torso at the glint I catch in his eyes. "One more question," he says, barely able to contain the smile that lights up his face with too much electrified energy. He jerks his chin in my direction, his eyes fused to my elbow. "Does Wallie rent out padding, too? The granite around here is pretty unforgiving. Wouldn't want to sideline myself with an injury when I have so much work to do, you know . . . ? Say . . . is that how you got that nasty scar? Mountain biking?"

"No," I say, that single word hanging in the air as I lay my napkin next to my empty plate. I slide my hand back under the table, clenching my fist in the shadows.

"A story for another time, I guess." Sam tips the brim of his hat, and when I give him the slightest nod in reply, he turns on his heel and leaves.

I watch the door, barely blinking. When I'm sure he won't traipse back through it, I stride to my room with singular focus guiding my path. As soon as I have my tools in hand, I head to the opposite side of the hotel, taking the steps to the second floor by twos. When I arrive at Room 202, I cast a quick look over my shoulder and then slide the snap gun and pin into the lock. With just a few clicks, the mechanism inside the lock gives way.

I push the door open just enough to scan the darkened interior, and then I slip into Sam's hotel room.

Sam has a smaller room than mine, and he doesn't keep it very organized. His luggage is propped open, clothes strewn haphazardly in its interior and hanging off the lid. Papers are scattered across the desk. A small printer sits on the dresser next to discarded socks and stacks of fresh paper. The scent of stale food lingers in the stagnant air. There's a tangle of charging cables and extra camera batteries plugged into the wall sockets. A pizza box sits on the counter of the little kitchenette, dirty dishes piled onto its grease-stained lid.

I crinkle my nose as I survey the space, then head toward the desk.

I'm not sure what I'm looking for. I just know I need *something*. An indication of what he's really after. A next move. Something that will tell me how to protect Harper.

The first papers I skim are notes about shots he's already taken for the documentary, places for cuts and voice-overs. There's a log of dates and locations, including Lancaster Manor and the Ballantyne River property. A list of names for interview subjects.

I skim paper after paper, but nothing clicks into place.

Not until I find a printout of a tide chart. Low tides and high tides. Times of day. Measurements in feet and meters.

At the next spring tide, Arthur Lancaster's biggest secret will surface, and even he doesn't realize just how big it is, Sam's words from the day I saw him filming Lancaster Manor in the fog hook into my thoughts, refusing to come loose.

I take out my phone and capture a photo of the chart, then move on to the next paper in the stack, this one a grainy, black-and-white photograph that's been blown up so that it focuses on the background of the shot and not its subjects. The edge of the social media platform frame is still visible on the bottom half of the page, the username partially cut off, but still legible. The focal point in the center of the paper is a slice of the coastline, the cliffs plunging into the sea. The water has peeled back from the stone, leaving a sliver of glistening beach behind. And peeking from the edge of the waves, reaching from the shallows, is something buried in the sand. Something unnatural, made by a human hand. The distinctive top of what looks like a crumpled camper van.

My frown deepens and I flip the page over. There are dates scrawled on the back beneath a header that says, *Spring Tides, Extreme Lows*. And then a list.

May 11th. May 27th. June 10th. June 25th. July 11th.

The dates extend all the way to the end of August, following the cyclical progression of low spring tides, when the sun, moon, and Earth are in a straight line to exert the most force on ocean waters. But it's the next upcoming date that concerns me the most. It's circled, and beneath it:

5:32 AM low tide, 44.6692° N, 67.2594° W

I take a picture of both sides of the page, then I flip through the next papers. A few are old photos of a younger Arthur. A couple are newspaper articles from when Arthur's daughter was murdered. And then I find something that chills my blood into jagged crystals of ice.

Photographs of Harper.

Harper walking down the street in her plaid shirt. Harper hanging baskets of flowers on Main Street. Harper buying supplies at Craft-A-Corpse, a fake torso tucked under her arm, mannequin limbs jutting from the bag in her other hand. Harper in the skirt she wore last night, waiting in line outside the theater. The pages have been printed out from digital images, the back of each one labeled with notes. Dates. Times. Locations. Observations about her mood or behavior. *Looks upset, maybe crying, walking fast, leaving Maya's Magical Mixtures*, the note says on the back of the photo of her in the plaid shirt. Even notes about her mannerisms. *Biting her bottom lip. Anxious? Check against older videos.*

My hands shake with the effort of not tearing the paper to shreds.

Sam Porter shouldn't know these intimate details. What she looks like when she's upset. How her eyes seem to glow when she's angry. That she was in tears when she left our conversation at Maya's shop. That she bites her lip when she's worried. He has no right to know these things. To follow her. Watch her. Hoard these little details. He hasn't earned them. Not her ephemeral trust, not her fierce loyalty. She didn't give those to him. Not like she has to me.

He's crept into her territory. And he thinks he knows these things and what they mean. But there's one detail he clearly hasn't captured:

She is *mine*.

I slam my fist onto the desk.

How much more does he know? What has he seen? She can't be safe here, and I know she's never going to leave Arthur on his own with someone like Porter lurking in her domain. I'm desperate to tear his bones out through his skin, but I believe what Harper said. If we kill him, we could risk the whole Sleuthseeker organization descending on this town. Though I cycle through every option, I can't see a clear solution.

I manage to gather my thoughts just long enough to skim the rest of the documents, though I barely digest what I'm reading through the haze of swirling rage and panic. Satisfied that I've seen enough, I put the papers back the way I found them. After a quick search of the wardrobe and dresser turns up empty, I head to the door, taking a moment to try to regain some semblance of composure. I run my fingers through my hair, but my hand still shakes. I take a calming breath, but my heart hammers at every bone. When I finally give up trying to wrangle my distress, I check the peephole, then open the door and step across the threshold.

I'm halfway down the hallway when I hear footsteps climbing the stairs. I freeze, but there's nowhere to go. Nowhere to hide. There's no way I can get back into Sam's room in time, the door already closed and locked behind me. And if it's him . . . ?

I keep walking, hoping it will look like I'm meant to be here as my heart claws across my rib cage, protesting my innocence with every beat.

I'm nearly at the end of the corridor when Sheriff Yates comes into view.

There's a momentary burst of surprise in his eyes, before a faint smile appears, one that's both professional but detached, none of it reaching his eyes.

"Mr. Roan," he says with a nod.

"Rhodes," I correct him, and his smile brightens.

"Ah, yes," he says. "*Rhodes*. All okay?"

No. I'm a fucking mess and I'm not sure what my face is doing. "Yes, sir. Yourself?"

Yates scratches his graying stubble, glancing past me to the door I just walked through a moment ago. "You know, busy day planned with the carnival. Thought I'd see if I could catch Mr. Porter for a moment before he goes off on his next adventure for the day. You're on this floor too? Don't know as I'd want Mr. Porter for a neighbor, personally."

"No, sir. Just stopped by to give him some information on

mountain biking in the area," I say, figuring there's no point in lying about my room location just in case Sheriff Yates calls my bluff. Though I keep my expression neutral, the panic churning through my guts only moments ago becomes a whirlpool I can't swim my way free from. Has Yates come to see Sam before, when I was occupied and didn't know it? What if he's been tracking Sam's movements too? What if they're collaborating and I somehow missed the signs? "Well," I say, resisting the urge to curl my hands into tight fists. "I just tried knocking but no one answered, so I think you might be too late."

"Huh. Could've sworn I heard a door close, not a knock."

"Sound travels strangely in these old places, I guess."

His smile might stretch just a little, but I don't get the impression that Yates is convinced. "Yeah. You're probably right."

With a tight nod, I resume my path toward the stairs, coming closer to Yates with every step. He seems to fill up too much space with his height and his uniform and his probing eyes that follow my motion. Just as I'm about to pass him, he clamps a hand down on my shoulder. I try not to flinch as he squeezes, his grip just over the wound still healing there. "Heard you went on a date with Miss Harper Starling, is that correct?"

"Not sure if you could call it a date, sir," I say, unease prickling across my skin. My wound sings to him with pain, as though it's whispering all my secrets into his palm. "But we had dinner last night, yes."

"Well, I hope it was a nice evening, because she sure could use a break. She's a good girl. Heard she was with Mr. Lancaster in the hospital when a tourist caused a ruckus in the emergency room. I hope she wasn't too rattled." He gives a shake of his head, concern creasing his brow before it smooths. "Say, you wouldn't know anything about a man named Sean McMillan, would you?"

My eyes narrow. I shake my head. "Doesn't ring any bells, sir."

"Hmm. Didn't think so." He squeezes my shoulder and then removes his hand, giving me a final pat before his hand drops to his side to rest on his holster. "Just seems odd. First Jake disappears. Now this McMillan character seems to vanish without a trace."

"Sorry I can't be of more help."

"No matter. They'll turn up somewhere eventually, I'm sure."

We're locked into a stare that lasts a beat too long, like a single note that lingers when the rest of the song has finished. "I'll be sure to let you know if I hear anything," I finally say, and Yates's face transforms with a welcoming smile. It's unnerving after the cold that seemed to spread through the air between us just a moment ago.

"I appreciate you, son. Take care." I give him a single nod. And then I walk away. I'm nearly at the end of the corridor when he stops me dead as he says, "Oh, and wish Harper luck at the races for me today. She's got a lot on her plate. I know you'll be good to her . . . right . . . ?"

I pin him with an assessing look over my shoulder. "Yes. Of course, sir."

That smile of his broadens. But it still doesn't reach his eyes.

With a final tip of my head, I leave Yates standing in the hall.

When I'm at the bottom of the stairs, I wait in the shadows, listening for Yates to follow. But he doesn't show.

GALES

Harper

"Corpsie the Copilot, reporting for duty," I say as I shove my crafted corpse into the rear seat of the Pocket Rocket. My refurbished soapbox racer might not be the most elaborate contraption, but Corpsie looks pretty badass with her goggles and pigtails and the bloody slash across her throat. I release the elastic bands around the long ribbons attached to the wands that I stitched to her palms, unfurling the colorful strips of fabric to rest them on the back of the car so they can trail in our wake when we hurtle down the hill.

"It's very . . . lifelike. Or deathlike, I guess . . ." Nolan says, his brow furrowed as he pokes a finger into her silicone cheek. His eyes slide to mine, but the crease between his brows remains, an echo of worry etched in his skin.

"But you wouldn't know anything about that, right?" I wink, and regret it immediately. I probably look deranged, some unhinged winking murder woman with a corpse mannequin copilot stuffed into the back seat of her soapbox racer. I resist the urge to look down at my retro aeronaut outfit, a white button-up shirt complemented with an old pair of Arthur's pleated pants and suspenders. I look *super hot.*

. . . I don't look super hot. *At all.*

Nolan's frown deepens as he scrutinizes my soapbox racer before his gaze pans across the competitors ahead of me in line. "Are you sure this is safe?"

"I tested it on Arthur's driveway. It seemed fine."

"The driveway?" His glare becomes brutally cold. "That's not really the same as the course. I'm not sure this is a good idea."

I scoff, looking down the twisting road that leads toward the glittering sea in the distance, the sidewalk flanked by onlookers. A prickle of unease dances along my ribs as I take in the steep hill before me, the angle of which seems so much worse when I lower myself into the cockpit. My bravado is entirely forced when I shrug and say, "No one has died yet."

"That doesn't inspire much confidence in me."

"There are straw bales at the sharper bends and at the finish line. I'm sure tourists will buffer me if anything else goes awry. You can stand at the second curve and we can test it out, if you like?"

"Just . . . be careful," Nolan says, leveling me with a hard stare, the kind of look that leaves you with no room to move. Even when I peel my focus away, I feel him. Somehow, his shadow is warmer than the sun. There's a heat in it that pulls me back.

"Why are you so worried?" I ask.

"I'm not."

"You sure about that?"

He doesn't answer. I square my shoulders and grip the steering wheel, even though there are five competitors left to go before me. When I dart a swift glance in his direction, I glean nothing from the stoic expression painted across his face. I can't decipher his emotions from his hardened features. It could be apprehension I see, or it could be anger. It could be regret. Whatever it is, it's enormously frustrating. Maybe it would be easier if I threw my own insecurities out into the open. Like, *What if I'm making the wrong decision to trust you?* Or, *I don't understand your motivations, and that scares me.* But it's not so easy to step into the light when you've been hiding in a sanctuary of shadows.

The silence stretches so long that I land on the only viable interpretation of Nolan's inscrutable expression, that maybe he's worried about what might happen to his book and weapons if I'm injured on the course. I'm tempted to say something sharp, something meant to wound. Maybe I just want a reaction. To cut beneath the flesh and see if he bleeds. But in the end, I just say, "Everything will be fine. Just go and get a beer and chill, or something. You're freaking me out."

He glances around us. Swallows. "We need to talk later. About Sam. I—"

"You ready, Harp?"

Lukas strides past the nearby competitors, a wide smile plastered to his face. He's wearing a matching outfit with suspenders over a white button-up shirt and old-fashioned, pleated brown pants, a set of goggles dangling from his neck. He turns enough that we can read the words *Pocket Rocket Corpse Crew* embroidered on his back.

I force an untroubled smile. "I hope you're ready to see Sarah Winkle's face when we win that fucking cake. She's going to be so pissed."

"That's the spirit. Nothing's a better motivator than spite." Lukas comes to a stop next to Nolan, offering a handshake that he accepts. "You helping to crew for the Pocket Rocket?"

274

"Nah, he's going to grab a beer and cheer from the sidelines," I say before he can answer. "I think we're covered."

Nolan seems to hesitate, leaning away while his feet stay rooted to the ground. He looks at Lukas before he wishes me luck and walks away. I watch as he slips into the crowd, and it isn't until he disappears that I feel like I'm able to take a full breath.

"Everything okay?" Lukas asks as he comes up beside me, readying to move the wooden block wedged beneath my front tires. My cheeks heat as he scrutinizes my face.

"Yeah. All good."

"That Nolan guy seems . . . intense."

I look in Nolan's direction, though I can't see him through the crowd. Lukas's words seem to hang in my thoughts like barbed hooks. *Intense.* I wonder if that's what other people see too when Nolan looks at me. Someone *intense.* Maybe dangerous. And even without his belongings in my possession, maybe they'd look to him if something happened to me. Maya saw our interaction in her shop. She could raise questions. Lukas has seen his dark edge, even if he doesn't understand it. Nolan can be charming, sure, but only when he wants to be. And it's the first time I really realize that the damning evidence I have against Nolan doesn't just keep me safe in case he suddenly decides to change course and make good on his plans to kill me. It also puts him in danger.

"He's just really worried I'm going to crash or something," I finally say, buckling myself in and clipping the harness into my seat belt. "He's fine."

"Something going on there with you two?"

"Going on . . . ?"

"You know. *Going on.*"

Maybe? I don't know? Does swing sex count . . . ? "No."

Lukas smiles. "Okay. I just heard you had dinner at Nightfog, that's all."

I roll my eyes, blush creeping into my cheeks. I love this town, but the locals are nosy as hell. "So? It's just food."

"At *Nightfog*. You know as much as anyone else that's the date place."

"If you're hoping to annoy me into rolling faster down the hill, it's working." I settle the retro aviator goggles over my eyes as Lukas puts his hands up in defeat, though his smile is one of teasing satisfaction. I let a few minutes pass. Lukas strikes up a conversation with a few nearby tourists who are also waiting for their turn, but I don't join in, my attention consumed by my blossoming fears. It's not until the next competitor heads down the hill and Lukas rolls me a space closer to the starting line that I finally say, "You know that bag that I gave you to put somewhere safe?"

A shadow falls across his features. "Yeah . . . ?"

"Where is it?"

Lukas frowns at the crowd around us, as though he knows it's important enough that he shouldn't let anyone hear him. "It's somewhere you would never look."

He might not know everything about me. About how I keep this town safe. What that takes. What I'm capable of. But Lukas does know enough about my past to know where I would never, *ever* want to go.

"In the basement at the main house?" I whisper, my heart already climbing into my throat at the mere idea of searching it out.

He nods once. "In a box on the shelves next to the boiler."

I nod and look at my hands, my fingers tensing and releasing from the steering wheel, the skin over my knuckles bleaching.

Maybe I'm about to make a big mistake. Or perhaps that risk is just the price of taking at least one step into the light. "If anything happens to me, destroy it. Make sure no one ever finds it. Okay?"

Lukas's brow furrows. "Are you sure?"

"Yeah," I say. "Promise me?"

It takes him a long second to consider it. A Lancaster vow is never delivered lightly. But finally, he says, "I promise."

"And our next contender coming down the pike is Harper Starling," Bert booms over the speakers. Our connection breaks, both of us looking toward the makeshift tower where Bert and Bob are sitting. "She's piloting the Pocket Rocket, in her interpretation of Amelia Earhart, with Corpsie the Copilot riding shotgun." The crowd snickers and cheers. "Are you ready, Miss Starling?"

I give him the thumbs-up with one of Corpsie's hands.

"Let's count her down, folks," he booms. "Five . . . Four . . ."

Lukas pulls the plank of wood from in front of my tires. The brakes groan against the weight of the wood and metal.

"Three . . . two . . ."

Lukas jogs to the back of my cart. The fuselage shifts as his hands land on the back edge.

"*One.*"

There's a bang as the starting pistol fires and I release the brake. Lukas gives the car a powerful shove. Onlookers cheer. My heart thunders. The wheels whir as I sail down the road, quickly gathering momentum on the thin bicycle tires. Bert's announcer voice fades into the background as he narrates the race over the speakers mounted along the route. I'm so focused on making it around the first corner without tipping over that I almost forget about the smoke canisters Lukas installed beneath the wings, and I grin as I hit the button. Smoke hisses behind me and the crowd cheers. I look over my shoulder at the trail of blue fog in my wake and cackle at Corpsie, with her arms flailing in the wind and ribbons flapping behind her.

I round the second corner and head down a deliciously straight patch of Maple Street, gathering even more speed. My car is *fast*. I don't catch my exact time as I pass the first of four milestone markers along the route, but I can hear the excitement in Bert's voice. Something about a record. I could win this thing. I wonder why the hell I haven't done this before. Sailing down the road with the crowd cheering and a deranged copilot silently hyping me up in a soapbox airplane? This is fucking *perfect*. The screaming kids. The smell of barbecue. Bert's enthusiastic commentary. The speed. The wind roaring past my ears. I'm having the time of my life. This is freedom. It's "no fucks given" fun. I laugh. It's a laugh that comes from a deep place I forgot I had. I used to laugh like this a lot. And I like it. I missed this part of me.

I zip around the next turn, having so much fun I barely touch the brakes, nearly colliding with the straw bales set along the exterior edge of the curve. A collective *ooh* sounds from the crowd at the near miss and I howl with delight.

But I've gathered too much speed.

I nearly crash again into the next section of the curve that directly follows, and I turn the wheel hard left to avoid the row of straw bales lining the sidewalk. Another rush of awe and excitement rises from the onlookers as I veer toward the inner side of the curve. I curse and slam my foot down on the brake . . .

. . . but nothing happens.

"Oh *shit*."

I pump the brakes. Nothing. I wrench the wheels back to the

right so I can slow my descent along the wall of straw. And then there's a *snap*. Panic seizes my chest.

"Fuck—not good—"

The car veers hard left.

"Look out—"

People on the left side of the road scream. They pick up their kids. Spill their beer. Toss their popcorn and grip their turkey legs. They gasp and shout and jump out of the path as I careen toward the sidewalk. There are no straw bales on this side of the curve. Nothing to stop me.

Not even Nolan.

He's the one person I recognize among the tourists scrambling to get out of my way. He's the only one standing nearly still, moving only enough to follow the motion of my car as I pass him in a moment that seems like it's been stretched so thin that time and all the world have disappeared. It's long enough to freeze the panic on his face. Despite his stillness, his expression seems frantic, as though his energy has been funneled into the fear that paints his face and haunts his eyes.

And that moment is ripped apart in a single heartbeat as I hit the curb with a jarring thud and then jump onto the sidewalk.

"Harper—" I hear him yell after me.

"Not safe!" is all I have time to reply.

And then I'm crossing the lawn to join Piper Boulevard, an even steeper road.

"Shit, totally not safe," I say to myself between tight breaths that pull my chest taut. I jerk the steering wheel from one side to the next, but it has no effect. I pump the brakes, but nothing happens. My car barrels straight down the steep road. Bert's worried commentary fades into the distance. The only thing I hear is the rattle of my wheels and the clatter of Corpsie behind me and the occasional shout of startled passersby on the sidewalk as I rocket down Piper Boulevard, gathering speed.

That is, until I hear Nolan shouting my name, his voice growing impossibly closer.

"Harper," he calls, dinging a bicycle bell to get my attention. I turn to see him pedaling furiously on a kid's pink bike with multi-colored tassels fluttering from the ends of the handlebars. "Aim for a hedge and cover your face!"

"No steering," I call back, jostling the steering wheel with no effect. "No brakes!"

He gets closer, only a few feet behind me. Corpsie's ribbons whip him in the face and he manages to grab a fistful and tug, pulling hard enough to detach the mannequin's arm, which he discards on the road. When he refocuses on me, the panic is still etched into his features, his eyes not leaving mine. Not until they look past me and widen.

I turn and face ahead. I'm closer to the end of the cul-de-sac than I thought I was. Closer to the path that leads to Widow's Point. To the cliff that drops into the sea.

Fuck.

"Nolan—"

"Undo your harness!"

I press the first button. The buckle sticks in the mechanism.

I'm picking up speed. The end of the road is only a block ahead.

"Your harness—"

"It's stuck—"

"I thought you said you'd checked this thing—"

"Now is *not the time*!" I frantically jam my thumb against the button and tug on the straps, but the harness only tightens across my body. The sound of the waves crashing against the cliff rises above the squeak of my wheels and Nolan's furious pedaling and the heartbeat roaring in my ears. I can smell the water and my breath catches as though I'm already drowning. I'm rocketing straight for the short path that leads to the edge, getting closer with every ragged inhalation. *No, no, no.*

"Keep trying. Loosen the harness all the way and climb out—"

"Nolan," he's just behind me when I turn toward his voice, wrestling with the belt, trying and failing to loosen it with shaking hands. I choke down a panicked sob. "I can't swim!"

There's a flicker of pure panic in his eyes. And then, as quickly as it appears, it snuffs out, replaced with unflinching resolve. His legs pump. He doubles his efforts to catch up. He manages to come alongside my car, as his hand is outstretched, reaching for me. I reach back. His voice is trapped in a slow-motion haze. *Take my hand.* All the other details fade away. I just see the lines on his palm. The tattoo on his forearm, the snake's mouth wrapped around its own scales. The fear in his eyes. And just as his fingers graze mine, I hit the curb.

I scream as the car lurches onto the path. Every bone in my body vibrates with the impact, but it hardly even slows me down. Nolan disappears from view. I hear him yell out in pain and frustration and glance behind me to see his body tangled with the bike on the rocks.

I bump over the uneven dirt and stone. The water shimmers in hues of gold on the horizon. It was silver on black water when I sent the real Harper Starling over a cliff and into the sea. And now destiny is eating its tail, consuming itself. Taking me with it.

The car veers off the path. It jostles, careening onto two wheels just long enough to give me hope that it might tip over. But it rights itself. It straightens, landing on the smooth granite ledge at the edge of the cliff.

Four feet. Three. Two. One.

I grip my harness and close my eyes as the car rockets off the ledge.

Wind whips across my face. I'm weightless. The ocean crashes beneath me. I remember the sound of Harper Starling's scream in the instant before her car hit the rocks and flipped, catapulting into the violent, churning surf.

And there's only one word that escapes me when I hit the water. A name. One that surprises me almost as much as the impact that steals my breath. It's the word I scream as the freezing water rushes into the cab and sinks my broken car faster than I thought possible. It's still an echo in my mind as a wave folds over my head and roars into my ears, into my open mouth. It's the one clear thought I have as I reach toward the surface even though there's nothing to grab, the metal that encases me dragging me down, the last of the ribbons swirling in the current above me as I fall into the abyss.

Nolan.

ABYSS

Nolan

I SHOVE THE BIKE OFF me and start running, my palms burning, stones embedded in the scrapes along my arms lighting a fire in my torn skin. But the pain is nothing compared to the fear that seizes my chest as I watch Harper sail off the cliff, pink and purple and gold ribbons trailing behind her in the wind. That burn is nothing compared to the sound of her screaming my name.

She disappears from view. I'm still yards away when I hear her crash into the sea.

The last thing I see as I run off the edge of the cliff is Harper thrashing in the restraints. Desperate. Panicked. The car is already submerged, the fuselage flooded. A wave laps at her neck.

I fold my hands above my head to dive. Take a deep breath. Close my eyes. She's still crying out my name as I hit the water.

The cold shocks every muscle. It fills my ears. Floods my clothes, weighing me down. I fight the pull of deep currents and swim. When I rise above the waves, I'm met with the sound of lapping water. Distant gulls. Nearby boats. Laughter from the festivities that carries on the wind. But there's no Harper. No echo of my name. Only her silence. Impossibly, it's even worse than the sound of her desperate scream.

A wave lifts me enough to catch a glimpse of shattered pieces of wood and her goggles floating on the surface. And then, the end of a gold ribbon before it sinks into the black water.

"*Harper.*"

I dive after it and open my eyes, following its trail.

Shafts of sunlight fracture in the waves. They illuminate threads of color and rising bubbles. Harper's hands as she reaches for the surface. She twists and turns but can't escape the car that's dragging her into the depths. Her shoulders are free of the harness but the belt must still be stuck across her legs. The light behind me penetrates into the darkness, but I can't see the bottom. There's only a black void pulling her away from me.

The weight of my clothes and my frantic kicking push me after her. But I already know I won't reach her in time.

I've seen fear in faces before. I've seen death. I've delivered it with my own two hands. But I've never felt someone's terror cut through my muscle and bone to lash at my heart. Her eyes are so wide. Her mouth is open in a scream, the last of her air rushing from her lungs in a flurry of bubbles. I want to scream back at her. *Hold on. I'm coming.* She thrashes at the belt before stretching for me once more. Her tears are lost to the ocean, but I know they're there.

I can't lose her. Not like this.

Her movement changes. A spasm starts in her chest. Spreads into her shoulders. She folds at the waist only to straighten again. It's uncontrolled reflexes, the final fire of electricity in cells. The magic of life ebbing away. The tension dissolves from her fingers as they graze mine. Her arms go slack, following the current as the car drags her deeper. The fear spirits away from her face. It leaves a momentary sorrow behind. The imprint of a final thought. And then, just as I grab her hand, the light in her eyes goes out.

I use her arm to pull myself closer until I'm at her limp body. My ears pop with the mounting pressure. My lungs burn as I draw the switchblade from my pocket and start cutting the belt from across her legs. I accidentally slice her side in my desperation. She doesn't react to any pain. Blood plumes through the water around us. But I don't stop, not even for a heartbeat. I keep sawing through the thick weave of fabric until the last thread finally gives way and Harper's body floats free of the seat and into my arms.

I let go of the knife. It sinks, following the car into the darkness as I wrap Harper in my arms and kick toward the light.

She doesn't kick with me. She doesn't grip me back.

Panic chokes up my throat. Every muscle is filled with fire. My lungs have nothing left. I keep struggling for the light wavering at a surface that seems too far for me to reach.

I break through with a gasp, coughing, my heart surging a deafening hum in my head. I flip Harper's head skyward, pushing the hair from her face. Her beautiful features are motionless. Serene. Her eyes are half open, glazed with a vacant stare. Her damp lashes don't flutter with the warm caress of the sun. Water trickles from her parted blue lips, dripping from her nose.

"Wake up. Come on." I kick harder so I can pull my free hand from treading water long enough to slap her cheek. She doesn't react. "No, Harper. *No.*" I slap her again, but the impact doesn't even color her skin. There's no blood beating through her heart to rise to the strike. A chasm deep in my chest splits open and a sound escapes. An anguished cry. One I've only heard myself make once before, when my brother died at my side, and all I could do was lie there and watch it happen. "Someone, help!"

"Here, son," a voice calls from behind me. I turn to see a sailboat coasting toward us. A man stands behind the wheel, his teenage boy at the bow with a life ring clutched in his hands. He tosses it to me and I grab it on the first throw. He pulls us in with surprising strength, his father joining by his side to grab Harper beneath her arms. I lift her as much as I can in the turbulent water, but the weight of her motionless body threatens to drag us both down, as though the sea isn't ready to let her go.

But there's no way I'm letting it take her. Not without a fight.

I haul myself onto the deck with the boy's help, and the moment I'm onboard, I scramble to Harper's side.

"Do you have a defibrillator on board?" I ask as I tear her shirt open, buttons pinging across the deck, her suspenders slipping from her shoulders.

The man shakes his head. Dismay is a heavy weight in his weathered features when I look his way. "No, just a standard first aid kit."

"Bring it."

As the man takes off below deck, I return my attention to Harper, her eyes half-lidded and unfocused. Years of training are there, ingrained in my actions. But it's as though the motions happen on the other side of a veil. I check for a pulse. I tell the man to send out a distress call. I ask the boy to bring blankets. I start chest compressions, counting each rhythmic press of my hands to Harper's chest, each thrust pushing water from her mouth and nose. But on the other side of it all is the riot of desperate panic.

I'm watching her die. The thing I once thought I wanted. It's what I came all this way and waited all this time for, and now I would give anything to stop it from happening.

"Not like this, Harper," I whisper as I push down on her chest.

"Anything?" the man asks when I pause just long enough to check her for a pulse. I shake my head as I resume chest compressions, and he lays a hand on my shoulder and squeezes. "Don't give up, son."

Tears glaze my eyes. Though my hope is fading with every moment that passes, I won't give up. I won't stop until someone pulls me off of her, and even then I know I'll fight them to get back to her side. To keep trying.

I stare down at her beautiful face, begging the universe for a sign. A beacon. A candle in the fog.

Images of Harper scatter through my thoughts. The way she smiled at me the first time we met. The ferocity of her glare as we faced off in her garden. But now, it feels like the abyss is still stealing my thoughts of her. When I push my weight into my palms, I'm haunted by the way her chest spasmed as it filled with water. When I press my lips to hers to force air into her lungs, I catch her taste and her scent, but they're marred by salt and the fragrance of the sea.

"You can't leave like this," I grit out as I pump her chest with a metronomic pulse. "We have unfinished business, Harper Starling. You don't get to tap out. Come on. *Come on.*"

I pinch her nose and tilt her head back and deliver a breath. Then another.

And as I'm pulling away, I feel it. A convulsion in her chest. A spasm that becomes a cough. White foam bubbles from her lips and nose, and I turn her to the side, each cough growing more violent. I lodge my fingers beneath her jaw and feel the faint thrum of her heart. It grows steadier with every passing beat.

I hold her head, keeping it steady as she vomits and coughs, frothy liquid spilling from her mouth. Every blink feels like a fucking miracle when just a moment ago she was unseeing.

"Can you hear me?" I ask, and her eyes squeeze shut in pain before focusing on me. She's disoriented, in shock, floating on the edge of consciousness. "Squeeze my hand."

Her eyes flutter open and she looks down at her hand engulfed in mine, and though it's weak, she squeezes back. I hear a boat racing toward us, hitting the waves with force as it turns. The captain of the sailboat pats my shoulder. "Good job, son," he says, then heads for the bow to exchange information with the Coast Guard crew as they cut the engine and pull alongside our boat.

When I look back down at Harper, her steady, exhausted gaze follows me, a thread whose pull I feel deep in a dormant place in my chest.

"I thought . . ." My words drift away, carried from my lips on the breeze that rustles the slack sails above us. *I thought I'd lost you. I thought I couldn't get you back.* Those words all float away. "I thought you were calling it quits on our deal there for a minute, Meatball."

A weak smile fleets across her lips. My own chest aches when I see it, as though someone has just beaten me up to keep me alive. "Couldn't go . . ." she whispers through lips that tremble with shock. I tuck the blankets around her and rub her arm as she shakes, in part to keep her conscious and warm, but in part because I feel suddenly unsure of what to say or do or how to act. "Unfinished business. Need to stab you for that nickname." When I meet her eyes, they solder to mine. The gray seems brighter, the gleam that was missing only moments ago now shining in the sun. "Thank you."

I give her a single nod and break my focus away, but still I feel her watching.

Two crew members from the Coast Guard ship board our boat with a portable defibrillator, and I talk them through what happened and Harper's condition in a way that feels oddly reassuring in its familiarity. When they've had a chance to assess her, they organize with the sailor and his son to keep her aboard so they can escort us to the marina where an ambulance will be waiting. And though they keep an eye on Harper's vitals and ensure she remains stable, a residual panic still ebbs and flows through my veins. Relief that I can feel her pulse beneath my fingertips as I keep hold of her wrist. Distress and desperation every time her eyes drift closed with fatigue. Intense, all-consuming fears chew through my thoughts with every moment that passes. *What about secondary drowning? Aspiration pneumonia? What about infection? Fuck knows what bacteria is already climbing around in her lungs. What if I broke her ribs during CPR? Her sternum? Will she have chronic lung damage? What about PTSD? What if—*

"*Son,*" the sailor says, shaking my shoulder. I blink, a haze dispelling from my mind as I look up at him and realize he's been talking to me for I don't even know how long. He gives me a gentle smile as he extends some folded clothes balanced on his other palm. "I brought you a change of clothes. Might be a little small for you but they'll fit close enough. Do you want to go below deck and get yourself settled for a minute?"

Cold. Stress. It's the first time I become aware that I'm still soaking wet, shaking beneath a towel that's appeared on my shoulders without me even realizing it. I look down at Harper, her eyes barely open, her breathing still erratic, a cough racking her body every few minutes.

I shake my head and squeeze her wrist, her pulse still a steady thrum that answers back. "I'm okay. Thank you."

The man nods, giving my shoulder a sympathetic pat. "I'll put them in a bag. You can take them with you to the hospital and change there. We're nearly at the marina," he says, nodding toward the shore. I follow his gesture to where an ambulance waits by the docks, its lights flashing. "How does that sound?"

"That sounds great, thank you, sir. I appreciate it."

The man leaves to pack up his gift, and my gaze lingers on the door he disappears through until Harper coughs, drawing my attention back to her. "I'll be fine," she whispers. "You can go get changed. I'll survive a few minutes on my own, don't worry."

"I'm not going anywhere."

"You don't have to come with me to the hospital."

I glare down at her. The spark brightens just a little in her eyes when I do. "Like hell I'm not."

"But you'll smell like the sea."

"That's supposed to be calming."

"On the beach, sure." She coughs, squeezing my hand as she does. I'm not sure if it's intentional or just a reflexive tightening of her muscles, but it makes my heart jump all the same. "You're going to smell like you rolled around naked in a fish market. They'll kick you out for disturbing the other patients."

I roll my eyes, and this time she gifts me a weak smile. "I see a near-death experience hasn't dampened your humor. Pun intended."

"That was awful. I don't think they can let you in. You smell like fish and make terrible, ill-timed puns."

"Do you not want me to come?"

Harper pauses. My heart sinks as though she's just tossed it right back into the deep water I just pulled her from. "I don't want you there if it brings back bad memories," she finally says. "Don't put yourself through that for me."

I stare at her, that image of her unseeing eyes still lingering like a nightmare that clings to consciousness long after waking. And I realize I hadn't even thought about the hospital and the painful past it could evoke. But she did. Only moments ago, she died in my arms. Beneath my hands. And she'd rather face the chaos and stress of a hospital alone than put me through memories that are difficult to bear.

The woman who put me there. The one who left me to die alone in the dark.

I cup her cheek. Her eyes drift closed. She leans into my touch. Squeezes my hand, and this time I know it was on purpose. Her warmth still feels like magic. I brought her back, and nothing I've done in my life feels like as much of an accomplishment as that.

"I'm coming with you," I say, leaning down to place a lingering kiss on her forehead.

When I pull away and look down at her face, it's as though everything I thought I'd come here for has been stripped away, leaving only one truth behind. One I'm not ready to put into the world. But one that consumes me nonetheless.

I'm in love with the woman I came here to kill.

SHROUDS

Harper

My eyes peel open, adjusting to the light in my bedroom. Scattered thoughts and fractured nightmares arrange into my first conscious thoughts.

Something is wrong.

There's motion in the bed. A tremor. A foreign sound.

I roll onto my side and see Nolan facing away from me, his body shaking. His back is exposed, his skin covered in a thin film of sweat. Though I've caught glimpses of it before, I can now see the full length of the straight scar that runs down his neck, dotted on either side with the healed marks of sutures or staples. A sound resonates from him, like a word he can't quite form in sleep. It's desperate. Like a plea.

I lay a hand on his shoulder. "Nolan . . ." He lets out another low, rumbling note of distress that forms a crevice in my heart. "Nolan . . . wake up . . ."

In a sudden flurry of movement, he flips over, his hand landing on my neck. His fingers notch beneath my jaw as he looms over me. His hair is damp with sweat, his eyes wild. Fear is painted across his features. When a few beats of my hammering pulse thrum into his fingertips, he finally blinks away the nightmare, processing the world in front of him. A shudder racks his body, and then he hangs his head, his forehead resting on my collarbone as he expels a long breath. "I'm sorry," he whispers against my skin.

"It was just a nightmare," I say, laying a tentative hand on the nape of his neck. His skin is hot and slick beneath my palm.

"Are you okay?"

"I'm fine." I gently squeeze the back of his neck, but he doesn't seem reassured, as though whatever he saw in his dreams is still too vivid to let go. And I know what that's like. At first, I was too exhausted to dream. But the last two nights, he's the one who's woken me from visions of hitting the water. Every time I thrashed or called out, he was there with a quiet word to wake me. But this is the first time I've seen him sleep. I wonder if he's been suffering nightmares all this time, and I just never knew. "Are you?"

Nolan lifts his head. His haunted eyes travel over my face, his fingers still collecting every beat of my heart as though it could stop without his touch. Though Arthur and Lukas and even Irene and Maya came to visit, it was Nolan who stayed. He spent three days at my side in the hospital. I don't know how he convinced the staff to let him stay, but he did, and he remained at my side the whole time. Whether it was waiting in the hall while I had X-rays to check for broken bones and fluid in my lungs, or watching from my bedside as I was given oxygen and IVs to combat edema and infection, or simply providing a steadying hand to help me out of bed to go to the bathroom, Nolan was there. And it seems like he's still not convinced that it's enough.

He wasn't enthusiastic about my insistence on leaving the

hospital so quickly. And he was *absolutely not* receptive to my suggestion that we resume our exhumations last night either. We finally arrived at a compromise: I would tell him the location of the next three burial sites, and he would handle the dig on his own, returning to my cottage when he was done. I tried to stay up and wait for him to get back, but the fatigue is still so consuming that I collapsed into bed shortly after dark and I never woke when he returned. I didn't expect him to lie in bed next to me, but now that he's here, there's a rightness to it. It feels like he's meant to be here. And I never expected it, but now I'm afraid of how much it will hurt when he's not.

"It's all I can see," he finally says. His touch travels from my neck to lie on my chest. My sternum and ribs are sore and bruised beneath my thin tank top. But my heart beats through the pain because of him. "Why can't you swim?"

I let out a breath of a laugh. "I fell into a pool when I was a toddler and nearly drowned. I refused to learn after that. I guess my parents didn't want to deal with the theatrical tantrum I threw whenever they tried to take me for swimming lessons, so they just . . . gave up."

"I hate that very much."

"I'm not sure it would have made much of a difference given the circumstances, but yeah. I think I hate it too," I say. A crease deepens between his brows as Nolan shifts to the side, lifting the hem of my shirt to inspect the bandage that covers the slice made by his knife. "How'd it go at the river?"

"Fine," he says, his attention still caught on the wound. "I found two bodies. I'll get the other one tomorrow. I brought them back here and hid them in the garden shed for now. What have you been doing with them?"

"Woodchipper."

Nolan's eyes flick to mine. "You know the bones don't just *dissolve*, right?"

"It's not like I'm making them into wall hangings and selling them on Etsy. I am *burying* them."

My joke doesn't seem to soften his hard expression. "And what if someone decides they want to come along and dig them up?"

"They'd have to suspect me first."

Nolan lets out a long sigh as he sits up, running a hand through his hair. I let my eyes travel over every inch of his skin. I've never had the chance to look at his body up close in the light before. And now he's casually sitting in my bed like he's always been here, all his bruises and scars on display. Those scars don't just stop at his skin. They run deep. I can almost see it, the way they tug and pull and warp his thoughts. He's afraid.

"What's wrong?" I ask, propping myself up on an elbow.

"Sam is watching you," Nolan says, turning enough to give me a single eye, his expression one of torment. "He has pictures. Notes and dates and times. Observations of your behavior."

I swallow, my pulse quickening. "I figured."

"Why didn't you say anything?"

"I did, about the drone. And considering he had no qualms about trespassing on the Ballantyne River property, it was probably a given that he'd take no issue with following me around on occasion."

"He could have followed us to the river. He could have seen something suspicious. We're digging up dead bodies on Arthur's land that he buried in rye sacks from the distillery, for fucksakes."

"I have no choice," I say as Nolan drags a hand down his face and levels me with a hard stare. "There are only days left before the sale closes. We have to get all of them out before that happens.

Viceroy could start work right away, and what happens then? Arthur's last years on this planet will not be spent in prison. I can't let that happen." I lay a hand on his arm, squeezing the snake beneath my palm. "It's only four bodies left. We can do that in a couple of nights, if we work together. But I have to get it done. Even if I dig alone and you keep an eye on Sam, we can figure something out."

"I'm not letting you do it by yourself." The sharp edge in his eyes softens just a little, and though it's obvious he's not pleased, it's more worry than anger that I see. "I only saw a few photos of Arthur. Most of them were of you. Why?"

"Proximity probably has something to do with it," I hedge. "But maybe he's trying to work me out. I'm sure he already has a lot banked up on Arthur."

"Is there something I need to know?"

I hesitate for a beat, sitting up with a wince that I hope he'll attribute to my bruised ribs. "You know the most important parts already," I say. "You know I'm not . . . good. I've done horrible things. You know I'll do whatever it takes to protect Arthur and Lukas and Cape Carnage." Nolan gives me a subtle, thoughtful nod, his eyes dropping from mine, resting on my lips for just a moment before his gaze lands on the bed. He doesn't say it, but I think he knows there's so much more that I just can't reveal. But he also seems to know that asking again won't yield a different result. "You know how to bring me back to life."

His focus snaps right back to me.

"I don't just mean pulling me from the water, Nolan. I mean . . . I forgot what it was like. What I was missing. It's been a long time since I let myself feel this way."

"Feel what way?"

My lip slides between my teeth. His gaze drops to the motion and I'm sure he thinks I'll just clamp down on my words. Maybe I should, but when I reflect on our interactions, every time I've defied the rational voice that told me to stay away from him, the risk has paid off. If I hadn't walked with him the first time we met, maybe he would have found me and killed me right away. If I hadn't risked forcing an alliance, we wouldn't be sitting in my bed, trying to figure out what we really mean to each other.

So I place my hand on his. I wait until he meets my eyes. "It feels like I can take a risk and trust you with all the worst versions of myself without scaring you away. Like even when I want to fight against you, I'm still fighting *with* you, because I know you're still on my side. Like I can let you in at my own pace, even though I'm afraid." I let my hand travel up his arm, my touch slowing over the ouroboros tattoo, a gentle caress over its infinite battle to consume itself. I trace the tense muscles, rising to his shoulder, not stopping until I fold my hand around the back of his neck. My eyes never leave Nolan's as I draw him closer, until I can see every variegated shade in the wedge of brown. "It feels like I can finally take a deep breath."

Maybe I can't say everything I truly feel. That he's chipping away at my heart, and I don't know how it's happening, but I don't want it to stop. I show him my worst and he's still here. And every day that passes, I think it has less to do with what I have over him, and more to do with me. But even though I might not be ready to put every thought out into the open, I can still show him how I feel. So I rise to my knees. I lay my hands on his warm face. I close the distance between us, pressing my lips to his as my eyes drift closed. And I kiss him with every emotion that I'm still struggling to understand. I pour what I can't say right into my touch.

Nolan's hand threads into my hair. But when I try to pull him down onto the bed with me, he resists. "I don't want to hurt you," he says when I draw away.

A wicked smile stalks across my face. I grab the hem of my shirt and drag it up my body, tossing it on the floor like a dare. My shorts go next. "Liar."

Nolan's eyes darken and he levels me with a serious stare. It looks like it takes effort to keep his eyes on mine as he lays a hand to my sternum. "You know what I mean. You're still recovering."

"But I like when you make it hurt," I whisper against his skin before I bite his bottom lip, raking my teeth over the tender flesh as I let it go. His pupils consume all but a thin band of color in his eyes. "You like a little pain too."

Nolan hesitates for only a heartbeat before he dives back into the kiss, biting me back as he pinches one of my nipples between his fingers, delivering a hit of pain with the pleasure, sparking the need for more. When I break the kiss on a gasp, he seals his mouth over the peak of my breast, taking my nipple between his teeth. My nails rake across his scalp as my desperate moan fills the room.

"I can take more," I whisper when he breaks away to press a line of kisses and gentle bites up my chest and onto my neck.

"I know you can. And you will. I have plans for you." One swift bite clamps down on my neck, and though I whimper with need, he lets go. I know it's a promise, one meant for another time. "But not today."

His arms fold around me, his eyes not leaving mine as he lays me down. Every motion is gentle. Careful. As though I'm not someone to harm, but someone to cherish.

"Do you remember what I told you?" he asks as one of his calloused palms lands on my thigh, traveling up my skin with agonizing slowness. He traces a line to my clit, swirling slowly over the sensitive bundle of nerves.

"That I was a brat?" I snicker as a low growl rumbles in his chest. He gives my clit a pinch before resuming a gentle caress. Antagonizing Nolan in any form possible has become my favorite game. "Yeah, I remember that pretty clearly."

"No," he says, drawing the word out like a warning. Again, his expression becomes serious as he tugs his gray sweatpants over his hips and kicks them off. "I said the next time I fucked you, I was going to claim you."

He lines his erection up to my pussy, notching the head at my entrance but not pushing deeper. "Claim me?" I whisper as he keeps his touch on my clit and his cock at my center. "What does that mean?"

Nolan's brow furrows as his gaze travels over my skin, leaving a trail of heat behind. "It means I promised I would hunt you until the end of time. And what I get at the end of that hunt might change, but one thing remains the same. You're *mine*, Harper. I'll never let anyone take you from me. Not some asshole like McMillan. Not Sam Porter. Not even the sea."

I swallow, feeling like I'm running to the edge of another cliff. "What if I don't want to belong to anyone but myself?"

"You don't understand." He pushes just a little deeper, but not enough. He knows I need more. "You can do what you want. Run and hide. Stay and fight. Love me or hate me—it doesn't matter. It's not going to change a fucking thing for me."

I should be terrified. He stares right into me as he makes his vow. And it could be deadly. All I have to go on is trust. Trust in my instincts. Trust in him. But maybe that's part of the thrill. This man who would have scoured every corner of the world to kill me will tear it apart to save me.

I lay both hands on his face and draw him closer. "Prove you mean every word."

With just a breath of time, the world reduces to my room. My bed. This man and me. He slides into me, filling me slowly, my body stretching around his girth until I don't know where he ends and I begin. And his eyes are on me the whole time. It isn't until he's as deep as he can go that he finally slants his lips to mine.

This isn't the vicious torrent of anger. Or the bite of desire. This is longing. Every kiss is slow. Every touch is purposeful. Every part of me aches as he glides in slow strokes within me. Even the parts he can't see or taste or feel. When he threads his fingers with mine and holds my hand tight, there's a twinge of pain, but it blooms deep in my chest. It takes root in a place that's been dark for so long that it burns as it's touched by light.

I map every muscle of his back. I trace every scar. The softness of his skin, the hardness of bone. I consume every inch of his flesh with my touch. Sandalwood and cedar flood every breath I take. I'm drowning. Drowning in his scent and his touch and his kiss. In his promises.

The rhythm of his slow thrusts grows stronger. I hook one leg over his back and he grabs my thigh, his fingers pressing into my flesh but his touch is still gentle, reverential. He breaks from my lips to layer kisses across my jaw, down my throat. A soft bite lands on my pulse. When I moan with the need for more, I can feel his smile in the kiss that lingers on my neck.

"I'll make it hurt next time, if that's what you want," he whispers into my ear in a decadent vow. I shudder at the thought, my core clenching with immediate need. "But this time, you're going to be my good girl and take it sweet."

Something seems hidden beneath his words. I tilt my head and force him to meet my eyes. "Why?"

Nolan sweeps the hair away from my face. His thrusts slow to a halt. A crease flickers between his brows as his eyes linger on the sweat gathering at my hairline. When they return to mine, that fissure of darkness seems to glow against the green. "I need to know I can have you without destroying you."

My lungs trap a breath beneath my bones. It takes a long moment before I can let it go. "I trust you," I finally say. I run my fingers through his damp hair. Press my palms harder to his back. "I mean it."

I draw him down into my kiss. I show him that I mean every word. It could be reckless. Dangerous. Deadly. But that's the price I'm willing to pay to feel alive.

Our kiss doesn't break as Nolan's cadence of thrusts resumes, gliding with rocking strokes. Every touch feels reverential, from the caress of his tongue across mine to the way his thumb traces a pattern across my thigh. I map his scars, committing each one to memory. When I trace the one down the back of his neck, he shudders. For a moment, I think I've made a mistake, bringing him back to a memory he thinks he has of me when a quiet growl rumbles in his chest. But the longing in his kiss only deepens. His fingers caress my cheek. His strokes grow more powerful. I do it again and he breaks the kiss just long enough to whisper my name. My heart feels like it's shedding a layer of ice, thawing beneath his warmth.

He keeps hold of my leg and raises my ass from the bed, angling my hips to take him even deeper. His pace grows stronger. More urgent. I whimper as he pistons into me, every muscle coiling tighter as I edge closer and closer to unraveling. And then he pulls my hand away from his neck long enough to prompt it down to my center, a wordless request for me to touch myself. I slide my fingers between us and I press my touch to my clit and moan into his mouth.

Nolan pulls just far enough away to stare down into my face. "You consume every waking thought. Every fucking dream. I tried to hate you for it. But I can't. I don't." His touch trails over my pulse. I wonder whether he thinks about how desperately he once hoped to snuff it out, or that my heart beats because of him. "Come apart for me."

It's as though he commands my body. Like he can conjure whatever he wants. The moment the demand leaves his lips, an orgasm builds until it washes through me. My lips part. My eyes close. Pleasure shatters through me, igniting every cell. My back bows from the bed and I feel the desperate unraveling of Nolan above me. He grits out my name as his final thrusts strike deep and hard, a tremor racking his body as he fills me with his cum.

Though it feels as though it could last forever, the orgasm gradually passes. His strokes slow to a stop, but he stays buried in my pussy. "So fucking beautiful," Nolan whispers, and with a kiss to the lashes of each of my closed eyes, he lets his weight sink onto me. It's a delicious pressure that I savor. Heat and heartbeats. Scents and caresses.

I trace long, slow lines down his spine. The sun is starting to color the world outside the window with shades of overcast gray. I'd like to imagine the outside world will never creep into this sanctuary, but there are too many fears and adversaries lying beyond that door for us to stay here much longer. And even though we remain entangled for a long while, it still feels too soon when Nolan checks his watch with a defeated groan and pulls away.

"I'd like to stay, but I should really go," he says, dragging his bag closer to the bed to pull a pair of briefs from its depths. I realize I must be showing more disappointment than I intended, because his expression softens. "I want to keep tabs on Sam. You should get some rest anyway, and I'm not sure that'll happen if I'm here."

I scoff, though I know he's probably right. "I can control myself."

"I can't."

When I smile, he does too, the dimples appearing in his cheeks. I think this is the lightest I've seen him since that day we met at A Shipwrecked Bean. But even now, I can see the mounting worries that haunt his eyes. "I'll see you later?" I ask.

Nolan runs his hand over my hair. Presses a kiss to my forehead. "Yeah. You will. Try to get some rest."

I stay in bed to leave him some space to gather himself up and depart. But my thoughts follow him like a storm that hugs the horizon. I know I'm putting him in danger, especially if it's true that Sam is following me around and taking photos and notes. Sam has already broken more than one law in pursuit of his story. Who's to say he won't find a way into Lancaster Manor to look for something concrete that will finally connect Arthur to La Plume? I don't want anything damning in my possession, or Arthur's, that could be linked to Nolan if he does.

I slide my phone off my nightstand, chewing my bottom lip as I send a text to Lukas.

Hey, Lukas.

A short moment later, I receive a text with a meme of an octopus chasing a scuba diver onto a boat and a joke I'm sure Lukas has been dying to make:

I've seen enough hentai to know where this is going.

Har har har. You're so hilarious, Lukas.

I've been waiting to use that! How are you feeling?

A little sore, but getting there. I need to ask a favor.

Sure, what's up?

The thing I gave you for safekeeping. Can you please get it for me and drop it by the cottage?

Sure, but it'll have to wait until next week if that's okay? I'm in Chicago for a whiskey conference.

I expel a long breath, pressing my eyes closed. I don't like what I see when I do. It's not just memories that surface on the black canvas, it's threats to an uncertain future too.

> On the shelves by the boiler, right?

> Yeah . . . you can't wait until I get back?

I wish I could, but I'm not willing to put Nolan at risk. I already left him once to the hands of fate. I'm not going to do it again.

> I'll be okay.

With a final note of thanks to Lukas, I head to the shower. In half an hour I'm entering Lancaster Manor, where "Leonore Overture No. 3" from Beethoven's opera *Fidelio* rolls down the hallway from Arthur's sitting room, one of his favorites. But I don't go to see him. Instead, I'm standing at the entrance of the basement door by the kitchen.

Every beat of my heart scrapes at my bones. Sweat slips down my spine. My breaths come in short pants. My palms are slick before I've even gripped the brass handle. It takes everything in me to turn it. Only one thought keeps me going.

I need to give it back.

I flip on the light switch, the old incandescent bulb doing little to illuminate the cavernous dark. The smell of dampness and mildew rises to greet me like a noxious fog. I avoid this place for a reason. It smells exactly the same as my worst nightmares. I'm desperate to shut the door and run. But I grip the cold iron railing and take my first step on the wooden plank.

One more step. One more step. One more.

By the time both my feet are on the packed dirt floor of the cellar, my whole body is shaking. The stone walls emanate the musky smell of earth that never dries. The exposed rafters overhead are covered with white curtains of spiderwebs that waft in the breeze as I walk beneath them. Decaying boxes rest on rusted shelves. The skeleton of a mouse lies curled next to a set of long-forgotten gardening tools.

"It's not the same place," I tell myself between shuddering breaths. I repeat that mantra with every step I take toward the furnace and boiler. I can see Nolan's bag, the one item on the shelf not covered with a layer of dust. I'm nearly there when I catch sight of the cellar doors that lead to the exterior of the house.

They're exactly the same as the ones in Harvey Mead's house.

I turn and vomit on the floor.

I'm shaking. Blinking at the floor. But I still see them. Those two cellar doors and the light that slid between the slats during the day, a heavy chain locking them closed from the outside. There weren't any stairs. I could just barely touch the doors when I jumped. The first two days we were trapped there, I would get up on Adam's shoulders and try to test the hinges or smash the wooden planks with my fist. Then Harvey Mead broke both Adam's legs so we couldn't reach them anymore.

I hear my own voice. Begging from memory. "He has an infection," I'd pleaded on Adam's behalf, pounding on the second door that led to the bowels of the house. This one we had no hope of breaching. It was made of iron with a slat in the middle where Mead would toss us bottles of cloudy water and half-eaten hamburgers, the patties covered in fly eggs. By that point, we'd become so desperately hungry that we stopped bothering to pick them off and consumed whatever he gave us, eggs and all. "Please help him."

Eventually, he came to the door. Unlocked it. Dragged Adam away. And I should have fought him with my bare hands. I should have done *something*. But I was too afraid. Just like I was too afraid to sit with Nolan on the road and put myself square in the public eye that I was so desperate to escape from. I was the social media influencer who'd escaped a serial killer there at the scene of a hit-and-run. A target for the press and the public. I thought I couldn't take the pressure of the publicity that would descend on me a second time. I feared the scrutiny I'd been trying so hard to avoid.

Tears streak down my face. I don't know if I'll ever get over the guilt of being the one who lived, or the woman who walked away. Or the grief of everything I lost. Or even my fear of waking alone in the dark.

But I can do something now.

I stumble to the shelves, grab the bag, and run, nearly toppling Arthur over when I bolt through the door and into the kitchen.

"*Harper*," he breathes, catching my arms. I'm gasping for air, as though I've run a marathon. The stern stare that's always etched into his skin from a lifetime of frowning softens when he takes in the state of me. "What are you doing? You were in the cellar . . . ?" I nod. "Why . . . ?"

"I had Lukas put something down there for safekeeping," I say between ragged inhalations. "It belongs to Nolan. The guy at the theater . . . ?" He looks at me blankly, and I can tell he's unable to recall the specifics. "It doesn't matter. I just had to give it back."

"So you went downstairs . . . ?" I nod, wiping my eyes with my sleeve. He knows I can hardly even look at the door. There are too many horrifying memories that lie in wait behind it. "My dear Harper," Arthur says, folding me into an embrace. "You could have asked. I would have come. You don't need to brave those demons alone."

I weep, for the first time in a long, long time. And as the weight of the backpack and the secrets it carries shift over my spine, I think maybe he's right.

Maybe I don't have to brave them alone anymore.

FOUL GROUND

Nolan

It's early evening, the sun still hidden behind a thick gray veil when I walk to Harper's cottage. I hear the electric hedge trimmer in the distance as I head up the flagstone walk and take the path that hugs the cottage and leads to the back garden. The sound grows louder as I cross the patio. *Christ*, I hope she's not slicing up another tourist to put through her woodchipper—though something about that idea fills me with unexpected excitement. I'm sure she'd have a good reason and a delightfully unhinged plan. I think.

I'm just about to pass through the garden gate when Arthur appears before me, a startling specter in his three-piece suit and polished shoes with a bespoke cane. His shock of white hair is perfectly coiffed, his bushy brows lowered as he regards me.

"Hello, Mr. Lancaster. You startled me," I say, opening the gate for him as he's clearly determined to pass through it.

"You're the man from the theater," Arthur says, his sharp eyes slicing across my face.

"That's right. Nolan Rhodes, sir." I extend a hand and his

expression softens. He gives me a slight nod and leans his weight on his cane as he accepts the handshake. "Is Harper around?"

"Yes. She's working on the topiaries."

"How's that going?"

"Horribly. The moose is an atrocity."

"I expected as much."

Arthur gives me a grunt and I tip my head to him, starting to walk in the direction of the sound. His sudden grip on my wrist stops me. "Before you move along, I wonder if you wouldn't mind doing me a favor?" he asks.

"Certainly. What do you need?"

Arthur doesn't let go of my arm, instead using it to prompt me back in the direction of Harper's house. "I'm looking for my bag that Harper was keeping for me. She said I could retrieve it from the cottage, but it might be upstairs and I have difficulty with the staircase. I'm old, you see."

I chuckle at his dry wit. "No problem," I say as we make our way toward the cottage with more vigor than I expected from my elderly companion. "What does it look like?"

"Black leather. Looks somewhat like an old doctor's bag. It has two robins embossed on the side, between the handles."

"Do you remember where it is, exactly?"

"I . . . I don't recall. The guest room, possibly."

"Okay. I'll have a look." I help him lower to a seat at the patio table, then I head into the unlocked back door of the cottage. The scent of palo santo lingers in the air. The interior is clean and unfussy, just like it always is. As I'm heading toward the staircase, I notice one of the white pawns has been moved on the chessboard. It's jumped ahead two spaces, waiting for an unseen opponent to play.

I take the stairs by twos, reluctant to leave Arthur waiting in the cooling air and growing fog. I've seen the guest room before, but this is the first time I've been inside. It's a simple layout, just a bed and a small dresser, a worn desk with some sewing supplies and papers resting beneath a window. I check the closet first, and I find the bag almost immediately beneath the folded blankets and winter clothes, taking it downstairs and out the back to where Arthur waits at the table, fidgeting with his crooked fingers. As soon as he sees it in my hands, his expression brightens, and he rises to his feet.

"Good lad," he says, nearly yanking the bag out of my hand when I offer it. "Thank you. You saved my poor knees. I'm old, you see."

"Yes, I think you might have mentioned that."

"Your short-term memory is the pits when you're so old your bones are crumbling to dust." He waves me off as I offer an arm with a chuckle. I'd assumed he wanted to go back to the house, but instead he heads toward the path that leads to the front of the cottage.

"Where are you going?" I call after him.

"Things to attend to, my boy. Many thanks for your assistance." Arthur doesn't turn as he raises his cane in a wave, then disappears around the side of the cottage, the bag gripped tight in his free hand. I wait until the metronomic cadence of his cane tapping the flagstones disappears. Once I'm reasonably sure he's successfully made it safely off the property, I go on the hunt for Harper, finding her near the main driveway to the house.

She doesn't realize I'm close by, so I take a moment to just watch her. She's partway up a stepladder, her hair pulled back in a messy bun, a pair of safety goggles over her eyes. Her favorite

Welcome to Cape Carnage shirt and black overalls are covered in leafy debris. She's wielding an orange hedge trimmer with great concentration but very little skill. If this bush was ever meant to be a moose, I can't see it. It looks more like an abstract, rabid dog. But she doesn't give up. Not even when she accidentally cuts off half its head.

It takes me a moment to realize I'm smiling.

I still don't understand how or when this happened. Weeks ago, I'd have given anything to get this close and use her own tool as a weapon against her. And now I'm standing here with a grin, admiring her determination. She's nothing like what I expected. I don't see a monster when I look at her now. I see someone so loyal that I know she'll stay here until dark if she has to, trying to get it right for Arthur. I see someone who is resilient. Someone who is fierce when she needs to be, but kind when it's deserved. Maybe, in my case, even when it's not. And I can't get enough of her, even if it just means watching from a distance.

When she gives up her efforts long enough to pause for a vicious cough, one that still plagues her after the near-drowning a few days ago, I finally approach.

Though it takes a moment to convince her to relinquish the trimmer and call it a day, she does. I take her back to the cottage. Make us dinner as she has a shower. I grab her as soon as she's out of the bathroom and haul her over my shoulder to the sound of her laughing shriek. I deposit her on the couch and spread her legs wide and eat her pussy until she's screaming my name. Then I flip her over and fuck her hard, just the way she likes. When I twist my fist in her hair and tug, she moans. When I slap her ass, she cries out for more. When I slide a hand across her throat and squeeze, her pussy tightens around my cock and she comes again, pulling me into oblivion with her as I fill her until I have nothing left to give.

I don't tell her, but I want to do this every day. Not just fuck her until she's boneless and trembling against me. It's everything else too. Taking care of her afterward. Reheating our cooling pasta. Sitting across from each other. Talking. Learning the things she likes. Things she worries about. I find myself wondering how I could take some of the other burdens she carries now that there are only four bodies left to find. We'll be done in a matter of days, and then what happens? She could clearly use help, whether it's with Arthur or navigating the tourist season or even those fucking topiaries. But I don't live even remotely close to Carnage. My life in Tennessee seems so distant from my reality these past few weeks. And every time I try to remind myself that my stay here is only temporary, I find I only push those thoughts away. *There are more important things to focus on right now*, I tell myself. *You can worry about home later.*

But what if I still don't want to worry about home when everything else passes? I already told Harper that I'm not letting her get away from me. And I meant it. But what does that look like? How does that work? Is it something she even thinks about?

I'm still tossing these questions around after dinner. We're biding our time until evening deepens to night, at which point I'll head back to the inn to retrieve the car for our next escapade at the Ballantyne River. At least, that's the plan until a call comes through on Harper's phone.

"Hey, Lukas," she says, her tone nonchalant as she rises from our game of cribbage to put the kettle on for a fresh pot of tea. "What's up?"

"Have you talked to Arthur?" he says over the speaker. I can detect the tone of concern, though he tries to hide it. And I can see in her face that she's worried, too.

"A few hours ago, yeah. Maybe about seven o'clock. Why?"

"I texted him a few times to check in, but he hasn't responded. He didn't pick up when I called, either. Would you mind checking the house? I'm worried he had another fall."

Harper is already grabbing her jacket and sliding her work boots on when she gives him a quick reply and hangs up. And I'm right on her heels.

"This isn't like him," she says as she marches through the back garden. A heavy fog has descended upon us, and I can't even see the main house through the thick, moonlit mist. There are no lights on inside to guide us either.

"Maybe he got tied up with something in town."

Harper looks up at me with a raised brow. "What do you mean?"

Unease trickles through my veins. I swallow, laying a hand on Harper's arm to stop her.

I already know it. I've made a fucking colossal mistake.

"I saw him when I first arrived," I say. "He said you told him to grab his bag from the cottage—"

"No—"

"And he asked if I could find it upstairs for him—"

"*Oh no no no*—"

"So . . . I gave it to him. And then he said he had 'things to attend to.'"

"Nolan," she shrieks, whacking my arm with a thud. "That's his fucking *murder bag*. He hates going into the cottage, and he played you like an amateur to get it."

I groan, swiping a hand down my face. Though I look back

toward the cottage simply because that's the last place I saw him, I have no fucking clue where to start. "Fuck. I'm sorry."

"You can't believe anything he says. Seriously. Not *anything*."

"I just didn't expect it. He kept telling me he's an 'old man'—"

"*I know*," she says, exasperation heavy in her voice. "He loves to tell people that. 'I'm *so* old, help an old man pick up his cane, would you, dear?'—and then *bam*. He knifes you in the fucking throat." Harper shoots me a glare before whipping her phone from her jacket pocket. Her thumbs tap furiously over the screen. "Don't mistake advanced age for weakness. Arthur has spent decades refining his craft. If anything, his age has worked to his advantage."

Though I'm irritated at myself and worried for Harper, I'm kind of impressed. "I'm sorry, Harper. Truly. I won't make that mistake again."

The only acknowledgment she gives me is a worried flick of her eyes as she chews on her bottom lip. She frowns at the screen, and a heartbeat later her expression clears, leaving only determination behind. "He's at the cemetery. Take these." Harper thrusts her keys in my direction. "The Jag is parked in the garage. Bring it down the main driveway and stop at the gate. I just have to grab something from my place and I'll meet you there."

With a nod, she turns and runs toward the cottage, and I watch her for just a beat before I pivot in the opposite direction and run for the house. The old sedan rumbles to life and I bring it down the drive, stopping where Harper instructed. A moment later, she appears, running from the back of the cottage with a backpack slung over her shoulders. She shrugs it off as she gets close to the car, but it's not until she's inside that I recognize it for what it is.

My backpack.

"I guess we're all about the murder bags today," she says quietly, passing it over the center console to me. I'm so stunned that it takes me a moment to accept it. "Your book is inside too. Everything is there." She lifts one shoulder. "But I won't be offended if you want to check."

I set it on my lap, my eyes not leaving hers. I should be celebrating. I should feel relieved. Maybe I should even feel ready for the revenge I came for. But I don't. It's as though everything has washed away, leaving only the core of my obsession behind. Harper was always at its center. But what she means to me has transformed, and now all I feel is fear for what this could mean. "Why?"

She tries to shrug again, but it comes off jerky and nervous. "Just in case."

"Just in case of what?" That anxiety is swirling now, a squall behind my sternum. "Just in case of Sam? Or something else?"

"I don't know. I just . . ." She shakes her head, turning her attention to her hands as they fidget in her lap. "I just don't want you to be pulled into it if things come down on Arthur and me." She tries to smile, but it seems brittle around the edges. "I've done enough damage already, don't you think?"

I don't answer that. I can't. I don't know how the accident happened or why she chose to leave Billy and me on the road. Maybe she has reasons I don't understand. And I can't quantify how much damage she's done, nor how much I've grown because of her, even when I didn't want to. How can I possibly measure loss against love? The grief I've endured against the life I've gained? I can't change the past. But hasn't she given me purpose in its aftermath?

I set the bag in the footwell behind her, and then I grasp her chin, staring into her shining eyes so she knows I mean it when I say, "Thank you, Harper."

With a swift and gentle kiss to her lips, I focus on the fog ahead, putting the car in drive.

The roads are empty given the hour and poor weather. The air feels thick with tension between us, Harper relaying directions before slipping back into contemplative silence. When we arrive at the cemetery, the iron gate that bars entry to the twisting road at night is ajar, enough for someone to walk through, a heavy padlock hanging open on the chain.

"Any idea what he's doing at the graveyard?"

Harper expels a long breath. "Hopefully having a peaceful moment of reflection and solitude." I glance in her direction and she gives me a flat look in reply. "Considering he has the murder bag, I seriously doubt it's anything good. I'll get the gate."

She steps out of the car and pushes it wide enough for me to drive through, and I wait on the other side as she shuts it. As she slides back into her seat, I hear the yapping bark of a small dog in the distance ahead.

"Looks like he's probably at the Lancaster family plot," Harper says, zooming in on the map on her screen to pinpoint the location of Arthur's phone. She pockets the device and points to the dark road that twists up a hill of graves. "Up there."

I roll forward, a slow and careful procession through the mist. When we're nearly at the top of the hill, a small dog with bows at its ears bounds across our path, a leash trailing behind it.

"That's probably not good," I say, lurching to a stop.

"No. Probably not."

I throw the car into park and turn it off, leaving the keys in the ignition. We get out and quietly push the doors closed, though it would be hard to hear us over the insistent bark of the tiny canine bounding around my legs. I pick it up and it settles, and we exchange a grim look before Harper turns toward a section of the cemetery bordered by a low fence with an open gate that leads to the headstones just visible through the thick fog. At first, it seems still. Empty. And then there's a moan.

We rush toward the gate.

Two men lie supine among the graves. But only one of them moves.

Harper drops to her knees at Arthur's side, checking his cheek where the skin is split and bleeding. "Arthur, oh my God, are you all right?" He groans and tries to sit up, but doesn't answer. I set the dog down and check the other man's pulse, but I can already tell by his open, unseeing eyes and his cool skin that there's no hope of resuscitating him.

Arthur's black bag is next to him, the zipper open, a syringe lying nearby. I pick up one of several vials strewn across the grass next to it. *Midazolam*, this one says beneath a bloody fingerprint. A powerful, fast-acting sedative. One that can kill.

I shift my attention to Arthur, who is clearly injured and disoriented. Questions swirl through my mind. *How the hell did this all happen? And why did he want to kill this man?* But judging by Arthur's groans and anxious mumbling, I'm not sure the answers are going to be easy to find.

I set the vial down and move to Arthur's side. We get him to his feet, and when I'm sure he won't fall over, I pass his cane to him.

"Are you okay?" Harper asks, grasping his trembling shoulders, her eyes shifting between his. A whimper escapes his lips. He seems deeply distressed, his face twisted in pain. "What happened?"

"Poppy." Arthur's bloodstained fingers trail across Harper's cheek, his whisper a plume of fog in the cooling night. "I thought you were gone."

Harper's focus cuts to mine for only an instant, but that brief glance is laced with sorrow. She hides her pain with a weak smile when she returns her attention to Arthur. "I'm right here," she says, catching Arthur's hand to whisper a kiss across his knuckles. "Everything is going to be okay."

Her words are sweet but fragile, like blossoms of color beneath the snow. But as much as Arthur wants to hold on to Harper's promises, the confusion is evident in his cloudy eyes. It surfaces in the way his gaze shifts over her face, in the fear and distrust harrowed in the patchwork of wrinkles that net across his skin.

"But I saw you. In the cottage." His voice wavers, his hand trembling on his cane. He tries to pull away from her and pace in agitation but finds it too difficult over the uneven ground. "There was so much blood."

"Just a nightmare."

"He wrote in your *skin*—"

"It's all okay."

Arthur shakes his head, tears welling in his eyes. "You were gone. My Poppy. I *saw* you."

"Shh," Harper whispers as Arthur repeats his words, the frustration climbing in his voice, making each note of distress grow louder. He runs a hand across his head as though trying to force the broken fragments of his thoughts into a picture he can recognize. "I can take you home now."

"Who are you?"

Harper grips his hand in both of hers, her eyes shimmering in the moonlight. "I'm Harper. I'm your friend."

"Where's Poppy?" Arthur's eyes cut to me as I lay my palm on

319

Harper's back, where the muscles are tense with the effort to hold back her emotion. "Who are *you*?"

"I'm Nolan." I reach out a hand in greeting and he eyes it with suspicion. "I think we've met once before, but you might not remember. It was a while ago. Nice to see you again, Mr. Lancaster."

Arthur's confusion deepens, but the distraction of my words seems to set him on a new path, just like I'd hoped. He shifts his cane to his left hand and takes my handshake with surprising strength.

"Harper came to take you home to Lancaster Manor. In the morning, she can show you the topiaries."

"Yeah, we have a gardening competition to win, don't we, Arthur?" she says, her tone infused with forced brightness. Every word feels ready to break open, to split apart and reveal the depth of her heartache. Her eyes quickly cut to the body beside her before she forces a smile. "We don't want to lose to Sarah Winkle. It was pretty close last year."

Arthur's jaw works as he chews through his thoughts, his white brows lowering as a look of wrath descends on his face. "Sarah Winkle. That insipid, talentless busybody."

Harper breathes a laugh, but sniffles as she nods. Though she tries to be discreet as she swipes the edge of her finger beneath her lashes, grief and worry still shine in her eyes. "Yeah. She's a hack. We'd better be sure you like the moose, it's been giving me some trouble. Maybe you can give me some pointers."

"A moose, yes." Though he looks tired, Arthur seems intrigued by the idea. The light that was absent from his eyes returns just a little, like a dim spark among ashes. For a long moment, he stares at the nearest gravestone, still chewing at his bottom lip just the same way Harper does when she's lost in thought. And watching her watch him, I can understand. It's not just a friendship. It's a kinship.

Harper takes a step closer, looping Arthur's hand over her arm. "I can take you home now. We can get you cleaned up. I'll polish up those Christina Riccis for you. Looks like you got a little blood on them."

"Stefano Riccis, you recalcitrant clown."

"My bad. So, do you want to tell me what happened?"

"That man," he says as she starts leading him toward the car. "The man with the hideous little dog. He *hit* me."

"I can see that. You're a little cut up."

"I'm an old man, Harper. He hit an *elderly man*. Uncouth fiend, coming into our town to let his witless canine defecate everywhere and then strike the elderly of Cape Carnage. I despise him."

"Well, he deserved what he got," Harper says, letting a weighted beat of silence pass between them. "He did deserve it . . . right . . . ?"

"Yes. *Of course* he did. Violent, terrible little man."

I gather up the syringe and the scattered vials, placing them in Arthur's bag before I follow. I slide the bag behind the driver's seat. As soon as I'm done, I return to the body so I don't risk further agitating Arthur with my presence. The rest of their conversation only comes in bits and pieces as Harper settles Arthur into the passenger seat, bringing a blanket from the trunk to lay over his lap before helping him with the seat belt. When she seems sure he's comfortable, she closes the door and strides back to the family plot, returning to face me where I stand next to the cooling corpse.

"Oh my God, this is bad," she says, her voice hushed and strained as she drags her hands down her face. "It's so super bad. Arthur might as well have carved his name right into the dude's forehead. I can actually see the shape of his fucking cane handle."

We both lean a little closer to the body. Sure enough, the outline of the distinctive curved handle and wolf's head embellishment of Arthur's cane is imprinted right there on his skin.

"Christ," I hiss on a long exhale as we both straighten. "What do we do with the dog?"

Harper frowns, then bends to pick it up. "I'll take"—she reads the dog's name tag, then rolls her eyes—"Killer Queenie—Jesus fucking Christ, that's the worst—back to Maria's house. That's where the guy was staying. If I leave the gate open a bit, his wife will probably figure Queenie here made her way home on her own. Hopefully . . ." She shifts her attention toward the car and then to the body before returning her gaze to me. "Are you sure about this?"

"Yeah, absolutely. Take Arthur home and get him settled, and I'll be back as soon as I can. I'll keep you posted." Harper nods once, but she doesn't move, not even when I come closer. "Be careful," I say, staring down at her. She gives me a weak smile. I run my hand over her hair and press a kiss to her forehead before I let her go. "Everything will be fine."

With another slight nod, she takes a step back, and another, and then finally she turns and walks away.

As soon as she's gone, I run.

I leave the main cemetery gate ajar just enough that I hope it will remain unnoticed, but will be quick for me to open when I return with my vehicle. And then I race to the inn as fast as my body will let me.

By the time I reach my room, my knee is throbbing and my shirt is sticking to my skin, dampened with sweat. I don't just grab the things I think I'll need to get rid of the unknown man. I grab *everything*. I'd already gotten rid of most of the food in the fridge and packed some of my bags in the process of working my way toward this decision. But now I know.

I could run. I could disappear in the fog and never think of Cape Carnage again.

But I will not leave Harper.

Not with Sam closing in. Not with Arthur causing chaos. She can't do this on her own. Whether she likes it or not, I'm staying at her place. I'll sleep on the fucking floor if I have to. If tonight has proven anything, it's that she is not safe. Even Arthur is becoming a threat to her well-being. And I will not let her endure this alone.

I rush with my suitcases through the empty lobby, placing them in my rental car before I head back to my room for my final two bags, the ones that are stocked with our nightly supplies—rope and collapsible shovels, duct tape and bug spray, the camp stove and hot chocolate. With a bag in each hand, I jog back to my vehicle and start loading them into the back, my thoughts consumed by Harper and everything I have to do at the cemetery to get rid of the body and ensure her secrets stay hidden.

"Well, I'll say," I hear Sam's voice from behind me. "That looks like a serial killer kit if I ever saw one."

I turn slowly, coming face-to-face with the muzzle of a gun.

"Evening, Sam. That's an aggressive way to say hello." I slowly start to raise my hands. When they're at chest height, I strike out with my right hand, hoping to snatch the gun from his hand.

But Sam is faster than I expected.

With a kick I don't even see coming, he nails my left knee with a vicious strike. I go down hard on the asphalt.

"Oops. That wouldn't be your bad leg, would it?"

Deep breaths shudder through my lungs. I struggle to focus on the asphalt beneath my palms. It's not just the agonizing burn in my knee. It's not the wound that's never fully healed that darkens the edges of my vision. It's the rage. Sam knows my weaknesses and he's willing to strike them.

A terrible question blares through my thoughts like an alarm: *How many weaknesses is he ready to exploit?*

Though it takes me a moment, I force myself through the searing pain. With a hand braced to the bumper, I rise and face Sam once more.

"I started looking into you," Sam says. His gun is steady. His eyes determined. A little smile of triumph lifts one corner of his lips. "The more I started digging, the more interesting things I started to find."

"I don't know what you're talking about."

His smile grows darker. More boastful. He shifts his weight, the camera bag on his hip following the motion. "I'm sure you don't. But you're going to get into your car and drive exactly where I tell you to go. And then we'll have a talk and see if I can jog your memory."

I take a step closer, and he takes one back, firming his grip on his weapon. "And if I don't?" I ask.

"Well, I guess I shoot you. It would probably be pretty believable that I acted in self-defense, all things considered. Especially since Sheriff Yates isn't known for his investigative skills, you know? So whether you live or die is up to you. But either way, if you don't come with me, I'll hand everything I have straight to the FBI. I'll expose everything I know about you," he says as his thumb shifts to release the safety from the gun. "*And* Harper Starling."

TEMPEST

Harper

| How's it going?

I OPEN MY LAST TEXT to Nolan, my thumb hovering over the screen. I start typing a new message. *Are you okay?* But just as I'm about to press send, I notice what's missing. The little gray Delivered notification below my last question.

A thread of unease knits through my veins.

I send my other message, though I already know the result won't be different. The second message isn't delivered either. I call Nolan's phone. It goes straight to voicemail.

"Fuck," I whisper.

I drag a hand through my hair and stare down at Arthur, his mouth agape, his breathing deep and even. Part of me wants to stay in case he becomes restless in the night. But something gnaws at me. Though I try to tell myself that Nolan might have his phone off to minimize disruptions or to avoid detection, my instincts are telling me otherwise. Something feels wrong.

With a final frown at my sleeping friend, I send Arthur a text in case he wakes and checks his phone, and then I leave, taking the Jaguar to venture into the fog. From Lancaster Manor, I first head toward the inn where I'll be able to turn left and progress straight west to Spruce Road, the cemetery only three blocks away.

I slow as I reach the Capeside Inn. The mist is a little clearer here with the breeze that rolls across the waves to climb the cliffs. I stop the vehicle at the entrance to the parking lot, where I can see all the spaces. It's nearly full, but Nolan's rental is nowhere in sight.

The unease that creeps through me starts to churn, rolling through my guts like a twisting serpent.

I turn and head west toward Spruce Road and the Cape Carnage Cemetery. The streets are empty. The mist is thick, a silver shroud that blankets my headlights. As I drive through the quiet streets, I couldn't be more grateful for its oppressive haze. Especially when I arrive at the graveyard to find one of the gates still open, the chain dangling from the wrought iron vines.

I swallow and take my foot off the brake, letting the car creep forward until I nudge the gate open farther and roll onto the unlit drive.

The road winds through elms and oaks and sculpted hedges, past statues of angels and crosses, some tilting at angles. It snakes to the top of the hill, where a low fence of black metal spearheads encloses the private gravesite. I roll to a stop and turn off the car, opening the door to the scent of the sea air heavy in the mist. I listen, but nothing comes. No rustle. No whisper. Not even my own exhalations, my breath trapped in my chest.

It feels like I'm walking in slow motion. I already know what I'll find when I push the low gate open and step into the Lancaster family plot.

A man's body, lying on the ground. Right where we left it.

Air rushes from my lungs and I gulp it back down like I'm drowning all over again. I scan the darkness around me, but there's no sign of Nolan. There's nothing to indicate he was ever here.

He wasn't at the inn.

He never returned to the cemetery.

And he has his book. All the evidence I held against him. I told him I trusted him and gave it all back.

I thread my fingers into my hair and lower to a squat, as though I could curl myself into another dimension. Tears sting my eyes. How could he just leave? I don't want to believe he could simply disappear, not after everything he said. His words had burrowed right into me when he made me a promise. *You're mine*, he'd said. *I'll never let anyone take you from me.*

It felt so . . . *real*. I was sure it was the truth. How could I be so wrong . . . ?

It takes a long moment before I raise my eyes from the earth. My gaze lands on the familiar headstone a few feet away, its unusual half-circle shape easily distinguishable from the other monuments. I can't see the swirls of green in the jade marble, but the bracelets glint in the dim light where they hang from tiny hooks beneath the curve of the carved crescent moon.

I force myself to stand, my vision wavering behind tears as I stop in front of the headstone that was a gift from Arthur, one he gave me in the first few months of our friendship. I didn't have a body to lay here. Only memories. Just a name. Adam Cunningham.

I let my finger coast across the trinkets that dangle from the hooks. One of them is missing—the engraved silver bracelet. I realize that this is the first time I've thought of Adam without feeling the sting of loss or the crush of guilt. Instead, my first thought is about how lovely it is that Morpheus brought it back to me. A wild creature, ferrying memories across the town. Maybe he's put that bracelet where it will return to the strata of time. And that thought doesn't bring me sadness. Somehow, it brings me *relief*.

I can't pinpoint the exact moment when that loss finally started to transform, even just a little. But I know the reason why. Ever since Nolan came to Cape Carnage, I've wanted more than to just survive in the shadows. I want to bloom in them. Even if Nolan is gone. Even if his promise was just a brittle illusion, maybe that's all I really needed. A little bit of its glow, like a lantern in the night.

With a swipe of my knuckles beneath my damp lashes, I rise. Nolan's promise might have been a fragile vow. But mine isn't. I will not let Arthur down.

I head toward the corpse that's cooling on the ground. It's already been nearly two hours since Arthur killed him, so I probably won't have too much longer before his limbs start to stiffen. My frown deepens as I look to the car. I don't have the equipment to make this easier. I hang my head and let out a deep sigh, then remove the man's shoes.

"I realize this is very undignified," I say, checking the pockets of his pants, all of which are empty. Next I unfasten his belt and undo his button and zipper. "But I don't have many options here. And you probably did hit Arthur, after all, so let's just say you deserve it."

I start tugging his trousers over his hips and down his legs, yanking them off. Once they're free, I twist the pant legs to create a makeshift rope that I knot around his ankles. Grabbing the free end, I start dragging him toward the waiting car. "This is not really how either of us intended to spend our night," I whisper between grunts and tugs. "I thought I'd maybe have a glass of wine and some super-hot sex with my serial killer almost-boyfriend. Not getting ghosted and cleaning up bodies. You tourists really do have to ruin everything."

I keep tugging, a mist of sweat coating my skin, breaths sawing from my lungs with the exertion of dragging a limp-bodied man across uneven ground. Once I've got him through the gate, I give him a shove to roll him down the little slope. He lurches to a halt in the shallow ditch, and then I'm dragging him once more until I'm at the rear driver's-side door of the sedan. When I've got his feet and lower legs positioned in the footwell, I get into the car and start tugging him inside.

"You could make things a little easier on me," I tell him, grabbing his floppy arms to pull his torso upright. "Stiffen up a bit already."

With a little rearranging and more than one attempt, I manage to embrace his torso and heave him across the footwells of the rear seats. I take a minute to let my heart rate settle, and then I stride to the trunk to grab a pair of Arthur's beloved Burberry wool blankets to spread over the body.

As soon as I'm done, we head back to the Capeside Inn.

I know I should be focused on more important things, like perhaps ensuring Arthur doesn't go on more murdery escapades. Or maybe getting rid of this unknown tourist's body should be a priority. But I can't help it. Part of me knows the logical explanation is that Nolan left now that he has what he wants from me. But another part of me just can't believe it. The words he said the other night didn't feel like counterfeit promises made in the heat of the moment. I refuse to believe that rational voice in my head. Not until I see it with my own eyes.

I roll to a stop close to the entrance of the Capeside Inn parking lot, but I don't go in. I park on the street instead, in the shadows of the unlit section of the road. With a final check to ensure the body is covered behind me, I get out of the car and walk toward the hotel.

Nolan's car is still missing from its spot. Most of the other spaces are full. When I enter the lobby, there's no one there, not even Irene. I pause only long enough to confirm she's not snoring in her darkened room, and then I keep going, headed for the corridor that leads to Nolan's room.

I listen at the door. Nothing comes from the other side. I give it three light knocks on the wood. No one comes to answer. Then I slide my key into the lock and step inside.

My rational mind told me this is what I would find. But my heart hurts just the same.

There's no bottle of pills on the nightstand. No luggage on the rack. No food in the fridge. When I head to the wardrobe, no clothes are hanging inside. I don't check anything after that. I just sit on the edge of the bed, feeling like something has been torn from the center of my chest. Maybe it shouldn't hurt so much. After all, how well do I really know Nolan Rhodes? He came here to destroy me. He just found another way to drive a knife home, that's all.

But it does hurt. It aches. I feel raw, like all my bloody wounds are exposed. Aside from Arthur, he was the only person I showed my true self to. He saw the very worst in me. And I thought he accepted me the way I am, but at the first opportunity, he left.

Society never accepts every facet of a woman's true nature—especially their grief and trauma and darkness—though it feasts on those things until it consumes them, leaving only a polished facade behind. The world wants a perfect victim. Not the creature a woman like me might choose to become to survive. The best we can hope for is to find another soul who can stand in our path with open arms to embrace us.

I thought I'd found that in Nolan. He didn't even need my tragic backstory. He didn't turn away like I know everyone else would. He accepted the woman I chose to be the day I walked away from the ashes of my former life.

Or so I thought.

I run my finger beneath my lashes, catching tears that only reappear the moment they're wiped away. It takes a long moment to subdue the loneliness that threatens to choke up my throat. But in time, I do. And I will. I've survived worse, and I'll survive this too.

I rise. Head to the door. With a check through the peephole, I exit the room and head down the corridor.

When I arrive at the lobby, I hesitate. Something compels me to approach the registration desk. Ducking under the hinged countertop, I make my way to Irene's guest ledger. I flip the pages until I find Nolan's entry, running a finger across the line of his details. His dates of planned stay. His arrival time. According to the ledger, he hasn't checked out.

I frown at the book, trying to work out the information, comparing Nolan's details to the entries for other guests who have come and gone. Nothing in the book indicates that he's left, even though his room is as neat as a pin. It looked ready for the next guest, like he'd never stayed in it at all. Another ghost of Cape

Carnage that's blown away in a gale that's swept across the wrecks hiding beneath the waves.

Questions are rolling through my mind when a voice approaches from upstairs. Footsteps pound down the staircase. Someone is in a rush. I duck behind the counter, making myself small in the shadows.

". . . you sure about this?" an unfamiliar voice asks. There's a delay, as though he's speaking on the phone. "What if Rhodes doesn't talk?"

My blood freezes. I peek around the space beneath the hinged countertop, where it's unlikely I'll be spotted. I see a man traveling quickly down the last few steps. There's a hint of fear in his eyes. But there's determination too. He has a bag in one hand, a logo of two *P*'s in a circle embroidered on one side.

My quiet gasp is lost beneath his heavy footfalls as I take my wallet from my pocket and pull out the business card I slid inside. The same logo is embossed next to Sam Porter's name. *Porter Productions*, the card says.

The alarm that chilled my blood only moments ago transforms. I'm suddenly burning. I'm an incendiary, ready to destroy everyone in my path. Starting with this man, who must be Sam's drone operator.

"This sounds risky. You sure it's worth it?" He travels past the front desk, toward the door. "What about the location? The distillery is echoey as shit."

He heads out the door, his focus taken up by his destination and conversation. He doesn't look back to see me take the ancient three-hole punch from Irene's desk and dart beneath the counter to follow.

When I exit the inn, he's halfway across the parking lot, the phone pressed between his ear and shoulder. He digs his keys from his pocket and unlocks a Honda CR-V parked a few spaces from Nolan's favorite spot.

"I do trust you, man." He slows as he nears the vehicle. As soon as the trunk is open, he loads his bag inside, then hurries toward the driver's door. "I'll be there as soon as I can," he says, and then disconnects the call.

No, you fucking won't, I think as I rush forward.

He doesn't hear me coming. Doesn't even turn around. I hit him with every ounce of strength I have, crashing the hole punch into the side of his head with a satisfying *whack*.

He falls unconscious to the asphalt.

I quickly scan my surroundings. It's eerily still, only the sound of the ocean rising to meet us. Just a brief breath of calm, and then I'm a frenzied storm of motion. First, I take his phone, running to the nearby cliff edge to toss it and the hole punch into the sea. Next, I take his wallet and keys. Opening the trunk of his vehicle, I grab the bag, along with any other equipment I can find. I have no intention of wasting time I don't have dragging another limp man here, there, and everywhere. But I can at least make it look like a robbery and take all his expensive gear.

When I'm done, I give the man a quick check. He's breathing. Blood trickles from his nose. He must have smacked his face hard on the way down. I'm not sure what kind of damage I just caused, and I'm not about to wait around to find out. It could be a while before he awakens, if he ever does. It could be only moments.

I leave him where he is and run to Arthur's car, pulling away from the Capeside Inn and heading out of town as quickly as I dare with a body in my back seat. The fog grows thicker the farther I go from the sea. It consumes the headlights as I turn down the road that leads to the Lancaster Distillery.

Nolan Rhodes said he would walk through hell to drag me out if I ever tried to run.

But I don't hide in hell.

I bring it to life.

SQUALL

Nolan

SAM'S FOOTSTEPS ECHO ACROSS THE space that stretches around us, trapped between the beams of the distillery's vaulted ceiling. Though I strain against the handcuffs, I don't make any headway. The metal is flush against my skin. I try twisting my ankles, but that's useless too, the duct tape wound in thick layers to bind my legs to the chair.

"There's a great synergy to recording in this place," Sam says as he brings a long, thin bag over from the mouth of the corridor and pulls a tripod from its interior. He takes a deep, dramatic sigh, inhaling the scent of fresh paint and freshly cut lumber. "Considering it was once the heart of Arthur Lancaster's empire, interviewing another murderer here in the distillery that Lukas Lancaster is trying to bring back to life is a perfect way to tie all the pieces together. Don't you think?"

I don't answer. I have no intention of telling this man shit. Especially not on camera.

Sam smiles. It's as though he can divine my thoughts right out of my head when he says, "We are going to talk, you and me. Or everything I know about Harper Starling will be thrown into this documentary, and trust me when I say, her life will be blown apart."

"How do I know you won't do that anyway, even if I do talk to you?"

"I guess you'll just have to trust me." He shrugs, adjusting the tripod and then bending to retrieve his camera bag off a drop cloth. His eyes don't leave mine any longer than they have to, as though he doesn't fully trust how thoroughly he's incapacitated me. "Give me what I want, and I promise I'll leave her out of it."

"And what do you want, exactly?"

His smile stretches. "The story of a lifetime, of course. And the recognition I deserve."

I scoff, and Sam's eyes narrow to slits of malice. "Recognition? Or do you mean 'fame'?"

"I mean, *acknowledgment*. That my group has done what no one else could." Sam presses a button on one of the black cords that surround him, and two portable studio lights flicker on. I squint against their blinding white glare. "We've solved cold cases when the authorities couldn't. We've exposed criminals—"

"And now you've become one." I jostle my wrists behind me, my arms hooked beneath the metal armrests of my chair. "Or did you conveniently forget that there are laws about abducting people at gunpoint and holding them against their will, to name a few?"

Sam approaches me with a wireless lapel microphone clutched in his fingers. He attaches it to my shirt, avoiding my unyielding glare. When he's done, he returns to the mounted camera, putting his own microphone on before settling a pair of headphones over his ears. "You know, since before I even started the Sleuthseekers, I believed some rules needed to be bent for justice to be fairly served. But of all people in this fucked-up town, I thought that *you* would agree with that."

Sam adjusts the lens and buttons on his camera until he seems satisfied with what he's seeing on the viewfinder, and then he grabs the film slate from the floor. He positions himself between me and the camera, the clapperboard clutched in his hands.

"*Action*," he declares, whacking the black-and-white striped arm down onto the body of the slate before he rushes behind the camera, exchanging the clapperboard for his notebook. I wait until he's looking at the viewfinder before I roll my eyes. "Is your name Nolan Caius Rhodes?"

"You already know my name."

Sam glares at me from behind the camera. "We can skip right to Harper Starling, if you prefer."

My blood boils. I strain against the handcuffs. I'm desperate to tear his fucking throat out. To dig my fingers into his flesh and feel it split apart in my grip.

"Yes," I grit out. "My name is Nolan Caius Rhodes."

"Where do you live?"

"Gatlinburg, Tennessee."

"Tell me about what brought you to Cape Carnage?"

I release a heavy sigh, as though this is the most ridiculous fucking thing I've ever been forced to endure. "Bird-watching."

"Bird-watching," Sam echoes, failing to keep his triumphant smirk from bleeding into his voice. He's hardly the impartial interviewer, not that I expected any level of professionalism here. "That's right, Irene mentioned something about that to me. I guess that makes a lot more sense now. Tell me, do you ever observe starlings?"

I cut him with a vicious glare.

337

"Did you know that a starling can mimic the songs of up to twenty different bird species?" he continues. "They can even impersonate human speech."

There's something else behind the slow smile he gives me. Like he holds all the cards. Even the ones I don't know about.

A suffocating blanket of unease seems to descend around me. "Ask me a relevant question," I snarl.

"Sure thing." The false brightness in his tone sets me even more on edge. Sam flips a page in his notebook, tapping a pen to his chin. "Ah, yes. I have a relevant question. *Why did you murder Trevor Fisher?*"

My lips seal tight.

"What about Dylan Jacobs? Or Marc Beaumont?"

I say nothing.

"Or what about Jake Hornell? Would you happen to know anything about his disappearance on June seventh? Or how about you tell me what you were doing at the Ballantyne River last night? Because it seemed pretty fucking suspicious to me."

Fuck. I never heard anything. Never saw a light or another car. It was a normal night at the river, except for the fact that Harper wasn't with me, which I'm so fucking grateful for now. But clearly I wasn't as alone as I thought.

When I still don't answer, frustration rolls from Sam, his shoulders stiff with tension. I don't believe he'll ever leave Harper out of this. I'll never take him for his word. But if I can rile him up enough, if I can force him from frustration and into rage, maybe I can coax him closer . . .

"Since you're determined to make this difficult, Mr. Rhodes, we're going to talk about what you know about Harper Starling. And then we'll talk about what *I* know about her." He flips a page in his notebook. "Harper was driving the car that crashed into you and your younger brother, Billy, four years ago. After the incident occurred, she drove away and left you to die. Isn't that—"

A sudden sound echoes from the far side of the distillery. We both startle, Sam letting out a long breath as he shakes his head. "Fucking finally." He checks his watch before pressing a button on his camera to pause the recording. "*Vinny, I'm on the landing,*" he calls out.

But there's no answer.

Sam carefully withdraws his gun from where he's shoved it between his belt and his back. Silence descends around us. It's shattered by another metallic *whack*, like something striking one of the copper stills.

"Goddamnit," Sam whispers. He checks my wrists and ankles, then moves toward the stairs that lead to the floor below, casting me a wary glare before he disappears. I hear his footsteps descend the rest of the stairs, and then he starts crossing the room, heading in the direction of the sound.

I resume my struggle against my bonds. But I stop the instant I see her.

"What are you doing here?" I hiss as Harper comes out of the shadows and into the bright studio lights. She crouches low, rushing toward me. There's a slight tremor in her hand when she wraps it around my arm as she examines my predicament.

"Saving your ass, obviously," she replies, letting go of my wrist. She drops to my feet, starting to slice at the duct tape where it's stuck against the chair leg. "At least, I thought I was. How did you let yourself get handcuffed?"

"*Let myself?* Who *lets themselves* get handcuffed?"

"You do, apparently. Like a fucking rookie. And if I recall correctly, this is the second time you've been played today."

"Now is *not the time*, Harper." I feel the give in the tape as it splits and she moves to my other leg. "You have to get out of here," I whisper. "He's unhinged. He's got a gun."

"I noticed."

"If he sees you here—" My words are cut short as we hear Sam's boots scuff against the lower stairs. Harper manages to free my other ankle. "*Hide.*"

Our eyes meet for only an instant, but in that moment, I see fear in them. I've seen it in her before. I'll never forget the terror and hopelessness that stared back at me from the abyss of the sea. But I also know that this time it's different. She's not afraid for herself. She's afraid for *me*.

"Go," I mouth, not letting any sound escape my lips.

Harper sneaks back to the corridor, her footfalls silent. She disappears into the shadows beyond the bright lights just a moment before Sam appears on the landing, the gun still clutched in his hand. He looks a little shaken, a little cautious. But his determination seems to take over as he returns to his camera and presses a button. A tiny red light flicks on.

"Now," he says, then clears his throat, "where were we?"

"I believe we were at the part where I tell you that you're fucking unhinged. You abducted me and you're holding me against my will, and you can go fuck yourself."

Though Sam keeps the gun lowered at his side, he flicks the safety on and off as a reminder of his power over me. Knowing Harper is somewhere in the shadows is the only thing about his quiet threat that gives me true fear. But if I can just draw him a little closer . . .

"You know the thing about guys like you?" I ask, settling into my chair as though I have all night to play this game. "You're not that much different than the people you claim to hunt down. You've just taken your true crime 'infotainment' ten steps too far. But you don't have the actual skill to back it up."

Sam might not move from behind the camera, but I can almost feel the heat of his rage.

"You don't know shit about how to interview a witness. Or how to legally do . . . well . . . *anything*. Do you really think flying drones over Lancaster Manor or trespassing on private property or, I dunno, fucking *kidnapping* will stand up in court?"

"I don't care about what you *think*." Sam surges closer. He trains the muzzle of the gun on my smirking face. "I care about the *truth*."

His thumb shifts. The safety clicks off.

"Tell me the *fucking truth*," he snarls.

"You want to know the truth?" My heart pounds so hard against my bones that they could break. "The truth is, I'm not the one you should be worried about."

"*I am*."

The instant Sam turns at the sound of Harper's voice behind him, I stand and spin. The metal chair smashes against the backs of his legs. He loses his balance, pitching forward. The gun falls from his hand. A deafening bang crashes through the distillery when it smacks the floor and slides into the shadows.

I go down hard on my knees, my shoulder and face hitting the floor. But my eyes never stray from Harper. She rushes at Sam, keeping her body low as she seizes her opportunity. She slams into him while he's still unbalanced and wraps her arms around his legs. Her cry of fury echoes across concrete and metal as she uses every ounce of her strength to push him toward me.

Harper releases Sam with a final shove. He tumbles backward onto me.

And then I lift with my knees to catapult him over the railing.

His arms and legs wheel through the air. I think we're in the clear until one of his feet catches between the metal rungs and then twists. His boot locks at a sideways angle against one of the cross rails. The audible pop of dislocating bones and torn tendons fills the air, followed by his agonizing screams as he dangles from the landing.

"Fucksakes," Harper says between panting breaths, her hands braced on her knees. "That must really hurt."

Sam begs for help.

"Are you okay?" she asks me, ignoring Sam's pleas for assistance as she helps me to my feet instead. Worry is vibrant in her eyes. She holds my face between her palms, skimming a thumb over the blood that drips onto my cheek from a cut above my eye. "The gun—"

"I'm fine. Just lost my balance. Are you?"

"Yeah. I'm good." Harper's gaze softens, dropping to my lips and lingering there. "I thought you left."

My brows furrow. Harper's eyes meet mine only briefly, her cheeks flushing crimson. "Left?" I ask, and she lifts a shoulder. "No. Of course not. Why would I leave?"

She doesn't look at me, her attention caught on the shadowed corridor. "Why *wouldn't* you?"

I know that whatever is happening between us might feel different to me than it does to her. The only reason she's had to trust me was because she didn't have a choice, so it makes sense that she thinks I would cut and run if I had the chance. But she doesn't understand that she's all I've thought about for the last four years.

Every single day, her presence in my mind has given me something to fight for. It's given me purpose. Maybe that obsession looked very different when it started. But it hasn't stopped. It's just transformed.

"Harper . . ." I sigh when she looks away with a shake of her head, trying to hide the shine at her lashes. "First, how about you get me a key?"

"Right. Key." She snaps out of her momentary crisis of confidence to head for Sam, where he flails from the railing, his panicked cries and furious expletives bouncing through the room. She lies on her belly and reaches down to his pockets, letting out a triumphant squeak when she finds what she's looking for. When she returns with the key, she unlocks the handcuffs, and the moment they're free, I let the chair drop from my arms and wrap her in an embrace.

"No," I say, burying my face against her neck and crushing her to me. I inhale the sweet aroma of her distinctive scent. I relish every breath she takes against me, every touch as her hands slide across my back to hold me just as tightly. "I did not leave. I told you already. You're mine, and I'm not letting you go."

She nods. Maybe she thinks they're just pretty words. She might not realize that it's a promise. A vow that has no end. But when I pull back just enough to capture her mouth in a searing kiss, I *show* her. I press my lips to hers and steal her breath and lavish her tongue with mine. My hand threads into her hair and I hold her close. I know she's not ready to hear the words. They hardly even make sense to me. But I love her, and with my touch, I prove it.

"*Fucking* help me, *you fucking psychopaths*," Sam screeches, shattering our moment.

I rest my forehead against Harper's, leaving a bloody stamp

behind when we part. "I guess we should do something about that asshole."

Harper lets out a long sigh, her eyes fluttering closed for just a moment as though she's still savoring my touch. "Yeah," she says before she steps back. "You're probably right."

With a brighter smile, Harper pivots on her heel and heads for Sam, kneeling to slide her hands between the rungs of the railing on either side of Sam's boot.

"W-what are you doing?" he stammers.

"Helping, clearly." She tugs at his laces, loosening the bow. "But I didn't say *who*."

Harper rises and gives a swift kick to his boot. Sam's foot slides free of the shoe. His screech is cut short as he lands on the floor one level below.

"*Christ*. The silence is nice, isn't it," I say as we peer over the railing to look at his unmoving body. Blood seeps from beneath his head to creep across the concrete.

"Yeah, he was getting on my last nerve." Harper grabs his boot to chuck it over the landing. It smacks his face before bouncing off to the side. "That's going to be a bitch to clean up. We'd better get to it. We're pretty far out of town—the nearest property is old Mr. Talbot's farm a half mile south, and he's pretty hard of hearing, but you never know. Someone still could have heard that gunshot and called it in."

"Hey." I lay a hand on her wrist, stopping her progress toward the lights that still shine behind us. She looks up at me with a question in her gunmetal eyes. "I know you thought I could have left you, but you could have left me too. I'm not sure how you figured out how to find me. I'm grateful that you did."

She nods. It takes her a beat before she finally says, "Sure. What are friends for, right?"

I give her a dead-eyed glare. "We are *not* 'friends.'"

"Yeah, I think I remember you saying that already," she replies, but I know she can tell what I really mean. That she's so much more than that. It's in the way she flashes me a shy smile that lodges like a splinter in my heart before she turns away to start working on dismantling the lights. I know we both went back to that moment when we first faced off in her garden. It was supposed to be the defining confrontation that would seal our destiny. Bounty and executioner. Crime and justice. But maybe I'm just ready to leave that behind for the other memories that are starting to eclipse it. Anger served a purpose for me in the beginning. But in the end, it was a cage. And guilt is an equally vicious prison, one Harper is clearly still trapped in.

For the first time, I wonder if I can help her escape it when I had a hand in putting her there.

That thought haunts me as we pack Sam's equipment, bringing anything that connects him with us to my rental and Arthur's Jaguar where they're parked at the back of the building, out of sight from the road.

After debating the best plan for the body, we agree that we should leave Sam here at the distillery, but take a final sweep through the space to ensure we've erased our presence so it looks like the unfortunate accident it was . . . almost.

If we remove him from the scene, it will only pique the interest of the Sleuthseekers. They'll be rabid for details, and they won't stop until they unravel the mystery. But if it's an accident, we might have hope for fewer problems. And if Vinny wakes from where Harper clocked him in the head back at the inn, it will be his word against mine. His wild story about his unhinged boss kidnapping me for an interview probably won't hold much weight with the pragmatic Sheriff Yates, particularly not against my alibi of sleeping soundly at Lancaster Manor's cottage with my girl-friend at my side.

We're heading down the slope to the lower entrance of the distillery for a last check of the scene, still talking through the finer details of our plan, when we hear the sound of a car engine and gravel crunching beneath tires.

Harper and I both stop abruptly, holding our breath. But there's no way we're mistaken, not when we hear the engine cut out, followed by the creak and thud of a car door closing.

Someone has pulled to a stop at the main parking lot of the Lancaster Distillery.

"Maybe it's the drone guy," Harper whispers as we peer through the windows at the body just visible in the dim light.

"Maybe," I agree, though I clasp a hand around her wrist, ready to pull her back toward the path that leads to the vehicles. A flashlight sweeps across the windows at the opposite side of the building. Slow, careful footsteps make their way toward the entrance, followed by the creak of the door as it opens and shuts.

We turn and jog toward the cars.

"But I don't think we should wait around to find out."

CHART DATUM

Nolan

MAYBE I SHOULD BE WORRIED that we missed something. Terrified that Yates will finally figure out how to do his job and come knocking at our door. I should feel like running away from this place.

But I don't. I feel *alive*.

It's nearly three in the morning, and the adrenaline has been going all night. First it was the encounter with Sam. Then escaping from the distillery. Then racing to the Capeside Inn. We swept through Sam's and Vinny's rooms to either erase or steal anything we could find that appeared too connected to Harper and me, and then we took the murdered tourist and all the evidence to Lancaster Manor, hiding it all in the shed. Even after we managed to get the tourist's stiffening body into the oversized chest freezer, we both felt far too energized for sleep.

So we decided on the next best thing.

Ropes cross Harper's skin, each soft cord carefully and precisely laid against her flesh. One loop sits across her neck. Two intertwined cords drop down the center of her chest, ending just above her pelvis. Perpendicular lines fan from a series of knots. Above her breasts. Below them. Across her waist. Even down each thigh. An intricate network binds her arms behind her back. I took my time to tie each knot and position each rope exactly where I wanted. Over an hour later, her upper body is immobilized, and she's completely at my mercy.

With the final knot tied, I savor my work, letting my gaze travel slowly over every inch of her flesh. I catalog every detail. The flush in her skin. The goose bumps on her thighs. The shimmer of arousal gathered at her entrance. The way she shudders as I drag a finger across her pussy and to her clit. The sound of her moan, the desperate edge to it when I remove my hand.

"Open," I say as I hold my finger between us. Her lips part, and I lay my finger on her tongue. "Suck it off."

Her lips close and she sucks hard on my finger, my cock hardening as her tongue rolls across my skin. When I remove my finger from her mouth, I trace it across her lips.

"Are you sure about this?" I ask.

Harper nods without hesitation. "I was pretty bad tonight." She feigns a pout, batting her lashes at me. "First I removed a body from a crime scene, and then I killed a man. I deserve to be punished."

"I thought the rumor was going to be that the first man got lost walking his dog at night and the other was a workplace accident," I say, reaching over to her nightstand where my supplies are laid out. I clean my hands with a sterile wipe, and then pull a pair of latex gloves out of the box, sliding them on.

"You can't believe everything you hear."

I smirk, my pulse already climbing in anticipation. Pillows already piled behind me, I lie back on her bed, my upper body propped up on the mattress. "Then I guess you'd better get on my cock and receive your punishment."

Harper's eyes darken with need. She's on her knees near the center of the bed, close to my lower legs. She rises higher so she can start crawling closer, her balance unsteady with her arms bound so tightly to her body. I make no effort to help her, content to watch her struggle. She keeps her eyes on my erection, managing to get her left knee over my thighs with a little effort, then shimmies her way up my body until her pussy is lined up with my cock. With a bit of maneuvering and still no assistance from me, she sinks herself onto my length, enveloping me with her slick heat.

"Ride it," I command. And she does. With slow and careful motion, she rises and falls, rolling her hips as she bites her lip. When she starts to gather a steady rhythm, I reach over for another sterile alcohol pad. "What's your safe word?"

"Ballmeat."

"That sounds pretty bratty to me."

"Just a little bit."

"Hmm," I say. She shudders as I swipe a cold towelette over her nipple until I'm satisfied her skin is clean. "Maybe I'll let it slide this time since I'm about to cause you pain."

I toss the pad aside, then pick up the forceps, clamping them around her left nipple to the sound of her sharp inhale. Then I grab the hollow needle.

"You ready?" I ask, keeping the sharpened surgical steel held between us like a warning.

"Yes."

"Then stay still."

She rests on my length, her skin flushed pink with arousal and the anticipation of pain. God, she looks fucking perfect. Those cords around her skin. Her plump lip clutched between her teeth. Her nipple in my grasp and her pussy wrapped around my cock. I want to keep this image in my memory forever.

I rest the point of the needle against her flesh.

"Take a deep breath."

She does as I ask. And then I push it in.

A delicious whimper. A sharp inhale. Her pussy tightens around my rock-hard erection. I slide the needle horizontally through her nipple until it pokes out the other side, and then I slowly pull it out, letting her embrace the pain she craves. When it's free, I replace it with a threadless bar, pushing the beveled opal ends into each side.

"How did that feel?" I ask. But I already know. I can tell by the way she shudders. By the arousal that floods from her pussy.

"Good," she whispers, breathless. "So fucking good."

"Show me."

She rides my cock, and I watch for a long moment, my eyes riveted to that metal bar through her nipple, her skin flushed. I don't think I've ever seen anything hotter. When I manage to tear my focus away, I reach for a fresh alcohol pad and wipe down her other breast before opening a fresh needle.

"Stay still," I command. Harper halts her motion, and I clamp the forceps over the nipple. "You liked that pain, didn't you?"

She nods. "Yes."

"Good." I let the tip of the needle rest against her skin and she takes a shuddering breath. "Because I'm going to take my time."

I keep the needle right where it is, the cold metal pressed against her, the clamp tight around her flesh. It's only when a shiver of anticipation finally racks her body that I start to push it in. And I stay true to my word. I go slower than I need to, pushing it through her sensitive flesh as she whimpers. When I survey the subtle details of her face, it's ecstasy I see in her darkened eyes and parted lips. It's want, and need.

As soon as the needle is through the other side, I draw it back out just as slowly, and then replace it with a matching bar and opal balls. When it's finished, I wipe away the droplets of blood and we stare at the beautiful result.

"That's really fucking hot," she says, her voice unsteady.

"You like it?"

"I fucking love it."

"Then show me how grateful you are and ride my cock like you mean it."

Hunger ignites in her eyes. I grip the knots at the center of her chest to steady her, and she fucking spears herself on my erection. I can't take my eyes off her. Whether it's the glistening arousal on my cock when she rises enough to slam down again or the shining gems that bracket her nipples, I feast on every inch of her that I see. I endlessly crave her, wanting more and more and more of her and never having enough.

"For a demon who murders innocent men and then acts like a brat, you fuck like a goddess. Maybe you deserve a little reward," I say, reaching over for one last thing from the nightstand. Harper tracks the motion of my hand, never breaking her cadence as she rides my length. I grab the vibrator wand and turn it on, holding it up between us. "What do you think?"

"Yes," she says on the heels of a moan.

"Yes what?"

She struggles to subdue a smile. "Yes, pretty please."

"You're being such a good girl. I like it, but I have a feeling I shouldn't get used to it. Am I right?" My question earns me a coy little shrug, but her eyes don't leave the buzzing toy.

"Didn't think so. But I'm glad. I like taming you." I lay the head of the toy just beneath the hollow between her collarbones, then drag it down, letting it pass over the cords as I make my way to her right breast. "I like punishing you as much as you like receiving it."

I touch the vibration to the very tip of her nipple and she gasps. Then I let it graze the jeweled end of the bar and her pussy tightens around my cock, her silky arousal a flood of warmth.

"You're soaking wet for that pain, aren't you?" I say as I do the same to the bar on her other breast. She drops her head with a moan. She's nearly mindless with pleasure. "You love when it hurts."

"Yes," she whispers. "But only with you."

My breath catches. It feels like a quiet confession. Not just the words, but the way she watches me as though she's just given me something precious. A secret. No matter what happens in the future, whether she one day casts me out or not, this is something she'll only ever share with me.

I lower the wand. "Only with you," I say, and then I press it to her clit.

I hold it against her sensitive bud of nerves with one hand while I grip her ropes with the other, helping her keep her balance as she gives me everything she has. Even when her head falls back and her eyes drift closed, she keeps a desperate rhythm with the kind of need that's mindless. She glides on my cock and whimpers and moans until we both come undone, falling into the pleasure that consumes us. My grip tightens on the knots at her chest as I keep her locked down on me until every last pulse of my cock subsides, filling her with my cum, not taking the toy away until I'm sure her orgasm has fully passed. Even then, I keep her there, not letting her go until our ragged inhalations start to calm. And then I lift her away, slowly and carefully, and set her gently on the bed where I can safely remove the ropes.

I take my time to unwrap her before I carry her to the bath. This is how I worship her. With warm water and careful strokes of a soft cloth. With candles and quiet words and delicate touches. I want to hurt her and I'm grateful she lets me, that she wants me to do it. But as much as we both crave the pain, I want to look after her too. Maybe more than I ever expected.

When I'm sure she's all right, we climb into bed, and I pull her into my arms. She falls asleep quickly.

But I don't.

I quietly slip away before dawn, placing a short note on her pillow with the promise that I'll return, just in case she has lingering doubts. Within twenty minutes, I'm standing on the granite ledge, looking toward the light that's coloring the horizon before the sun crests the distant line between the water and the sky.

And then I start my descent.

My boots sink into the sand as I step down from the last jagged edge of the cliff face and onto the thin strip of beach. It's June 25. I'm standing at latitude 44.6692° N and longitude 67.2594° W. The spring tide is still slowly rolling back from the shore. I check my watch. 5:22 a.m. Only another ten minutes until it reaches its lowest point, but already I can see the very top of the van from Sam's blown-up photograph breaking through the waves.

For whatever reason, it was vitally important to Sam to find this vehicle, which must only be visible during the spring low tides when the water is at its lowest. And I need to know why.

I set my bag down and take off my shoes. Within another few minutes, I've stripped off my clothes that cover the wetsuit I rented from Wallie's Water Sports. I pull my flippers on, strapping a dive light to my wrist. And then I'm headed for the surf, settling my mask and snorkel over my face as I wade into the crashing white waves.

Even through the wetsuit, the cold sea is a shock. It soaks through the cuffs and neck, water filling the space between skin and neoprene with a cold film until my body starts to warm it. Treacherous rocks poke through the water. Seaweed rolls around me on every swirling wave. I keep my head up. Stay focused on that dented sheet of rusted metal. Try not to think about the last time I dove into the sea, or what I nearly lost. I just keep kicking, fighting the pull of the current that tries to drag me down the shore.

I grab the sharp edge of the fiberglass where the window has long since shattered and fallen away, and I hold on.

Not much of the vehicle is visible above the waves, but even with what does sit above the surface, I can tell it's the roof extender of a camper van. The original color has bleached, the surface blistered and cracked. None of the windows have survived, leaving only the holes that once let light into the living space. I keep a hand gripped to the vehicle as I adjust my snorkel and sink beneath the waves, hoping to find a license plate. I'm not surprised to find nothing there.

When I've surfaced, I start making my way forward. The fiberglass flexes and groans against the corroded welds and screws that hold it to the steel frame of the vehicle as I pull myself along its length.

When I get to the front of the vehicle, I take a deep breath and dive.

Small fish scatter as I keep a hand on the missing driver's side window and cast my light across the interior. Seaweed and barnacles and creatures I can't name have already claimed much of the space. The metal frame is coated in layers of rust. The fabric of the seats has decayed, leaving behind only strips of upholstery. There's a small kitchen area. A bench and table. What looks like a cast iron wood stove, the thick glass cracked but still in place. There's a bed toward the back of the van and a door just beyond it that might lead to a small toilet or storage. The space is covered in shades of green, filaments of life that seem so vivid in a place that feels like a tomb.

I rise to the surface, take a breath, and dive again.

This time, I head through the front window and enter the interior. Fish scatter. I scan the bottom surface of the van, looking for anything left behind. I even check the kitchen cupboards, one of the doors hanging on to the frame by a single rusted hinge. But there's nothing.

With another trip to the surface, I dive again.

This time, I head toward the passenger side, staying close to the bottom of the window. I find the plate that's fixed to the dashboard. I clear away the debris with my gloved thumb. I shine my light on the vehicle identification number. I can just make out the seventeen-digit alphanumeric code. I repeat the number over and over until I'm sure I'll remember it. I even dive more than once to check that I've gotten it correct. My heart is humming, even though I don't know what it will tell me. Maybe nothing. But my instincts say otherwise.

With a final glance around the van's interior, I rise and swim to shore.

I chant the VIN to myself as I strip off the wetsuit on the

deserted thread of beach. I change quickly, shivering in the cold morning breeze. As soon as I'm changed, I enter the VIN into my phone, then hook the backpack over my shoulders and start climbing from the sand that will soon be consumed by the incoming tide.

I drive back to Cape Carnage, following the winding road that hugs the cliff. Before long, I pass the lighthouse, a handful of tourists already hiking up the steps that lead to the red-and-white beacon to the sea. I drive past houses that are now becoming familiar, with colorful planked siding and intricate trim. Instead of heading back to Harper's cottage, I turn toward the Capeside Inn, rolling to a stop in my favorite spot in the parking lot that faces the ocean. When I turn off my car, I sit and watch in silence for a moment, thinking about that first day I looked across those sparkling waves and imagined all the righteous sins I'd waited so long to commit. I came here looking to dredge at least one long-hidden secret from the depths of Cape Carnage, but I caught more than I ever bargained for.

I grab my bag and make my way inside the inn, past the little dining area where patrons are smiling over French toast or chatting about the day's plans as the happy aroma of maple syrup and fresh coffee wafts through the air. Maybe they don't even know what's happened over the last few days. Maybe they do and just don't care. They're on holiday, after all. Somehow, it seems fitting that Cape Carnage continues on as though untroubled by the dark current snaking through its streets.

I make it to the corridor that leads to my room before Irene can spot me and those questions might end up out in the open.

When I get to my room, I drop my bag by the door and stride toward the small table next to the window with my laptop in

hand. My leg bounces as it powers up. It goes through the slowest update of its entire fucking electronic life, because *of course it would pick this exact moment*. By the time I'm finally able to log in, I'm nearly vibrating with impatience.

I google a VIN lookup service and enter the code for the vehicle, followed by my credit card information for a full report. My finger hesitates for a beat before I hit the return button. A report comes up with eight previous unnamed owners, the location of the title transfer, and the service history for a 1985 Chevy G20 camper van. The last change of ownership was five years ago, a private sale in Lubbock, Texas.

I frown at the screen. That vehicle has come a long way.

Though I might have a location and date of sale for what is a rather uncommon vehicle, that's still not going to tell me who the last owner was. I run my fingers across my lips, thinking about the way Harper bites her own flesh when she's nervous or deep in thought. If Sam had an interest in this particular Chevy G20 . . . maybe he's said so.

The Sleuthseekers have accounts on a few social media sites, and though I check through them, I find nothing related to the van. What they post publicly is kept pretty vague. But they must have a place where they speak more openly with one another. Where they share secrets and theories.

With a little more hunting, I find mention of a Discord server.

I create a new account and try to tamp down the disappointment when I have to answer a number of questions and wait for an admin to approve my request to join the Sleuthseekers server. Who knows how long that will take. With a groan, I rise and put the kettle on, a text from Harper coming through on my phone as I'm waiting for the water to boil.

> You'll probably be happy to know that I'm
> thinking of you literally every time I move.

I smirk, starting to type a reply when an image quickly follows her message. It's a photo of her naked upper body, the bars through her nipples gleaming.

> I think I'm obsessed.

My cock hardens and I shift, trying to relieve the sudden ache of need.

> You're trying to torture me, aren't
> you?

> Absolutely. One thousand percent YES.

> They're a little tender but it looks pretty hot,
> don't you think?

> If they're sore, maybe I should come
> and take a closer look.

> I'm free after lunch. 1pm?

I check my watch. It's not quite eight in the morning. The wait is going to be fucking agonizing.

> 12:30?

> You know, I think I'm busy at 1pm, actually.
> How about 3pm?

I drag a hand down my face, ready to claw my skin off. She's a fucking monster. And to drive the point home, she sends through two more photos of her breasts, one from the side and another a close-up of one nipple.

> Okay okay okay. 1pm.

> Fucking brat.

The kettle whistles and I pocket my phone. As I'm pouring the water, a notification comes through on my laptop. My heart lurches, a hit of adrenaline flooding its chambers. Tea in hand, I head to the table and wake the screen to find my request approved.

With a grim smile, I start exploring the information on the server.

First, I start with Sam's recent posts. He's been teasing his trip to Cape Carnage, posting the occasional image of the town or his film equipment or shots of him and Vinny as they focus on their work. I come to learn that Vinny is a trusted friend to Sam in his escapades to unearth the town's secrets. Much of the recent discourse centers on La Plume and the interviews Sam has conducted to confirm his suspicions that Arthur is the infamous serial killer. Nothing of the latest posts tells me about the Chevy van.

So I start trawling the archives.

Once I search for a Chevy G20, a new picture starts to emerge. The earliest posts referencing the G20 are from three years ago, mentions of a van that had been refurbished before setting out on a road trip across the southern states, starting in Texas. "AC bought the G20 in September, and they spent the winter overhauling it," one of the posts says, along with a photo of the old van that must have come from the used car dealership's listing. I check the VIN report, and it lists a transfer of ownership in September six years ago. There are some questions in response to the post. And then, "His parents gave it to AB the October after Mead."

I have no idea what that means, but the dates line up with the VIN report. It's useless trying to search up "AB" or "AC." I blow out a long breath, readying myself to start delving into the bigger picture to understand the context in which the van occurs. Just as I'm about to start trawling through the posts, a new message comes through on the general chat, and I click on it.

Anybody hear from Sam or Vinny? it reads.

A few replies confirm that no one has heard from either Sam or Vinny yet. Sam's absence is no surprise to me, of course, but it's odd that Vinny hasn't checked in with the group if that's what they would expect. Maybe Harper hit him harder than she thought and he's spent the night in the hospital.

Sam told me in confidence a couple of weeks ago that he was going to be looking for something at spring tide, which was this morning sometime, a user called KnightofTruth replies. *He might still be out on the water. I'll check in with his girlfriend and report back.*

This message generates some chatter in the group, an atmosphere of excitement. Another user asks a question that strikes my interest. *Something to do with autumn?*

I don't know what could be happening in the autumn here. Aside from the Taste of Terror festival near the end of summer, there's not much planned in the fall when the coastal weather starts to turn. If there's something coming up that Sam would take an interest in, it's a mystery to me.

I frown at the screen and start a new search for autumn.

But what I find is not at all what I expected.

There are numerous results for "autumn," some as recent as yesterday, some dating back to four years ago. But it's not a season. It's a person. Autumn Bower. The name brings up a vague recollection of news stories and speculation. She was fodder for the press. A popular influencer in her niche who survived a prolific serial killer, what could be a more enticing story than that? She was a seemingly unassuming woman who somehow escaped from the cellar of a house of horrors and walked seven miles to the nearest town barefoot in nothing but a fucking plaid shirt, leaving the remains of her slain boyfriend and his murderer burned in her wake.

And then, several months later, she just . . . disappeared.

I keep scrolling through entries, so many of them from shortly after her mysterious disappearance focused on trying to track her down. *Autumn's last video*, one entry says, with a YouTube link. I click on it.

And smiling back at me is Harper Starling.

"Hi," she says, with a wave to the camera. "I'm Autumn, and welcome to Autumn and Adam's Vanventures with Goonie, our 1985 Chevy G20 camper van conversion. Now that we've been living in Goonie for a month, we have a better idea of what we've done well in our rebuild and what we'll probably change. Today I'm going to show you my top-five favorite things in the van so far. Come on in . . ."

The rest of her words are lost to the roaring heartbeats in my ears. I'm staring at Harper. But I'm not. She seems so different. And it's not just the long blond hair or the lighter eyebrows or the sun-kissed glow. It's not a Texas accent I can hear in her voice, one I've never heard when she speaks. It's the ease in her. The openness. It's her welcoming smile, her enthusiasm.

She shows the interior of the van, from the kitchen to the little wood stove, the layout identical to the van that lies at the bottom of the sea. I start the video again and pause it when her face is centered in the shot, and then I bring up my pictures of Harper Starling from before the accident, placing them side by side on the screen. The resemblance is there. They must be about the same age. Their face shape is similar. Even the width of their noses and the angle of their jaws. They look like they could be sisters if their hair color was different. But they are not the same woman.

I close my eyes and try to force a memory that refuses to surface. When I look back at the glimpse of the driver of the car that hit Billy and me, it's the woman I know that I see behind the wheel. But is it? When I recall the feeling of the asphalt against my face, it's her voice I hear arguing with the men whose souls I've already claimed. But can I be sure?

What if my memory is wrong?

It was only a flash of a moment, her features illuminated by the dashboard lights in the instant before the crash. Could I have warped this memory with my hatred until it matched what I wanted to see and hear?

I navigate to the channel page and click on the introductory video.

It's her again, this time with a man her age, his arm around her shoulders. He has a surfer vibe: a wide, bright smile and a mop of unruly blond hair. He's the kind of guy everyone loves. It bleeds right through the screen. There are photos and video shots of them working on the van, with a voice-over. "I'm Adam Cunningham," he says.

"And I'm Autumn Bower," she chimes in.

"And welcome to Autumn and Adam's Vanventures . . ."

I press a shaking finger to the keyboard and pause the video. And then I stand so quickly that I knock the table, rattling my laptop and cup and saucer with a shock of sound that just barely penetrates the thoughts that are clicking together like magnets snapping into place. I rush to my jacket where I tossed it over my backpack and take out the silver bracelet I put there the day the raven dropped it in the sink.

A^2BC.

Autumn Bower. Adam Cunningham.

I slowly sit on the edge of the bed.

She's not the woman who struck me and left me for dead.

She's Autumn Bower.

The hint of blond roots I noticed in her hair just the other day. The way she feared Sam as though she knew exactly what he could do to her life.

Tears blur the metal links laid across my open palms.

All the fucking horrible things I spent years wanting to do to her. The way I've hated her. The way I've treated her. Until only recently, I've always approached her with the expectation that *she* was the one who owed *me*. And every harsh word, every glare, every threat and vow to wreak havoc upon her, she took it all.

Somehow, she made her way here. And in the process, though I have no recollection of when or how, we crossed paths. She must have stolen Harper Starling's identity, maybe in the hopes of evading a past that refused to let her have what she'd fought for and earned. *A life.*

And I almost took that from her. I came here to destroy her. But she isn't even the woman I was seeking, and yet she never said a word.

. . . or did she?

I'm not who you think I am, she'd said, defiance vibrantly gleaming in her silver eyes. And I didn't listen, not really. I didn't hear what she was trying to say.

She has survived loss. Captivity. Horror and death. And she was ready to survive me.

Me.

I've fallen in love with a phantom. A woman I hardly know. One who never told me the truth. She'll let me pierce her skin and pledge my loyalty with the pain she craves, but she won't tell me her fucking name.

What happened to the actual Harper Starling? And how the hell did Autumn take her identity and wind up *here*?

I don't know what I'm supposed to feel in this squall that crashes through the cavity of my chest. The guilt and shame for how I treated her and what I nearly did. Betrayal and anger that she never told me who she really was, even after I promised I was never going to give her up. Worry and hope. Longing and sorrow and regret. With a heavy sigh, I curl my fist around the bracelet and hang my head, trying to figure my way out of this storm. But I don't see a clear path through it.

A notification dings from my computer. Then another. And another. My brow furrows, and I push myself off the bed, returning to the table. When I click on the tab for the Discord server, KnightofTruth has sent a message to the chat.

Sleuthseekers, it's time to fucking mobilize.

A chill dances through my flesh. Goose bumps rise on my arms.

A slew of messages comes through from other users in the server. Questions. Excitement. Guesses and theories.

I type out a question of my own: *Mobilize for what?*

KnightofTruth sends a reply to my query that sets off another storm of questions.

War.

Anxiety bleeds through the chat. The same question echoes in different iterations. *Why?*

Maybe some instinct within me expects KnightofTruth's reply, at least in part. But it still hits me like the car that started this tempest four years ago. An unstoppable impact that slams right into my chest. It crushes muscle and bone, sucking the air from my lungs.

Sam and Vinny are both dead, KnightofTruth says. *It's time to blow this case wide open.*

We're going to Cape Carnage.

EPILOGUE

I PULL MY GUN FROM the holster at my side, holding the flashlight over the barrel as I shoulder the iron door open, keeping it ajar with my foot as I enter the old distillery. There's a rustle in the dark. I shine my light on the plastic taped to the wall, flapping in the breeze. Sheets of drywall are stacked in the center of the reception room that surrounds me, waiting to be hung. The smell of paint and malt and freshly cut lumber lingers in the air. I pan my light around the space, but there's no evidence that anyone is here.

I let the door close behind me with a dull thud.

I've been to the Lancaster Distillery only once, years ago, before I even lived in Cape Carnage. But I still remember the layout with perfect clarity. I head first to the tasting room and retail space to my right, beyond the reception area. There are polished countertops, new lighting and fixtures, but everything has been selected with care to maintain the feel of history in a building that has been here almost as long as the town itself. Lukas Lancaster does nothing by half measures, after all. Mediocrity is not a Lancaster trait. It's something I've come to admire about them.

Lord knows, I've been watching them long enough.

When I determine there's no one to find, I backtrack into the reception room, heading down the corridor that leads toward the stills.

The building is silent as I enter the room where exposed beams frame the vaulted ceiling shaped to mimic the hull of a ship. I stop on the landing that overlooks the main production area. Copper stills reflect the moonlight that stalks through the leaded windows. My light pans across the concrete, swept clean, no prints to guide me. But I don't need them. Not when I step to the railing and my light crosses a body lying motionless on the floor below.

"Mr. Porter," I say to myself, tipping my hat up my forehead as I stare down at him. Blood pools around his head like a halo. One of his arms rests at an impossible angle. I shake my head and *tsk*. "You found yourself in some kind of unfortunate predicament."

I'm about to head down the stairs to investigate further when I hear a sound from the entrance of the distillery. I raise my gun and point it in the direction of a flashlight that approaches. "Sam . . . ?" a man's voice calls. "I'm sorry I'm so late, man. I—"

"Stop right there. Hands in the air." Vinny Meschino. Sam's drone operator and helper. He raises his hands. "Come forward slowly. Let me get a good look at you." He does as I ask, stopping when I gesture with my free hand for him to stop just before the end of the hallway. One side of his face is scraped with fresh cuts. Dried blood rims his nostrils. The guy has had a rough night, by the looks of things. "Want to tell me what you're doing here, son?" I ask.

He swallows. Shifts his feet. His eyes dart around the corridor as though he might be able to pluck a suitable lie off the walls.

That's a guilty man if I've ever seen one. And I've seen a fair few in my time.

"I got all night, kid. Go on."

"I was coming to find Sam," he finally admits. "We were going to do some filming here."

"With permission of the Lancaster family?"

He doesn't answer.

"So that's a no," I confirm, and a defeated expression passes over his face.

"Look, I just go where Sam tells me, Officer."

"Sheriff."

"*Sheriff.*" He shakes his head, lowering his hands just a little. "I'm sorry, sir. Somebody hit me in the parking lot of the Capeside Inn and stole all my gear and my phone. When I came to, I drove straight here to check on Sam. Can I file a police report?"

I slip my flashlight into its loop at my belt, then lower my gun and take a few steps closer. A reassuring smile rises on my lips. "I think we'll have a few of those to fill out, son," I say as I lay a hand on his shoulder, giving it a fatherly pat.

Before his next blink, I dig my fingers in and use all my force to smash his head into the concrete wall.

He lands hard on the floor. I'm on him with a knee lodged against his chest as soon as he lands, my gun pointed at his forehead. A spike of adrenaline drives through my veins.

"Wh . . . what's happening?" he asks, his speech slurred as he hangs on the edge of consciousness. His limbs scrape across the floor.

"Oh my. Seems you've gotten yourself in a bit of a pickle, Mr. Meschino." He struggles beneath me, but it's a half-hearted effort that dies when I press my knee harder to his chest. "Tell me why you're really here."

"N . . . Nolan. Nolan Rhodes. Sam . . . Sam took him. He was going to . . . to force him to t-talk before handing him to . . . you."

"Where is Rhodes now?"

"D-don't know."

I make a mental note to check the premises for any sign of Rhodes, though I doubt he would have left much behind. But there is plenty of evidence of Sam's presence in a building that doesn't belong to him. And now there's his companion. Two men who were obviously up to no good. It's easy for emotions to run high when right and wrong are involved. Morals are tested. Allegiances break.

"N-Nolan Rhodes . . . is a killer . . ." Meschino says. "And Harp . . . Harper Starling, she's not who she s-says she is. And Arthur Lancaster—"

"Ah yes," I reply, my tone grim. "Arthur Lancaster. I've heard that one before."

"B-but . . . the p-property at the Ballantyne River—"

"Do you know about the Symbolist movement in literature?" I interrupt as I pat down Meschino's pockets. He moans a non-answer.

"Didn't think so. The Symbolist movement believed art should unlock the fundamental truths of humanity by systematically 'deranging the senses.' Isn't that wonderful? *Systematic derangement.* Think about it." I give his temple a light tap with the muzzle of my gun and he whimpers. With a deep sigh, I lean back, pulling a knife from my belt with my free hand. "*Je suis un berceau, qu'une main balance, au creux d'un caveau:* Silence, silence!" I grin down at Meschino, watching as his confusion bleeds into fear. An alchemical transformation of the soul. It's a delicious concoction. My favorite elixir.

"Please . . . I have a family. A d-daughter . . ."

"How fitting. Life. Death. The cyclical nature of time." I push my hat up with my gun and cast my gaze around us, checking the corners, listening for anything beyond the quiet sobs of the injured man beneath my knee. "That tattoo on Mr. Rhodes is prophetic, don't you think? He was meant to come to Carnage. Just like Harper Starling fits right in at Lancaster Manor, doesn't she?" I slip the handle of the knife against Meschino's palm. He's too weak to fight me off. A faint smile hooks the corners of my mouth as confusion filters into his eyes. It's the first genuine smile I've felt in a long while. The first stir of my heart against my ribs as I tighten his grip around the handle of the blade. "Or should I say, Autumn Bower."

I raise Vinny's hand, tilting the tip of the knife so it faces me. His eyes dart between mine and the polished blade that I bring closer to my body. "W-what are you doing?"

"Taking care of my toys."

He's too weak to stop me as I push the tip of the blade into my uniform, piercing just beneath my collarbone. I welcome the pain. "You know, I really should commend you. I didn't know her true identity. I never looked at it closely. I just figured the old man had a soft spot for a woman much like the daughter he lost. But you and Sam are the ones who pieced it together."

I consume Meschino's confusion as I push the knife deeper into my flesh. The burn blooms, its caress a systematic derangement of nerves beneath my skin. I am art. Poetry come to life to challenge Vinny's perception of the world as it slips through his grasp. Every shake of his head, every word of disbelief, every breath of mounting terror feeds a darkness that I spend too much time trying to hide.

"I hear you've been looking for La Plume," I say as I rise to my feet, aiming my gun at Vinny's shaking, blood-streaked head. He begs for his life as I squeeze the trigger. With a single shot that echoes across brick and copper, his pleas fall silent.

"You found him."

Acknowledgments

FIRSTLY, THANK YOU TO YOU, dear reader, for spending some of your time with Harper (or NOT Harper, in this case!), Nolan, Arthur, and the rest of the cast and crew of Cape Carnage. It's always so exciting to start a new series, and I truly felt like the town sucked me right in from the start. Parts of Carnage were loosely based on some of the small towns across Nova Scotia that I've had the privilege to live or spend time in. They're quirky and close-knit, with colorful characters and unusual histories. Don't worry, they're not murdery (at least, not that I know of!), and you should absolutely go visit. I hope you enjoyed your time in Cape Carnage and that you fell in love with Harper and Nolan as much as I did. There's so much left to their journey, and I can't wait for book two!

Thank you to Chris McKay, whose question about *Butcher & Blackbird* during our very first *B&B* movie discussion set off the whole idea for this series: "What happened to Autumn?" I'm so grateful you asked. That question stuck with me, and it's resulted in one of my favorite books I've ever written. So, THANK YOU!

Huge thanks to Kim Whalen from the Whalen Agency. You deserve all the champagne in the world. You're always there, no matter if it's something big or something small. You work so fucking hard. I hope you know how much I appreciate everything you do for me. Thank you also to Mary Pender at WME for all your ongoing support. You're such a pleasure to work with!

To Molly Stern, Sierra Stovall, Hayley Wagreich, Andrew Rein, Julia McGarry, and the Zando team, thank you for helping me bring the Seasons of Carnage series to life, and for taking a chance on it when it was still in the "I can't tell you what it is yet because I don't really know" stage, HAHA. You are always up for entertaining some wild ideas, and I'm very grateful for all the work you put in behind the scenes to put my books in the hands of readers. Thank you also to Ellie Russell and Becky West at Little, Brown UK, as well as Glenn Tavennec and Benoit André from Label Verso (France) for continuing to be such huge supporters of my work—I can't wait to see Cape Carnage overseas! And I will always be so eternally grateful to András Kepets in Hungary. I'm not sure any of this would have happened without his help!

To my wonderful PA, Val Downs of Turning Pages Designs. Thank you so much for everything you do! From the amazing graphics you make to all the unseen support you give, you are such a delight to work with. I appreciate you so much. Thank you also to Jess Stamp, not only are you a great friend and a fab early vibe checker, but you keep my Facebook group from descending into chaos, and I'm so grateful, haha!

A HUGE shout-out to the amazing ARC readers and social media supporters who take the time to read and hype my work. Thank you so much for all you do to read, promote, and talk about these stories. Many of you have been on this journey with me for years! That's so hard to fathom!! It means so much to me that you're willing to take time out of your day to spend time with my characters, and I'm honored to be on this journey with you. A special note of thanks to Abbie, Chelsea, Lauren, and Kristie, whom I had the honor of becoming friends with on this wild ride; I'm so grateful this roller coaster brought you into my life.

To Samantha Brentmoor, audiobook narrator empress extraordinaire, thank you for your unfailing love and support. You're the greatest hype woman and girl's girl, and I'm so grateful for your friendship.

Similarly, a huge thank-you to all my author friends. I'm very fortunate, because you're too many to name for fear of leaving anyone out, though I do need to shout out a few who have played a particularly active role not only in the journey of this book, but in my life as I navigate the highs and lows of publishing. To Santana Knox and H. D. Carlton. My human centipede. You're both so generous with your time and your huge hearts, and I love you so much. To my local ladies, Emma Noyes and Stacia Stark: Where's My Hat?! To Lyla Sage, you are the only person I'll let lead me into a cult, and I'm not even paid by Zipfizz to say that.

To my longtime dear friends Sanja Kajic and Lynsey Wills, who always take time to read and check in and make trips to visit, I love you dearly. Every time we get together, it feels like we've never been apart, and that brings me joy!

To my maternal grandparents, Cy and Ethel, who both passed away long before this manuscript was ever written. They were integral to my upbringing. Their battles with dementia and Alzheimer's disease were full of grace, hardship, and, most of all, humanity. They taught me the importance of crafting a life of impact and the bittersweet fragility of personhood. I'm forever grateful for the path they set me on, inspiring my scientific career in Alzheimer's disease research before I transitioned to writing full time. I'd like to think they'd be proud of this story, but honestly, they'd probably hate the smut bahaha. But that's okay, because I know they'd be proud of *me*. And I am enormously proud of them. Grandma and Grandpa—I wish I'd told you more often how grateful I am for the way you stepped up to help raise me. I think of you all the time. I hope you know now how much you've steered the course of my ship and how deeply I love and miss you.

Last but never least, to my wonderful boys. Fun fact: I never would have figured out the flow of the Sam vs. railing scene if it wasn't for my husband, Daniel, moving the furniture and acting it out with me, HAHA. None of this would be possible without you, Daniel. Every moment of support you give, whether it's bringing me snacks or staying up late to quietly sit with me on deadline or helping to keep me sane (not an easy task), I see it. And I appreciate it more than I can ever express. I love you so very much. You are simply amazing in every way, and I'm so lucky that our chance meet-cute became a real-life happy ending. And to our son, Hayden, thank you for your incredible kindness, your empathy, your hugs, your pats on my cheek that I adore. I love you for all time. You're the best, "infinity-times-infinity-plus-one-no-returns." I know you're going to ask me when you're allowed to read this book. Convince Dad to let me get a pet raccoon and we'll talk. (Just kidding, the answer is still never.)

Can't get enough of Brynne Weaver?

Don't miss the Ruinous Love trilogy

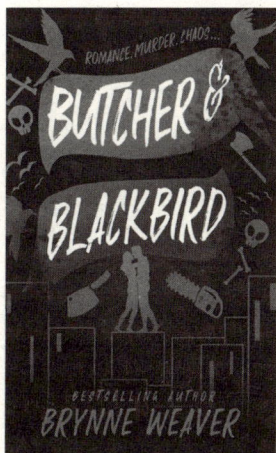

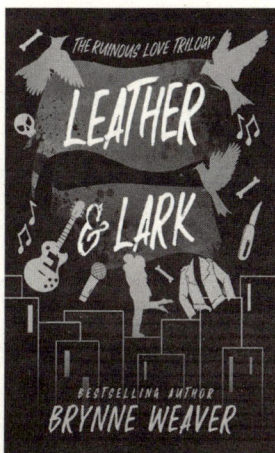

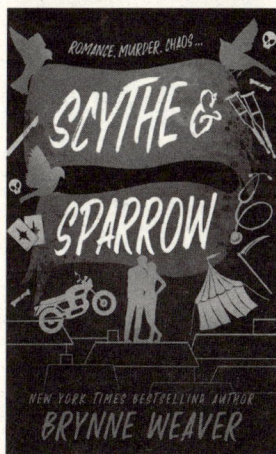